P9-DEV-571

AGAINST ALL ENEMIES

AGAINST ALL ENEMIES

A Novel by
Ervin S. Duggan and
Ben J. Wattenberg

DOUBLEDAY & COMPANY, INC., GARDEN CITY, NEW YORK
1977

ISBN: 0-385-03768-6
Library of Congress Catalog Card Number 73–22796

Printed in the United States of America

For Lillian Ervin Duggan
and to the memory of
Rachel Wattenberg

Contents

Who put up that cage?
Who hung it up with bars, doors?
Why do those on the inside want to get out?
Why do those on the outside want to get in?
What is this crying inside and out all the time?
What is this endless, useless beating of baffled
wings at these bars, doors, this cage?

—Carl Sandburg

NOVEMBER

In the West Wing

Monday the Twentieth

Precisely at noon, the Army bandsmen arrayed on the South Balcony hoisted their long heraldic trumpets. They blared a fanfare into the late November air, then swept smoothly into "Hail to the Chief." Carlton Rattigan emerged from his Oval Office, and a thousand guests huddled behind ropes on the lawn craned to see him.

The President and Lisa Rattigan, moving perfectly in step with the stately rhythm of the trumpets, marched toward the small red-carpeted platform that had been set up near the South Entrance. A murmur of awe and approval ran through the crowd.

Seeing Carl Rattigan in person for the first time, people were always struck by his size: His photographs, his tiny image on television, did not suggest his height. He stood six feet, four inches tall, and the upward tilt of his head emphasized his stature. Though he was fifty years old, he moved with the spring of a young man, and his neatly fitted suits outlined the lean, hard body of an athlete. Despite his years as a politician, despite the sedentary hours, the soggy banquet food, he had not gone soft; he wore the ruddy winter tan of a rich man.

Not only his looks set him apart. As he strode past the crowd on the South Lawn, nodding to the guests, acknowledging their applause, murmuring happily to his regal wife, he radiated energy, vitality, zest for his high office.

In three years he had endured dozens of these ceremonies, the elaborate welcoming rituals for visiting chiefs of state, but there was no trace of boredom or impatience on his face. He shook hands warmly with Brooks Healy, the Secretary of State, and waved to the chief of protocol. Then, seeing the ambassador of Paraguay, who stood awaiting the arrival of his country's President, Rattigan walked over, spoke a word or two in halting, prep-school Spanish, and seized the ambassador in a friendly *abrazo*.

The trumpeters finished their tribute; there was a moment of silence. The crowd waited restlessly, expectantly. Then, after a flurry of unheard and unseen signals by men hidden in the trees with tiny two-way radios, the musicians played again: this time, a fanfare grand enough for the welcome of a king.

From the Southwest Gate below came a great black car, the President's own. It rolled slowly up the drive and stopped alongside the little platform where the welcoming party stood. The fanfare ended, the chief of protocol opened the limousine's rear door, and Antonio Badillo Silvera, the military dictator of Paraguay, stepped out.

Lisa Rattigan leaned forward, handed a large bouquet to Badillo's wife, and the two women followed their husbands onto the platform. When the band began to play the Paraguayan national anthem, the First Lady winced, anticipating the frightening noise of the twenty-one-gun salute. These ceremonies, which her husband enjoyed so much, were an ordeal for her. She braced herself for the thunderclaps from the cannon on the Ellipse; they came, and a great cloud of smoke swept up the lawn toward the platform.

In the echo of the last cannon blast, the President stepped forward to make his welcoming speech.

The Secretary of State, watching the ceremonies from his vantage point at the rear of the tiny platform, frowned. Brooks Healy was perhaps the President's oldest friend, and he was one of the half-dozen men in Washington who knew the true significance of the Paraguayan dictator's visit. In Healy's opinion, it could not have come at a worse time.

The President's personal secretary, Sheila Roundtree, peered out across the Rose Garden, watching the ceremonies through the french doors of the Oval Office. She could hear little of the speeches; to her, the ceremony seemed identical to dozens of others she had seen. Soon she left her place at the door and returned to her desk in the next room. She arranged some letters for the President's signature, affixing to each one a yellow slip marking the spot where he should sign. Then she hurried on to the Cabinet Room to prepare for a meeting, which the President's appointments secretary had warned her would be strictly off the record. At each place around the table she placed a freshly sharpened pencil and a small memo pad imprinted at the top, in simple blue letters, "The White House." When the meeting was over, she knew, all of the little tablets would be gone. Not even the highest officials, as previous Presidents had learned, could resist taking away a souvenir of White House service.

On the South Lawn the President ended his remarks, and Badillo, a fat, dark man in military uniform, responded in fervent Spanish. The reporters, gathered in a little corral directly in front of the podium, found little of interest to record. Neither of the Presidents departed significantly from the advance text that had been handed to the press. There was nothing in their words, or on their faces, to suggest that Badillo's visit was anything more than routine.

The band struck up a slow march, and the two chiefs of state left the podium to review the ceremonial guard.

"Hey, Trip," a reporter called to the President's press secretary in a hoarse stage whisper, "can we go to lunch when this crap is finished?"

Gary Triplitano nodded yes, and a tiny muffled cheer went up from the little band of reporters.

Downstairs, in the West Wing, John Cardwell was rewriting the President's little speech for the fourth time: a five-hundred-word toast for the dinner honoring Badillo that evening.

Outside, echoing from the walls of the great gray building across West Executive Avenue, he could hear the burst and rattle of march music. He imagined the dictator, in shaded spectacles, medals clicking on his chest, reviewing the massed troops with the President.

"We are linked"—Cardwell frowned as he wrote—*"not only by warm ties of friendship, but also by strong bonds of alliance."* Then he paused, staring at the long yellow pad on the desk before him.

He made a quick mark on the yellow pad, changed "linked" to "joined," and continued to write.

"As friends, we have chosen to work together for economic development and the enlargement of liberty. As allies, we are pledged to stand together against the threat of . . ."

The threat of what? A sharp buzz from the telephone at his elbow destroyed the phrase forming in his mind, and Cardwell, picking up the receiver, spoke sharply: "Dot, please, no calls. I've got to get this thing upstairs!"

"I'm sorry, I thought you'd want this one. Sarah Tolman is calling about lunch. She's just back from a trip around the country for the *Times*. She's doing a series on the political climate, and she wants to talk to you. One o'clock at Sans Souci?"

"Tell her one-thirty. And come in for the next page of this toast."

He didn't like to miss a lunch with Sarah. Once before on a busy day he had called to cancel a lunch with her, and she had said gently, "Oh, come on. I do wonders for men under pressure."

He returned to his writing. "*. . . against the threat of aggression and subversion that hangs over our hemisphere.*"

Cardwell's frown deepened. He didn't like this vague, ominous language. But the President himself, for reasons known best to him, had ordered such words for the dinner tonight.

The door opened and Dot entered, brushing back a wisp of blond hair.

"One-thirty is fine. Is it all right if I have two corrections on page two, or should I type it over?"

"Leave it as it is. It'll do him good to see human error in black and white, right before his eyes."

Dot smiled, and Cardwell handed her the next page, a long yellow sheet filled with barely legible scrawls and a mass of heavy scratch-throughs. Then he attacked once more the closing paragraph: *"We must acknowledge that threat. It exists. We cannot ignore it—if we value human liberty in the Americas or around the world."*

The language was vague, threatening, militant—and decidedly out of character for Rattigan. The night before, reading an earlier draft, Rattigan had penciled in some terse notes:

"Stress fact we are military allies—without being too specific—and we can be counted on. No need to praise Badillo—he is tin-hat dictator—but praise his country, people, etc."

Beside another paragraph, the President had scribbled, in his large, bold scrawl: *"Too weak. Stress solidarity in hemisphere. We all have responsibility to protect stable, democratic countries under threat. No need to mention names."*

Cardwell's frown deepened, and he wrote on.

In truth, these toasts were not usually viewed by the White House press corps as important bits of oratory: They were social, not political, speeches. Although the President's words—like every other detail of the Badillo visit—would be front-page news in Paraguay, and would be studied by diplomats in Latin America, such speeches usually bored the White House regulars. Toasts were largely ceremonial, uttered late in the evening, too late for newspaper deadlines; and advance texts were seldom provided to reporters. Those reporters who covered state dinners were usually from the women's pages, more interested in the clothes, the food, and the entertainment than in the President's remarks.

But occasionally such a speech would find its way onto the front pages: if it held some hint of serious purpose, some omen of presidential decisions in the making; if the President uttered the toast with a special ring of urgency—or, as Cardwell knew, if one of the President's aides called a few reporters in advance to alert them that something important was about to be said.

This toast, Cardwell guessed, might be widely quoted. The more sensitive reporters would wonder why Rattigan seemed to be worrying to this extent about events in the hemisphere: *"We cannot ignore the threat . . ."*

The wall clock in his office stood at one-fifteen. Cardwell got up from his desk, took off the frayed sweater he wore when he was writing, put on his dark blue coat, and carried the final page into the outer office, a cubicle barely large enough for Dot's desk and a few file cabinets.

"Here's the last part," he said. "How does it sound so far?"

She wrinkled her nose. "Well, not very festive for a social occasion."

"This time he wants to be serious. What bothers me is that it sounds more like the ghost of John Foster Dulles than Carl Rattigan."

Nodding, she rolled a sheaf of paper into her electric typewriter.

"I'm going to lunch," he said. "Call a messenger right away, and don't worry about mistakes on the last page. Or take it up yourself if you want to meet the President in the hall." He headed for the door.

"Oh," Dot said, "you had a call from Arlene Sprague."

He paused. Arlene Templeton Sprague was the White House social secretary, an immensely powerful and awesomely competent middle-aged woman whose finishing-school accent and imperious air irritated Cardwell. From her office in the East Wing, Arlene generated a whirl of invitations, guest lists, place cards, and whispered stories to society reporters. Many felt that her influence rivaled that of the senior men in the West Wing.

Suddenly curious about what she wanted, Cardwell said, "See if you can get her now."

He returned to his desk and waited. In a moment the phone buzzed. He picked it up and said, "Hello, Arlene?"

"John, how *are* you?" The voice, with its lilting affectation, rushed on. "I understand you're working on the dinner speech for tonight, and I just wondered—"

"Arlene," he interrupted, his voice sharp, "if you're suggesting any changes, it's too late. The last page is already being typed—"

"Oh, no, John! Far be it from me to meddle with your deathless prose! The President just wondered if you and Nancy could come to the dinner tonight, since you've played such a big part in this visit."

Cardwell was flattered. "Great, Arlene." Then he thought, if I've played such a big part, why the last-minute invitation? "I'm sure we can be there," he said. "I'll call Nancy."

"John, how wonderful," Arlene breathed. "The Vice President's office called to say he's coming down with the flu or something, and I've been reshuffling tables like mad. Some day we're going to have a dinner with no last-minute cancellations, even if I have to drag—"

The invitation, he realized as she talked, was not straight from the President. At the most, Rattigan had probably approved a fast memo from Arlene, suggesting that Cardwell come because he wrote the toast.

"Thanks, Arlene. I've got to run. Eight o'clock?"

"A little earlier, if you can. I'll send the invitation to your office as soon as the calligraphers finish it. The aide at the door will give you the list for your table. Try to meet them all before dinner and make them feel at home."

"Right." He hung up and headed for the door. "Dot, call Nancy and tell her we're invited to the dinner tonight. I'll come home early, but tell her to have my clothes laid out because we've got to be here by seven forty-five. If she can't find my studs, ask her to buy some for me."

In a moment he was walking up Pennsylvania Avenue toward Seventeenth Street and the nearby Sans Souci, passing the lunchtime crowds that scurried along the windy streets.

As he walked, he thought of handsome women: young Dot Orme in his office; Sarah Tolman, waiting for him now at the restaurant—older than he, almost forty, but still an exciting woman. He realized that he frequently thought about beautiful women, and he felt slightly guilty. A faithful husband by habit, if not always by inclination, he admitted to himself.

He was frowning as he neared the restaurant.

Cardwell looked forward to lunch with Sarah Tolman. Between White House staff members and the journalists who covered the White House, there was a wary symbiotic relationship: The reporters, hungry for insights into the workings of the West Wing, saw even the most casual conversation with a White House man as an opportunity for news. The President's assistants, isolated and confined by their intense schedules, their long hours, and their exclusive view of the world through the President's eyes and interests, relished their meetings with reporters as opportunities to hear opinions from outside the Administration; to pick up news and gossip for the President; and to explain, quietly and confidentially, the real meaning of the President's last speech, his latest act, his most recently announced decision. And so almost every day at lunchtime the tables at Sans Souci and the Federal City Club were filled with Administration aides and reporters, their heads bent toward each other, talking earnestly in low and urgent tones.

His reporter friends, Cardwell knew, were impressed by his closeness to the President—a closeness that most of them tended to exaggerate. And he in turn was flattered to know reporters whose bylines were household words; he was impressed by their rich store of political anecdotes, delighted by their easy, irreverent wit.

After nearly three years, Cardwell was familiar with the pattern these meetings took. After some casual banter—the latest Washington jokes, the most recent snippet of political gossip—the conversation would turn inevitably to the President, to some recent act or statement of the Chief Executive, or to some perplexing facet of his personality. And Cardwell, even at his distance from the President, would earnestly try to explain, to justify the President's words and deeds. "That's not the way it is," he would say gently. "I'm not sure

I agree." Or, when the conversation turned to the character and personality of the President, he would find himself saying, "That's not what he's really like." For Carl Rattigan's staff—like every other President's loyal aides—believed that their chief was generally misunderstood by the press. And reporters, though they certainly liked and admired Rattigan more than his recent predecessors, were constantly prodding for his motives and probing his vulnerable points. It was, after all, their job.

Now, as he entered the bustling restaurant on Seventeenth Street, he wondered how many reporters, for how many years, had listened, in this ornate gold and green room, to other presidential assistants saying earnestly about other Presidents, "No, that's not the way it is. That's not what he's really like."

In the crowded dining room he saw Sarah Tolman, her dark hair pulled sleekly back, finishing a bloody mary and studying the faces in the room. She scanned the tables casually, but with a shrewd reporter's eye, he knew, noting who was leaking news to whom. She was one of the capital's best reporters and she enjoyed a small but satisfying fame: Ten years earlier she had won a Pulitzer Prize for her dispatches from Vietnam.

She was deeply tanned. The last point on her pulse-taking tour of the nation must have been Florida.

"Sarah!" Cardwell reached her table and touched her shoulder. "Who've you been interviewing? The lifeguard at the Fontainebleau?"

They shook hands warmly, and Cardwell sat down.

"Mr. Cardwell," she said in a mock press-conference voice, "what is the mood of the White House?"

"The mood of the White House," he declaimed, "is one of cautious optimism," and they laughed together. He ordered a drink to catch up, and before long they were deep in conversation, oblivious to the murmur of other voices in the large room.

Sarah Tolman and John Cardwell didn't trade facts and rumors, the standard currency of reporter and source. Their medium of exchange was mood, and it was a valuable one. Sarah had met Cardwell a year before, during the off-year congressional elections, when she had joined Rattigan's press entourage for a campaign swing through New York.

As the President's motorcade rumbled from the Bronx—her

birthplace—toward Westchester County, the young aide had taken a seat on the press bus beside her.

They had ridden, through an autumn rain that spoiled two outdoor rallies, up the Hutchinson River Parkway to New Rochelle and back to Manhattan, talking all the while. He had been impressed, first by her dark beauty and her low, sultry voice; later by her intelligence. She had a reporter's sharp insight, made richer by a sort of warm female wisdom. She seemed to know Rattigan and understand him, not only in the way a reporter sizes up a subject, but also in the way a woman knows a man who captures her interest.

On that first meeting Sarah Tolman learned that John Cardwell was not a first-ranking member of the President's staff; not as senior, for example, as Fred Leonhardt, Rattigan's chief speechwriter. But Cardwell, she saw, had a sure feel for the rhythm and the moods of the White House. His instinct, his grasp of nuance in politics, she knew, would make him invaluable to her for the sort of impressionistic reporting that was her stock in trade. So they became acquaintances, then friends.

Cardwell enjoyed lunching with Sarah because she, too, was expert at conveying moods and feelings as well as facts. And she traveled widely, which gave her a range of vision often missing from the Washington scene.

As they ordered she asked, "Really, how is it going over there at the Big House?"

He smiled. "Let me ask you some questions first. How are things in the country?"

"Strange." Her brow furrowed. "I'm always amazed at how different the rest of the country is from Washington. In this town you'd think politics was at the heart of the universe: It rules people's lives. Out there"—she waved her hand—"people manage to hold jobs, have babies, and wash their cars without thinking about Congress or the President or Washington for days—hell, years—on end."

"Isn't that partly why Washington exists—so they can be indifferent if they want to?"

"I don't mean they're indifferent. Actually they're quite interested to meet someone from Washington, full of questions and pretty well informed. They just have their own lives, a different set of values. It always shocks me. I'm so political. I come back dreaming of a cottage in the suburbs and babies around my feet."

A white-coated waiter filled their glasses with pale wine, then set the carafe between them, and Sarah continued.

"In Washington, we all take our mood from the President, whoever he is. The press, the government pick up his mood. He has this terrific hold on us all. And then you go out in the country and find that they don't feel that way: He doesn't have that hold."

"You mean Rattigan, or any President?" Cardwell's eyes were fixed on her.

"I mean Rattigan. In the campaign I used to watch his following—the liberals, the doves. They were so intense. More zealous, really, than Stevenson's were years ago during his first campaign. Now . . . well, they don't seem to feel that attachment any more. It's gone—as if winning had somehow spoiled it for them."

"My dad used to talk about the ritual cannibalism of liberals. He said they're more loyal to ideas than they are to men. Conviction makes them fickle."

"Whatever it is, it goes pretty deep. I was in Cambridge four days, and I didn't hear a good word for Rattigan, not even from the people who worked hardest for him in the campaign. Then I went up to Brown, to Providence—"

"My alma mater."

"—and it was the same thing. Three years ago, he was a hero to those kids and to the young faculty. Now he's just another politician."

She paused, tracing with her finger the rim of her wine glass, and Cardwell studied her face: her dark, heavily fringed eyes, her broad mouth; a strangely placid face for one so energetic, so intense.

"Sarah, what's the issue? Why are they so down on him?"

"That's the strange thing," she said. "So much of the criticism doesn't seem to touch an issue. There's just a sort of free-floating restlessness and apathy. I think people are tired—tired of the same headlines, the same politicians, the same problems that don't get solved. In New York I heard some really shocking rumors about the President—personal things, very snide. In Miami I went to the club where Joe Topps performs. I used to enjoy his spoofs—the stories, the impersonations of the President: It was always light and good-natured. Now it's bitter—and the audience loves it."

"That doesn't exactly make a trend."

"Maybe not. But when even your best friends are indifferent and your enemies are bitter, that's reason for concern, isn't it?"

The tables beneath the great central chandelier and the green leather banquettes along the wall were beginning to empty now; it was almost two-thirty.

They were silent for a moment, and she spoke again. "And it's not just the ideologues. All over the country I heard people getting personal, calling Rattigan the playboy President—the same people who voted for him because he was tough on crime, a tough DA. In the Midwest they don't like the vacations, the witty speeches, the good looks. They don't like it that there's still so much crime; they don't like high prices. If he ever had anything that could be called a coalition, it was certainly a shaky one."

"Was?"

"The Vice President has been making speeches out there in his old home grounds, and they like the contrast: He's sober, hard-working, folksy. He makes Rattigan look flashy and superficial."

"Sarah, nobody solves the issues overnight, and it's unfair to—"

"Fair or not, he came in creating such expectations, such hope—it's frustrating for people to want so much and see so little happen. Sooner or later the frustration gets personalized, and that's what I think is happening. His stock of support, of public enthusiasm, seems to be just drying up. When that happens, it won't be too many months before the long knives are drawn. Any issue can do it."

"Is that what you're going to write?"

"I'm afraid so."

"You're telling me that people are disenchanted with the President *because* he's the President?"

"Because he's the President in a very difficult and frustrating time. I said the feeling was strange. I guess a better word would be ominous, as if one big issue could bring everything down, bring all the troublemakers out of the woodwork—hawks, doves, intellectuals, fascists, screwballs."

When she talked about the President she sounded almost protective, and Cardwell was grateful to her.

"You know," he said, "you've never told me anything I couldn't rely on absolutely, and I've never read anything of yours that didn't seem sound. But I'm sitting here hoping you're wrong."

Sarah laughed, and Cardwell glanced at his watch.

"I've got to go soon," he said. "The Vice President is sick, so Nancy and I are filling some chairs at the dinner tonight."

"Sick?" She looked up sharply, and a flicker of concern crossed her face.

"Nothing serious. A cold, the flu."

They finished lunch. Sarah signed the check—a gesture that once had disturbed Cardwell, but no longer did. She was on an expense account; he was not.

"You let me do all the talking!" Sarah said suddenly. "And I brought you to lunch so I could ask some questions."

"Walk back with me," Cardwell said. "You can ask your questions on the way."

He helped her on with her coat. Where her dark hair was caught at the nape by a multicolored scarf, a few tendrils had escaped. He noticed her perfume, heavier than Nancy's, somehow oriental.

She smiled. "If we keep having such serious conversations over lunch, our colleagues will think we're having an affair."

He laughed. "Your colleagues will think that. Mine will think I'm leaking White House secrets."

Smiling, they walked out into the November chill.

"Okay, fire away," said Cardwell.

"Well, as soon as I finish this series I'm going to South America, to check out some rumors and hints at the office—a story that Chilean troops are crossing the border to help the rebels in Bolivia. Are you getting any of this at the White House?"

"Bolivia?" He deflected her question. "You really live dangerously, don't you?"

"It's this very unfeminine quality I have. When I was seventeen I went to New Jersey one Saturday and jumped out of an airplane. My mother almost died."

He had a brief picture of her falling, her arms outstretched against the rushing air.

"You didn't answer my question," she said.

Cardwell stared at the ground as he walked, then said softly, "Sarah, I don't know. Bolivia's hardly my specialty, and I'm not that much on the inside."

A long line of black limousines waited in front of the Blair House: Badillo's caravan. Two young Marines guarded the door, and a cluster of policemen huddled on the curb nearby. Flags, bracketed on lampposts for the welcome, snapped in the November wind.

Sarah was looking at him, questioning, expectant.

He thought of the toast, with its strangely militant language, and then looked up at Sarah.

"I just don't know, Sarah."

"I'm sure you do know that the Vice President has stepped up his speaking schedule," she said. "He's been doing almost nothing else for two months, and he's being very well received."

"What does that have to do with Bolivia?"

She smiled mischievously. "John, I don't know. I'm not that much on the inside." And they laughed.

They reached the driveway near the West Wing, and as they shook hands, Sarah's tone was serious. "I don't know whether he's really in trouble or not, John. It's just my guess. But I hope he'll be careful. He shouldn't do anything to lose his own people. Why is he playing up to this awful creature from Paraguay, Badillo?"

"He's not playing up to Badillo. It's a fairly routine visit. For all we know Badillo isn't asking for anything, and he won't get anything."

"They're all asking for something."

"Well, I don't know."

"Besides, John, it just looks bad, Carl Rattigan embracing this . . . this—"

"Dictator?"

"Worse. Can't you see how his liberal friends would feel betrayed?"

"Sarah, for God's sake," Cardwell said slowly and earnestly, "he's President of the United States. There are some things he might know that even your sources are dry on. And countries aren't people. You can pick and choose the people you want to associate with, but diplomacy's a little more complicated."

Sarah laughed, amused by his earnestness.

"You really love your job, don't you?"

He laughed, too, surprised by her question. "I guess I do," he said. "I really do."

It was true. It had been three years since Rattigan was elected, but to Cardwell it seemed no time at all.

On most mornings when he entered the White House, he felt a

rush of emotions: an almost charged, physical excitement, and amazement that chance, accident, had brought him to this place. The aura of power that pervaded the halls and offices of the White House hung like an essence in the air, the way the scent of money fills and dominates a bank. And he loved it, loved the excitement, the exhilaration of playing for high stakes. Even though he was a middle-level assistant, one of the more anonymous of Rattigan's entourage, he loved the sense of being close to the center of power.

"How about your wife?" Sarah said.

"Nancy? She hates it. She loved Louisville, and she's never gotten used to Washington. She never sees me. She can't understand why I love politics, love the long hours."

"Well," she said, "there are wives and there are political wives. It's hard on the ones who don't love politics."

He nodded, remembering.

Just after Rattigan's election, while carpenters labored in the cold to complete the inaugural grandstand in front of the White House, they had found a house in Bethesda that Nancy liked. But within a matter of months, Cardwell was in the West Wing, close to the inner mechanisms that made the White House go, and Nancy was pining for their old house in Louisville, for her old friends, for the days when her husband was not so tense and so preoccupied.

"I've got to run," said Sarah. "Have a good time tonight."

"Have a safe trip," he said. He stared as she walked toward the Northwest Gate.

One of the West Wing's prettiest secretaries, returning late from lunch, passed him. "Hello, Mr. Cardwell."

"Hello. Nice to see you," he said. But he scarcely noticed her at all.

The sun struggled to see through the slate-gray sky. The White House seemed caught in shadow.

He walked inside.

Meanwhile a secret meeting was beginning in the White House. The silk draperies were drawn in the Cabinet Room, where six men waited, scattered around the long, dark table. When the two Presidents entered, followed by their interpreter, the men rose, came together for hurried, muted introductions, then rearranged themselves about the table after the Presidents sat down.

Brooks Healy, State, and James Woodson, the Secretary of Defense, flanked Rattigan. Badillo took the empty chair directly across the table; his Foreign Minister, Costa-Murillo, and the interpreter took seats beside him. At the far end of the table three additional Americans sat down.

"Gentlemen," Rattigan said, "I don't think it's necessary to dwell on the gravity of the matter before us, or to stress that this meeting is strictly off the record. We have a critical request from Bolivia for military equipment, air support, and combat troops. President Badillo is offering to put in a Paraguayan contingent if we go in. Your Excellency—" he looked across the table to Badillo "—you may want to start first, or we can begin with the briefing."

After a whispered colloquy with his Foreign Minister, Badillo waved toward a large easel at the table's end and spoke in a gravelly voice to the interpreter.

"First the briefing, if you please," the interpreter said.

On the easel there was a large map: the looming, pendulous shape of South America. Shaded in red at its center, positioned and shaped like a human heart, was the outline of Bolivia, marked by arrows.

"Mr. Karnow?"

At the President's nod, his senior adviser for national security affairs rose from the trio of men who sat at the end of the table. He stepped to the easel.

"Mr. President, Your Excellency." Sheldon Karnow spoke in a voice of calm authority, like a professor delivering a lecture. "Director Harkness will join me in this briefing, which includes intelligence received as late as noon today."

Harkness, the CIA director, looked nothing like a spy: His face was the round, pink, genial face of a favorite uncle.

"Ambassador Williams flew in from La Paz last night," Karnow said. "He can answer our questions about the situation up close." The President nodded. Bert Williams was a friend of Rattigan's from Harvard days. Rattigan remembered him as crisp and well tailored, but today he seemed almost disheveled: puffy-eyed, gray. When summoned secretly to Washington, the ambassador had announced a diplomatic cold, canceled his appointments, and rushed in darkness to a waiting Air Force jet. Now no one knew of his presence in the capital; he had snatched a few hours of sleep at Andrews Air Force Base, then he had been rushed directly to this room.

"The most intense activity in Bolivia, as you know," said Karnow, "has been in the southeastern portion of the country. The Bolivian Army has been almost totally preoccupied with the guerrilla problem down here. Now, Mr. President—" Karnow swung his pointer to the left edge of the red-shaded mass and stopped it on the thin, irregular line separating Bolivia and Chile "—now we are concerned about activity farther west—" he paused, an ominous pause "—outside Bolivia."

Leaning forward, eyes narrowed, the men in the room followed the line that Karnow traced.

"We have noticed in the past three weeks tremendous activity in northern Chile—an almost constant movement of troops and equipment by railway into the area along the frontier, together with a sudden flurry of construction work. The photographs show some of the building in the past two weeks."

He removed the map, revealing a board on which four square, mottled aerial photographs were mounted. There was silence except for the busy whispering of the interpreter.

"As you can see, gentlemen, three weeks ago this area was almost virgin territory, except for the railroad; salt flats, bare land, virtually uninhabited. Here you can see the start of construction: long, tin-roofed sheds, probably barracks, thrown up in a very short time. And in this photograph—"

So this is how it happens, Rattigan thought. He leaned hard on the right arm of his chair, held by Karnow's impressive voice, and felt the familiar sensation beginning again: the feeling of weight, of heaviness.

When crisis came, the President felt it as a physical burden, a tightness in the chest. Reaching for the telephone at four in the morning, seeing the dial's ghostly glow in the dark: "Mr. President—" Karnow speaking softly "—I'm sorry to wake you, but we have some trouble . . ." But until now, none of the troubles his Administration had encountered had burst into full-blown crisis.

I've been lucky, the President thought.

Early in his presidency, the right-wing generals in Chile had finally been toppled. And when a moderately left-wing government was freely elected, Carl Rattigan had applauded; he had signaled his approval by sending Abner Hoffman to represent the United States at the installation of Chile's new President. And things had gone quietly enough, for a year. . . .

He looked down the table toward the easel. Harkness had risen, was talking: "All this could indicate that instead of just a gun-running operation, they're planning something major: a heavy movement of equipment across the border—"

"Or troops?" Secretary Woodson asked.

"Or troops," Harkness replied.

His answer hung on the silence, and the interpreter whispered to Badillo.

There had been signs, of course: premonitions. After that first quiet year, the CIA had begun sending reports to Rattigan that hard-line leftists were streaming back to Chile from their exiles in Cuba and East Germany. But Rattigan had seen nothing in the reports to justify action by the United States.

Then, eighteen months after the free elections, it had happened: an outbreak of political bloodshed in Santiago—and in one convulsive week, the political pendulum in Chile had jerked violently from left-of-center to extreme left. Strange how things happen. . . .

Now, sitting in the Cabinet Room, Rattigan remembered the week of the coup. After all the briefings had ended, he had called Healy to the Mansion and asked his advice.

"Well, Brooks?" he had said, "what now?" The view from his White House bedroom swept across the South Lawn past the Washington Monument to the Jefferson Memorial, a soft, round glow by the Tidal Basin. Even from a mile away you could almost see Jefferson's face, caught in the sharp glare of a spotlight.

"Let's keep cool," Healy had said. "The hawks will grumble about Soviet influence in Chile and quote the Monroe Doctrine. But you shouldn't overreact. Let's cut off relations and leave it at that. If worse comes to worst, we can isolate Chile—organize a trade boycott."

Healy. He was a good Cabinet man for the same reason he had been a great lawyer: He knew his job was not only to advise, but also to reassure his client. Rattigan, reassured, had kept cool—but slowly, worse *had* come to worst, until now they all sat here.

Lucky as hell, Rattigan thought—until now.

Harkness continued, his voice easy and informal, in contrast to

Karnow's professorial tone: "Chile, of course, has been sending in equipment, medicine, and some irregulars to help the rebels. So far this has been a small-scale operation. But now it's beginning to have impact: The thing is on the edge. You can see that it's a great temptation or a great opportunity for them to mount a large effort from outside."

Looking past the portly Harkness, Rattigan stared at the photographs with their strangely abstract images. Tin sheds? They could be concrete slabs, pools of water, anything. He felt a sudden rage at the fuzziness, the imprecision of the photographs; rage at the glib certainty of Karnow; a sudden wild desire to fly to the troubled land himself, see for himself if there were buildings, troops, aircraft being landed.

I'm not going to risk a war, he thought, over a few blurry pictures.

Then his rage subsided, leaving only the feeling of weight, of tightness.

Harkness finished and looked expectantly at the President.

"Thank you, Ken," he said softly. "Can we hear something now from Ambassador Williams? Bert? I'm sorry you had to leave La Paz so quickly, but I wanted you here for this."

Rattigan hungered for facts, for light, for some clue beyond the dim shapes in the photos—but he was weary of the talk. He knew what the men in the room would recommend; he did not want to hear it. An hour had passed since the meeting began in the closed room with its drawn gold curtains.

Ambassador Williams spoke from his chair, spreading his hands thoughtfully before him on the Cabinet table.

"I can't add much, Mr. President, except to say that I've been in Bolivia almost two years, and all I've seen in that time has been a kind of erosion, a weakening. Now, with the collapse of the world tin market, they're weaker than ever.

"You've got an army of ten thousand men with a history of defeat. The textbooks tell us that for any advantage at all, you've got to have ten army and police for every guerrilla. They had that for a while, but with the infiltration"—he shrugged and turned his hands up in a gesture of resignation—"it's like trying to bail out a boat with a hole in the bottom."

The President looked down the long table, eying Williams, Harkness, and Karnow.

"You're expecting trouble, then."

Harkness spoke in reply. "I'm not in the business of making flat predictions, Mr. President. But I think it's clear that we have a dangerous situation on our hands. Anything could happen, and—"

Across the table from Rattigan, Badillo—who had been listening silently to his interpreter's whispering—raised his hand and leaned forward to speak. His burst of loud, rapid Spanish in the quiet room caused all the men to turn abruptly toward him, and the interpreter began his translation.

"You are not in the business of predicting," Badillo said, nodding toward Harkness. "So I will make a prediction for you. If you do nothing, or if you do too little, these predators will move in, they will invade. It will not be in one grand movement, all at once, naked and obvious to the world: They will move by stealth, or they will claim some legal reasons. They will announce that they have been called upon to 'liberate' the Bolivians from their oppressors, or some such lie. But believe me, it will happen. They will move."

Even when Badillo paused for the translation of his words, the men in the room stared at him, scarcely aware of the interpreter.

"I do not think it is enough," he said, "merely to respond to their aggression, if and when they move. I think it is essential to prevent it —to make them wish they had never thought of it."

"You're suggesting some sort of pre-emptive strike?" asked Secretary Woodson softly, and the interpreter whispered busily.

"I know that what I say is impolitic," Badillo answered. "But I will say it: You have the means. You have airplanes, missiles. In the long run, you would be saving lives—by hitting now."

There was a stubborn silence in the room. The Secretary of Defense glanced at Rattigan, then explained, "Your Excellency, I'm afraid that is the one alternative we could never adopt. Even if it were effective, we could never properly explain it to the world—or to our own people, for that matter. And we might touch off a reaction from other Latin countries, from the Soviets—"

When Badillo spoke again, his tone was low and reflective:

"I am a military man, and when your newspapers describe me, they call me a dictator," he said. "But you would be very wrong to think me bloodthirsty, or to think that my ideals are different from yours."

Rattigan, fascinated, leaned forward. What's he getting at? he wondered.

"I love liberty!" Badillo exclaimed, almost rising from his chair with the final word, *libertad*.

"I did not send my sons to Spain or Portugal to the university, but to the United States," he said. "When I go tomorrow to place a wreath at your monument to Thomas Jefferson, some will think it a mockery. But they will be wrong: I want for my people some day to have what he gave you."

Badillo's Foreign Minister, seated beside him, nodded as if to confirm his agreement, and one or two of the men in the room shifted in their chairs.

"So, gentlemen," he continued, "I suggest decisive action against this aggression. Not because I am bloodthirsty, or because I believe in a quick resort to arms, but because I believe that if we are not hard on these animals, democracy will have no future—in my country, or in many others."

He paused, breathing heavily as his interpreter translated, and he looked from side to side as if awaiting an answer. When none came, he spoke again.

"My friends, I will not appeal only to your love of liberty. Let me remind you of your interest in stability, in order." He raised one finger for emphasis. "If you allow one nation to march upon another —openly or by stealth—our whole continent will catch fire. And this time you will feel the heat, the burning, because you are very close."

He looked across the table at Rattigan. "I am familiar with your political record, Mr. President. I know you do not approve of police actions by the United States, and I respect your motive in that. I can only observe that the question before your country is not whether to be a policeman in the world. You already are; there is no one else. You must determine what kind of policeman you will be. Will you be strong, or weak? Will you act, or be indifferent? Will your indifference lead to greater turmoil, to war?"

Rattigan, who had almost been moved by Badillo's words at first, was irritated by the lecturing tone of his visitor. He replied with an edge of severity in his voice.

"I think I'd prefer to hear some practical suggestions at this point,

Your Excellency. What do you recommend, short of a pre-emptive strike?"

"A force on the Altiplano and in Bolivian cities to stop any incursion—a force large enough to meet any eventuality." The interpreter, echoing Badillo's tone, spoke the words with exaggerated precision. "I can speak for the President of Bolivia in advocating this, and I have reason to believe we can get the co-operation of other nations in the hemisphere. At least some of them. I am prepared to send a contingent of my own."

The Defense Secretary, Woodson, spoke again. "You would consider it enough, sir, if the United States offered equipment, supplies, logistical support for such a protective force?"

"No!" Badillo said, and Rattigan noticed that he did not wait for a translation of Woodson's question. "No, gentlemen. To offer materiel without men is not enough. It says to the world that you, the United States, care about what happens, but only up to a point—a point short of risking your men. I believe it would be interpreted now as a sign of weakness. I am afraid you must face the necessity of committing troops. Not many, but some; enough to show that you mean it. And if you decide not to do it now, I can only suggest that you are postponing the inevitable."

There was silence in the room. A few of the Americans around the table looked toward their President, waiting for his reply. He said nothing.

"I am stopping in La Paz on my way home," Badillo said. "Must I report to President Rojas that I have no reassurance?"

Rattigan resisted Badillo's pressure. "Your Excellency, we are going to meet our responsibilities in this thing. But *we* are going to decide what those responsibilities are."

"You will make a public statement tomorrow?" Badillo pressed on.

"I think you'll be interested in what I say tonight," Rattigan replied.

"You will give some indication about a commitment of troops?"

Rattigan's face flushed with irritation, but before he could answer, the door opened. Anders Martin slipped in and said, "Mr. President, you've gone over two hours. If you're escorting General Badillo to his car, the press would like some pictures."

Rattigan nodded and stood up. "Gentlemen, we may want to continue this tomorrow afternoon. Thank you very much. Brooks—" he nodded toward the Secretary of State "—could you wait for me in my office?"

In the Press Room, the two chiefs of state met a barrage of questions. Rattigan held up his hand.

"There'll be a communiqué tomorrow," he said mildly.

"Your Excellency, how would you characterize the talks?"

Badillo surprised the crowd by speaking in English. "Friendly and cordial," he said, grinning a broad, toothy grin. "Very friendly and cordial."

When he returned to the Oval Office, the President saw Brooks Healy standing at the tall french doors, gazing out into the Rose Garden which lay bare and flowerless, abandoned for the winter.

"The old bastard speaks perfectly good English," Rattigan said.

"Yes," said Healy. "But with an interpreter he gets twice as long to think about what he's going to say."

Rattigan sank heavily into a slipcovered sofa, frustration creasing his face. "Say something to cheer me up, Mr. Secretary."

Healy smiled. "Well, it could be worse, Mr. President."

"I don't see how," Rattigan said grimly.

"If you go in on this one, you won't be helping some feudal regime," Healy said. "You'll be defending a democracy, and there's something to be said for that."

"I don't want to get sucked into this thing, Brooks."

"I don't blame you, Mr. President."

"You don't blame me! You sympathize. You feel for me." Rattigan's anger escaped in the sanctuary of his office. "But when push comes to shove, you're going to recommend that we move in there; every bastard in that room is going to recommend it. I'll get cut to ribbons, and you can all go out and sell your memoirs."

Healy stared hard at Rattigan but said nothing.

"I'm sorry, Brooks," Rattigan said softly.

There was a knock at the door and the President's secretary came in, a sheaf of papers in her hand.

"Excuse me, Mr. President. I have some things to be signed, and the toast for tonight."

She laid the papers on the long table behind the President's desk and walked out, closing the door carefully behind her.

"Brooks," the President said, "call Jim Woodson when you get back to your office. I don't want anything to drop between the cracks on this one; I want State and Defense to come in together this time. I want to know everything that can possibly happen down there—every response we can make, and the consequences for each one. Everything."

"Do you want us to send it through Karnow?"

"No," said Rattigan, "I want you to bring it straight to me. I'm going to have Karnow do a memo of his own."

"All right, sir."

"Can you get a paper in to me tomorrow? Close of business?"

"We'll do it," Healy said. And seeing that the meeting was ending, he moved toward the french doors. His long car was waiting on the South Lawn.

"And Brooks, I want something else."

"Yes, sir?"

"I want you to tell me what will happen if I don't do a goddamned thing. What the consequences will be five years, ten years, from now—for us, not the Bolivians. Tell me what happens if Bolivia falls. Do you expect an invasion of El Paso or Houston or New Orleans? Will the Cubans march on Miami Beach and subvert the lifeguards? Because I don't want to do a goddamned thing. I'm not sure it's necessary. I'm not sure it would be right. And even if it were, I'm not sure the people would support it."

For a long time after Healy was gone, Rattigan stood at the french doors, looking, without seeing, across the empty garden past the two great magnolias—Andrew Jackson's trees—that hugged the South Portico. Finally he went to the table behind the desk, picked up the speech draft with its small green transmittal slip, and settled into his padded chair to read, marking occasionally in the margins with his swift scrawl. Once, hearing the dull, shuddering roar of a jet as it lifted away from National Airport, he leaned back, closed his eyes, and wished himself aboard it: a glint of silver in the dying afternoon.

For Cardwell, the rest of the afternoon moved swiftly.

He received advance copies of the Gallup poll scheduled for publication on Sunday. Spreading the sheets before him on his desk, he studied the charts and columns, making occasional notes with his pencil. First he turned to the job rating: Fifty-two per cent of the nation approved of the President's handling of his duties; 39 per cent disapproved; 9 per cent were undecided. The results showed a rise of 6 per cent in the dissatisfied over a previous poll taken thirty days eariler. It was the third straight decline.

Cardwell leaned back in his chair and stared at the ceiling. The poll echoed Sarah Tolman's report of rising disenchantment with Rattigan. And poll results, he knew, must be read in terms of votes. He turned to the pairings: Rattigan against Broadman; Rattigan against Watkins, both Republicans. If the election were held today, the President would win—but his support seemed to be dwindling.

He buzzed for Dot and dictated a short note to Gary Triplitano to accompany a copy of the poll. Knowing the poll and the memo would soon find their way into the President's hands, Cardwell was brief.

"The election is less than a year away," he said. "The time to begin countering a declining poll is when the decline begins, not when it becomes serious. I would suggest, at the very least, a series of direct presidential speeches over the next sixty days and perhaps a more visible stance. More domestic travel and a foreign trip, if success could be reasonably guaranteed, could have a good effect—at least temporarily. We should get four or five members of the staff together to discuss this."

At three-thirty, Nancy called from the hairdresser's. "Why couldn't they give us a little notice?" she complained.

"Sweetheart, stop shouting," he said.

"I'm under the drier and I have to shout! Tell the President I want an engraved invitation next time."

"You tell him tonight. I'll see you around six."

At five-fifteen he walked into the outer office.

"Any calls?"

"Quiet as a tomb. Your wife called to tell me to get you home on time. And the President liked the speech, so you can go home."

"He liked it? Let me see."

She handed him the draft, which the President had returned with only two changes. There was a scrawled note from the President at the end: "Good job. CTR."

Cardwell smiled. "Let's get this on speech cards right away."

"I've already started," Dot said. "Now go home."

When he reached home, he was amazed to find Nancy ready, her hair freshly piled in curls atop her head. She wore a form-fitting, brilliant scarlet gown that made her seem taller. It was not new, but she had worn it only once before.

While he dressed, she sat on the edge of their bed and flipped idly through a magazine.

"Why do you think they asked us at the last minute like that?" she asked.

He fumbled with a cuff link, and she came to help.

"Basically, because the Vice President has the flu. That means the Secretary of State has to be moved to the No. 2 seat, which leaves a table in need of a host somewhere along the line. Most of the Cabinet are out of town, and a few of the staff people are always invited anyway. This time I wrote the toast."

"This almost makes Washington bearable," she said. She helped him on with his coat, eager to be off.

"I'd almost rather stay home," he said. "I always get stage fright when he's using my stuff—worse than if I were making the speech myself."

By seven o'clock, an hour before the dinner, they were driving down Wisconsin Avenue toward the center of the city. Usually he turned left at Massachusetts Avenue, near the Cathedral. But tonight, because they had started early, he drove through Georgetown, past the lighted shops on Wisconsin. At Q Street he turned left and drove to Twenty-ninth, then turned right and drove toward the Potomac—a route he took to avoid the heavy traffic of Georgetown's main streets.

Suddenly, sharply, he pulled the car to the curb and cut the engine.

"Johnny, what on earth!"

"Shh!" He pointed through the dusk and the shadows made by overhanging trees to a large brick house on the corner of N and Twenty-ninth.

The house, an old Federal-style mansion, was Abner Hoffman's. Three years ago, when he had been elected Vice President, he had flatly refused to move from Georgetown to the cavernous official residence on Massachusetts Avenue. "Too big, too fancy, and too drafty for two people," he had drawled. So he and Libby Hoffman, over the protests of the Secret Service, stayed in their old house; they used the government mansion only for official parties.

In the light of the doorway, the Vice President stood, smiling. He was greeting two people at the door: Sarah Tolman of the New York *Times* and Roger Tanham of the Washington *Post*.

"He doesn't look very sick, does he?" Nancy whispered in the silence.

Cardwell put a finger to his lips, watching Sarah Tolman. Why hadn't she mentioned this? In a few moments two men went up the high steps of the house and rang the bell. Despite the gathering darkness, Cardwell recognized Murphy Morrow, columnist and chief political correspondent of the Christian Science *Monitor*. The other man Cardwell didn't know. Again the door opened; the Vice President appeared briefly in the shaft of light, smiling; the door closed again.

"The son-of-a-bitch!" Cardwell started the engine, pulled into the street again, and drove across M Street, under the Whitehurst Freeway, onto Rock Creek Parkway and toward the White House.

"John, why would he lie to the President?"

"I'm not sure," Cardwell said. "But you can bet the President is going to hear about it."

They rode in silence. At seven-fifty, ten minutes before the party was to begin, they passed through the South Gate. John Cardwell nodded to the gatekeeper who checked off their names on his clipboard, and pulled around the great circular driveway to the South Portico: the Diplomatic Entrance.

The great house shone in the night. In the last moments before the dinner a steady line of cars, many of them long, black limousines, pulled up the sweeping drive. By eight, the last of the cars had come and gone; no matter how important the guest, it was *not* fashionable to be fashionably late to a White House dinner.

Their faces flushed with anticipation, the guests entered the President's house: the famous and the ambitious men of Washington;

members of the Paraguayan President's entourage; Americans from New York or Chicago or Houston with a special interest in Latin America; citizens whose names and faces were identified with great fortunes—and maximum contributions to President Rattigan's campaign.

They swept through the Diplomatic Entrance, presented themselves to a crisply uniformed guard, and received table cards from young military officers with close-cropped hair. Then, for a few expectant minutes, the people stood in little groups, murmuring in English or Spanish in the richly papered oval reception room downstairs.

Arlene Sprague, freshly coiffed and dressed in green, strode up to the Cardwells and kissed Nancy, whom she hardly knew. "Dear, you look so beautiful! John, have you got your table list? We'll be moving upstairs in a minute. Nancy, you'll be at Table 10—by Senator Merrill." Her voice dropped to a hoarse whisper. "He's awfully charming, but watch out if he has too much to drink. He's a Mormon at home, but a terror in Washington."

Then she was off, circling expertly among the guests, smiling always, but glancing about with wary eyes as waiters passed cocktails from silver trays.

A moment later the waiters disappeared, as though at a signal, and the young military aides—imperceptibly at first, and then quite obviously—began moving the guests through the downstairs hall, up a flight of marble stairs, and onto the main floor of the Mansion. The presidential party would receive in the Blue Room.

"I feel like a small-town girl," Nancy whispered as they moved up the stairs.

Cardwell, preoccupied, did not answer. The scene at Abner Hoffman's house had burned itself into his mind. Could the President possibly know that he had been lied to? The Vice President, he was sure, was ducking the dinner, and the news would soon be out—in this town there could be no doubt of that. Cardwell knew he would have to tell Rattigan what he had seen, and as soon as possible.

Suddenly there was a blast of trumpets and a great blaze of television floodlights in the center hall. The Marine Band, its martial blare softened by violins, swung into "Hail to the Chief." A slow-stepping color guard of four young Marines descended the grand staircase from the President's apartment.

Behind them, gleaming and triumphant in black tie, came Carl

Rattigan, his wife, Lisa, on his arm. Both were smiling. President Badillo and his wife, a leathery-faced Latin woman of sixty, followed.

From the waiting guests came a ragged, spontaneous burst of applause, and the party walked into the Blue Room.

The receiving line moved quickly. Both the President and his lady had, in their years of political life, mastered the "politician's pull"—the handshake that at once greets the guest and subtly pulls him along, making way for the next guest to be greeted.

Almost inaudibly, a young officer near the President murmured instructions to the guests in line: "Husbands first, sir, followed by your wife. Please give your names to the aide as you go by."

But when Cardwell stepped up, followed by his wife, the President didn't need any prompting. "John!" he said in a voice of genuine enthusiasm, "that was a beautiful job. Thank you for coming. And . . . Mrs. Cardwell."

Cardwell noticed with a twinge of disappointment that the President could not remember—or did not know—Nancy's name. But Nancy, flushed with the excitement of the moment, noticed not at all.

In the Red Room, Cardwell spotted Anders Martin, a usually unsmiling man with piercing eyes who was as close to Rattigan as any member of the staff, and who was therefore resented by much of the staff.

Tonight, Martin was grinning affably.

He stood in the Red Room, a sort of one-man receiving line, greeting guests as they entered the flamboyant room. But, as always, he was in view of Rattigan through the doorway, ready to respond to the slightest sign from the President: to step quickly to his side, receive whispered instructions, and move quietly into action on the President's behalf. Martin's devotion to the President was total, and he was at his job—receiving instructions, passing along orders, managing the President's schedule, guarding his door—from early morning until late each night, when the cleaning crews took over the West Wing and the White House finally slept.

"Johnny! Great to see you! Who's this beautiful girl? Nancy, sweetheart, you're gorgeous. Johnny, how are you?"

"Fine, Andy," he said. Then he pulled Martin gently aside. "Look Andy, I think I've got to see the President, right away."

"Well, we'll see what we can do. Give me a call in the morning. Mr. Ambassador, how are you?" Martin was already looking toward the next approaching couple. Cardwell had been dismissed. *"Señora* Fuentes," Martin said. "What a pleasure!" When the Brazilian ambassador and his broad-beamed wife had gone past, Cardwell went back to Martin, nodding to Nancy to step away.

"Andy, I've got to see him sooner—tonight, if possible."

Martin frowned, distracted for the moment from his social duties. "What is this, John? Can't you send him a memo?"

"No, I'm sorry."

"Grave matter of national security?"

"Grave matter of political security—the President's."

For the first time, Martin seemed to take the younger man seriously.

"Okay, I'll see what I can do, John. But it had better be damned important."

Then Martin turned back to his greeting and Cardwell joined Nancy, noticing that the color of her dress almost matched the satin wall covering of the Red Room. Then, arm in arm, they strolled from the Red Room through the center hall of the mansion, where the Marine Band played beneath the soft glitter of a pair of eighteenth-century Waterford chandeliers.

They passed the tail of the receiving line and joined a group near the Green Room door: Senator Merrill of Utah, Don Tievolo, a young Democratic congressman from New Jersey, their wives, and a diplomat from Paraguay—a slight, dark man in tinted glasses. After the introductions, the senator resumed his previous comments.

"I was saying, Mr. Cardwell, that the Vice President is making a tremendous impression around the country. Abner spoke in Utah over Veterans' Day, and I can tell you, my people were impressed. And he talks sense. I just wish the President would get out and see the people more. Can't you persuade him, Mr. Cardwell?"

Before Cardwell could answer, the little knots of guests began to move. The high walnut doors at the end of the hall had been flung open, and the crowd was moving toward the State Dining Room.

As they walked toward the dining room, the Paraguayan said, "I have not seen the Vice President. Is he traveling again tonight?"

"No," said the senator. "This afternoon's *Star* says he's in bed with flu. I guess it's this changeable weather."

"Right," Cardwell said. "The climate can certainly change unexpectedly." He glanced at Nancy, who smiled at the secret exchange.

Cardwell headed for Table 4, found his place, and met his guests, who included Sterling Worman, a wealthy Democratic stalwart from New York City; Mrs. Al Loewy, wife of the manager of the Cincinnati Reds, winners of this year's World Series; Robert Foreman, a congressman from Missouri; the Paraguayan minister-counselor, who stuttered; and Mrs. Annette Michaelson, seventy-two-year-old *grande dame* of Washington.

"How do you do. I'm John Cardwell," he said, extending his hand to each.

Downstairs, Cardwell knew, waiters were frantically serving food onto heated plates, passing nervously in review before the chef. A few steps beyond the State Dining Room, in the room known as the Family Dining Room, a makeshift butler's pantry had been set up. Fine carpets had been covered with canvas, priceless antiques draped in heavy cloth, and warming tables set up in the center of the room. The meal, days in preparation, would be served perfectly to 140 guests—a feat requiring dozens of cooks and butlers, and a chef with the logistical genius of a general.

Mrs. Michaelson kept Cardwell's table sparkling. She was a handsome woman, her upswept hair white with age but her eyes and voice deceptively young. Her husband, Oscar Michaelson, had committed suicide twenty-two years before, leaving his wife to spend the generous proceeds of his career as a Washington lawyer. Wise, witty, worldly, and rich, she was a frequent guest at Washington parties, from the White House to the smallest embassies.

"Tell me, my young host, how ever did you come to the White House? Did you write a letter to the President and tell him your qualifications? Did you put an ad in the Washington *Post?*"

"Oh, no," he said, "the President found me by accident."

"How interesting!"

Before the first course ended—a tiny pastry shell filled with steaming lobster thermidor, served with a white California wine—Cardwell had told Annette Michaelson and his other tablemates the story of his unexpected phone call from Carl Rattigan.

He had been fascinated by votes and by politics since he was a teen-ager in Kentucky, reading history, poring over polls and election data. He remembered sitting rapt for hours—at home in Louisville or in his father's green-carpeted office downtown—while his father, a newspaper publisher whose backstage passion was politics, talked earnestly to governors, mayors, legislators.

The boy had watched, fascinated, as men worked to translate words into votes, votes into power.

By the time he was in college he had begun to form his own political beliefs, and in his sophomore year he dropped his classes for several weeks to campaign for Eugene McCarthy.

Then he graduated from Brown, returned to his place on his father's newspaper, and began to watch again, somewhat mystified, for he felt he was a mere observer of the machinery of power, his father the user of it. But gradually his instincts sharpened, and soon he was an expert, sure of his own insights.

The call from Rattigan had come in mid-March, when Rattigan's campaign in the primaries was still young. Cardwell's father, a proud Democrat, had printed a number of his son's editorials in a pamphlet entitled, *New Directions, New Issues, New Candidates*. The candidate, somehow, had seen and liked it; he called Cardwell from his chartered airplane and invited him to join the campaign. Cardwell, with his father's permission and his wife's uncertain consent, left the newspaper the next week to join the jet-borne caravan.

"You mean he just called you like that, out of the blue?" Mrs. Michaelson asked.

"Well, I think he knew my father, or knew of him. But he did call out of the blue—literally," Cardwell said, and the group laughed.

Cardwell glanced anxiously about the room. Where was Andy Martin? Had he spoken to the President? What if the President had ordered the Vice President to skip the dinner and brief key reporters? Cardwell knew he would look unforgiveably foolish if that were the case—but he knew too that such a possibility was remote. Something was going on, and the President should know it.

The dinner was a triumph: tournedos bathed in a sauce of wine and mushrooms, two wines, and a cream-filled, strawberry-topped pastry served with champagne and christened *Crème Emelda,* after the Paraguayan President's wife.

Before dessert was finished, a butler brought a tabletop lectern to the President's place, and the room lights were brightened. The din subsided: It was time for the toast.

Cardwell felt a knot low in his stomach, a twinge of stage fright.

"President and Mrs. Badillo, Your Excellencies, ladies and gentlemen."

Rattigan's voice was rich and steady; he was a superb and forceful speaker. With a smile the President was into the speech, speaking rapidly and convincingly, referring only occasionally to the text on the lectern.

He's done his homework, Cardwell thought with a sigh. He's made it his.

"In the defense of liberty, Your Excellency, the United States will not be found wanting. Of that, you and your people, and all men everywhere . . ."

By now the text of the speech would be available in the Press Room to the few reporters who were interested. Perhaps at this moment the story would be moving across the country's late-night news wires. What was the real meaning of this speech? Not even Cardwell, who had written it, could be sure.

"Ladies and gentlemen—" President Rattigan raised his glass, a warm smile playing on his lips "—will you join me in a toast to His Excellency . . ." The assemblage rose as the President finished speaking. There was a chorus of "Hear, hear!" from a few of the men, old hands at the White House dinners, and Cardwell noticed that most of the women were gazing at the President, who stood smiling, his glass raised.

He hypnotizes them, the old devil, Cardwell thought. He wondered involuntarily about the rumors of Rattigan's escapades with women. Such rumors flew about the heads of many important men in Washington, but Cardwell found the gossip hard to believe.

Certainly no one could doubt Rattigan's charm or his eye for beautiful women. He sought them out, even in press conferences calling upon the most attractive female reporters; he charmed them casually, with smiles and compliments, and with the aura of power that was all about him. But no matter how filled with dalliances his past might have been, this President would find them difficult now, Cardwell thought: He was too preoccupied—and too exposed.

The guests settled back in their gilt chairs for President Badillo's speech, which was loud, ornate and interminable—with pauses for interpretation.

Cardwell glanced at his watch: eleven o'clock. There would be dancing after dinner, but Cardwell speculated that the party would end before midnight: The toasts had run rather long, Badillo was not a young man, and the crowd, mostly middle-aged, serious types, was far from swinging.

When, then, would he get to see the President? He looked about the room for Andy Martin. Had Martin spoken to the President? Sent him a note? Cardwell decided that sometime during the dancing he would try to catch the President's eye, take him aside, give him some information of the Vice President's intrigues.

The applause for Badillo's toast was brief and perfunctory—as was the dancing that followed in the East Room.

Cardwell danced with Nancy, but all the while he kept looking toward the President, wondering if a moment would come during the evening for a brief word with him. And all the while, he cursed Andy Martin.

The moment did not come. Just before midnight the state visitors departed, shaking hands in the foyer with the President and his wife, who immediately disappeared. The crowd, first in couples and then in larger numbers, began to depart. It was twelve o'clock.

"Wasn't it beautiful?" Nancy asked as they retrieved their coats downstairs.

"It was okay." His resentment and disappointment had formed a knot in his stomach. "Let's go home."

Then, as they walked out, a black-coated usher stepped up.

"Mr. Cardwell?"

Cardwell nodded.

"The President wants to see you. He's upstairs in the West Hall. We have a car for Mrs. Cardwell."

Cardwell stepped off the elevator into the wide hall and stood waiting, not quite sure where to go.

The great center hall, running the length of the mansion from east to west, was in semidarkness. Nearby, a large antique clock, ticking slowly, showed the time: a few minutes past midnight.

"John? Come on in and have a drink." The President's voice came from the west sitting room—really not a room, but the west end of the long hall.

"Good evening, Mr. President."

As Cardwell walked in, the President, his jacket tossed aside, rose from his large wing chair. His formal shirt was half-unbuttoned and he was wearing horn-rimmed glasses—which he never wore in public.

Rattigan looks tired, Cardwell thought. Gone now were the vitality and easy charm he had displayed downstairs.

They shook hands, and the President motioned toward a chair. A pile of newspapers—tomorrow's Washington *Post,* and the earliest edition of the New York *Times*—lay scattered on the floor nearby, and on a low table there were a bottle of scotch, a small silver ice bucket, and several glasses. None had been touched.

"That was a nice job on the toast, John. I'm sorry to make your wife go home alone."

"That's all right, sir."

The President leaned forward and poured two drinks, pushed a glass over to Cardwell, and then leaned back without touching his glass.

"Okay, what's all this secret business?"

Cardwell hesitated an instant.

"Well, Mr. President, this may turn out to be nothing, but I thought you'd better know. I don't think the Vice President missed the dinner tonight because he was in bed with the flu."

The President looked up sharply.

"I drove past his house tonight on the way down, and I saw him usher four reporters through his front door."

"Who were they?"

"Sarah Tolman of the *Times,* Tanham of the *Post,* Murphy Morrow, and one other whom I didn't know. There could have been others, but I didn't see them. I wasn't sure: Is this something he was doing on your behalf?"

"Hell, no. He told me he had the flu." The President's eyes went hard behind the glasses. "Giving a backgrounder on the night of a state dinner after we announced he's sick. He knows it'll get around that he snubbed Badillo."

He reached for his glass and took a long drink. The silence in the half-darkened room was heavy. Cardwell glanced around the room with its gold-framed paintings and pairs of double doors. Behind one set of tall doors Lisa Rattigan lay asleep after a strenuous official evening. Behind another, in the butler's pantry off the dining room, there was an usher on night duty, waiting, dozing lightly, ready to serve. But the surrounding silence made Cardwell feel that he and the President were isolated in the enormous house—shut off, alone.

"It might not be anything important," Cardwell said, trying to fill the silence.

"No, I should have seen this coming," the President said. "I should have seen it coming." Then he looked up, half smiling, and said, "I'm afraid Abner Hoffman hates my guts."

Cardwell said nothing. Since their days in the Senate, Rattigan and Hoffman had been known as close political allies.

"We've never exchanged a cross word," Rattigan continued, "but I knew it a long time ago."

"Why?"

The President set down his drink. "Because everything he wanted, everything he worked his ass off to get, came easy for me."

Cardwell leaned forward, and the President went on.

"He wanted to be the Majority Leader. He was older than I, had more seniority, and I beat him. I'll hand it to him, he never showed a hint of resentment."

Again the President paused, and Cardwell could feel the silence like a third presence in the room.

"He wanted the nomination. He wanted to be President, really thought he could get it by winning some late primaries. But before he could make a move we had the early primaries wrapped up."

"I didn't know he was that serious."

"Oh, hell, yes. He wanted to be President." Rattigan finished his drink, set down his glass. "You know, it's funny, I never suspected Abner resented me. He was so—affable. When I knew I had the nomination I asked Brooks Healy who I should pick for a running mate, and he said, 'There's only one choice: Abner Hoffman.' I was dumbfounded, then Brooks told me his reasons. 'First, because he's the smartest man in the Senate. And second, because he hates your guts.'

"I said, 'Brooks, why on earth should I pick a man who hates me?' And he gave me the best advice I ever got: 'Suppose you pick somebody else. Abner will go back to the Senate, and he'll be the Majority Leader. He'll see you living in the White House, flying around on Air Force One, and it will be too much for him. Either he'll go on a sit-down strike, or he'll starts cutting you up.' "

The President sighed. "So I decided on Abner. I put him where he could do the least harm. We agreed on all the issues."

"Why do you think he accepted?" Cardwell asked.

"I don't know. I was surprised myself. Of course, I really did a selling job. I told him he wouldn't be just another Vice President—that he would be at my side on every decision. I told him this was a chance to put his fingerprints on history. I guess I believed it then." He shook his head.

"Well, he's a proud man, an ambitious man. A man like that can take just so many dam dedications and fund-raising dinners." Again the President fell silent, and in a moment he said, "I should have seen it coming. He's finally taking his chance to cut me up a little. He was against the Badillo visit. He doesn't feel he's listened to—and he's probably right. He's just severely frustrated. I don't know. But one thing you can be sure of." His voice went hard. "It won't happen a second time."

Cardwell sensed that he was staying too long, hearing too much. But as he started to rise, the President spoke again.

"No, stay. I'm sorry to unburden myself so." He rewarded Cardwell with a friendly smile. "What about you? How are you getting on? What are you doing to help the cause?"

Cardwell settled back into his chair.

"Mr. President, I sent Trip a memo today about the polls. Have you seen it yet?"

"Not yet. Good news or bad?"

"Well, you're down, for the third month. There's no way of knowing if it's a trend, especially this long before the election. These things jump all around; they're swayed by small things."

The President was interested. "But you think it may be a trend?"

"I don't know. Maybe just a spell of the doldrums. But it's three straight months now." He finished his drink and set it down by the President's empty glass. "The significant thing in these polls is the pairings. Both the top Republicans are gaining when they're paired with you. Broadman has 38 per cent. I think, and Watkins has 40 per cent. They're picking up some strength from you, some from the undecided."

The President broke in, half smiling, "You specialize in good news, don't you, John?"

"Well, you're still way ahead. But if this is a trend, it's not a good one. It means voters are growing uneasy, restless, dissatisfied. They may not even know exactly why they're dissatisfied—but if it lasts, if it gets worse, it will probably find an issue. There's always an issue."

The President nodded. "I can think of a dozen."

"Well, sir, it seems to me that the important thing is to find a way now, before the convention, to fight the downtrend. This is one of those times when popularity is an issue in itself, when style also becomes substance. This is when you've got to make every effort to get to the people—to win them in advance." He realized that he was pushing too hard at the tag end of a long day. He smiled and said, "It's all in my memo, in carefully chosen words." He rose.

The President stood up with him and walked along to the elevator.

"I'll be looking forward to seeing your memo. But I'm not turning any cartwheels down Pennsylvania Avenue just to boost a Gallup poll. No Indian headdresses."

Cardwell grinned. "We have some better ideas than that, Mr. President."

"All right. And don't tell anybody—*anybody*—what you saw at the Vice President's house. I'm going to wait until I see it in the papers—and then I'll call him in for a nice heart-to-heart."

"Right, sir. Good night."

"Give my best to your wife."

Noiselessly, the elevator dropped him to the ground floor of the silent White House. When the door rolled back, he stepped into the red-carpeted ground floor hall and nodded to the lone guard, who noted his departure in a black log-book.

Cardwell was troubled by the conversation with the President, but try as he might, he could not suppress his exhilaration: After more than three years, tonight he had glimpsed the center of the action.

Outside the Diplomatic Entrance, Cardwell climbed into his car, nosed it through the wide black gates, and sped through dark and silent streets toward home.

At the Pentagon, the lights burned late. The working group had begun its deliberations within three hours after Brooks Healy left the President on Monday. Healy had returned to his office, spoken briefly with Woodson, then placed calls to the other officials whose help would be needed in preparing the paper for the President.

They decided to meet at the Pentagon, in the Secretary's conference room. There, across the river from Washington, their comings and going would be less likely to be noticed.

By nightfall Monday the group had gathered: Healy; Woodson; Harkness from the CIA; Bert Williams, the ambassador to Bolivia; General Roundcastle, chairman of the Joint Chiefs. They were joined by four lesser officials: Thomas Blankenship, the Assistant Secretary of State for Inter-American Affairs; Joseph Tapling, Assistant Secretary of Defense for International Security Affairs; Bernard Weynkamp, the State Department's Bolivian desk man; and Thomas Hertlinger, chief of the State Department's Bureau of Intelligence and Research. Their wives and secretaries had canceled Monday evening's social engagements with bright, persuasive lies; the men, charged with the high energy of crisis, assembled and fell into their discussions, prepared to work through the night and on into Tuesday.

Brooks Healy, who had received the President's order, presided. He slipped away from the high-ceilinged meeting room in the E Ring only to attend the State Dinner, then rejoined the group at midnight, still in his evening clothes. As the discussions went on, bleary-eyed aides and secretaries moved quietly in and out, receiving orders, taking notes, placing calls. Two stocky Army sergeants hauled in maps and easels and stood by, ready to run errands. One by one, the members of the working group threw off their coats, then their ties, and leaned over the table in shirtsleeves, wearily propping their heads on their hands. By 3:00 A.M. on Tuesday, when most of the group went home for a few hours' rest, coffee cups and filled ash trays littered the long conference table.

Brooks Healy did not go home. Alone, he paced Woodson's spacious office, stood for a long minute gazing at a portrait of James Forrestal, then walked to a window and stared out. Beyond the Pentagon's mall, across the river, the city slept beneath its softly glowing monuments, unaware. Late-night traffic rumbled up the Shirley Highway toward the city. In the next room electric typewriters clattered relentlessly: Four extra secretaries had been called in—older women, reliable, accustomed to crisis labor.

A strange business, Healy thought. The more serious the crisis, the smaller the number of officials called in to work on it. Nine men would prepare the working paper; only three—he, Woodson, and Harkness—would sign it, taking full responsibility for what their subordinates contributed. And only one man, the President, would act upon it.

Rattigan had few alternatives, really. He could do nothing. He could attempt to deal with the crisis diplomatically, sending a stern note to Chile through the Swiss Embassy in Santiago, then appealing to the Soviets to restrain their client state. If these efforts failed, he could call for urgent meetings of the OAS and perhaps the UN Security Council. He could send military equipment—without troops. He could send part or all of the troops recommended by Badillo. And finally, he could choose to intervene massively, to launch a pre-emptive strike that would crush any action on the part of the Chileans. This last alternative—which only General Roundcastle was willing to discuss as a real possibility—had come to be known around the table as "fire in the sky."

He stepped to the door and said to the nearest secretary, "I'm going to sleep for a while."

"All right, sir. Does our typing bother you?"

"Not at all."

He took off his shirt, fell onto James Woodson's long leather couch, and lapsed into sleep with the office lights still blazing.

Healy awoke at 10:00 A.M. to find the typed draft completed: an estimate of the current Bolivian situation by Williams, Harkness, and Weynkamp; an analysis of diplomatic and military alternatives by Roundcastle, Tapling, and Blankenship; a paper, "The Consequences of Inaction," by Hertlinger; and additional comments by Healy and Woodson.

He dictated a short note to accompany each copy:

"TOP SECRET. I would greatly appreciate your comments on this draft, expressed as suggested changes, by 2:00 P.M. today. The working group will reassemble at 4:00 P.M. for its final meeting in Secretary Woodson's office to make final changes and to approve the final draft."

The last meeting of the group was uneventful. The nine men were agreed on most of the language, and the changes were minor.

After some earnest discussion, they brought Roundcastle around: A pre-emptive strike was really impossible, not worthy of consideration by the President. A final paragraph was added to the covering memorandum: "Although there are differences among us as to the most desirable course of action, it is the unanimous conclusion of the working group that both Alternative 1, inaction, and Alternative 6, a pre-emptive strike against the government of Chile, are unacceptable in the light of national interest."

The typists fell to work again, and by nine o'clock on Tuesday evening their work was done. Shortly afterward an olive-drab sedan pulled up to the White House West Basement, and a young Marine messenger stepped out with two envelopes in his hand. He signed a log book at the guard's desk, then delivered both envelopes to the Situation Room, one labeled "For the President's Eyes Only" and the other "For Mr. Karnow's Eyes Only." From the Pentagon, the weary members of the working group made their way home, to eat, to sleep, and to await the President's decision.

Wednesday the Twenty-second

When the President wakened on Wednesday morning he had made his decision: He would not send the troops. He couldn't.

He woke at seven, snapped on the lamp beside his high bed, and finished reading the stack of memos and reports piled on the table beside him. By eight, most of the papers lay in a heap around the bed.

But he kept one beside him: the thick document from Healy's working group. Another document, typed on White House paper, lay beside him: Sheldon Karnow's memorandum.

The President reached for the white telephone beside his bed and pressed a direct-line button. "Sheldon? Can you come up?"

By the time Karnow had arrived from the West Wing, the President had showered and shaved. Rattigan sat clad in a blue bathrobe, eating his breakfast from a tray beside the window. Late editions of the morning newspapers lay in a heap beside his chair, and the Bolivian memoranda rested beside the tray.

"How about some coffee?" the President asked.

"No, I just had breakfast, thank you."

"Well, I've seen these memos," the President said. "Looks as though you all came down at the same place. I want somebody—you or Brooks Healy—to get in touch with Badillo before he leaves the country," Rattigan said. "Tell him I'm withholding a decision on troops or equipment—don't tell him I've decided against them. Where does he go next?"

"New York, I think, sir."

"Well, maybe we'd better send somebody up there to talk to him." Rattigan pushed his tray away, rose, and walked to his bed. Earlier, while he was shaving, a valet had laid his clothes out neatly on the bed: a blue suit and shirt, a blue and scarlet tie. He sat on the edge of the bed and pulled on his high black socks.

"It's Alternative 2, then? The diplomatic route?" Karnow asked.

"Yes, I think so. Call Brooks and tell him, if you will. How soon can you have a note drafted for the Swiss?"

"No later than two o'clock."

"Keep it simple. Just tell them we consider any attack—no, any hostile action—against Bolivia a matter of grave concern to our interests. We will not sit idly by. Chile must bear the consequences, et cetera."

Karnow sank into a large wing chair, removed a small notebook from his breast pocket, and took notes busily.

"I'd like to have it dispatched by this evening. And tell Brooks Healy to call Lubshanko to his office tonight; completely off the record. I want Lubshanko to see the note to the Chileans. Then tell him that he can prevent a tragic mistake if he can persuade Chile to keep hands off."

The President held up the tie, threw it back onto the bed, then walked to the closet to select a new one. "If Healy thinks that's not enough, let me know, and *I'll* call Lubshanko in."

Karnow scribbled quickly, then asked, "What about the OAS and the Security Council?"

"I don't want to call them yet. Let's see what we can do with a quiet approach first."

The President put on his coat, and Karnow rose to leave. "I'll bring the note up around two, and a talking paper for Secretary Healy to use with Lubshanko."

"Good," said Rattigan. He looked in a mirror above a tall mahogany dresser, tightened the knot of his tie, and patted it lightly.

There was a knock at the door. Karnow stepped across the deeply carpeted room to open it, and Gary Triplitano walked in.

"Good morning, Trip. Sheldon, thank you," the President said.

Karnow, notebook in hand, nodded and left.

"How are you this morning, Mr. President?" Triplitano said.

"I'm mad as hell." Rattigan pointed to the heap of newspapers on the floor. Each one carried, on its front page, a barely veiled account of Abner Hoffman's backgrounder.

"I'd like to kick Abner's ass over the Washington Monument," the President said.

Meanwhile, in the West Wing, Cardwell was reading his morning mail. There was a note from Sarah Tolman, written in her sweeping hand on New York *Times* stationery: "John: Thanks for lunch. Am packing madly for South America. Will see you in a week or two. Yours, Sarah."

Then, across the bottom of the page: "P.S. I saw the V.P. after we talked. No signs of flu, but many of frustration. You'll know the story soon.

"P.S. again: Read my series and tell me what you think. S.T."

Cardwell pushed his coffee cup aside and spread the New York

Times on his desk. Sarah's story, the first installment of her series, was just below the fold on page 1:

PRESIDENTIAL MAGIC FADES
A YEAR BEFORE ELECTION

Growing Problems, Disunity
Cloud Democratic Horizon

The article summed up what Sarah had told him earlier about her travels: Three years in the presidency had dimmed Carlton Rattigan's heroic image.

Cardwell's eye stopped on one paragraph in the second half of Sarah's story: "Disaffection can be detected not only among the voters around the country, but within the Administration itself. Vice President Abner Hoffman, for example, is known to be deeply troubled by his lack of influence in the high councils of policy and increasingly restless in the essentially ceremonial post he holds.

"Hoffman has confided to associates that his advice to the President counts for little, especially in matters of foreign policy.

"Close advisers have urged him to air his ideas publicly and independently, thus forcing the President's attention. But Hoffman, who thus far has borne his frustrations in silence, has resisted such advice."

He turned to the Washington *Post*. Here, too, Hoffman's backgrounder had produced results. Under a two-column headline on page 1—"Rift Rumored Between President, Veep"—the *Post* article came close to exploding Hoffman's pretended case of flu:

"One current disagreement arises from the Rattigan administration's hospitality to Antonio Badillo Silvera, the military ruler of Paraguay, who left Washington late yesterday for a tour of the nation. The Vice President, who usually participates in festivities surrounding such official visits, was pointedly absent from Monday's state dinner. Hoffman pleaded illness, but some observers felt that his ailment might be more political than physical."

Cardwell shook his head: You had to admire Hoffman's nerve and skill. Most readers of these stories would have no idea that the stories had come straight from Hoffman.

He was about to buzz Dot for a second cup of coffee when the telephone rang at his elbow: The interoffice phone button was blinking.

He picked up: "Yes?"

"Have you read the stuff from Hoffman's backgrounder?" It was Gary Triplitano.

"I'm just finishing it. Have you talked to the President?"

"I just did," said Triplitano. "I went up to give him my brilliant analysis—that Hoffman had been squealing to the press—and he told me the whole story. How'd you catch Abner with his hand in the cookie jar?"

"Pure happenstance," Cardwell said. "How's he going to handle it?"

"One, let the story die as fast as possible. Two, answer press queries with a statement of full confidence in Hoffman. And then he's seeing the bastard at two o'clock in his office. Off the record. He's hopping mad, and he's gonna give him hell."

"I'm not sure that's a good idea. Abner's trying to get him riled. Why give him the satisfaction?"

"Johnny, you need to study the Triplitano Golden Rule. In politics, the guy who turns the other cheek gets his ass kicked."

Cardwell laughed.

"Look," said Triplitano, "I was calling about lunch. I showed him your memo on the polls. He wants us to talk about travel plans, give him some ideas."

"Great. I'm free when you are."

"How about one o'clock in the Mess? You get the table."

They met at one in the Staff Mess. The low-ceilinged room in the basement of the West Wing would seat scarcely more than fifty, and at this most popular hour for lunch, every table was filled. Cardwell and Triplitano had a small table against the wall, beneath a large painting of a ship under full sail.

"Fifty-two per cent of the people are convinced he's doing well," Triplitano said. "Only 39 per cent say they're dissatisfied. That's a comfortable margin in my book."

"But the point is that his margin is *shrinking*. Three months ago he had 60 per cent. Last month it was 57 per cent. It won't be long until the Republicans start firing all their big guns. Jesus, if the decline goes on, his rating will soon be under 50 per cent. Do you think we should sit on our tails until that happens?"

"Look," said Triplitano, "all I'm saying is that I don't think he's ready to hit the hustings. He'll explore an idea like this, he'll walk all around it, but in the end he's going to do it his way. I know that guy. When things look tough, he starts withdrawing, brooding, sizing up the situation. Then he'll gather the old crowd around him, like Healy, and it's their advice he'll listen to. I want you to be prepared for that. They're going to tell him not to panic, not to worry about the polls—just to do the best job possible and worry about campaigning when it's time to campaign."

"And they'll be wrong," Cardwell said.

"He's got the best stage anybody can have right now," Triplitano continued, "the White House. On television, he's smooth as glass, and he can reach an audience of eighty million with a major speech. He's the President, for God's sake. Why does he have to go tearing around the country speaking in parking lots?"

"Trip," said Cardwell, "the President is a good performer. He's smart, he's eloquent, he's convincing. But seeing him staring out of a television set is not the same as seeing him in person, in the flesh, in your hometown."

"John, I think he's going to say it's gimmicky."

"I'm not talking about gimmicks," Cardwell insisted. "The only time he travels these days is to go to Palm Springs, and that's not enough. If he makes this trip, it will be to show what he's doing, draw attention to his programs, prove to people that he cares about them." It seemed so obvious to Cardwell, and so damned hard to explain.

Seeing his gloom, Triplitano smiled. "Look, John, that's just *my* reaction to what *his* reaction will finally be. Maybe I'm wrong. As of now, he's interested. I don't know what you said to him the other night, but he was impressed. He wants to see what you suggest."

Cardwell looked up sharply, flattered by Trip's words and tone.

"I don't think it's a good idea to suggest anything too elaborate," Trip said. "But you should work something up—a two-day trip maybe—and send it in. If it looks plausible, I'll put in a good word."

A waiter stepped to the table, carrying a white telephone. "For you, Mr. Triplitano."

While Trip talked, Cardwell concentrated on his food, trying not to look as though he were eavesdropping. In a minute, Triplitano hung up the phone and rose from the table.

"I've got to run. Angela says Murphy Morrow is upstairs asking to see me—private and urgent."

"What is it?"

"I can guess." Trip grinned. "When I was asked about Hoffman at the briefing this morning, I threw bouquets all over the place: The President admires and respects the Vice President. No number of rumors and speculative stories can shake the President's trust and affection. There may be occasional mild differences of opinion, but there is certainly no rift. Repeat, no rift."

Cardwell smiled.

"Well, that worried old Murphy. We're not rising to Hoffman's bait, so he figures we don't know what's been going on. So Murphy's going to sneak in and tell me everything that happened at Abner's house the other night. He's going to watch to see how I react to the shocking news that the Vice President has been seeing the press secretly to complain about the President."

"And what are you going to say?" Cardwell asked, grinning.

"Oh, I'm going to be very shocked, very shocked indeed." Trip said. "I'm going to say, 'Murphy, this is a very serious thing for us, very serious. You know, of course, that my reaction will be strictly off the record. But I think I can tell you what the President's response would be to news like this.' " Triplitano's voice dropped to a confidential whisper. " 'The President admires and respects the Vice President. Rumors and speculation can't lessen his trust and affection. There may be occasional mild differences, but there's no rift, et cetera, et cetera.' I'm going to drive old Murphy wild."

Triplitano left, smiling, without signing his check.

At two o'clock Anders Martin ushered Hoffman into the Oval Office—"Mr. President, the Vice President"—then backed out discreetly. Rattigan, who had been signing letters at his desk, did not rise, and the Vice President stood uncomfortably in the center of the large oval room.

"Mr. President, I—"

"Sit down, Ab," said Rattigan. He motioned to one of the sofas flanking the fireplace, then followed him over.

"I had a good lunch with the Speaker," Hoffman said casually, as Rattigan sat down. "It looks as though the House will take up the education bill right away, so we can count on a Christmas adjournment. I told him you were—"

"Abner," Rattigan said, "you made me look like a goddamned fool."

Hoffman saw the anger in the President's eyes, but he returned Rattigan's gaze and said nothing.

"I heard about your little party Monday night as soon as it happened. The whole business. And I read the papers today." He paused and studied Hoffman's expressionless face, and his anger deepened. "You knew I'd hear about it, so the only question is why you did it."

He stood up and walked to the center of the room, where he stood for a moment looking down at the presidential seal woven into the deep broadloom rug. Then he looked directly at Hoffman again.

"Well, I don't give a damn why you did it. All I care is that it never happen again. Never. If you're not satisfied with the treatment you're getting, or if you don't like the way things are going, there's only one man you have to tell." Rattigan raised one finger and tapped his own chest lightly. "So, if I ever see one more word in the paper like what I read today, I'm not going to issue any more statements about how much I respect you or how much confidence I have in you." He eyed Hoffman with cold anger. "I'm going to blow you right out of the water."

The two men stared at each other with narrowed eyes until Rattigan opened his mouth as if to speak again. Instead he looked down, shook his head impatiently, and said, "All right, that's all," dismissing Hoffman.

"No," said Hoffman, "that's not all."

Rattigan looked up in surprise. In three years as President he had grown accustomed to seeing on the face of almost every man he met an expression of deference, awe—sometimes even of fear. These were proper expressions to wear before a President, and most men assumed them instinctively. But Hoffman's face seemed set in stubborn anger.

"For three years I haven't had any more influence on you than the lowest secretary down the hall. I am never consulted, and I'm omitted from half the meetings I should be in on," Hoffman said.

Rattigan stared, disbelieving, and Hoffman went on.

"So, what can I do?" He spread his large freckled hands before him, then rested them on his knees. "I could come to you with my complaints and keep quiet in public. That's what you want me to do. But that's what I've been doing for three years, and it doesn't work." He shook his head.

"I could get up on my hind legs and attack you," he said. "And believe me, some people have urged me to do it. But I think that would hurt us both, and I want to avoid that."

Rattigan started to speak, but said nothing.

"So I called in a few reporters," Hoffman continued, "and I nudged you a little bit. Just a little bit." He stood up and shrugged. "If that seems disloyal to you, well . . . I'm sorry. But I may actually be doing you a big favor."

When the President replied, his voice was low and tight. "Abner," he said, "if you think you can blackmail me, you're very wrong. And if you try—"

Before the President could finish, there was a sharp buzz from the low round table before the fireplace. Rattigan leaned over, pulled open a drawer in the table, and lifted out a telephone.

"How can you be sure?" he said, after listening for a moment. "Were they in uniform?" He tapped the tabletop silently as he listened, then said, "No, I'll come down there. I have the Vice President with me."

When he hung up, he spoke to Hoffman with a preoccupied air, as if he had forgotten the conversation they had been having. "Let's go down to the Situation Room," he said. "I want you to see what's happening down there."

Even when he walked the guarded halls of the White House, the President was accompanied by Secret Service agents: tall, tight-lipped young men in trim, dark suits. Within five minutes after Sheldon Karnow's call, Rattigan and the Vice President were in the Situation Room. Their guards took up stations outside in the West Basement Hall.

The Situation Room was actually several rooms: offices, anterooms, and a communications center, alive with the clatter of teletype machines and staffed by shirt-sleeved clerks. Toward the rear was a small conference room, darkly paneled, hung with maps, furnished with a television set and a long, bare table. Karnow met the two men and took them to the conference room; he had spread the latest cables on the table.

The President, pulling his glasses from a breast pocket, eased into a chair and began to read, shoving the pages across the table to Hoffman. Sheldon Karnow watched the two men for a moment, then talked softly as they read.

"This was a pretty brave thing," he said, "and they almost made it. Apparently some Indians saw them and notified the Army. They were caught in the woods—three miles from the spot where they buried their parachutes."

"How do you know they're from Chile?" Hoffman asked.

"I suppose they can identify their equipment," Karnow said. "They were in civilian clothing, but the parachutes . . ." Then he added, making it sound like an afterthought, "Of course, all twelve were subjected to a most thorough . . . interrogation."

It was the first confirmation, the first unarguable evidence, that Chilean guerrillas were in Bolivia. Studying the summary, Rattigan propped his head on his hand, then sat back and rubbed his chin with his forefinger.

There were brief reports from the questioning of all twelve interlopers. The first—the only one the President read carefully—was the confession of Jorge Jesus Cuevas. He was twenty-seven years old. When capured with his compatriots in a wooded ravine in western Bolivia, he was carrying false Bolivian papers. But under questioning he admitted his true identity: He was a lieutenant in the Army of the Republic of Chile.

"I can have a map brought in if you like," Karnow said. "It's pretty remote."

"How many outfits like this have dropped in? Do they know?" the President asked.

"These guys either don't know or they aren't telling," Karnow said. "My guess is that it would take a good many to do the job."

With a glance at Hoffman, the President read aloud the cable he held: "To organize resistance, to disrupt communications, to pursue a campaign of selective terror and sabotage, the advance parties of the liberation . . ."

The Vice President said nothing. He sat impassive, his large hands folded on the table before him, his heavy-jowled face appearing almost sleepy in the subdued light. With a flick of his finger, Rattigan shot the last report across the table to Hoffman, who picked it up and began silently digesting its contents.

A young man entered. He handed Karnow a long strand of teletype paper, then disappeared.

"Bolivian radio has released the story," Karnow said. The teletype copy held was a dispatch from the Foreign Broadcast Intelligence Service. "The wires will have it soon."

Rattigan removed his glasses and rubbed his eyes with one hand, feeling once again the sensations of weight and weariness. When he had sought the presidency, he had thought only of the opportunities it offered. Now he saw not the powers of his office, but its limitations, its restraints.

"All right," he said. "Call in three or four columnists and background them. Tell them we're studying this development with deepest concern. We're contemplating our choices in the light of events. Nothing more specific than that."

"What about the troop request?" Karnow asked.

"Troops?" Abner Hoffman, who had been following this colloquy while reading the cables, looked sharply at the President.

"Nothing about that," Rattigan said. "Nothing about the note to Chile, and nothing about the Soviets. How's that coming, by the way?"

"Brooks Healy is reading the draft now. And he's got Lubshanko coming in tonight at seven. I'll check now to see if he's ready with that note."

When he was gone, Rattigan sat and stared across the table.

"What are you going to do?" the Vice President asked.

"Well, to begin with," Rattigan said wearily, "we're sending a hands-off note to Chile. And we've called Lubshanko in to let the Soviets know we mean business."

"And if that doesn't work?"

The President frowned. "I haven't thought about that yet."

But there was no way, he knew, to put off thinking about it any longer. If Chile ignored the warning, if the conflict in Bolivia continued to become more than a civil war, meetings of the Organization of American States and the UN Security Council could be called, protests made, more warnings issued. And if that didn't work, the pressure on the United States for money, for advisers, for equipment, and for troops could be unbearable.

"All right, Abner," Rattigan said, "what would you do?"

"Absolutely nothing," Hoffman said. He noticed the President's raised eyebrows, and went on: "If you do anything more—send equipment, send troops—you're risking far too much."

"And if they have a war anyway?"

"It's their war! You can go on television and tell the people we're keeping hands off, working to settle it in international forums, acting as peacemaker. When the fighting stops, they all can count on us for aid to rebuild. Can't you see that's just what Chile and the others would like for you to do—rush in there with troops? You'd get tied down for years and Uncle Sam would look like a bloodthirsty imperialist. It's just what they want."

"And what if we have to send troops?"

"You don't have to send troops," Hoffman said.

Rattigan eyed the Vice President coldly. "Ab, I'm not saying you're right or wrong. I just want you to remember one thing. It has to do with the way this country runs." His voice was almost a whisper. "I don't want to do anything in this situation. But I may have to. And if I do, I want you to remember one thing: I'm the President. I have to make the final decisions. I have two hundred thirty million constituents to answer to. You're the Vice President. You have one constituent, and he's—"

"The way I see it, Mr. President," Hoffman interrupted, "I have the same number of constituents you have. They didn't just vote for Carl Rattigan—they voted for me, too. And I have a responsibility to them."

"I don't need any lectures from you," said the President. Without another word, he stood up and left the Situation Room, leaving Abner Hoffman alone at the long table with its litter of cables.

Sarah Tolman's flight had left Dulles Airport early in the morning; there had been stops in Miami, Panama City, and Lima; now, as the great craft finally began its descent into La Paz, night had fallen over the high mountains of Bolivia. Sarah leaned to her right, almost pressing her forehead against the window in her effort to catch a glimpse of the countryside below. All she could see was the ghostly reflection of her own face.

Feeling the downward lurch of the plane, she fastened her seatbelt. She hoisted the blue flight bag from beneath her seat, took out a slim gold compact, and studied her face. She looked as grimy and exhausted as she felt. Not a very appealing face to present to Tony Jack—but then, perhaps she didn't want to appeal to him.

She tried to imagine what he would look like after all these years. But the only image she could conjure was the last memory she had of him, dressed in baggy damp fatigues, his cap shoved back over black hair, his eyes invisible behind a pair of sunglasses whose lenses reflected like two small mirrors. When she had left Saigon to return to the States, Tony had come to the airport to say good-bye.

"God, I'm sorry to see you leave so soon," he had said forlornly.

"Tony, why?" she had said, touched. They had only been good friends, fellow journalists.

"I think you're the only American woman in this godforsaken country I haven't laid—and the only one I'd really like to."

"Tony!" She had laughed, but secretly she was flattered.

He was the only man she had ever met who came close to being a soldier of fortune. A free-lance journalist and photographer whose special love was war, he lived out of a battered canvas flight bag, sniffed out the most dangerous battles, and dived into them. He had spent five years in Vietnam, and they had become fast friensds. When she won a Pulitzer Prize for her wartime reporting, she had felt—and she had told him—that the honor should have gone to him.

The plane touched down with a hard bump and a shudder. As it taxied to a halt, Sarah looked out of the window again and saw lights, clusters of people on the airport's open balcony—and a picket of armed guards standing at intervals in the glare of floodlights, guns hung loosely over their shoulders. She inhaled sharply, then smiled: The old excitement, the old love of risk and danger, was coming back. She felt suddenly younger, more alive.

The customs inspector, a fat, mustachioed man in a brown work uniform, searched her large suitcase minutely for a full ten minutes, then slapped a wet sticker on her bag, giving her a wide grin of approval.

Tony Jack was waiting, looking exactly as she remembered. He hugged her, then guided her away from the customs area, a strong hand on her elbow.

"You look marvelous!" she said. "You aren't a day older."

"I'm a wife and four kids older," he said. "How about you?"

She smiled, but her eyes fell. "No, still footloose and . . . still independent."

"I heard you had some mystery man in Washington," he said. "Whatever happened?"

"Tony," she said lightly, "I didn't know you were the sort who listened to gossip."

As they left the customs area, she noticed a thin man staring toward them. She watched the man as Tony struggled with her bags; once, glancing back, she stared into his eyes. A few steps later she looked back again. The man had disappeared.

"Tony," she said. "I think there was a man following us."

"There probably was," he said casually. "Everybody gets followed. You'll become paranoid very quickly."

"Do you think it was the government—or somebody else?"

Tony laughed. "Probably both," he said.

In five minutes they were rattling toward the city in Tony's battered Volkswagen.

"How about dinner?" he asked.

"We ate on the plane," she said. "All I want is a shower and a drink—in that order."

An hour later they sat in the dim and empty bar of her hotel, lingering over tall, weak drinks.

"Actually, we've got a perfect marriage." Tony was telling her the story of his life since Vietnam. "Six months after the ceremony, I was going crazy. I'd promised her I'd settle down, but I couldn't. I knew I could get a job as a stringer for *Time* and do some free-lancing on the side, so I came to South America." He grinned. "So I live in Caracas, write her the most passionate letters I can dream up, and go home every now and then to get her pregnant again."

Sarah laughed. "And she's happy?"

"I think so. She loves the kids, I love my work. We've both got what we want."

"Speaking of work," she said, "I'm here to cover an exotic little guerrilla war for my readers back in the States."

Tony finished his drink, signaled the solemn-faced bartender across the room to bring a refill, and then looked intently at Sarah.

"You're too late to cover the guerrilla war," he said.

"I don't understand."

"What I'm saying is that the guerrilla war is about over. Something bigger is about to happen."

"How do you know?"

"My hunch. The feeling in the air. All that's been happening in the past few weeks. I'm not the only one who thinks so. This guy Badillo is broadcasting it all over the States."

"He's not making much of a stir," Sarah said.

The bartender arrived with Tony's drink. When he turned to Sarah, she shook her head and waved him away.

"There's a fascinating game being played down here," Tony said. "On the one hand, you've got the guerrilla leader, Aguila. You know about him?"

"Just what I've read," said Sarah. "A sort of a Che Guevara figure."

"Not exactly. The thing to remember about Che is that he wasn't interested in local victories. He was after bigger fish. He wanted to set the whole continent on fire, remember? One, two, many Vietnams." He pulled his chair closer to the table. "His basic strategy was to involve the United States—to force a confrontation with the Yankee imperialists. That would galvanize the left wing all over the continent and pow! Uncle Sam would have had his hands full, like a man fighting a hive of bees."

Tony took a sip from his drink, then raised a finger.

"Well, Aguila is a Marxist, but he's a nationalist, too. He wants to knock over the government here and set up a new political order. Period. He's not interested in global revolutions as far as I can tell. I think the last thing he wants is a confrontation with the United States and the other Latin governments. He has problems enough as it is. Aguila doesn't want big trouble—just a socialist triumph in Bolivia and a better life for some of the poorest people on earth."

"Can he get it?"

"Not by himself. Not at the rate he's been going." Sarah noticed that despite the emptiness of the bar, Tony was speaking very softly. She pushed her glass toward the center of the table and leaned forward, resting her forearms on the table edge.

"This government may not be a very good example for the civics books," Tony said, "but by Latin standards, it's democratic, and it was popular enough before the bottom fell out economically. For a while the government was making real progress: schools, highways, land reform. So Aguila had trouble gaining a following for his guerrilla movement. And I think he's smart enough to know he can't succeed and stay a success without support from the people. That's rule No. 1."

Sarah was interested, but suddenly very tired. She felt a chill sweep across the large empty room and wished she had brought a sweater from her room upstairs.

"Can we get some coffee?" she asked.

Tony signaled the bartender, spoke to him briefly in Spanish, then returned to their conversation.

"So a new phase began. Aguila has forged some kind of alliance with the junta in Chile. They've been pouring in guns, food, money, medicine. And now people. Have you seen a paper tonight?"

"No."

"Well, the Bolivian Army picked up some guerrillas in the mountains last night. Only they weren't guerrillas. They were Chilean Army. The government has been blaring the news all day. And Chile has got some sort of military buildup going on way up north, right up against the Bolivian border. It makes a certain sense from their viewpoint; the government in La Paz could hardly be weaker."

The bartender brought two coffees. Sarah lifted hers to her lips. It was thick, black, and so bitter that she winced.

"Welcome to Bolivia," Tony smiled, and raised his cup in a toast.

She smiled, then returned to the subject. "So Aguila is going to take over, with help from Chile."

"That's what he hopes," Tony said. "But there's a joker in the deck. There's Aguila on the one hand—and Chile on the other. And Chile has a different idea. Not just to liberate, in their words, Bolivia—but to establish a secure beachhead on the continent, extend her influence, and break out of her isolation as the only Marxist state on the continent. It's global stuff."

"Che Guevara again."

"Exactly, my dear Sarah. And our friend Aguila will probably get lost in the shuffle."

"At least that's your theory."

"It's more than my theory. It's my conviction. And if you stay around long enough, you can watch it happen. By now Bolivia knows about all these Chilean troops on maneuvers nearby. Suppose they ask for American troops to put the fear of God into Chile?"

"Rattigan would never send them," she said. "There are other ways to deal with a threat like that."

"Such as?"

"The United Nations. The OAS."

Tony Jack eyed Sarah with an indulgent, mocking smile. "Of course, of course. And what if Chile invades Bolivia?"

She frowned. "Tony, I just find it impossible to believe that a weak little country like Chile would risk a fight with a nuclear power."

He smiled. "Do you remember a weak little country called North Vietnam?"

"You bastard," she said, and Tony laughed.

She downed the rest of her coffee. "Okay, you have me thoroughly fascinated, but I've got to have some sleep."

When they reached her door, Tony smiled. "Okay, up early tomorrow. I'll take you to the embassy to get acquainted with the cookie pushers, and then I'm your faithful guide. What's the first thing you want to do?"

"The first thing I want to do," she said, "is to meet Roberto Aguila."

Tony whistled. "Sarah, love, you've got more guts than any man I know."

"Do you know Aguila?"

"No," he said, "but maybe we can get an introduction." She could tell by his tone that he meant it.

In her room she felt herself giving away to weariness. She took off her dress and flung it down on a straight chair, then went into the bathroom to brush her teeth. When she had finished, she washed her face in the tepid water, rubbed the back of her neck hard with the face cloth, and returned to the bedroom.

Suddenly she stopped.

The closet door, which she remembered closing, was ajar. She could see her dark blue bag hanging inside.

Her breath quickened and she glanced around the room. Her suitcase lay on the easy chair by the door; she had left the suitcase open, with its lid resting against the chair back. Now it was closed, its dull metal locks securely fastened.

She rushed across the room and opened the suitcase. The contents were intact; nothing was missing. But she could feel the certainty, like a presence in the room, that it had been searched.

She opened the door to the hall. "Tony!" she called softly. But he was gone. The long corridor was deserted.

She closed the door, stood listening for a moment, then pushed the large chair against the door. When she sat breathless on the side of her bed, she remembered Tony's words: *Everybody gets followed. You'll become paranoid very quickly.*

For a long time after she snapped off the light she lay in darkness, listening for some sound from the empty hallway. At last, hearing nothing, she fell into a long and fitful sleep.

Cardwell worked long into the night. At nine-thirty, Dot placed the memorandum before him: four pages, with a fifth page attached at the end titled "Suggested Itinerary for Two-day Trip by the President."

"Do you want me to stay for corrections?" Dot was tired; faint lines of fatigue crossed her forehead.

"No, this looks fine, Dot. I really appreciate your staying."

She smiled and was gone, leaving him alone in his silent office to read and reread the memo. He smiled in satisfaction as he scanned it. It would be a great trip if the President decided to go.

He swept the pages into a neat stack, then walked over to Dot's desk, stapled the pages together, and placed the memo in a clean manila folder on which he wrote, "For the President's Night Reading." Then he affixed a small red cardboard square to the folder, a reminder to the messengers that this paper was urgent and must reach its addressee without delay.

"The trip I am suggesting," Cardwell had written to the President, "is not merely an image-making burst of activity, not simply a tactic to push up your rating in the polls. I am suggesting that you should, with this trip and others in the future, put yourself more directly in touch with the voters; that you should exploit, in addition to television and the press, another potent medium of communication: direct, frequent contact with the people to whom as President you owe your authority and to whom, in effect, you belong."

It was strange, Cardwell thought, that he should have to argue the point at all. And he realized it might sound a bit presumptuous. But the fact was there: Since the congressional elections last year, Carl Rattigan had not gone to the people very often, had not plunged into many shouting crowds, smiling and shaking hands, as he had done in the old days. There were reasons, of course: the wild pace of daily life for the President; the press of events in Washington; the endless round of ceremonies and meetings. And above all there was the convenient magic of television: to reach millions of people, the President need only give a few hours' notice and he could summon the network cameras to his Oval Office for a live broadcast.

And finally, like a barely visible shadow across the White House lawn, there was the threat of violence, of assassination. No one spoke of it. But to the Secret Service and the FBI, to all the wary men in whose keeping lay the President's physical safety, the White House with its guards, its fences, its secret surveillance systems was a fortress: a haven. They discouraged forays into dangerous territory—and in their eyes, city streets and public squares were places of danger.

There were good reasons, Cardwell knew, that the President did not travel. And for those same reasons, he felt, the President had become remote and distant from the people. Despite the trappings of the White House—the television cameras, the retinue of reporters, the helicopters, the planes—the President was becoming a prisoner of his office.

Cardwell left his office to take the slim folder to the messenger room. He walked through the dim and empty West Basement, down a ramp near the Staff Mess, and into a blast of noise and activity. The messengers worked all night, in a din of Xerox and mimeograph machines, copying documents, printing news releases, sorting mail. Somewhere from the rear of the large room came the sound of a television set: the late news.

He handed the folder to a brown-faced messenger at the desk inside the door. "I'd like to get this to the President right away."

The man grinned. "Yes, sir. We're gonna keep him awake tonight."

Cardwell smiled and walked out. The West Basement entrance had been closed for the night, so he would have to leave by the main entrance upstairs. He stopped by his office, grabbed his coat, and walked to the stairs, nodding as he passed a portly black cleaning woman who was crisscrossing the hall with a carpet sweeper. Except for her and the lone guard in the lobby, the West Wing was deserted. It was ten o'clock.

By day in the West Wing, Carlton Rattigan could work, could read, could meet his visitors in the oceanic calm of the Oval Office. But it was a deceptive calm. He was aware always of the storm outside: the waiting reporters, eager to feed again upon his words and deeds; the officials waiting nervously for their appointments with the President, a kind of lust lighting their eyes; the quivering jangle of wires and antennas connecting the White House to the world.

He did his best work at night, when he left the West Wing and returned to the guarded precincts of the Mansion. At dinnertime, accompanied only by a pair of Secret Service agents, he would leave the West Wing, stroll down the colonnade beside the Rose Garden and through the dim ground-floor hall of the Mansion, and ascend by a small elevator to his apartment upstairs.

When they were alone, he and Lisa would eat from trays in the West Hall, sometimes watching a television documentary, more often discussing quietly some inconsequential thing. An outsider, witnessing their evening ritual, might think them a typical middle-aged pair at day's end—except for their striking faces and the quiet richness of the surroundings.

He could depend on her not to ask about his work unless he brought it up; whether it was from indifference or some deliberate effort to offer him peace, surcease, he had never been sure—but he was grateful for it. And tonight, as on most nights when the trays were removed, she excused herself and went to her bedroom to study her appointment book and a stack of mail and memos sent over from her staff in the East Wing.

Tonight, seated in an easy chair, taking up the first of the folders in his foot-high stack of night reading, he could look down through an enormous fan-shaped window at the West Wing and the driveway that led to the Northwest Gate. The quiet that lay over the White House was real: The reporters and the favor-seekers were gone, the telephones stilled; by now the place was populated only by guards, the cleaning crew, the unsleeping duty officers who managed the Situation Room, and a few late-working staff.

He could work for hours, into the early morning, interrupting his swift reading only for a massage—a favorite ritual—and a look at the late television news. He had learned long ago that he could go without sleep: His bottomless energy was one of the subtle but important differences between the President and other men.

But tonight, though a hundred crises and a hundred decisions lay before him, the one that vexed him most had moved outside his reach. A warning note to Chile, a stern lecture to the Soviet ambassador—both had been delivered. He could not guess what effect these moves might have; he could only wait and see. And because he was helpless to influence events, he tried to turn his mind away from the crisis.

The stack of papers before him defined the range of a President's concern. There was an urgent memo from the Attorney General: Zealous budget-trimmers in the Executive Office Building were gutting next year's program of federal aid to local police departments. Would he intercede?

Affixed to a pale green transmittal slip, there was a brief speech draft for a ceremony the next morning: A group of labor union officials, gathered in the Cabinet Room, would present to the President a scroll celebrating a major upward shift in the housing market and a corresponding increase in jobs for construction workers.

Most of his predecessors in the White House, Rattigan knew, had barely tolerated these little ceremonies. But he enjoyed them, found them easy, a welcome respite from the tedium of the day.

A splendid misery, Jefferson had written of the office. Perhaps. But it was a job that had its advantages. What king could be better served? He had at his beckoning the minds and manpower of the most powerful government on earth. The cars, the aircraft, the incredible machinery of communications could fling him, his image, or his voice around the world on short notice. The White House was peopled with dozens of men—doctors, gardeners, chefs—whose only object was his care and comfort. There was the satisfaction of high endeavor, urgent activity, work well done.

And finally, there was the heady sense of living at the summit. There might be tedium, but none of it was trivial. The issues he decided were great ones; the subjects of his speeches were often momentous ones; when he stared into the blank red eye of a television camera, he commanded the attention of the world; when he signed a law, he touched and altered the lives of millions and their children. There could be no feeling like it: on the summit—and near the precipice.

Softly the telephone rang beside his chair: It would be Sorrel, the young Navy medic who manned the dispensary downstairs. He was the President's masseur.

"Yes?"

"Sorrel, Mr. President. Do you want me to come up tonight?"

"Any time, Sorrel."

"Working late tonight, sir?"

"I sure am."

There was a note from Karnow, in his crisp professorial tone. He had briefed reporters from the major newspapers on the ominous events in Bolivia: The capture of Chileans in the country. He had told them that the President viewed events in Bolivia with the deepest interest and concern; the United States would use every available diplomatic channel to warn the parties that grave consequences could ensue if Chile sought to exploit the weakness of her neighbor.

Karnow had underlined the word "diplomatic." A good man.

Bolivia again.

Badillo, the Paraguayan, was in New York. He was staying in a Waldorf Towers suite provided by the United States Government—a suite whose every room was monitored by tiny electronic ears. The CIA had sent, via Karnow, a transcript of a conversation between Badillo and the ambassador of Bolivia to the United Nations.

Rattigan was a coward, Badillo had said. He would not provide help to Bolivia until he was forced by events. But then help would come: The United States could not avoid it; the stakes were too high.

"The crazy bastard," Rattigan said aloud, "how can he know what I'm going to do when I don't know myself?"

In the hall, the elevator doors rolled back. Sorrel was there, carrying a portable massage table folded to suitcase size. He looked, in his civilian clothes, like a young medical student: clean, bespectacled, his blond hair cropped close.

"I'll be with you in a minute," Rattigan said, and the young man disappeared into the President's bedroom.

He laid the sheaf of papers aside, stood and stretched, and looked down again through the graceful fan-shaped window. Beyond the low West Wing, across West Executive Avenue, the Executive Office Building loomed gray and ghostly in the winter night.

A few lights burned in the tall windows of the EOB. On the second floor, the Vice President's office was ablaze with lights. The cleaning women? Or was Abner working late? Carlton Rattigan thought, without bitterness or anger, of their scene this afternoon—of Hoffman's long and bulky frame, the defiance in his eyes.

He wants to be President, Rattigan knew. The thought was almost funny—Abner wouldn't have a chance. He was fifty-nine or sixty, and in four more years . . . but his knowledge of Hoffman's innermost desire gave Rattigan a certain edge. If Abner Hoffman wanted the nomination four years from now, he would need the blessing of the chief. He must give his loyalty—in public, at least. Unquestioning, uncritical loyalty: the standard offering of Vice President to President.

There would be no more trouble with Hoffman. Rattigan was sure of it. And if there were—if there were another indiscreet meeting with the press, another hint of rupture, an angry public breach—well, it could be handled. Abner could be dropped from the ticket, and Brooks Healy could replace him. Brooks was not only his best friend, he was also the best man in the Cabinet.

The thought of destroying Abner Hoffman gave Rattigan neither pain nor pleasure. If it became necessary it would be done, like a piece of distasteful surgery. He had entered politics to serve, of course. But long ago he had learned that to serve, one must survive. And to survive on the summit, one might have to cut another climber's rope.

It was midnight; he had only half completed the stack of reading. An usher had laid the early editions of the newspapers and a few late-arriving memos on a table near the elevator. He could read them after his rubdown.

He walked toward his bedroom, loosening his tie as he went. He was not tired, not at all. But Carlton Rattigan was beginning to feel old.

Cardwell saw Nancy's car parked in the sloping driveway and felt a stab of guilt: late again. He sighed, parked behind her car, then walked through the dark garage, hearing his footsteps in the cold silence.

Inside, the house was quiet: only the heavy throb of the furnace, like a heartbeat.

The lamp beside her bed was lighted, but she was turned away from him, her face to the wall.

"Nan, you asleep?"

She turned toward him. "Have you had anything to eat?" Her voice was toneless, weary.

"I had a sandwich at the office. Look, I'm sorry."

She raised herself, leaned back against her pillow.

"John, I'm so tired of things like this. I'm really tired."

"Nancy, I'm sorry," he said. "But I'm not going to apologize to you for my job."

"I'm not asking you to apologize for your job!" she said fiercely. "I'm asking you to apologize for the way you treat me."

"Look, I don't want to fight about a trivial situation. Please, let's—"

"Trivial situation! The situation is that I'm miserable!"

"Nancy, for God's sake, I'm sorry. But I work for the President of the United States. There just might occasionally be something important that has to be—"

"There just might be something important about *us,*" she said, and he saw there was no point in continuing. Abruptly he left the room and walked slowly down the dark hall.

Without turning on the kitchen light, he walked to the refrigerator, pulled open the door, and stared into its dim, cold light. He pulled out a beer, snapped it open, and took a long drink, shuddering at the first cold swallow, then walked silently into the breakfast room and sat down in the dark, cupping his two hands lightly about the can on the table before him.

It wasn't Nancy's fault, really. She had tried for three years—first to overcome her dislike for their new life, his job, then to conceal her feelings. She had joined a few committees, thought of taking a job herself, some sort of volunteer work. But nothing could erase from her mind the image of her old life: In Louisville, by virtue of her father's name and wealth, she counted. In Washington, she felt, she was simply another bright, attractive wife of an earnest young man in politics; one of those who came and went. She couldn't help but feel the difference and resent it. It wasn't her fault.

But it was her fault. He felt his hand tighten around the can of beer. Other men's wives came to Washington as strangers, entered into the life of the capital, found a way to like it—even love it. They endured their husbands' schedules without complaint, found themselves fascinated by politics and politicians. But Nancy had refused to make the effort. Selfishly, he thought. Her refusal to accept Washington, to share his enthusiasm for the White House job, her demands, her complaints—were they real, or just weapons she used against him? They had what people called a good marriage; but the excitement was gone—had been gone, he suspected, before they left Louisville. When they made love now, it was out of habit rather than passion or desire.

But was it her fault that she had no taste for Washington, for politics, for his job, his hours? There are wives, and there are political wives: Sarah Tolman's words.

Sarah. Involuntarily his mind fastened upon her, conjured her face: her sad, intelligent eyes across the table at Sans Souci. He tried to imagine what she might be doing at this moment: sleeping in some jungle, perhaps.

The last of the beer was getting warm. He lifted the can and drained it slowly in the dark. Suddenly he was aware of the ringing of a telephone, as if it came from some great distance. It was one room away, in the den. He started up, and found the phone in the darkness.

"Mr. Cardwell?" It was the White House operator. "Just a moment for the President."

He reached to turn on a lamp and scrambled on the desktop for a pencil.

"John?"

"Good evening, Mr. President."

"I have your memo. You think I'm too isolated, eh?"

"Well, not really too isolated," Cardwell said, and immediately felt foolish, realizing he was backtracking. "I do think it's a real danger," he said, recovering.

"Well, you may be right, but I wonder about this trip," the President said. "I don't think we could put it together in less than a week. Do you know anything about this, or—"

"Trip says we can have advance men out tomorrow if you decide to go," Cardwell said. "I can have speech drafts assigned tomorrow, in my office by Saturday, and on your desk on Monday."

"You think it's worth the effort, then." It was a statement rather than a question.

"I certainly do, sir. I think it could be a great trip."

The President did not reply, and in the long silence Cardwell wondered if their connection had somehow been broken.

"All right, I'll go," the President said slowly. "I think we could all use a little diversion. Call Trip and Andy Martin and tell them in the morning."

"All right, sir."

"This is your show. I want you to go along. You can ride the press plane if you want to, or you can fly with me."

Before he could reply, Cardwell heard the line go blank: The President had hung up.

Cardwell stood in the warm circle of lamplight, staring down at the phone after he had cradled the receiver. The President had called him—and moved him from his place on the periphery into one of the smaller circles, closer to the center.

It was a strange, almost magical place, the White House. Elsewhere in government men fought for titles, raises in pay, a higher spot in the bureaucratic hierarchy—for these were the incontrovertible evidences of power. But in the West Wing the currency was mysterious, intangible: closeness to the President. Journalists used the phrase with a touch of awe: "Mr. Jones is known to be close to the President."

Cardwell snapped off the lamp and walked down the hall to the bedroom. "You can ride the press plane if you want to," the President had said, "or you can fly with me."

The bedroom lamp was off, but he sensed that she was awake.

"Who was that?" she asked.

"The President. He liked my memo. He's going to make the trip."

She made no reply.

"He wants me to ride with him on the plane."

No answer. She shifted in bed, and he could tell that her back was toward him. Swiftly he began to undress in the darkness, tearing off his tie with one hand, flinging his clothes onto a chair in the corner.

Stripped to his shorts, he climbed into bed and sensed the wide space between his body and Nancy's. Lying on his back, his hands tucked behind his head, he listened to the gentle throb of the furnace and waited for sleep to come.

Sunday the Twenty-sixth

Late on Thursday afternoon, Triplitano announced the President's plans: a two-day trip to New York, North Carolina, Chicago, and Denver, ending in Palm Springs.

Already, dozens of advance men had fanned out to the cities, surveying motor routes, setting up press facilities, monitoring security precautions—and exhorting local Democrats to bring out the faithful, get them onto the streets, swell the crowds to welcome their chief.

In a fever of excitement, Cardwell assigned, gathered, and edited six speech drafts; talked endlessly to the agents in the cities the President would visit; and worked Dot and two more typists from the White House Correspondence Section to near-exhaustion.

He worked late, reaching home long after midnight every night. He spent almost all weekend at the office—and Nancy, determined not to show her resentment but unable to conceal it, became elaborately formal and polite when they were together.

She called him at the office on Sunday afternoon. "Are plans for the great Odyssey almost complete?" she said.

"Almost. Why do you ask?"

"Because," she said coolly, "we haven't had dinner together all week, and I was wondering about tonight."

In a wave of remorse he said, "Tonight we dine at Sans Souci."

Three hours later, they were together in the Sunday evening calm of the restaurant. She tried to be pleasant, and he courted her, teasing her gently, ordering an outrageously expensive wine and then champagne, thinking only once or twice of Sarah Tolman and how strange it seemed to be in Sans Souci without her.

At home, for the first time in many nights, Nancy moved close to him in bed, took his hand, and he explored in the dark the familiar angles of her body.

When it was over she lay close to him, her head resting on his arm.

"That was good," she said, as much about the evening as of their making love.

"I'll tell you what," he said in the darkness. "When things slow down, we'll take a trip. Around Christmas."

"You mean it?"

"We can go to Mexico. Or skiing. Whatever you want."

He felt, lying in the darkness, that things between them were better. The promise of a trip, of this gift of time to her, was a peace offering. She had seized it happily.

He fell toward sleep.

Tuesday the Twenty-eighth

At dawn on Tuesday the President roared off on the trip Cardwell had planned.

In New York Rattigan spoke to a breakfast gathering of the Overseas Press Club, answered questions for a half hour, then lingered to shake hands with a crowd of well-wishers on the street.

They were airborne again by ten o'clock: Air Force One with its army of staff, Secret Service, and presidential guests; the press plane, crowded with reporters and cameramen who exchanged jokes and tossed down bloody marys despite the early hour. Next stop: Charlotte, North Carolina.

By noon the President's motorcade, having reached the big intersection of Trade and Tryon streets in Charlotte, was so engulfed by the welcoming crowd that it slowed almost to a halt. No matter that Rattigan, in the last election, had not carried North Carolina; no matter that his polls were slipping: Here he was mobbed by thousands who would not miss an opportunity to see a President—any President.

So slowly did the motorcade move, straining between the shifting walls of people, that reporters could climb down from the press bus at the rear, run up alongside the presidential limousine, record the scene, and then board their bus again.

Cardwell, from his place two cars behind the President's, listened to the thunder of the crowd. He could not see the President, but he could imagine Rattigan's expression: flushed, smiling, excited by the tumult of the welcome.

So far, so good. Cardwell, satisfied, smiled too.

At the same moment, four thousand miles away in La Paz, Ambassador Bert Williams left his office, on his way to an appointment he had kept each Tuesday during most of his two years in Bolivia.

"Good afternoon, sir!" The young Marine guard in the lobby stood as he passed, and Williams nodded, smiling.

He emerged into the flat afternoon sunlight of La Paz and glanced up and down the street. It was the hour of the siesta; the narrow street and the sidewalks were deserted, and the shops along the *avenida* were closed, their windows secured by heavy metal shutters. The only signs of life were the two cars that stood before the Embassy, their motors growling: his dark blue sedan and the black Mercury, filled with embassy plainclothesmen, which followed him everywhere—the State Department's idea of security.

"All set, sir?" Rip was waiting by the sedan; he flung open the rear door before Bert Williams could reach it, and the ambassador climbed in.

"Club Nacional, pronto," Rip said to the driver, and they were off, moving deliberately through the silent streets, past the white stucco houses with barred windows and red-tiled roofs, and occasionally an ancient church set hard against the sidewalk, its bell tower casting a wide, dark shadow into the street.

Even after two years, Williams felt like a tourist seeing the high, sunswept city for the first time. The light that suffused the capital was like nothing he knew elsewhere: a clear, shadowless light extending beyond the city to the mountains, not so much like sunlight as like a light given off by the landscape itself. It was the pure, hazeless air, the natives said. Settled in the rear seat of the sedan, he stared out, lost in thought.

"Think you'll win today?" Rip's voice from the front seat startled him.

"Lord, I hope so," said Williams. "If I don't stop losing I'll have to ask the Department for an advance on my pay."

Rip laughed. "Well, they ought to cover your losses anyway. You could call it official entertainment or something."

"I may do it," Williams said. He took up his sightseeing again, but Rip continued.

"I thought bridge was an American game," he said.

"It is," said Williams. "But these fellows play it with Latin intensity."

The Tuesday bridge sessions at the Nacional were a favorite feature of a job Williams loved. He liked the country, liked the people, and enjoyed the explosive joviality of the generals and the Cabinet ministers who played bridge as if it were a duel of honor.

Strange how things happened. Had it not been for a college friendship with Carlton Rattigan, he would never be here as ambassador. And they had not been close friends, either; only casual acquaintances who fell into conversation occasionally in Eliot House and nodded cordially when they met in Harvard Yard.

Bert Williams had never been much interested in politics; he had devoted himself, from the time he left the law school and returned to Seattle, to the practice he shared with his father and brother. But years after Harvard, when he read that Carl Rattigan was running for the Senate, he sent him a cordial note and a campaign contribution. And when Rattigan ran for President, Williams had headed the western division of Citizens for Rattigan; he made, this time, a contribution to his friend's campaign that was the maximum allowed by law. It was not just from friendship: He respected Rattigan, believed in him, wanted to see him President.

That was how it happened. He and Angela had been invited to the White House soon after the inauguration—a State Dinner—and soon afterward Bert turned down a job on the Federal Communications Commission. His father had died; the practice was growing; he could hardly leave the firm and go to Washington. And Angela and the girls loved Seattle, and hated the thought of moving East.

He smiled, remembering. A few months later, the White House called again, sending his secretary into quivers of excitement. This time it was the President himself.

"Bert, how's your Spanish?"

"Pretty rusty, Mr. President. Why do you ask?"

"I want you to be my ambassador to Bolivia."

"Mr. President, I—"

"I think I should tell you that it's considered bad form to turn down the President twice in a row."

"I'm afraid I don't know much about Bolivia."

The President had laughed loudly while Williams, puzzled, held the phone away from his ear.

"Bert, you told me you didn't know anything about politics, and you carried the West for us." He laughed again, then turned serious. "I want you to come to Washington right away, for a month. You can learn enough about Bolivia to get confirmed, and we'll backstop you in La Paz with the best men we have in the State Department."

"Thank you, sir."

"I think you know," Rattigan said, "I'm not asking you to go just because I like you. I'm asking you because I need the smartest, toughest man I can find, and you're the one."

There had been some hard questions in his Senate confirmation hearings. But two months after the President's call, Bert Williams was in La Paz. He had worked hard—damned hard—and last week, shaking hands with the President after the secret meeting in the Cabinet Room, he had received the highest compliment of his life: "I've never made a better choice," Rattigan had said. "I've got a half a dozen other countries where I could use you, if it were possible."

The job had its drawbacks, of course. Angela had a bit of trouble with her Spanish, though God knows her efforts to speak it had charmed the Bolivians. The fighting in the countryside made it impossible to travel. And the security—the guards, the floodlights around the residence, the black sedan, constantly following—these were nuisances. He had complained; it embarrassed him to move everywhere with bodyguards. But the Department, deaf in its rigid, cautious wisdom, overruled him. Worst of all, because of this jumpiness, they had had to leave the girls behind. His daughters had moved in with his brother's family; they were missing the greatest educational experience two kids could have.

In a poor section of the city, near the outskirts of La Paz, no more than ten minutes from the elegant Club Nacional, there was a street market—to Bert Williams, the most colorful sight in La Paz. During the siesta, the open bins of bright fruits and vegetables were covered, but the Indians, away from their homes in the hills and with no place to go during siesta, leaned against their stalls and chattered softly in their mysterious dialect. Their dark, impassive faces contrasted with their riotous costumes, the splashes of red and orange and purple.

Passing the market, Williams said to Rip, "Do you know any of that language?"

"A little," Rip said.

"How did you learn?"

"I just picked it up," he said.

He was listed on the embassy rolls as a political officer. But Rip, crewcut and taut-faced, was a bodyguard, trained by the CIA in all the arts of self-defense and death. The left side of his jacket always bulged slightly, and wherever the ambassador rode, Rip went too, making little birdlike glances from side to side and peering occasionally into the rear-view mirror to see if the follow-up car was close enough behind. Williams liked Rip, wondered about his life and how he had come to his strange occupation. But they seldom exchanged more than a few trivial words. Rip was not a talker.

Near the edge of the city, the empty streets glowed in the afternoon. At the Nacional, the players would be gathering, nodding and smiling while the waiters passed frosted pitchers of bitter domestic beer. They had accepted him like a brother—not because he was the American ambassador, but because he was a damned good bridge player. And he enjoyed the Tuesday sessions—not only because he occasionally won, but also because he learned more in these informal gatherings than in any official meetings. He usually spent Wednesday dictating cables, reporting to Washington the news he had gleaned over cards: about politics in the capital; about the mood of the country's leadership; about progress in the countryside in the war against the rebels.

"It's really beautiful here, isn't it?" he said to Rip. "I guess you'd call these slums, but—"

Even before they heard the crash, Rip wheeled violently around in his seat and screamed a curse. He had seen something from the corner of his eye: a car lunging from a side street toward the black sedan, the follow-up car. It hit the guard car squarely, in a scream of brakes.

They heard the crash, and Williams, turning back, saw the wreckage, the twisted cars against the curb.

A whipcrack: Someone was shooting.

"Let's go!" Rip screamed. The driver kicked the car forward so violently that Williams was thrown against the seat.

"Move!" Rip cried.

But it was too late.

Before them two more cars had blocked the street, and three dark-faced men, crouching as they ran, were moving toward them.

"Get down!" Rip shouted. Williams caught the dull glint of gun metal—the pistol in Rip's hand.

The ambassador did not hear the shot. He was aware only of a heavy shudder that moved the car, of Rip's head snapping back. A shower of blood and flesh from the wound in Rip's neck spattered the ambassador's gray suit.

The three men were near the car. Williams knew he could still run, crouching, putting the car between himself and the gunmen, perhaps escaping into a side street or a house. He scrambled for the far door, grabbed the handle, and lunged out.

He ran. There was a dome of silence: he could hear his wildly beating heart, his footsteps. Bert Williams ran. He had run no more than twenty yards when he realized that the street he had entered was a street without an exit: a dead end.

An hour behind schedule, Air Force One roared away from Charlotte, climbed beyond the autumn haze above the southern city, and headed for Chicago. The President disappeared into his compartment at the rear of the plane to wash up, to change his soaked shirt, and to entertain the Illinois congressional delegation, Republicans and Democrats, who were his guests aboard the plane.

In the staff compartment Secret Service agents doffed their jackets and played cards. Young Signal Corps technicians dozed in their seats; staff members talked above the sleepy drone of the engines and stared from the oval windows at the dappled land as dusk swept in five miles below.

Two hours to Chicago. An Air Force steward, natty in a pale blue blazer, passed a tray of drinks. Another steward, holding his elbows high to keep from bumping the seats, circulated a mammoth tray of sandwiches, cheeses, and canapes.

There were little reminders all about that this was no commercial plane: the seats, deep, comfortable, upholstered in a rich teal blue; at the ends of the compartment, fabric-covered desktops with typewriters and white telephones. Matchbooks were scattered about, bearing the presidential seal and a legend stamped in gold: "Welcome Aboard Air Force One."

John Cardwell leaned over one of the desks up forward, dictating to a secretary who sat belted into a seat before her typewriter.

"Okay," he said, "you can get this all on one card—one line for each member of the delegation: 'Senator Evard, a Republican but a progressive Republican.' 'Mrs. Evard; Senator—' "

Anders Martin emerged from the President's compartment, moved down the narrow aisle, and tapped Cardwell on the shoulder. "The President wants you to come back with him."

"Should I finish this introduction?"

"No, you can do that later."

The President, sitting in shirtsleeves in his high-backed swivel seat, leaned forward, smiling as Cardwell entered.

"Gentlemen," Rattigan said, "this is John Cardwell. He's responsible for the big reception we got back in Charlotte." It was Rattigan's way of thanking Cardwell. He smiled and shook hands with the congressmen, who sat together in a couchlike row of seats facing the President.

"Sit down," said Rattigan. Cardwell found a place.

"Mr. President," said Congressman Ardmore, a black leader from Chicago, "I wish we could match that reception in Chicago, but I'm afraid all our people will be out watching the Bears tonight."

"Maybe we should drop by the stadium," Rattigan said, smiling, and the little group laughed—too eagerly, Cardwell thought.

Cardwell leaned back, pretending to follow the jovial conversation of the President and his guests. But behind his expression of deferential interest, beneath his occasional laugh when the group laughed, his mind was at work; he was watching the President, studying him.

Two hours ago, borne triumphant through the crowd in his gleaming limousine, accepting the cheers with upraised arms, Rattigan had seemed more symbol than man. But now, aloft, he seemed only a man. He sat in shirtsleeves, a half-finished drink on the table before him, and idly fingered his glasses case. Watching him, Cardwell noticed the fine lines that had invaded the President's forehead, the network of tiny red veins across his eyes. Fatigue? Worry? Sleeplessness?

Cardwell glanced at the other men—all of them politicians, all of them men of a certain degree of fame—then turned back toward the President. How did Rattigan differ from a thousand other men?

The difference, Cardwell suspected, lay not in ability, nor eloquence, nor conviction, nor even love of power. Other men had these—some, perhaps, in greater measure than the President. What made Carlton Rattigan different—what made every man different who had sought and seized the presidency—lay hidden, deep beneath the public faces of the man: ceaseless, restless energy, the kind of fiery energy that ignored fatigue and sleeplessness. An ego wholly different from other men's egos: large, hungry, accepting as its due the most extravagant praise, the most tumultuous public adoration. And nerve—plenty of nerve. Rattigan had it. Had he never entered politics, had he become a criminal or a mountain climber, his boiling energy, his ego, his unblinking, almost casual nerve would have driven him to the top of Everest—or onto the most-wanted list. Cardwell had no doubt of it.

There was a pause in the banter, and Rattigan used it to give the conversation a serious tone. He asked a question that he always asked in all of his private conversations.

"Well, gentlemen," he said, "what should I be doing that I'm not doing?"

Anders Martin, sitting beside the President, slipped a small notebook out of his pocket, ready to take notes as the politicians talked.

Ardmore, the black congressman, spoke first. "Well, Mr. President, I'd like to see you go into the ghettos. Nobody can quarrel with what you've been doing for black people, but you've got to dramatize it, go on the street—"

"I'm not sure that's either safe or desirable," said Evard, the lone Republican. Ardmore looked from side to side, as if seeking support, and finding none, fell silent. Rattigan looked thoughtful, but said nothing.

"In any case, Mr. President," said Congressman Klominski, another Chicagoan, "trips like this one are a great idea, a great idea. I told my wife—"

"We're going to take more of them," the President said, and Cardwell felt a stirring of pleasure: He had won his point.

Strangely, no one else volunteered a suggestion. Cardwell was amazed: Faced with an opportunity to advise the President directly, these eminent men were embarrassed, inarticulate. He wondered how often it happened.

"Gentlemen, thank you," said the President, and he turned to Cardwell. "John, I'd like to go over this speech before we land." Anders Martin rose, signaling the congressmen that their visit was over; they stood, murmuring pleasantries, and filed into the outer cabin.

"I was making some changes in the introduction," Cardwell said when they were gone. "I can be finished in a minute."

"Take your time," said Rattigan, and he turned toward Martin, taking from the aide a folder of letters and memos to read. Not a moment could be wasted; the President's time was always well used.

"Tell them I can't come," Rattigan said, pushing the first letter toward Martin.

"Send this man a nice thank you," he said of another. Martin jotted notes on each piece of paper.

Cardwell worked in silence, printing in block letters on large index cards.

"Let's put this off," said the President to Martin. "I can think about this in the spring, and—"

When the telephone rang, the President kept on reading. Martin picked up the receiver, listened a moment, then nodded. "Sure, Sheldon, he's right here." He turned to Rattigan. "Karnow, Mr. President."

"Sheldon?"

Cardwell wrote on, absorbed, scarcely hearing the conversation.

"Oh, my God! How did it happen?" said Rattigan loudly. Cardwell looked up. Anders Martin was staring too, a sheaf of letters in his hand.

"That's incredible," said the President. "What about his security?" He rubbed his forehead. Cardwell, watching intently now, saw the fine lines deepen into wrinkles across the President's forehead. "Oh, Jesus," the President said.

For a long moment he was silent, holding the receiver, listening carefully to Karnow on the other end.

"Sheldon," he said finally, "I've got to decide what I'm going to do. Can you dictate all the information you have on this and then call me in fifteen minutes?" He turned to Martin and pointed to the phone. "Give this to one of the girls up front. Tell her to take it right on her typewriter."

Then, looking at Cardwell, he said, "They've shot Bert Williams."

"Is he—"

"He's dead. There was an ambush in the outskirts of La Paz."

Cardwell remembered Williams: the U.S. ambassador. He had gotten a rough time from the Foreign Relations Committee before he was confirmed. Cardwell remembered Williams' cool answers, his final victory.

"I can't believe it," the President said softly. "He was in my office a week ago."

Air Force One flew through darkness. Inside, the cabin lights were on, casting a soft fluorescent glow. Rattigan clenched his fist, unclenched it, and drummed lightly on the tabletop. An electronic clock above the cabin door, silently clicking off minutes, showed "Washington time" and "destination time." They were nearing Chicago; it was almost seven o'clock.

Anders Martin returned to the President's cabin, and Rattigan looked up.

"Maybe we'd better go back to Washington," he said. "How far are we from Chicago? How long before we land?"

"About half an hour," Martin answered. "We've already begun our descent."

"All right. We should put together a statement for the press." The President was himself again, in command. "John, can you draft a paragraph or two for Trip to read when we land? Just say I've received news of Ambassador Williams' death, and I've decided to return to Washington. I'll make the Chicago speech, but we leave right afterward. Andy, can you get word to Trip on the press plane to hold the press for an announcement?"

Martin nodded, moving toward the telephone, and Cardwell leaned over the table where the President sat. He wrote mechanically: "At about 7:00 P.M., Central Standard Time, the President received word from Washington that the United States ambassador to Bolivia, Bertrand D. Williams, was assassinated today in La Paz. . . ."

The plane sank into clouds, continued its descent, and bumped slightly in turbulent air; the seat belt sign flashed on.

Martin returned to the President's side.

"I got word to Trip. He's going to hold the press on the plane until we can read him the statement."

The telephone sounded again, and this time the President reached for it. Cardwell stopped his writing and looked up, fixing his eyes upon the little red "in use" light on the phone.

Rattigan almost shouted. "What the hell is going on down there?" Then, holding the telephone away from his ear as if to refuse the message he had heard, he told them:

"Our embassy in La Paz has been fire-bombed. It's burning now."

Sarah Tolman was no longer in La Paz; she and Tony Jack had moved on to Santa Cruz. Now, from the window of her shabby hotel room, Sarah could look down on the white city: a patchwork of red-tiled rooftops darkening as the sun went down. She had been in Bolivia almost a week: four days in La Paz, two in Santa Cruz. From the cluttered cable office in La Paz, she had filed three long dispatches on the war—and yet she had no real feeling of the presence of conflict, nothing more than a vague sense of menace when she saw, walking along the streets of La Paz pairs of helmeted policemen and soldiers, Sten guns slung over their shoulders.

She had noticed a curious quiet about the ancient city—and now, watching as the shadows came on, she could feel the quiet deepen. People disappeared from the streets; windows were shuttered in defense against the night.

She turned from her place at the window and walked across the room. A washstand stood against the wall, a bowl and pitcher atop it. There was no bathroom. She seized a cloth and scrubbed her face. Tony would be downstairs in a few minutes, waiting to take her to dinner. She felt like a tourist on a leisurely side trip, not like a reporter in a land where people were being killed.

And yet, all the officials she had met in La Paz seemed to feel the war's presence. The American ambassador, Bert Williams, had seemed surprised when she told him she planned to travel in the country.

"Be careful," he had said. "Yankees aren't very popular these days, and they won't be impressed by your press card." And then he had laughed. "Hell, I envy you. They won't let me walk down the street. I feel like a prisoner."

On a console behind his desk she had seen a picture of his family: his wife, a pleasant-looking woman, and two daughters with long blond hair.

She remembered the chief of the tiny U.S. military aid mission, a handsome colonel named Redwine who wore civilian clothes with the slightly uncomfortable look of a military man out of uniform. She and Tony Jack had spent a long lunch hour in La Paz listening to what Redwine called a "briefing," a routine anti-Communist diatribe in which the rebels, from Aguila on down, were agents of Peking and Moscow, and Bolivia was a vital free-world bastion. He actually used those words.

Sarah had looked at the colonel in disbelief. How, she wanted to ask him, could this high, forgotten land be vital to anyone? What did they care, these stolid, unlettered Indians in the streets, whether they were ruled by capitalists or Communists? To whom were these mountains and arid plains vital? If the country was a bastion of anything, it was a bastion of silence, of backwardness, of poverty.

"What an awful bore," Sarah had said to Tony later. "I can't imagine why they'd give him an assignment like this."

"Don't sell him short," Tony had warned her. "Redwine may be a bore, but he's a hell of a soldier and he's doing a good job. He has one quality that makes him perfect for a job like this: He believes in what he's doing. He really believes it's all no more than God and the free world against atheistic Commies. It may not correspond to reality, but he holds his faith as deeply as any Marxist. He's got all the men in his mission fired up, and they're getting to the Bolivian Army."

"It sounds like what we used to call Yanqui imperialism," Sarah had said with a smile.

"Call it what you will, but eventually old Redwine will make it uncomfortable for Aguila, and that's his job."

At the mention of the rebel leader's name, Sarah had looked at Tony with raised eyebrows.

"No luck yet," he had answered. "Wait till we get out in the countryside. When we get to Santa Cruz, I'm going to ask around the university. It's full of sympathizers; somebody's bound to know how we can get to him."

"I have permission from the *Times* to stay down here until I find him."

"Ah, then we may grow old together after all."

While Sarah stayed in her hotel room in Santa Cruz, sifting through her notes and drafting her next dispatch, Tony had spent the first day loitering around the university buildings, chatting with students in his perfect Spanish, hoping to meet one person who could help him: who could perhaps introduce him to a leftist student leader, who in turn might point out a contact in the movement, who in turn . . .

"Any luck?" she had asked when they met for dinner the night before.

"Zero," he had said. "I came close, though. I saw a law student, about thirty, sneaking a Marxist poster onto a bulletin board. When I asked him about Aguila he looked like he'd seen a ghost. I guess he thought I'm from the CIA."

Now, leaning forward to see her reflection in the small, cloudy hotel mirror, Sarah swept her dark hair back and tied it with a ribbon. A far cry from combat gear, she thought, and frowned at her image in the glass.

There was a knock at her door.

"Who is it?"

"Anthony Paul Jack, journalist and *bon vivant.*"

"Tony!" She opened the door. "I was going to meet you downstairs."

"I am a true gentleman," he said. "And besides, I wanted to get into your room and overpower you."

When they reached the narrow street below, he took her elbow and steered her to the left, away from the hill on which their hotel stood.

"Any contacts?" she asked.

"No," he said, "but I found a fantastic little restaurant near the university. Mutton stew, a few dangerous-looking characters, all the beer you can drink—"

"And dysentery tomorrow."

"Trust me," he said.

It was almost nightfall, and in places where shadows filled the narrow cobbled streets it was dark already. They walked slowly past closed and shuttered shops, catching scents, from the houses they passed, of smoke, of food cooking. The sidewalks were almost empty.

"I get the feeling we're war correspondents without a war to report," she said.

"How so?"

"Well, you promised me all sorts of excitement, and here we are, walking peacefully down the street like a pair of tourists. You even told me I'd gotten here in time for the real fireworks. I want to see some action."

She was joking, but he answered her seriously.

"Observation No. 1," he said. "In countries like this one, when things seem really quiet, things are really happening.

"Like what?"

"You have to wait and see," he said.

He guided her around a corner, down a narrow sidewalk past a few parked cars.

What had she hoped to find?

She had come to Bolivia, after years of reporting the bloodless battles of Washington, hoping to find her youth—to find the exhilaration she had known in Saigon when, with a group of friends, she could climb at night to the roof of the Caravelle Hotel to see the rockets flashing in the darkness beyond the city.

"When you say you want to see some action," Tony said, "you mean you want to see battles, blood, men getting killed. You're rather bloodthirsty to be such a pretty girl, aren't you?"

"Forgive me," she said.

"Don't look at me," he laughed. "You're talking to the original war lover."

"Well, it's been a nice trip," she said. "I can go back to Washington and write a long piece about the elusive guerrillas, the shadowy war in the countryside, and then get back to normal: committee hearings, speeches in the Senate, the comings and goings of the great."

"How do you stand it?" he asked.

"Actually, I love it," she said. "I'm good at my work, I have complete freedom, and I'm crazy about Washington."

"Politicians," he said.

"I can't be cynical about them," she said. "You don't see many great men, but you see good men, up against real problems. It's true, they make dull speeches and dull conversation. But the issues aren't dull."

"Sarah," Tony said suddenly, "how old are you?"

"Thirty-eight," she said.

"Old enough to be married, have kids," he said.

She shrugged.

"Well, what about it? There must be guys all over Washington after you. Jesus, there were in Saigon. You're smart, you've got fantastic class, you look great, you—"

Sarah Tolman said nothing.

"Well, like I always say, superior women marry late."

"And superior men marry other people," Sarah said.

They had walked about a mile, Tony touching her elbow lightly, looking at her and listening. They entered a small square near the university; a few more people were on the street.

"Remember the other night when you asked about my mystery man in Washington? Well, you were right," she said. "I met him in Saigon, and when I went back to Washington he was there."

"But it didn't work out," Tony said.

"He was married to somebody else, and there was no possibility of a divorce."

"Do you ever see him?"

"I see him, but I don't. We move in the same circle, in a way, but we . . . avoid each other."

"Okay, so that's over," Tony said. "But surely you've met somebody—"

Suddenly Sarah grabbed Tony's arm and held it hard.

"Hey, what's the matter?"

"Tony, did you see that man?"

"What man?"

"Don't say anything, just keep walking."

The instant she had seen the man at the edge of the square she had recognized him. "Tony," she whispered urgently, "that's the man who was following us in La Paz. He's even wearing the same suit."

"Is he following us?" Tony asked.

"I don't know, but he looked right at us," Sarah said.

"Well, let's find out," Tony said. Abruptly he steered her off the square into a side street.

"Okay, don't look back until we've gone a block," he said.

At the end of the block they both looked back. Less than a hundred yards behind, walking deliberately toward them, they saw the thin man. He was looking directly at them, walking with one hand in his pocket.

"Tony, I'm frightened."

"So am I, baby," Tony said tightly. The narrow street was deserted, silent. They could hear their footsteps in the shadows.

"In here." Tony gave her a push to the right. They passed through a vast dark entryway, through massive wooden doors: a church.

"St. Christopher be my guide," Tony said, and they stood for a moment in the half light, searching the vast space of the sanctuary. The church was almost empty; they could make out, at the altar, the forms of two old women kneeling, black-clad, praying.

"Over there," he said, and they moved to the side of the church, to a place behind two pillars where rows of candles burned.

"Can we sit down?" she asked. She was breathless, spent.

He shook his head. "I think we're okay," he said. "But let's watch the door."

Sarah felt herself recovering. Deliberately she began breathing deeply. Tony moved into the shadow of one pillar, staring across the high pews toward the door.

Then the door swung open; the thin man entered. He stood gazing down the long aisle toward the altar, his dark eyes narrowed beneath the heavy brows.

"Okay," Tony whispered. "Let's get down to that altar and pray like hell. Kneel right between those two old ladies, and if he tries anything, scream."

Quickly, in full view of the man, they moved toward the altar, their footsteps clattering on the cold stone floor. Sarah dropped to her knees beside one of the dark-faced women. She felt her chest pounding, shut her eyes tightly, and she realized she *was* praying.

Then she heard his footsteps behind her and she almost stopped breathing. The man knelt beside her at the altar, and she was about to scream. Then she heard his voice, murmuring a prayer, almost whispering, slurring the familiar Latin phrases.

When she stole a quick look at him from the corner of her eye, the man was looking straight into her face.

"You want to see Roberto Aguila," he said in good, clear English. "I can take you to his place."

Air Force One, racing back to Washington, hit rough air.

Cardwell leaned forward, lifted his drink, and the plane lurched, rattling the ice in the plastic cup. He drank carefully, then settled back again.

Gary Triplitano emerged from the President's compartment and moved down the aisle, holding onto seat backs as he walked to keep his footing.

"May I join you?"

"Sure thing."

He sank into the empty seat by Cardwell and said quietly, "That was rotten luck. I know how hard you worked."

"There's always next time," Cardwell said.

"Let's hope so." Feeling the plane move wildly in the turbulence, Triplitano quickly fastened his seat belt.

"How much do you know about this Bolivian thing?" he asked.

"Only what I read in the papers, and that's not much."

"Well, it's a hell of a mess. We were hoping we could cool it down—manage it all behind the scenes." He shrugged. "And now this."

And so, whispering in the half light of the speeding plane, Triplitano sketched for Cardwell the outline of the crisis: the disturbing intelligence from Chile; the secret meeting in the Cabinet Room; Bolivia's desperate request, delivered by Badillo, for troops; the President's diplomatic probes, still unanswered; and now these acts of violence.

In the quiet of his compartment, the President tried to focus on the stack of letters and memos Andy Martin had brought along. But again and again the image of Bert Williams swam into his head, fixed itself before him: Williams, alive eight days ago, talking earnestly in the Cabinet Room.

He imagined the scene in La Paz now: troops and police surrounding the burned-out embassy, streets roped off. He was trying to avoid involvement, trying to resist sending troops to Bolivia. But a dead ambassador, the bombed-out embassy—there were men on Capitol Hill, and across the country, who would cry for retaliation. And weren't they right? Could there be any more direct provocation than this?

The plane shuddered through a series of slight jolts, and Rattigan returned to the papers before him: *Try not to think about it now,* he told himself. *Wait until you have all the facts.* It would be a long night in the Situation Room.

Rattigan prided himself on his power of concentration, his ability to dismiss one problem absolutely while he took up another. Now he locked his eyes on a long memo from the Attorney General, forced himself to read—but it was no use.

Bert Williams was dead—and Carl Rattigan, despite the hard rein he kept on his thoughts, could not escape a feeling of guilt for his death. Hadn't he called him from a safe life in Seattle, put him where he could be killed?

Anders Martin, coatless, was dozing nearby.

"Andy?"

"Mr. President?" He stirred instantly.

"Could you call one of the girls? I'd like to dictate."

In a moment Sheila Roundtree sat beside him, an open tablet in her lap. "This is to Ambassador Williams' wife," he said.

"Dear Angela," he began. He wondered how to say anything that would help; he wanted to say something personal, expressing his feelings exactly. "Bert's tragic death came as a blow to me," he said, then stopped. It sounded hollow.

"I'm sorry," he said after a moment. "Get somebody to draft something and I'll sign it." The secretary left and he returned, bleakly, to his thoughts.

There had been no answer from Chile to his warning of eight days ago. The Swiss embassy in Santiago had delivered it, receiving silence in reply. And the Russians? Since Healy's confrontation with Lubshanko, there had been no word. What were they thinking?

He felt the plane shift slightly, angling downward, beginning its descent.

"What time is it?" he asked Andy Martin.

"Eleven o'clock, sir," said Martin. "We'll be landing soon."

For Rattigan, the great issues, the great decisions, always reduced themselves to personal terms. A crisis loomed in Bolivia, war threatened; but try as he might, he could not be detached, could not see the situation in terms of red pins on a map or blurred photos on an easel. From now on, when he thought of Bolivia, he would see Bert Williams' face and feel a stab of pain and guilt. He wondered whether other Presidents had felt the same, taken events so personally.

Anders Martin went forward, stayed a minute, then returned.

"Landing in five minutes, Mr. President. We'll hit some high winds on the ground."

The President strapped himself in tighter and stared out the window at his side: Wisps of cloud, of fog, rushed by in the darkness.

The pilot, fighting the winds, kept the throttle forward, and the big plane hurtled downward, eastward toward the long runway at Andrews Air Force Base.

In the staff cabin up forward, Cardwell listened to Triplitano, amazed at what he was hearing: Neither the country nor the press, not even most of the President's own staff, knew the full depth of the difficulty Rattigan faced.

"So there you have it," Triplitano said, concluding.

"Jesus," Cardwell whispered. Then, after a pause, "All right. He's warned Chile. He's asked the Russians to intercede. What if that doesn't work?"

Triplitano sighed. "We can appeal to the OAS, call the Security Council into session . . ." He shrugged.

"And if that doesn't work?"

Trip frowned. "I don't know. He can send money, arms, ammunition. Or he can give them the troops they're asking for. Any way you look at it, it's bad."

Cardwell said nothing. He was thinking of the strange workings of the West Wing, where dozens of men saw the President each day, yet each saw only a fraction of the man. Cardwell, busy writing speeches, reading the Gallup poll, had seen only that part of Rattigan concerned with speeches, politics, the polls. Yet all the while, the President faced other, greater worries.

The plane was landing: They saw, winking in the darkness, the blue lights of Andrews. Eleven-fifteen.

A steward, holding a clipboard, dropped quickly into the seat across the aisle, fastening his belt as the plane landed. "Gentlemen," he said, leaning toward the two aides, "you're on the helicopter manifest. You'll be leaving the plane by the rear door."

They nodded. The plane roared, straining to slow itself. In a few minutes they would be aboard the chopper with the President, clattering through the late November fog to the makeshift heliport on the South Lawn.

Air Force One rolled to the ramp. There were black cars out in the darkness: White House sedans. In the plane the sleepers waked; there was shuffling in the aisles. Cardwell and Triplitano stood and moved rearward, toward the President's compartment.

"I feel sorry for him," Cardwell said.

"Don't," said Triplitano. "He asked for the job."

The President had already left the plane. They moved through the empty compartment, down the steps, rushing through the cold to the waiting helicopter.

My name is Rafael," the man had said in answer to Sarah Tolman's question. "I can take you to him."

Now, with the stranger driving, Sarah and Tony Jack had bounced along for more than an hour in the rear compartment of a Jeep-like truck. There was a single slit for a window, but when Sarah peered out, she could see only darkness.

"Well, this is one way to get an interview," she said.

"Or get ourselves killed," Tony answered.

"Oh, come on," Sarah said. "You know you love this." But she was nervous, too. She searched the darkness for Tony's face, but could see only his shadow.

"I can't believe we were so willing to go along with this guy," Tony said. She could hear the tightness in his voice. "Suppose they want us as hostages or something."

"Tony!" she said, surprised by his tone. "That's not like you. I thought you were fearless."

"Semifearless," Tony said. "And very careful. I just don't like the way we got into this."

They had left Santa Cruz long ago; the truck bumped along a graveled highway, swung around hairpin curves. They started down a steep hill and, up front, Rafael shifted suddenly into low gear. His two passengers were thrown violently forward.

"Hey, watch it up there!" Tony shouted. But their driver did not answer.

"How far do you think we've come?" Sarah asked.

"I don't know. Thirty, forty miles. I can't tell."

Sarah leaned back, bracing herself against the jostling of the truck, trying, with her eyes closed, to imagine the landscape they were passing, the steep, black hills and heavy forests.

Sarah Tolman was afraid, as she had been many times in her life. She had learned long ago the precise sensations that danger aroused in her: a quickened heartbeat, a slight feeling of breathlessness, a cool prickly sensation at the back of her neck—and finally a sense of excitement, of heightened expectation. Her body knew, if her mind did not, the secret that soldiers and adventurers know—that danger is a sensual experience, deeply sensual.

Tony spoke in the darkness. "I'll give you a cigarette if you'll admit you're scared."

"For a cigarette, I'll admit I'm terrified," she said.

He laughed. "I knew it." Leaning toward her in the dark, he held out the cigarette pack; reaching for it, she touched his hand.

At that moment the truck slowed—stopped.

"We're there?" she asked.

"No," Tony said. "I think he's turning."

They could tell by the truck's motion that Rafael had left the graveled highway, turning right onto a rough, ungraded road.

"We're in the sticks," Tony said. He leaned forward, struck a match, and lit their cigarettes, the flame trembling in his cupped hands.

The road was rough, and they could hear the slap and brush of tree limbs against the truck's sides, the clatter of rocks beneath the wheels.

In ten minutes Rafael cut the engine. The rear door of the truck opened and a light glared into their faces, making Sarah blink.

"From here we walk," Rafael said.

Cold, aching from the ride, they followed him, trying to see beyond the faint wedge of light his flashlight cast.

"We should be in fatigues," Tony said. They made a strange sight: the two men in suits, Sarah in a light dress and shoes too flimsy for a hike in the darkness.

They headed down into a steep ravine. Following Rafael, with Tony close behind her, Sarah snagged a heel, slipped, and fell backward. Tony caught her and they halted, breathless.

"How much farther?" Tony asked.

"We are there," said Rafael. He was wagging his flashlight, signaling someone who waited in the darkness.

"Pombo," he said.

"Rafael." They passed the guard.

The guerrilla camp was well concealed: a cluster of shanties in a basin at the end of a canyon. A fringe of trees on the cliffs above roofed the canyon. Even by daylight, the camp would be invisible.

In the doorway of a broad, squat building, silhouetted against the dim light from within, a man was waiting.

"I'm glad you have come," he said. "I am Roberto Aguila." He spoke good English. They followed him inside, joined by Rafael, and in a wary, wordless ritual, shook hands.

"Sit down."

Aguila motioned them into chairs around a square table, then sat down facing them.

"Coffee?"

"Please," said Sarah. And Rafael, nodding deferentially, went outside. The two reporters studied their host.

Sarah was sure she had seen photos of Aguila; she tried to remember, but the face of the man before her was something new, unexpected. His hair was not dark but almost blond, and his eyes, which burned from deep sockets, were blue. Except for the heavily muscled shoulders beneath his brown work shirt, he had the lean, ascetic form of a saint—or a revolutionary. It was a compelling face.

Tony, too, was staring at Aguila, as if to commit his face to memory. A lantern lit the room where they sat, casting flashes off a tin ceiling.

"Was it uncomfortable?" Aguila said.

"No, it was all right," said Sarah.

"When the revolution comes," he said, half smiling, "we will be in La Paz, and when you visit I will send a big black car for you."

She caught the hint of a smile on Tony's face, and she smiled too. Extraordinary that he could joke, here, as if among friends. She wished she had a pencil, a notebook; pledged herself to remember every detail—was, in fact, already beginning mentally to write her account of this meeting.

Rafael returned with four tin mugs of thick, bitter coffee. He set them on the table, then took a chair.

"I'm sorry if we frightened you," Aguila said. "I knew you were looking for me, but today it became urgent that I talk to you."

He paused and Sarah darted a look toward Tony, then back to Aguila.

"Rafael has been with you since La Paz," he said, and Rafael smiled slightly. "He is in the Ministry of Information."

"Theirs, or yours?" asked Tony.

"Theirs," said Aguila. "But he is one of us."

Sarah wondered how many Bolivians—farmers, civil servants, plain citizens by day—were secret soldiers at night, or watchers, for Aguila. And she was amazed at his indiscretion—revealing Rafael's double role. How could he be sure they would not betray him? Then she had a frightening thought: Perhaps he could talk freely because he planned to keep them here, make them prisoners. She shivered slightly.

"You had to see us," Tony said, all business now. "Why is it so urgent?"

"First the rules," Aguila said. "You are both reporters. Everything I tell you, you can write. But you must transmit your stories from La Paz, and you must not tell when you saw me, or where."

"The Army knows you're camped near Santa Cruz," said Tony Jack.

"They need not be certain of it. Just say 'somewhere in Bolivia.' Otherwise . . ."

"Otherwise," said Aguila mildly, "I cannot talk to you. You are a man of your word?"

"Okay," Tony nodded.

Aguila laid his hands upon the table and spoke slowly, gravely. "In La Paz today, it did not go according to our plans. It was an accident—a tragedy. I think it is important that your people know—"

"Excuse me," said Tony. He shot a puzzled glance toward Sarah, and both stared blankly at Aguila. "We've been in Santa Cruz, and we haven't heard anything about—"

"Forgive me. The United States ambassador was killed today—shot in La Paz."

"Oh, my God!" said Sarah.

"We were going to—take him into custody," said Aguila. "But he tried to run away. It was an accident. A stupid accident, and I regret it. If only he had not tried to run away. . . . I am afraid somebody else also panicked, one of our people, I am investigating now to be sure. . . ."

Sarah thought of their meeting—of Williams' office, with the family pictures behind his desk.

"You were going to take him into custody?" Tony said.

"For ransom," said Aguila. "For—indemnity. We honestly meant him no harm."

"But you killed him."

"There were several people killed," Aguila said softly. "It is most unfortunate. An hour later, the American embassy was set afire—but *not* by my people. Of *that* I *am* certain. It is most unfortunate. We have been listening to the radio," Aguila went on. "The embassy is surrounded by riot police. The Army has begun a sweep through the city. And they are begging once again for outside help: American troops."

"I'd say you've done a good bit to strengthen their case," Tony said, but his tone was not unfriendly.

Aguila said nothing for a moment. He sat, hands folded on the table, looking first at Tony, then at Sarah, as if digesting Tony's remark. Then he raised his hands and let them drop, a gesture of resignation.

"It was a very good plan, very audacious. For the release of your ambassador, two million American dollars, delivered in cash, in Chile. When we got the money, we would have released him safe. Unharmed."

"I don't think you'd have ever gotten the money," Sarah said.

"Then we would have kept the ambassador," Aguila said.

"And you would have killed him?" She was sorry she had said it—she did not want to offend this man.

"I don't know," he said. "It is of small consequence now, isn't it?"

They said nothing.

"I brought you here," said Aguila, "to tell you the truth. I think it is important that your government know the ambassador's death was an accident. An accident—not a provocation. And the burning—that was by other people."

"Well you can't expect them to just sit," Tony said.

"It would be a great mistake," said Aguila, "for your President to react too harshly. A great mistake."

"With that, I agree," said Sarah.

Aguila nodded. "For your country," he said, "Bolivia is not of great consequence. A poor country. A little beggar of a country. I do not think your President would make such a mistake, would he?"

"I think," said Sarah, "that he would do whatever he felt he had to do."

"You know him?" Aguila said, fascinated.

"Yes," she said.

"You know him well?"

"Not so well now," she said.

"What do you think he will do?"

"I think he would like to avoid getting involved in Bolivia. But in the end, he'll do what he feels he has to do." She hesitated, searching for words. "He's not entirely free to do as he'd like. All sorts of things—events, political pressures—can force him . . ."

"I think I understand," Aguila said gravely. And then sadly, abstractly, he looked at her. "A leader is not always free to do as he would like. There are factions, divisions, rivalries. There are enemies to be overcome and allies to be held in check. One cannot always control events."

"You mean," said Sarah slowly, "that you already know somebody deliberately killed the ambassador."

Aguila stared at her.

"And somebody . . . somebody you know," Sarah said, "set fire to that building."

Aguila said nothing, but Sarah saw in his eyes a look of profound sadness.

"Your friends from Chile," Sarah said.

For a long moment Aguila said nothing. When he spoke his voice was low, almost wistful.

"For many years," he said, "it was my dream that there would be a true revolution." He looked at Sarah. "I hoped that it could be accomplished by Bolivians, on their own, without outside help—and without outside opposition."

The lantern flickered dully off the tin ceiling. Sarah stole a glance at Rafael. He was listening, transfixed, his heavy brows knit together.

"But what cannot be, cannot be," said Aguila. "Our friends from Chile offer money, arms, men. They have different aims, but they want to help." He shrugged. "One cannot always control events."

Suddenly he stood up, and his face brightened.

"It is late," he said. "The interview is over. You can take my picture, as proof that you were here, and Rafael will drive you back."

Sarah and Tony stared at one another.

"What? You are reporters and you have no camera?" Aguila was smiling. "Rafael." He spoke in Spanish, and Rafael rushed out.

In a moment Rafael returned. With him was a short, swarthy youth in soiled fatigues. He held a camera—a small, cheap American model of the sort schoolchildren use.

"Stand here," said Aguila beckoning to them, strapping to his chest an ammunition belt. "Stand beside me."

He struck a stiffly formal pose and glared into the camera. Standing by him, Sarah caught his scent of sweat and gunpowder.

"I am not often photographed," he said, smiling. "We must do it right."

The youth snapped several pictures, blinding them each time with the flashbulbs' glare: Sarah with Aguila; Tony with Aguila; the three of them; Aguila alone. When it was over, Aguila took the camera, removed the film, and pressed the roll into her hand.

"You are very beautiful," he said.

It was late; time to go. Rafael stood, moved toward the door, and they followed him.

"Con Dios, Rafaelito," Aguila said.

"Buena suerte," he replied. Good luck.

"He is my half brother," Aguila said to them. "I would die for him."

They went outside. They entered the woods, climbed the steep path behind Rafael's dim light, and left the camp behind them, lost in darkness.

It fell to Anders Martin, the appointments secretary, to bring order out of the chaos created by the President's sudden decision to come home.

"Do you think we should send somebody to make your speech in Denver?" he had asked Rattigan in the helicopter from Andrews.

"Call the Vice President," Rattigan had said. "Tell him I want him to do it."

Martin's office was the one nearest the President's. Most of Rattigan's official visitors passed through it on their way to see the President: Martin took them in, introduced them, then retired, making a bold mark across the clipboard. And if they stayed too long—as almost every visitor did—he would re-enter the Oval Office, hover near the President and his guest, and stare pointedly at the visitor. It always worked.

Now, in his empty office, he picked up the telephone and waited for the operator's reply.

"Yes, Mr. Martin?"

"I'm back in my office. Do you have any calls?"

"Oh, yes, sir," she said, "we have several."

He recognized all the names she gave and knew he could let them wait—except one.

"—and Governor Hocking of Colorado. He said it was urgent. He wanted us to reach you on the plane, but—"

"All right." The governor would be frantic, wondering who would represent the President. "Get in touch with the governor and tell him I'll be calling him within the hour. And meanwhile, get me the Vice President."

"You know he's in Oklahoma?" the operator said.

"I know," said Martin. "Let's get him."

He knew he would not have to wait long. The operators were so efficient and the system so superb that the White House could reach almost any government official, anywhere, in seconds.

"I have the Vice President," she said.

"Andy?" Hoffman's voice was a rich political basso.

"Mr. Vice President. Sorry to bother you while you're on vacation."

"That's all right. What's up?"

"You know we're back in Washington."

"I heard the news. I'm awfully sorry about Williams. Awfully shocked. What's the situation down there now? Can you—"

"Actually, I don't know," Martin said. "The President's having a meeting—"

"A meeting? Look, if you want me up there, I can leave right away. Actually I've been doing a great deal of thinking about that situation down there, and there're some things I'd like to say. Suppose I—"

Poor old Abner, Martin thought. For the Vice President, Martin felt no particular emotion except a touch of pity seasoned with contempt. The Vice President, except for his title, simply didn't count. There were other men on whom the President depended in a crisis, and they were with him now.

"I know he'd appreciate that, sir," said Martin, breaking in, "but there's something else he needs."

Hoffman was silent on the other end.

"The President was wondering," Martin said, "if you could take this speech for him in Denver in the morning." He paused, waiting for Hoffman to reply, but the phone was silent.

"The governor has put together a rather big affair," Martin said. "It would be pretty bad if it fell through."

Silence.

"And the President said he knew you could do a fantastic job." Martin regretted this last—he had intended to pay Hoffman a compliment, but it sounded hollow, patronizing.

"Andy," said the Vice President slowly, "it would be difficult for me to go; I've got some appointments of my own. I hope you can get somebody else."

Old fella, you just don't understand, Martin thought. Though Hoffman far outranked the White House appointments secretary, though Martin could never give an *order* to the Vice President, they both knew that he spoke for the President—and that one fact meant more than the formality of rank or title.

"Mr. Vice President," Martin said gently, "I'm really sorry to hear that, and I hope you can reconsider. The President talked to Governor Hocking and told him you'd be coming, so this puts us in an awkward—"

"He said that?" Hoffman asked. Martin was lying, of course, but there was no way Hoffman could be sure of that.

"Yes, sir," said Martin. "The governor said he had to give the press some word this evening or he'd lose his crowd."

"Andy—"

"Maybe you'd better talk to the President," Martin said smoothly, "so we can straighten this thing out."

"Andy," said Hoffman in a low, choked voice, "I am goddamned sick and tired of the way you people treat me."

Martin said nothing.

"I am sick of being doormat, flunky, errand boy, and stand-in for Carlton Rattigan."

"Mr. Vice President—"

"Will you tell him that for me?"

"I think," said Martin formally, "that's something the two of you may want to talk about in private."

"We already have," said Hoffman.

"Meanwhile," said Martin, making no pretense now at diplomacy, "my main concern is this speech tomorrow."

"I'll make the goddamned speech," said Hoffman coldly. "Send it to me on the wire. And tell Bob Hocking to call me tonight about the arrangements." He hung up.

Quickly Martin wrote, in large block letters, a memo to the President: "I talked to the Vice President. He will make the speech in Denver, but was very angry and insulting. Perhaps you should call him."

Then he lifted the telephone receiver. "All right," he said when the operator answered. "We can talk to Governor Hocking now."

Cardwell, excited by the presence of crisis, could not go home. He went to his office, switched on the lights, and settled into the big chair behind his desk. Fifty feet away, the President and his most senior aides huddled to discuss the crisis; Cardwell sat—with nothing to do.

He switched on the television set and watched a pool of blue light flow onto the screen, but the late news was over.

Cardwell snapped off the set: The picture shrank to a bright point of silence, then went dark.

Dot, expecting him to be gone five days, had arranged five folders on his desk: one for each day's mail. He flipped open the only one that was filled and read the letters: all routine.

The quiet of his office was strange to him: He missed the daytime bustle of Dot's typing, the ringing of telephones. The stillness, the emptiness of his office, matched the emptiness he felt.

He sat, feeling the quiet, thinking of the storm that raged tonight, bringing the President back to Washington, keeping him awake and at work.

He heard the door open in the outer office.

"Mr. Cardwell?"

"Right here."

It was a White House policeman, the West Basement guard.

"The truck just came with the baggage, sir. I've got your suitcase beside my desk."

"Thank you, Sergeant."

He thought again of the trip. When the President left Washington, his entourage numbered almost two hundred: aides, agents, communications experts, telephone operators, secretaries, reporters. All of them, he suspected, would think of the aborted journey as a gift: They could spend the weekend at home, with their families.

He snapped off the lights and walked into the dim hall.

There was no agent outside the Situation Room door: The President's meeting was over.

"Has everybody gone home?" Cardwell asked the sergeant.

"There's still a crowd upstairs," the guard said.

Cardwell pressed the elevator button and went upstairs.

Triplitano was finishing his final briefing: The weary reporters huddled around him, scribbling awkwardly in their tiny notebooks. Cardwell edged through the door and leaned against the wall, listening.

"Trip, is the President back in the Mansion?"

"As far as I know, yes."

"You know how long they met?"

"They broke up around twelve."

"Can you give us a rundown on the nature of this meeting?"

"I would characterize it as a review of the events of this afternoon in La Paz. It's an informational meeting—not one to make decisions or plan actions. The President simply wanted to have all the available information—intelligence—he could get."

"What should I tell my editor?"

"Tell him 'Good night,'" Triplitano said.

"Can we have a lid?"

"You have one." The reporters turned and crowded toward the door. It was twelve forty-five.

"I don't know how you do it," Cardwell said when they had all left.

Triplitano looked up, surprised by his presence.

"I have nerves of steel," he said. "And a bottle of scotch in my desk drawer."

He rolled open a deep drawer, brought out the bottle and two glasses, poured two drinks, shoved one toward Cardwell, and sank heavily into his big chair.

"Still feeling sorry for the President?"

Cardwell grinned.

"Why not feel sorry for me?" Trip said. "I work harder. He gets rubdowns, big cars, and the cheers of the crowd. I get ulcers, fallen arches, and questions from the press."

"What do you think he'll do?" Cardwell said.

"I think," said Triplitano, holding his glass up to the light, peering through it, "he'll ride this one out, do nothing. I think he'll issue a statement tomorrow deploring the violence, then hope everybody forgets about it."

He turned up his glass and drank almost half of the warm scotch in one swallow.

"He's lucky," Trip said. "Congress is still home for Thanksgiving. If they were in town, they'd raise hell for three days, and this thing would be dragged out—the pressure would be on. But as it is, we can let it drop in a day or two."

"Assuming it doesn't get worse," said Cardwell.

"Exactly." Triplitano finished his drink and poured another one. It was one o'clock. The place was empty now. The reporters had all gone home.

"You realize," said Triplitano, "that he didn't come home tonight just because Williams got killed. You understand?"

"No," said Cardwell, "I don't understand."

"That wasn't it. At least not entirely," Trip said. "Put yourself in his place. You have information—good information—that all hell is about to break loose down there. Or at least *can* break loose. Suddenly, within a couple of hours, your ambassador is murdered and your embassy fire-bombed. This is it, you think: They're doing it after all. Are you going to be caught dedicating a dam in Ashtabula, or back at your battle station? That's why he came home. He'll be jumpy as hell all week, waiting for the other shoe to drop."

"Well, I hope it doesn't drop," said Cardwell.

"But when it does?"

"If it does," said Cardwell, "I still hope he stays out."

"You mean," said Triplitano, "you'd let Chile march in there and shoot up the place, and you wouldn't lift a finger? Why?"

"Because it would go against everything he's ever stood for, everything he's promised. And because there's an election less than a year away."

Triplitano smiled at him, took a swallow of his drink, and shook his head from side to side.

"You mean it would go against everything you believe."

"That, too," said Cardwell.

"Suppose it happened," Triplitano said. "Suppose he sends in ten thousand troops—fifty thousand troops. What would you do?"

"What would I do?" said Cardwell. "What could I do? I'm not the Secretary of State."

"I mean, would you quit, leave the White House? I'm asking how strongly you feel about it."

"No," said Cardwell. "No, I wouldn't."

"Why not?"

"Loyalty, I guess," said Cardwell.

"Bullshit."

"No, I really believe that," Cardwell said.

"Okay," said Triplitano, "maybe you do, and maybe you're right. Hell, I'm loyal too. But there's more to it than that. He could invade Canada, drop the bomb on Mexico City, and most of us would stay. You know why?"

Cardwell said nothing, listening.

"Because we're hooked."

"Hooked?"

"Yes, sir. We're hooked. We've all had a taste of the White House. I don't mean the cars, the trips, all that. I mean the chance to play President." He lifted the half-empty bottle from its place on the desk and leaned over, placing it once again in the deep drawer below.

"You know what I mean," he said. "We all play President, every day. When I brief the press—why, I'm the President. When Andy Martin tells a senator the President can't possibly see him until next month, or when he calls up some middle-level bureaucrat and chews his ass, he's the President! And you speechwriters . . ." Triplitano grinned. "I think you've got it worst of all."

"That's funny," Cardwell said. "When I hear him make a speech

I've written, I get stage fright. I stand there and go through it all, just as though I'm the one making the speech."

"You see?" said Triplitano. "It's true with every guy I know, everyone who's ever gotten close to a President. Their egos get all screwed up, all tied up with his—and they call it loyalty, call it a sense of public duty, call it everything except what it really is."

He put his feet up on his desk and leaned back, his hands folded behind his head.

"Remember Vietnam? There must have been a dozen guys—in the White House, in the Cabinet—who stayed until the end, and then leaked the word, ever so subtly, that they were doves all along: They really were against it all the time, they really didn't agree with Johnson at all."

"I remember," Cardwell said.

"Well," said Triplitano, "maybe they weren't lying. Maybe they *were* against the whole thing. But they were hooked, they couldn't let go. They couldn't quit over a principle, because they couldn't bear to face life without being able to look across the table at old Lyndon and say those magic words: 'If I were you, Mr. President . . .' So they rationalized. They told themselves they could fight better from within—"

"And then they didn't fight," Cardwell said.

"They were good men, decent men," Triplitano said. "And you, Mr. Cardwell, are no better than they were."

It was almost one-thirty. Cardwell finished his drink, set the glass on Trip's desk, and stood. "Jesus, it's late," he said. "Thanks for the drink." He turned to go, but Triplitano pointed to his chair, signaling him to sit down again.

"No, don't go," he said. "I want to talk to you."

Cardwell leaned against the chair.

"About you," Triplitano said.

He sat down.

"John Cardwell, thirty-two years old," Triplitano said, as if he were reading the data from a file.

"Thirty-four," said Cardwell.

"You seem younger," Triplitano said. "White, male, Protestant. Probably Presbyterian or Episcopalian."

"The latter."

"One of those polite, restrained denominations," Triplitano said. "Family wealthy, well-to-do?"

"Comfortable," Cardwell said, puzzled. "What have you been doing? Reading my FBI file?"

"No," said Triplitano, "I've been reading you. It's my famous insight." He tapped his forehead, smiling.

"The President likes you. You're smart—goddamned smart. You have judgment, a sort of political sixth sense—and in this business, there's no asset that means more than that. But"—he picked up a pen from his desk and pointed it, like a pistol, toward Cardwell —"you don't fight."

Cardwell hesitated, wondering whether to speak, to defend himself.

"You do damned well," Triplitano said. "You put that trip together in record time, without a flaw. I know how much effort that took. But around this place, it's not mere effort that counts, in the long run."

Cardwell waited.

"It's influence. It's who talks to the President when he gets up in the morning and when he goes to bed at night. It's the ones he trusts the most, depends on the most: the guys he calls when he's got a problem. There can only be a few like that, so there's lots of shoving going on."

"I know that," Cardwell said.

"But you don't shove. You've got this extraordinary restraint, this politeness. I think it must have something to do with the way you were reared: Nice guys don't brawl, don't fight, don't use their elbows. Am I right?"

Cardwell was astounded. He felt vaguely uncomfortable, as though Trip knew him better than he knew himself.

"Perhaps, but not entirely," Cardwell said. "I look at all the people around here who've been with him longer—experts, guys with experience, credentials, and I—"

"That doesn't mean a damn thing," Trip said softly. "When it comes to the big problems, the problems he's supposed to decide, there aren't any experts. Who can tell him whether they're going to invade tomorrow or the next day, or at all? Who can tell him what to do if it happens? Who can guarantee it won't be an awful mistake?"

"Not me," said Cardwell.

"Not anybody," Triplitano said. "All he can hope for is that he's got some guys around him with good judgment. He can hire speechwriters, advance men, spear carriers—they're a dime a dozen. But the guys with judgment, the guys with nerve, the guys he counts on—they come few and far between."

"Why are you telling me all this?" Cardwell said.

"Because," said Triplitano, "I think you ought to be one of those guys."

"Use my elbows," Cardwell said.

"Elbows, knees, switchblade, broken bottle, anything it takes," Triplitano said. "I'm not telling you this because I want you to be a big shot. I'm saying it because I think he can use you; you can help him."

"Suppose I elbow you aside?" Cardwell said, smiling.

"Nobody elbows me aside," Triplitano said.

The telephone on his desk rang and he picked up the receiver.

"Okay, I'm on my way." He hung up. "My driver's here," he said, "do you need a ride?"

"I have my car," said Cardwell.

When he reached home, Nancy was asleep. He climbed into bed beside her and listened for a moment to the heavy pull of her breathing, then felt himself sinking toward sleep.

Toward dawn he had a long and vivid dream. In a city that could be any city, on a street that seemed to have no end, a crowd was cheering the President. He rode slowly among them, sitting high in his gleaming limousine, nodding right and left, smiling broadly, lifting first one hand and then the other in a gesture of triumph.

The street and the crowd went on and on; the cheers blended into one unending roll of thunder. And John Cardwell, deep in sleep, could not be sure whether he was one of those who watched the President . . . or whether, in his dream, he was the man who rode among them, hearing their cheers.

On Wednesday, the White House issued a statement deploring the violence that had flared the day before in La Paz, and warning that the United States "cannot stand idly by in the face of violence against its diplomatic personnel and installations on foreign soil."

Newspapers and broadcasts characterized the President's response as a "cautious, wait-and-see" attitude; some commentators praised his prudence and restraint.

And for one whole day and night, all was quiet in Bolivia.

Thursday the Thirtieth

Roughly halfway between La Paz and the old city of Santa Cruz, the narrow, graveled highway ends its twisting and stretches straight and open for two miles. The road becomes a bridge, crosses a tangled, deep ravine, then snakes again into the ragged hills.

The bridge and its flat approach have become a landmark and a stopping place. By day, the Indians and other travelers on the road stop their carts and cars and battered pickups near the bridge to rest. Some—mothers and their children—drink and wash their faces in the stream that runs beside the road south of the bridge; others, mostly young men, gather in clusters by the road to talk. And a few old men can usually be seen idling on the narrow bridge itself, leaning their forearms upon the railing, gazing quietly across the ravine. They rest awhile, enjoying the cool air rising up from the shadows far below, and then move on. By nightfall, the straight place and the bridge are quiet. The road is not a good one; few people travel it at night.

But two hours before dawn on November 30, less than forty-eight hours after the murder of the American ambassador to Bolivia, there was one heavy line of traffic on the road. A convoy of Bolivian Army trucks heaved and rumbled around the hills: the 29th Ranger Battalion, an elite Bolivian unit, had been ordered from its garrison in La Paz to join an intensified search for Roberto Aguila, to flush him from his hiding place in the hills near Santa Cruz, and thus to break the back of his insurgent movement.

The trucks moved as though linked together; their lights cleaved a path through the darkness, leaving a wake of darkness behind. Their engines growled and roared, straining against the steepness. And when the convoy reached the straight place, the laboring of the engines became an easy hum and the trucks approached the bridge.

In the high, dim cab of the lead truck rode the commander of the 29th Ranger Battalion, Colonel Juan Jesus Adeño, holding a lighted cigarette between two thick fingers, making no conversation with the driver, a blank-faced private. Adeño sat erect, still wearing the black cap of the Bolivian Special Forces, and stared into the wedge of brightness thrown onto the road by the big truck's lights.

He stared, but saw nothing. His mind was somewhere up ahead, in the tangled woods of eastern Bolivia where Aguila kept his hiding place. He saw himself, followed by a band of his best troopers, moving quietly through the woods, stalking the outlaw, surprising Aguila and his rebels in a sunlit clearing. In his mind's eye he raised his carbine, pointed it—then saw the rebel leader lift his hands, drop his weapon, surrendering. Adeño was forty years old, a fearless and intelligent soldier. Ever since his boyhood in La Paz, with only a stick for a rifle, he had filled his mind with visions of himself as a hero. Now, as his convoy lumbered toward Santa Cruz, he lifted his cigarette and drew impatiently upon it; the cab filled brightly with its warm red glow, and Colonel Adeño savored the image he had conjured up of himself as captor of Aguila, the elusive rebel chief.

The first trucks pulled onto the bridge and inched across it. The sound of their engines filled the ravine below, and an echo came back, doubling the drone. Adeño leaned forward, stubbed out his cigarette, then settled back into his seat, feeling the heavy rattle of the truck across the bridge.

He did not hear—nor did his four hundred men, riding in the trucks behind—the low, faint whine that started high to their rear. Then the whine grew into a roar as four jets, streaking in across the mountains from the west, screamed down upon the convoy, swept up the line of headlights with a thunder of fire and bullets, climbed sharply up the sky, then circled and came screaming down again.

In the split second before he died, Colonel Adeño saw a wall of fire, intensely orange, sweeping toward him. Instinctively he and his young driver flung their arms up to shield their faces, and, in a roar, their truck was consumed. The bomb opened an enormous hole in the bridge before them, and bits of the truck's flaming wreckage dropped through, falling like flares into the chasm below. The planes roared off.

On the bridge and on the road several trucks burst into flames. Others struggled off the side of the road, overturned into ditches, disgorged maimed and shouting soldiers. A few engines labored heavily, then fell silent. Amid the shouting, the crackle of radios began: urgent calls for help, reports of the attack. Dawn approached.

The planes, which no one in the convoy had heard or seen before the attack, streaked homeward, flying low. They flew in a straight line westward—away from the rising sun; toward Chile.

In the White House, Lisa Rattigan awakened, saw slivers of gray light showing through the drawn curtains, and guessed it was about seven-thirty. She reached for the telephone beside her bed and said to the operator, "I'll have breakfast with the President in his room. Will you tell the kitchen for me?"

Lisa Rattigan climbed down from her high canopied bed, wrapped herself in a blue quilted robe, gave her hair several strokes with a silver-backed brush, fixed a bright smile upon her face, and stepped through the doors.

"Good morning," she said.

"Good morning." He looked up, smiling slightly, from the large wing chair beside his bed. Already he was working: He held a blue-bordered intelligence report titled "The President's Daily Brief," one of several stacked beside the chair.

"Am I intruding?"

"Oh no. Come in." His eyes behind his thick-rimmed glasses told her she was welcome.

"I thought I'd come and pour your coffee for you." She leaned over, kissed him lightly on the cheek and, as she rose, picked up a newspaper from beside his chair. "And maybe bring you a little cheer," she added.

"I could use both," he said, and she sat down in the chair facing him.

They read quietly for a minute, until a waiter knocked and brought in a rolling table with their breakfast. When he had placed the table before them and drawn wide the draperies of the President's room, she spoke again.

"Yesterday must have been terrible for you."

He nodded. She poured coffee for the two of them, then studied his face for a moment as he ate, searching for his reaction. Although they seldom discussed his work, she knew this was one time that it would be best to draw him out, to let him talk about the burdens, the frustrations. He could say to her things he could say to no one else. She decided to press on, gently.

"It's so baffling," she said. "I can't tell from reading the papers why they would kill Bert Williams, or who's responsible. The *Times* says they were trying to kidnap him, but . . ."

"That's the whole trouble," he said. "We can't tell anything ourselves—how all this hangs together, or whether it does—this guerrilla thing, Bert Williams, Chile."

"Chile?"

"They've got some troops in Bolivia. We know that. I sent them a warning, and we asked the Russians to intercede, to call them off." He shook his head. "And all we've got so far is silence—and Bert Williams' head on a platter."

Involuntarily she winced at his words. He picked restlessly at the food on his plate, then stood up and walked to the window.

A mile to the south a bit of winter sunlight whitened the dome of the Jefferson Memorial and cast a flat glitter on the gray Potomac.

"In the Cabinet Room yesterday," Rattigan said, "I asked the whole crowd of them to imagine the worst: to assume that Chile would come in, help the rebels, bring down the government. How would that hurt us?" He seemed almost to be talking to himself. "Nobody said anything for a long time, and then Brooks Healy spoke up. 'It might not hurt us at all,' he said. 'It would simply mean the end of a poor, weak country that asked our help and didn't get it. A free country.' "

"You can't be sure that would happen," Lisa Rattigan said.

"But you can't be sure it wouldn't," he said.

He turned, walked back to his chair, and brushed with his slippered foot the heap of newspapers beside it.

"Come finish breakfast," she said.

He sat down and reached for his coffee.

"I know you can't dismiss it from your mind," she said. "But I hope you can relax today. I've asked Brooks and Anna Healy to Camp David—on the condition that you and he won't talk business."

He managed a smile.

"We can fly right up this morning," she said. "After the . . . funeral."

At the word she saw his face tighten.

"I wonder if I should even go out there," he said. "I'm not sure—"

"Of course you should."

"I'm not sure his wife will want to see me."

"Carl! Of course she will," Lisa said quickly. And she realized for the first time how deeply shaken he was by Bert Williams' death. *He feels responsible,* she thought.

"I don't know what to say to her," he said. "I tried to write her a letter when it happened, but I couldn't think of anything to say."

"Perhaps there's nothing you can say. Just being there will be enough."

Before he could reply, the telephone rang. He reached back to the table beside his bed and picked it up.

"Hello?"

Lisa started to pour a second cup of coffee.

"Sheldon, good morning," he said.

When she glanced up she saw his face go hard and she knew before he spoke that more trouble had come, another tightening of the vise that held him.

"Are you in the building?" the President said to Karnow. "Okay, then, get up here as soon as you can."

When he hung up, he stared at her, his eyes blank.

"You can forget about Camp David," he said quietly.

"Bad news?" She knew the answer.

"The worst," he said.

At the house on Willow Road in Bethesda, John Cardwell slept until nine-thirty. He had decided, since the President's trip had been aborted, to take the next two days off, and Nancy was delighted. For several minutes he lay still, curled in the spot of warmth his body made, trying to sink toward sleep again. Then he heard, as if from a great distance, the kitchen radio: a last wisp of music, then a voice. Nancy was fixing breakfast.

He climbed from bed, pulled from a bureau drawer a pair of ancient khaki pants and a sweatshirt. Without shaving or combing his hair he wandered to the kitchen, feeling heavy, drugged with sleep.

"Good morning," Nancy said brightly.

"Morning," he said, settling into a chair. She moved, from stove to sink to counter and back again, in time with the music from the radio. In the bright light of the kitchen, beneath the pale flesh-colored peignoir that she wore, he could see her body: a few shadows, the gentle angle of her hips.

"The paper's on the counter," she said, and he reached for it, leaning to his left, not rising from his chair.

She rattled about while he breakfasted and read the paper, looking up occasionally to nod or murmur a reply. AMBASSADOR'S RITES TODAY: PRESIDENT WILL ATTEND, said a headline. How much of Rattigan's time was spent in rituals like this? Lay a wreath, say a prayer, bury the dead. Cardwell searched the *Post* for news of developments in Bolivia, found none: The murder of Bert Williams had been followed by a day of silence. Good.

"I thought we could have a late dinner," Nancy was saying, "and then go into town for some fun." He half listened; the sound of her voice blended with the pleasant, impersonal drone of the radio. "What would you like to do?" Cardwell asked.

"Well, I'm not sure," said Nancy. "Let me check the papers, and I'll—"

"This just in," said the radio news voice. "The official government radio of Chile this morning denied that Chile was responsible for a daring series of air strikes against Bolivian troops and bases."

"Can I see the paper?"

"Shh, wait," he said.

"But Bolivian and U.S. sources charged that the strikes were clearly made by Chile in support of Bolivian guerrillas—"

"I've got to get dressed," he said, standing up abruptly.

"What's the matter?"

"I've got to go to the office. Didn't you hear the radio?"

She said nothing.

"Look," he said, "I'll probably be back in time for dinner. I've just got to go down there for a while."

With Nancy looking after him he walked down the short hall to their room.

Shaving, with the fast-running water sending up a cloud of steam before him, he remembered hearing Triplitano two nights before, asking almost casually over his glass of warm scotch: "Who can tell him whether things will heat up down there or suddenly cool off? And who can tell him what to do if the worst should happen?"

There would be no traffic. He could dress and drive to the White House in less than thirty minutes.

"The colonel should be here any minute. You can wait in his office if you like."

Sarah and Tony Jack smiled. Redwine's office, since the embassy staff had moved into the Cordoba Hotel, was a bedroom. His secretary, an efficient-looking brunette in her early forties, seemed strangely serene, as if unfazed by the murder of Williams and his bodyguards, the burning of the embassy, this morning's news of jet attacks by Chile.

"You're awfully calm," said Tony pleasantly.

"I'm just in shock," the secretary said.

They moved from her desk in the hallway into Redwine's office, found chairs, and waited.

"Still bored?" said Tony, lighting a cigarette.

"Bored?" said Sarah.

"Two days ago you were complaining about a lack of action."

"Forgive me," Sarah said. Wearily she shook her head, too tired for banter, and stared for a moment through the room's large window, down into the empty street below. A line of soldiers and policemen stood outside, guarding the Americans in their makeshift embassy.

"I only wish that things could slow down now," she said.

Since yesterday, when she and Tony had rushed back to La Paz from Santa Cruz, she had worked constantly. She had cabled pages of copy to New York: the story of her meeting with Roberto Aguila and his claim that Williams' death on Tuesday was an accident. Then, fighting a deadline, she filed again, describing the tension in La Paz: the ruined embassy; the sight of troops with loaded weapons on every street; the farewell, at the airport, to the slain Americans. That scene had burned itself into her mind.

"Poor guys," Tony had said. Then three embassy cars had rolled up, bringing the wives. Sarah had recognized Angela Williams from the picture she had seen of her on the ambassador's desk: a slender woman with tawny hair, her eyes stunned now. In a moment they were up the ramp; the door swung shut, and the big jet had rolled away.

Sarah had not slept last night: Her mind refused to rest, refused to give up the images colliding in her mind. She tossed until early morning, then napped, then heard the phone.

"You'd better get dressed," Tony had said. "All hell has broken loose." Within an hour, they both had filed dispatches: bare, skeletal accounts of the predawn bombing raids.

"Hi, Colonel!" Tony's voice shattered her reverie.

Redwine walked in, wearing his uniform.

"I have about twenty minutes," Redwine said, greeting them with a nod, "but I'll be glad to tell you what I know. You know the place where they hit the convoy?"

"We drove right over it yesterday morning," Tony said.

"A complete rout," Redwine said. "Obviously they knew that convoy would be moving. They just swept down the road until they saw it, and zap! It's their way of protecting their boy Aguila."

"What do you know about casualties?" Sarah said.

"It's not as bad as they thought at first," Redwine said. "The convoy got shot up pretty badly—lots of killed and wounded. But the two Army camps got off light. I don't have numbers."

Redwine sat facing them, behind a large table that served as his desk. Most of the furniture in the large room, except for the table and several chairs, had been pushed to one side; a bed had been dismantled, its springs and mattress propped against the wall. The colonel seemed oblivious to the disarray.

"The worst part of it isn't even the casualties," he said. "It's what this does to the people down here. All of a sudden their weakness is exposed: a army that can't fight, borders they can't guard, cities and bases they can't protect. The government down here is practically defenseless, and everybody knows it. And Chile must have decided that we're not going to help, that we're a paper tiger."

Sarah scribbled notes and Redwine added, "What I say is not for attribution. Is that okay?" She nodded.

"Has there been a request from Bolivia for help from Washington?" Sarah asked.

"Oh, hell yes," Redwine said. "They've been begging for help for months, and we haven't done a goddamned thing."

"I mean today," said Sarah. "In the wake of this move by Chile. Has there been a formal request for help?"

"Off the record, the answer's yes. As soon as it's received in Washington, the Bolivians will announce it."

"What are they asking for?" Tony said.

"Planes, ammunition, equipment," Redwine said. "And ten thousand combat troops."

"Ten thousand troops." The President spoke the words unemotionally, as if he were simply fixing the figure in his mind.

Brooks Healy, strapped into the seat facing Rattigan in the helicopter, raised his voice against the heavy drone of the rotors. "That's the request," he said. "If you think of it in terms of their need, it's not so many. Maybe not enough. But in terms of our situation, it's altogether a different matter."

Rattigan nodded. "It's the same figure Badillo used the other day," he said. He turned to stare through the window beside him. The President's helicopter skimmed along at twelve hundred feet; beneath them the rushing landscape changed—from Washington's row houses and tenement roofs to the flat, shining river, then to the open land of Maryland: driveways, neat suburban lawns, tract houses. They were nearing Andrews.

The ceremony honoring the dead men would start late: Rattigan had been delayed an hour—reviewing, with Karnow and his aides, the cables from La Paz. Meanwhile, as news of the air strikes swept the city, reporters and cameramen rushed to Andrews, hoping to catch a glimpse of the President in crisis—to press him for some statement, some word, some hint of his reaction.

"When we get back," said Rattigan, "you start the meeting. I'm going to come in a few minutes late."

Healy nodded. The meeting had been called to review Bolivia's formal request for troops and stepped-up military help.

"Tell them what Karnow said this morning," the President said. "This was an attack, not an invasion. We're not going to overreact. I don't want us to lose our heads."

Andrews. The 'copter floated down, landed on a flat expanse of asphalt, and let its rotors die. Outside, two long cars stood waiting to speed them to the chapel: the President and Lisa Rattigan, Healy, Anders Martin, the ever-present Secret Service agents.

Climbing into his car, Rattigan asked an agent, "How many press are at the chapel?"

"About three dozen, sir, but we're only letting a pool inside the chapel. If you want to dodge them, we can take you through a rear door."

"No, that's all right."

An honor guard of white-gloved Air Police lined the curb before the red-brick chapel. When the President's car pulled up, they snapped to attention and saluted. Reporters and cameramen rushed toward the car.

"Mr. President!" called one. "What can you tell us about the air strikes in Bolivia?"

Rattigan stepped from his car, then helped his wife alight. She laid a black-gloved hand upon his arm, and they walked toward the chapel. The knot of cameramen moved with them, backing up the walk, fighting for position.

"Will you have any statement?"

The Rattigans, followed by Healy, Martin, and their agents, moved up the walk.

"Any statement at all?"

"What sort of response are you contemplating?"

The President said nothing. He reached the steps; the knot of photographers parted to let him pass, and he said softly, "We may have a statement late today, this evening."

Inside, five caskets crowded the space before the altar, the five flags over them intensely bright.

Rattigan sat down; the congregation sat. A choir sang; then there was an interval of silence before the chaplain, a colonel with red jowls, stood up to speak.

Rattigan switched his mind inward: The chaplain's voice, a stagy pulpit bass, seemed suddenly far away.

He thought of the Cabinet Room, where already members of the National Security Council and the Joint Chiefs were gathering to hear Karnow's recapitulation of the morning's events.

Rattigan would join them later, to sift the facts and seek their advice. Yet even now he could predict what each man around the table would say. He knew them well.

The White House men—Leonhardt and Karnow—would be most cautious, would counsel patience, would be most eager to save Rattigan from any rash mistakes. Leonhardt, especially. He had written the speeches that spelled out Rattigan's doctrine: no more crusades; no more brash attempts to be the world's *gendarme*.

Leonhardt would sit, puffing nervously on his pipe, and point out all the dangers of any course of action. And then—whatever the final decision—he would, because he was the President's man, draft the speech proclaiming the policy.

Roundcastle: Backed by his colleagues, the Joint Chiefs, the old general would tend to call for Armageddon, say again that power "is the only language these outlaws understand." He would suggest retaliation: swift, decisive, merciless; an eye for an eye. The general was one year away from retirement. "Old Bill," Healy once said, "wants one more war before he goes."

Between the caution of the White House men and the militancy of the generals, the President could look to Woodson and Healy, the Cabinet men. He could count on Woodson, the Secretary of Defense, to give sensible advice: He was a former governor, a shrewd politician.

And Healy. Of all the men in the Administration, the closest in view and temperament to Rattigan himself. He had not only a lawyer's talent for advocacy and compromise, he also had wisdom.

At the thought of his friend, the President looked toward the altar. The chaplain's portion of the service ended, and Healy rose to speak. As he spoke, Rattigan thought, *He's the best man I have.* He had wanted, more than three years ago, to name Healy his running mate, but he could not. Healy was a lawyer, a private man; he had never held office, never campaigned. The two men were too close, too similar. And yet he felt for Healy what he had never felt for Hoffman: affection, trust, respect.

"The day before yesterday," Healy said quietly, looking into the first few rows of the chapel, "a cruel fate overtook these men, and not only they, but we, too, became victims of the violence that took their lives. Now we gather to pay them our respects, and to seek some comfort for ourselves."

Healy spoke simply, sincerely, but with no great show of emotion;

he was offering, to Angela Williams and the wives of the other dead men, strength—not pity. "They chose to serve in a place and at a time of great danger. And though we may live in a cynical age, most of us still believe that those who face great danger deserve great honor."

Rattigan wondered if Healy's words could have any meaning for these women who sat listening, dry-eyed, probably still in shock.

He noticed that Healy was looking toward him, probably nearing the end of what he had to say. The President shifted in his seat, ready to move forward for the presentation of the medals.

"Finally," Healy said, "I hope you will find some comfort in my assurance that this nation, facing some grave and puzzling events in Bolivia, will be steadfast. We intend to honor these men not only with our words, but in the choices and decisions we make—today, and in the future."

The Secretary of State stepped to the side of the pulpit, preparing to read the citations. Rattigan, followed by Lisa, rose and moved forward to the altar.

"Bertrand Deland Williams." Healy read the first citation. "Attorney, public servant, ambassador of the United States to Bolivia—"

Five small leather cases rested on the pulpit: the medals. The President turned and lifted the one that bore Bert Williams' name. When he looked up, he was facing Angela Williams. He handed her the medal, clasped her hand, and was wondering what to say when she whispered, "Mr. President, Bert thought so much of you." She faltered, as if she would cry. Instantly, Lisa Rattigan reached out, embraced her, whispered a few words, and it was over.

"Joseph Henry Rippard." Rattigan remembered the name vaguely, from the list of the dead: the bodyguard; the CIA man.

He reached for the medal, faced the man's widow, shook hands, murmured woodenly some platitude of sympathy, and repeated the sequence for the others. But all the while, until the ceremony ended and the choir sang again, too loudly, some words of Karnow's burned in his mind: "The only question now," Karnow had told him this morning, "is whether we stop Chile by persuasion, or by force."

Gary Triplitano joined them for the flight back to the White House. When they were airborne, the President leaned toward the window by his seat and, as the helicopter banked, stared silently down at the scene below: houses and streets; a freeway only sparsely lined with cars.

Despite the cold, a few sailboats were on the Potomac, tiny white triangles on the wind-raked water.

Watching him, Brooks Healy wondered what the President saw; whether he felt, as he stared down on the quiet suburbs, any connection between himself and the people in those houses, so far removed from him. What does he feel? Healy wondered.

Lisa Rattigan removed her black kid gloves and picked up a newspaper. No one spoke. What they had seen—the caskets—and what lay ahead today subdued them.

Finally Rattigan spoke, leaning toward Anders Martin:

"They'll all be there when I get back?"

"Yes, sir," Martin said. "Most of them were coming in when we left. Karnow was going to start the meeting and brief them while they waited for you."

"This meeting will last until three-thirty," Rattigan said to Triplitano. "I'll need Karnow until then. But after that I want him to background the press. I want him to sketch the situation, the facts, as we know them. They can credit 'high government officials,' but I want them to know what we're up against."

"They'll never let him go," Triplitano said, "without asking about this meeting. They're already raising hell to know what your response is going to be."

Rattigan shrugged. "We can't tell them that," he said, "until we know ourselves." Again, for a moment, he gazed through the window.

"I want you to clear some network time tonight," Rattigan said. "You can announce that I'm going to speak on the whole situation in Bolivia and Chile. Including our response."

"How much time, sir?"

"I don't know. Tell the networks to be prepared for thirty minutes."

Triplitano rummaged in his pockets for a pen. Finding one, he jotted notes on an envelope he carried.

"How about the OAS?" Rattigan asked.

"We've already asked for a meeting," Healy said, "but I don't know. It'll probably be tomorrow before we can get them together."

"What time do you want to go on?" Triplitano asked.

"Late," said Rattigan. "Nine-thirty or ten. We're going to have a long day." Triplitano looked relieved: Clearing network time, drafting a speech, moving furniture out of and the networks' equipment into the Oval Office—all this would be a labor of many hours. But by nine-thirty or ten, it could be done.

The helicopter swept past the Washington Monument and swung down toward the South Lawn, over the fence, above the trees. The great wind from the rotors fanned out across the lawn and flattened momentarily the plume of water from the South Lawn's fountain. The 'copter settled down, just before the South Portico.

"If you think it's worth it," Rattigan said to Healy as he loosened his seat belt, "we can call in some ambassadors—the OAS countries. You could brief them in the Mansion while I'm working with the leadership."

"I think it's worth it," Healy said.

They disembarked. Triplitano and Martin rushed toward the West Wing, while the President and Healy saw Lisa to the Diplomatic Entrance.

"I hope you'll have some time for dinner," she said. "I'm going to call Anna to come down here."

Neither man answered. Lisa Rattigan squeezed her husband's hand and disappeared into the Mansion.

"I get the impression," Healy said as they strode across the Rose Garden toward the Cabinet Room, "that you've got the situation in control."

"No," said Rattigan. "What makes you say that?" They paused outside the french doors that led from the colonnade into the Cabinet Room.

"All the orders on the helicopter," Healy said. "It almost sounded as if you already know what you're going to do."

"No," said Rattigan. "I just know I have to do something."

Healy opened the door, and the men inside, seeing the President, rose from their seats around the table.

In his silent office John Cardwell scanned the noon edition of the Washington *Star*. MAJOR LATIN CRISIS ERUPTS, the banner headline read—and then, in smaller type below: PRESIDENT, ADVISERS HUDDLE, PONDER U.S. REACTION.

Then, hungry for more news, he left his office and took the stairs, two at a time, up to the press office. There, at least, would be activity: He could read the wire reports, perhaps catch some new scrap of news or rumor.

In the outer office, Trip's secretary leaned over a table near her desk, out-of-town newspapers in a neat overlapping pile.

"Mr. Cardwell, hi."

"Hi. Have you got the wire clips?"

"They're on his desk." She pointed into Trip's empty office then returned to her chore, and Cardwell walked to Trip's desk. Three clipboards, each laden with neatly cut wire-service copy, lay there side by side: the Associated Press, United Press International, Reuters. He leaned over them, flipping the pages over impatiently.

The whole thing, Cardwell thought, had an air of fantasy. Yet the planes, however much Chile might deny their existence, were real. And the meeting in progress in the Cabinet Room was real—acutely real. Cardwell turned the pages on the middle clipboard. As he read, he sank into Triplitano's chair.

"Are you trying to take my job?"

He looked up. Triplitano entered through his side door, and closed the door into the outer office. Cardwell rose from his chair.

"Is the meeting over?" Cardwell asked.

"No, I just ducked out. He's going on the networks tonight, so I've got to set that up."

"What's he going to say?"

"He's going to say, 'Hands off, Chile, you greedy bastards, or else!' " Triplitano said.

"Or else what?" said Cardwell.

"That's what they're discussing now," the press secretary said. He moved to the chair behind his desk, shoved the clipboards aside, and sat down. "The big guns in there are advising him to send some troops down there."

"To Chile?"

"Oh, my God, no. Bolivia. You know, put some troops in La Paz and hope Chile will back off from a confrontation. The only questions are how many troops, and what will they do when they get there, and there's a hell of an argument about that. But it looks as if we can't get the Latin countries to help Bolivia unless we lead."

"Who's doing the speech?" Cardwell asked.

"Leonhardt. He's in the meeting."

Cardwell, seeing that Triplitano was rushed, moved toward the door. He hesitated, then said what was on his mind: "I'd like to help with the speech."

Triplitano looked up, then shook his head.

"I don't see how you can," he said. "Leonhardt's in the meeting, so he's the one who knows what to write. It's going to be a short speech anyway."

Cardwell turned to leave.

"Wait a minute," Triplitano said. "Come back here." He pointed to the chair across from his desk, but Cardwell did not sit down.

"You know a lot of people are going to raise hell about this thing."

Cardwell nodded.

"Some of them will say the President's impulsive to send troops in," Trip said. "And the others will say he didn't send enough in view of the provocation."

"Right," Cardwell said.

"Well," said Triplitano, "I want to beat them to the draw—in tomorrow's papers, at least. Draft about a dozen statements of support: 'The President's action tonight was timely, courageous, and necessary. He has my wholehearted support.' You know." Triplitano pulled a small brown notebook from his pocket; he flipped it open to a page of reminders he had written to himself. "We can plant them with some key senators and Cabinet people," he said, "so everything that moves on the wires after the speech will be in support. Could you manage?"

"I guess so."

"Good man." Triplitano reached hurriedly for his telephone and buzzed for his secretary. He was eager to complete his urgent errands and return to the President's meeting.

"Hey, Trip," said Cardwell, leaving, "if I'm going to write statements of support, I need to know what it is that we're supporting."

"Okay," said Triplitano. "Leonhardt will probably dictate this speech and send it to the President page by page. He can send you the carbons. I'll tell him." With his free hand he waved to Cardwell; then, in a gesture of impatience, he stabbed the buzzer once again.

Back in his office, Cardwell tossed his coat onto the sofa and reached into the closet for his worn gray sweater. It was after two o'clock.

He called the White House operator.

"Yes, Mr. Cardwell?"

"I'd like you to reach my secretary," he said. "Miss Orme. Tell her I need her here as soon as she can come. And meanwhile, I'll need a typist from the correspondence section. If they can't send anybody, can you call me?"

He started to call Nancy, to tell her that he would be home too late for dinner, but then he checked himself. He could call her later. Meanwhile he must get started: there was work to be done.

The meeting in the Cabinet Room wore on.

"It seems to me," said the Secretary of State, "that we face three alternatives, none of them entirely pleasant.

"The first, and perhaps the least drastic," he said, "is to withhold any action and simply deliver a strong, clear, public warning to Chile."

"The second alternative," Healy said, "is advanced by the Chiefs." Everyone listened for a hint from Healy that he was unsympathetic to the military men, but he went on, speaking politely and impartially. "It is, without doubt, the more drastic choice, but it has the advantages of being decisive and of clearly seizing the initiative from the other side."

Now Roundcastle was nodding vehemently.

"In its simplest form, this plan involves sending in the full number of troops requested by Bolivia—"

"Or more," Roundcastle said. Roundcastle had even suggested a series of air strikes against Chilean bases.

"—with a mission to help the Bolivians in combat against the insurgents," Healy went on. "Now, the disadvantages of this scenario have been rather exhaustively aired." And Healy began, in his mild, conciliatory tone, to discuss them.

Rattigan was suddenly impatient. He knew, better than most of the men around the table, the defects of the military choice: the outrage it would cause among his own supporters; the wave of shock around the world. He was not about to choose a course of outright military intervention that would put U.S. troops into combat. He would not overreact—and Roundcastle's grisly solution, two eyes for an eye, went beyond overreaction. The President was ready to hear Healy's formulation of his last alternative.

"You left something out," Leonhardt said to Healy. "The moral objections to our committing combat troops—the whole question of our intervening in a civil war."

The President interrupted. "I don't want to get into a discussion about civil war," he said. "We're concerned with protecting Bolivia from Chile; we're not discussing the internal conflict."

Roundcastle, in his eagerness to speak, almost interrupted the President. "I don't want anyone to think that I don't care about moral considerations in this affair," he said, "but let me tell you when you start hearing the most about morality." He shifted in his seat and glared at Leonhardt: "I've been in some wars in my time," he said, "and it's been my observation that the moralists start squawking when Uncle Sam makes a fool of himself—not before. If we do something right"—his voice was rising—"if we *win* once in a while, nobody questions our morality. But if we do something halfway and it fails and we end up making fools of ourselves, that's when some damned fool on Capitol Hill questions whether what we did was moral or not."

Leonhardt tried to reply, but Roundcastle held up a hand to silence him.

"Do you think that anybody would have questioned the Bay of Pigs if it had been a success?" he asked. "Do you think anybody would have questioned our morality in Vietnam if we'd had a quick victory in ninety days out there instead of a disaster that went on for years? What I'm advising is that we do this thing all the way, for once, so we won't *have* to listen to a lot of rhetoric about morality!"

"Thank you, gentlemen," Brooks Healy said with finality. "We're extremely short of time." He turned to the President beside him.

"Finally, Mr. President," he said, "there is a choice that combines elements of the first two: first, dispatch of a relatively small number of troops to Bolivia as a symbolic expression of our willingness to help defend that country and to give the government in La Paz a psychological boost. They would not take any hostile action—"

Roundcastle, who thought this plan too weak, shook his head from side to side, and looked to his colleagues, three more generals and an admiral, who returned his gaze with sympathetic eyes.

"—but would give logistical support to the Bolivians; they would take up defensive positions in Bolivia, mostly around La Paz. Meanwhile, you would make clear to the other side that any further hostile action on their part would be met swiftly and decisively. The hope is that this show of force would be enough to convince Chile." Healy cleared his throat. "Now, the strong points of this approach—"

"Thank you, Brooks," the President said. He sat up straighter in his chair. "I don't think you need to go any farther."

The men in the room riveted their eyes upon the President. The meeting, they knew, was drawing to an end. A few, without looking down, began straightening the jumbled piles of paper and memoranda before them on the table.

"Actually," said Rattigan, "I wish I didn't have to make any decision. I think you know my personal reluctance to embroil this country in affairs like this abroad."

A few men nodded.

"God knows," the President said wearily, "we've been lucky up to now. But you've convinced me"—he nodded in the direction of Harkness and the easels near the table's end—"that we have no choice in this one; that to stay out will almost surely invite a full-scale invasion by Chile."

It was after three o'clock. Triplitano, who had taken a seat near the door, consulted his watch, caught Karnow's attention, and tapped the timepiece with his finger. There was to be a press briefing at three-thirty; the reporters would question Karnow.

"My greatest concern," the President said, "is that we give Chile a self-respecting way out of this thing. For that reason, I want to limit the pressure we bring to bear."

Leonhardt and Karnow glanced at one another with apparent satisfaction.

"I want to go with the third response."

They stared at him in silence, and Rattigan turned toward Woodson, the Defense Secretary.

"I want the troops to be moving when I speak tonight," he said to Woodson. "If you think it will take longer than six or seven hours to get them into the air, I can delay the speech."

"We can have them airborne in an hour," Woodson said.

Someone whistled. It was over four thousand miles to La Paz.

At the President's nod, the men began moving away from the table, toward the doors.

Only General Roundcastle lingered, and he eyed the President.

"Just one thing to remember, Mr. President. If you send troops, you've got to be willing to use them in combat. And if you're going to use them, you've got to send enough. And if you don't send enough—you'll have to send more."

Rattigan looked at him, saying nothing. Then he turned to Leonhardt.

"Fred," he said, "I'd like the speech as soon as possible. You can send it to me page by page. I'll be in the Mansion."

"I think I should point out," Leonhardt said, "that you're going to have tremendous difficulty politically with this choice."

The President colored.

"Well," Rattigan said, "I can't think about that now, and I don't want you to. Now please get out of here and write that speech."

When, by five o'clock, her husband had not called, Nancy Cardwell dialed his office. His secretary answered.

"I'm sorry," Dot said. "The President's speaking tonight, and Mr. Cardwell's doing statements for congressmen to make afterward."

Nancy rose from her place beside the phone, smoothed down the front of her wool dress, and walked from the study to the kitchen. Ignoring the kitchen's litter of dishes and utensils, she passed through to the dining room and stared for a moment at the table. A drink. She moved to the sideboard and poured three fingers of scotch into a glass.

"Oh, God, I'm trying. I really am," she said aloud.

Suddenly she felt drained—beyond anger or frustration.

The little things. Years ago her mother, laughing, had warned her: "It's the little things. If your husband drinks too much or beats you or goes with other women, why, you can stand that. You can complain and be a martyr, and your friends will sympathize. But suppose he whistles all the time, or splashes water all over the bathroom floor, or wears funny-looking undershorts. It's little things like that that drive you crazy."

"Oh, Mother," she had said. "Be serious."

But her mother had been right. Recalling eight years of marriage to John Cardwell, Nancy could remember no violent disagreement, no major quarrel, no bitter and traumatic conflicts. Theirs had been an apparently placid marriage, what their friends would call a solid marriage. Then "little things" began to ruin it: his absences, more and more frequent; his love for politics, her lack of it. And now the little things had become big things. They slept together; there was not much more. They had little to talk about when they were together.

Mother, you were so right, she thought. And suddenly she decided to call home, if only to hear a friendly voice. She walked into the study, sat down, and dialed.

Her mother answered, surprised and flattered. "How are you?"

"Fine," she lied.

"Well, we miss you, but we know you're having fun," her mother said. Then, mercifully, she rattled on, reviewing all the details of their elaborate Thanksgiving Day feast. "Of course, your father spent the whole day watching football on televison." Nancy half listened to inconsequential bits of family news, grateful for her mother's trivial chatter, for some companionship.

"How's John?" her mother finally asked.

"All right, I guess."

"You guess?"

"Mother, I hardly see him anymore. He's always at the office. There's always a crisis."

"Oh, baby," her mother said. "I hate to think of you there, all alone."

"Oh, I have lots to keep me busy," Nancy lied. "One thing about Washington, there's always so much going on."

"Why don't you come on down and visit us awhile? Sometimes a change is just the thing to perk you up, if—"

"Look," said Nancy quickly, "I just wanted to say hello. I've got to go." She didn't want to get into a long discussion of her troubles.

"Nancy? Are you all right?"

"I'm all right, Mother. 'Bye."

Five-twenty. She could use another drink. She was refilling her glass with scotch when the telephone rang.

"Nancy? I tried to call you. The line's been busy."

"I called home," she told her husband.

"Look," said Cardwell, "I'm sorry. I don't want to have a scene. I know you're upset, and I don't blame you. But I'm just not going to be able to get home until late tonight."

"I'm not upset," she said, trying to sound indifferent. "Why should I be upset?"

"I'm sorry about dinner."

"Oh, don't worry," she said. "I can eat alone. I'm fully used to that by now."

She heard him sigh. "I'll come home as soon as I can," he said, and hung up.

For a moment she held the dead receiver in her hand. Then she hung up, turned, and—feeling suddenly tired of the silence in the house—walked across the study and turned on the television set. Noise filled the room: an old movie.

Nancy Cardwell had no real interest in it, but she decided to watch until it ended, and then to watch whatever followed. She fetched her drink from beside the telephone and sank into a cushioned chair nearby.

When a commercial came on—one in which a couple, smiling vacuously, danced and sang the praises of a household cleanser—Nancy felt suddenly, inexplicably angry. She had a wild impulse to throw her glass across the room, scotch, ice, and all—to hit the singing couple. But when she brought her arm forward, some inhibition checked her: She kept the glass, but sent its contents flying.

A few bits of ice bounced wildly off the screen onto the carpet. The commercial gave way to the movie again; drops of scotch slid down the screen.

Nancy Cardwell, leaning forward, stared at the dark blots on the rug. Then she began to cry.

Carl Rattigan spun his leather chair around to face the tall windows behind his desk. Dusk was gathering outside. He could see only bare trees, their limbs rising and falling with the occasional wind.

He buzzed Sheila Roundtree.

"Get Fred Leonhardt down here."

Rattigan spun his chair again and lifted from his desktop the typewritten pages he had been reading: tonight's speech—or the first half of it—drafted by Leonhardt.

"Mr. President, good evening." Leonhardt strolled in, an expectant smile on his face.

Carl Rattigan stared at him a moment. Then he tossed the five white pages across the desk toward Leonhardt.

"I can't use this," he said.

Leonhardt made no move to retrieve the fallen pages, which lay scattered before the President's desk.

"Why not?"

"I can't go on television before the whole world and apologize and whine and snivel. I'm not going to do it."

Fred Leonhardt hesitated, clenching his teeth so suddenly upon his unlit pipe that it tilted sharply upward.

"I don't think it's sniveling," he finally said. "You're breaking into people's homes with a sudden announcement that you're sending troops off to Bolivia. You're announcing the possibility that we could go to war. You can't exactly sound pleased about that."

"Fred," said Rattigan softly, "do you think I *want* to do all this? Do you think—"

"I know you don't, Mr. President," Leonhardt said, "and I think it's to your advantage to let people know that you're reluctant to—"

"To my advantage! To my advantage!" Rattigan flung up his hands in exasperation and walked around to the space before his desk. "I'm not concerned about my advantage! I'm concerned about convincing a bunch of generals in Chile that we'll fight them if they persist. And I can't do *that* with *this*. Now take this back"—he bent as if to pick up the scattered pages, but Leonhardt retrieved them first—"and do it over. And you can cut out all those phrases like 'tragic necessity' and 'heavy heart' and 'painful decision,' because I'm not going to say them."

"Excuse me, gentlemen." Gary Triplitano stepped into the Oval Office and said to the President, "We're going to move you out soon, sir. We've got to set this place up."

"All right," said Rattigan mildly, "I'm going to the Mansion."

"Mr. President," said Fred Leonhardt, "the reason I've used conciliatory phrases is that I think you have made a decision that *is* painful and that *could* prove to be tragic. That's what I was trying to say this afternoon when we—"

"Listen, Fred." Rattigan dropped his voice and emphasized each word in anger. "If you think that, you can go out somewhere and make a speech of your own. But don't write it for me."

Leonhardt, wounded, blinked behind his owlish glasses.

Rattigan sighed, regretting his harsh tone. "Fred, how can I convince people I'm taking the right step if I don't sound convinced myself?"

"That's a good question, Mr. President," said Leonhardt stiffly.

"Well," said Rattigan, "I want you to go upstairs and write me a different speech, and there's not much time, so go to it." His voice was firm now, but not angry. Leonhardt nodded and walked toward the door, carrying the speech draft with him.

When he had gone, Rattigan turned to Triplitano.

"Have you read this thing?"

"I saw the carbons," Triplitano said.

"He thinks I'm doing the wrong thing," Rattigan said. "Hell, he may be right, but I'm not going to agonize about it in front of sixty million people."

"I think you should let somebody else write a new draft," Triplitano said.

Rattigan shook his head. "It's too late for that."

"I've got a man," Triplitano said.

On the President's desk there was a Speakerphone—a small attachment near his telephone that made it possible to carry on a conversation from any spot in the room. Triplitano stepped to the desk, switched it on, and dialed John Cardwell's number.

"John?" he said to Cardwell, "have you looked at Leonhardt's draft?"

"I've got the carbons," Cardwell said.

"What do you think?"

"About sending troops?"

"No, about the speech."

"I think it's weak. It sounds as if he's confessing his sins instead of announcing his plans." He didn't know the President was listening.

"You think you could do a better job?"

"I could, Trip," Cardwell said, "if I had a chance."

"You've got your chance," the President said. He half smiled at the thought of surprising Cardwell with his voice. "If you think you can rewrite it in a hour or two, get up here. We've leaving my office for the Mansion."

There was a moment's hesitation before John Cardwell spoke.

"Yes, sir!" he said, sounding stunned. They heard him click off the line.

"He's a good man," Triplitano said. "He doesn't exactly have steel tips in his shoes, but he's a good man."

"Let's go," said Rattigan. "It's getting late."

Two hours later, John Cardwell neared the end of the speech he was reworking. The pages of Leonhardt's draft were spread before him, and in the outer office, two typists from the correspondence section worked furiously: They were taking Cardwell's dictation in relays, each recording a page at a time, then rushing out to type.

The new speech would be short, spare, straightforward: a stark announcement of today's decision. There was no time for eloquence, no opportunity for elaboration.

"'. . . that is all I have to report,'" Cardwell dictated. "'In the days and weeks to come, we will know more. . . .'"

It was seven-thirty: two hours before air time. Two hours for the President to read, approve, rehearse the speech; for the press office to photocopy and pass it out; for Trip and Sheldon Karnow to brief reporters about its meaning; for Healy to explain it to the diplomats.

At the same moment, far away, the Government of Bolivia and the United States embassy in that country clamped a strict and total embargo on all news from La Paz.

From her hotel in the center of the city, Sarah Tolman called Redwine.

"What's going on?" she asked.

"Nothing," the colonel said. But she could tell from his tone that much was happening.

"Can't you say anything?" she said, "even off the record?"

"You know that Rattigan is speaking tonight."

"Yes," she said. "I'd heard, but I wasn't sure it was about this."

"If you want to hear it," Redwine said, "call an embassy car in an hour and meet me at the airport. We'll have a short-wave radio."

"Why the airport?"

"That's where the planes come in," he said.

"Look, Colonel," Sarah said, "you might as well tell me what's happening. They won't let us file copy anyway, so nothing you tell me will go through. What planes?"

"That's off the record," Redwine said. "I'll see you at the airport." He hung up.

For a moment she held the dead receiver and watched as, outside her window, night fell in the city. Inch by inch the light receded, and the steep, narrow streets filled with darkness. It was as if the city, ringed with mountains, were a vessel being drained and refilled.

She watched for a moment, transfixed, then caught herself and dialed Tony Jack's number.

When the President walked into the cold Oval Office, the television lights were already blazing. A few reporters, called in to witness the speech, stood near one door.

He nodded, took the folder with his reading copy from Anders Martin, and sat down at his desk.

"Are you ready?" the President asked, blinking into the hot white lights.

"One minute, Mr. President," someone answered.

He took the speech out of the folder, laid it on the desk, then dropped the folder to the floor. The room was silent.

"Thirty seconds."

Carlton Rattigan raised his chin and cleared his throat quickly, testing the sound of his voice.

"Fifteen."

From the corner of his eye he saw a man's hand slice through the air, then point toward him. He stared toward the red light of a camera before him and began to speak.

"Good evening, my fellow Americans," he said. His voice was steady, almost casual.

"This morning I received word that targets in Bolivia had been attacked by jet aircraft. Though Chile has denied it, we know that those aircraft were flying from bases in Chile and flown by Chilean pilots.

"This news comes upon the heels of confirmation that irregular troops from Chile, in considerable strength, are now in action in Bolivia, in support of Bolivian guerrilla efforts to overthrow the government there."

The red light on one camera winked off, and another one came on. His voice grew slower, more emphatic.

"The Government of Bolivia," he said, "has asked for immediate aid from the Organization of American States and from the signatories to the Rio Treaty. Beyond that, it has asked directly for military aid—*specifically for troops*—from the United States.

"During this afternoon, our government consulted with the governments of the Organization of American States. We have reason to believe that several of these governments will soon join in helping Bolivia defend herself.

"With that assurance, with the knowledge that the OAS itself will be meeting tomorrow to co-ordinate hemispheric policy, and in response to Bolivia's direct request, I have decided to act immediately.

"Earlier today, elements of the 101st Airborne Division left Fort Campbell, Kentucky, bound for staging areas near La Paz. They are flying on C-5A transports and should be arriving shortly in Bolivia."

"Oh, my God," said Sarah Tolman.

She sat in a small room of the airport terminal near La Paz. Tony, Nathan Redwine, and four other men—three in uniform—stood in a circle around the radio, hearing, amid the static, the President's announcement.

"These troops will have a strictly limited mission: first, to help guard the capital of Bolivia and the legitimate government there against any hostile actions; second, to provide transportation and other logistical support to the armed forces of Bolivia. In short, their mission is a defensive one; they will participate in no offensive operations."

Sarah stood up, clasped her hands together, and walked impatiently toward the window. Outside, in the floodlights that cut a clearing in the darkness around the airport, she could see a line of people watching the first transport planes as they roared in: giant pot-bellied aircraft, bearing the insignia of the United States. Out in the darkness, she knew, Bolivian troops had taken up positions to secure the airfield.

As they landed, the planes taxied to a long, paved strip beside the runway. One by one, they formed a line that stretched off into the darkness toward the mountains.

"There are two reasons," the President was saying, "that I have acted as I have.

"First, I wanted all the governments of South America, and particularly the Chilean Government, to know, without any doubt, that the United States will meet its commitments. The government of Chile can still call off their action against a sovereign nation. If there has been any doubt on its part that the United States would fail to respond to this hostile act against a peaceful Bolivia, that doubt should be dispelled."

Standing there, looking out over the lighted airfield, Sarah felt suddenly sick.

"What's the matter?" Redwine said.

"They've got him," she replied.

"Got him? Who?"

"Your friends," she said bitterly. "You. You've got him."

The President took a deep breath and continued. The room was growing warmer.

"I acted for a second reason as well," he said.

"A world community that permits chaos also encourages it, and in so doing invites its own ultimate destruction. And a world that ignores the struggle of free nations to survive may soon become a world with ever fewer free nations.

"That, then, is why I am sending American troops to Bolivia this evening.

"It may be true that if the legitimate Government of Bolivia falls, nothing much will change tomorrow in Illinois or California. But it is also true that if our world is in flames, with no volunteer fire department, we soon will feel the heat all over America. The idea of a free and peaceful America as an island in a world without freedom or peace is both naïve and dangerous."

Downstairs, John Cardwell frowned. He wondered if the speech had been too short; the President was coming to the end.

He wondered where Leonhardt was—what he was thinking.

"A great nation such as the United States," said the President, "is deeply involved in the destiny of many nations around the world. *We are involved, whether we like it or not.* We were especially involved with free, democratic Bolivia even before today as a member in very good standing in our hemispheric family. We are even more involved in Bolivia's destiny because of our actions today. But we would be still more deeply involved—perhaps tragically so—in Bolivia's destiny if we failed to act."

Rattigan came to the end of his brief speech.

"Our only real choice at this time," he said, "was one of *how* to be involved: as one nation in a group of nations serving as a volunteer fire department, or as a nation that turns away and says that the alarm bell is ringing for someone else, that it's none of our business, that the fire probably won't spread anyway.

"My job as President, as has been the job of my predecessors, is to take the actions that will quench the fire before it spreads."

The few reporters in the Oval Office noticed a fine dew of perspiration on Rattigan's forehead. The lights burned the air, heated the room until it was oppressive.

But the President resisted the temptation to mop his forehead now.

"My fellow citizens," he said, "that is all I have to say tonight. In the days and weeks to come, we will know more about the developing situation in South America, and I will report to you more fully. Thank you, and good night."

The red light winked off, and Rattigan reached for his handkerchief.

"All right, Mr. President, you're finished," a cameraman called out.

"I hope you mean the speech," Rattigan said, not smiling. Among the people in the Oval Office, no one laughed.

Triplitano, who was near the door, spoke to his press pool: "That last," he said, "is strictly off the record."

For a time after the speech, Cardwell stayed in his office.

He watched the commentators for half an hour, heard them speculate. They were cautious, somewhat puzzled. The President had chosen a perilous course, one said, and then added that time may prove it a necessary one.

Platitudes.

He grew bored, turned off the set, and decided to go upstairs. There would be chaos: reporters filing, the network people rushing back and forth as they dismantled their equipment. The President would be back in the Mansion.

Cardwell climbed the stairs and walked past office doors toward the press center.

Halfway there he saw Fred Leonhardt coming down the hall. The older man walked quickly toward him, his pipe clenched between his teeth.

"Hi, Fred," said Cardwell as they neared each other. Cardwell did not mention the speech.

"Well, well," said Leonhardt, slowing his pace. "The young speech doctor."

Cardwell felt his face grow warm. He did not want a fight with Leonhardt. He said nothing.

"Tell me something," Leonhardt said. "If this is a fire department and he's the chief, just what does that make you? The firehouse dog?"

Cardwell tried to smile. "It was what he wanted, Fred," he said. "And he's the President."

It was after midnight when Cardwell got home.

"Nancy?"

No lights were on, but he could hear the television's blare.

"Nancy?"

Cardwell headed for the study, the source of the sound, wondering if she had watched the President's speech.

"Nan?"

He snapped on the hall light and peered into the study. An old movie was playing. Then he saw her sprawled asleep upon the sofa.

"Hey, wake up, I'm home."

She didn't stir. Cardwell moved across the room, flicked on a lamp, and killed the television image.

"Hey," he said, "come on, wake up. Please." He leaned above her, and when she did not move, he dropped down, took her shoulder, and shook her gently.

"Nancy?"

He pulled her to her feet and she stood uncertainly, as if she would sink down once again onto the sofa.

"Let's go to bed," he said. And, holding her shoulders, he propelled her gently down the hall toward their bedroom. She walked uncertainly, and he noticed as they moved into the shadows that she wore a puzzled expression, the expression that a child wears when awakened in a strange place.

Cardwell felt a curious relief; he had prepared himself for a bitter confrontation with his wife.

In their room, he let her sink onto the bed on his side. He turned on a lamp and tried to remove her pink wool dress, but she was asleep, a dead weight. A tendril of her hair had fallen across her face. Now, as she breathed, it rose and fell loosely. Cardwell stripped and headed for the bathroom.

What had gone wrong?

In the shower he let his mind reach backward, trying to remember the early days of their marriage, when they were reminded by everyone they knew that they were perfect for each other.

And weren't they? Their families were old friends; their fathers had played golf together for years. And though John and Nancy had known each other only slightly when they were younger—she had been away at school—they had been friends.

After Brown he had taken a year at the Columbia Journalism School; then he had come home and plunged into his work at the paper. He had worked hard, first as a reporter, then as a deskman in the crowded newsroom. Then—when he had gained their respect, proved to the staff that he was more than just the boss's son—he had moved upstairs to help his father.

He had been back for two years when Nancy Locke came home, fresh out of Sweet Briar. Friends brought them together; it was inevitable. They became a couple, invited together to dinner parties. Their parents, wise enough to do no more than hint, had encouraged them to marry. A lovely girl, his mother said. You don't want to be an old bachelor, now, do you?

One fall night in his disheveled apartment Nancy had cooked their dinner. They drank champagne, built a fire, slipped from their place upon the sofa onto the floor, and made love. Nancy was a virgin: frightened, tensing her body against his, resisting slightly. When it was over he filled her glass, then turned back to find her crying. Her face gleamed in the firelight.

It all seemed a long time ago, longer than eight years.

Cardwell reached, dripping, for his towel, rubbed himself slowly with it, then stepped out of the tub onto the cool tile floor. He stood before the lavatory naked, waiting for the fogged-up mirror to clear. Slowly he saw himself materialize, as the steam faded, and he touched himself, frowning: The mirror told him his hard swimmer's body was going soft.

What had gone wrong? He had thrived in these three years; he loved the heady aura of the White House. Now he was rolling, moving to the center; he had learned he could live away from Louisville, away from his family's name and power, and never miss them. But Nancy: She was like a plant uprooted, then set down in a strange and hostile climate.

He walked, wrapped in a towel, back to their bedroom and climbed into bed. But it was a long time before he got to sleep.

DECEMBER

Cracks in the Façade

Friday the First

On the way to the White House the next morning, John Cardwell drove almost unconsciously, his mind fixed upon the car radio. He turned to an all-news station and listened avidly, even after he had heard every scrap of news about the crisis, and the announcer had begun to repeat the items:

Congressional reaction to the President's dramatic disclosures of last night was mixed. Ryland Boyd, Speaker of the House, praised the President's dispatch of troops as . . .

Cardwell heard his own words quoted: The Speaker had been handed one of the statements he had drafted.

Meanwhile, three thousand U.S. troops took up positions near La Paz last night, ready to defend that Latin American capital against possible new moves by Chile.

There had been no fighting: good. Maybe the whole thing would blow over without violence and the troops could come home.

Pulled along in the stream of rush-hour traffic, Cardwell rode down into the city, along Wisconsin Avenue toward Georgetown. He passed the looming gray shadow of the Cathedral, then cut left onto Massachusetts Avenue, past brick houses with wide lawns, past mansions, embassies.

He crossed a bridge, turned sharply right, and crawled down with the line of cars onto the Rock Creek Parkway. The park was drained of color: gray trees, dead grass along the parkway.

A small band of pickets, protesting the President's decision, appeared this morning at the White House. A spokesman for the group, who declined to be identified, told newsmen that the President's decision to send troops to Bolivia was "ill-advised, and could be tragic . . ."

Cardwell turned left onto Virginia Avenue, heading for a stretch of freeway: a shortcut to the White House.

In other news, a local man was killed last night when the car he was driving spun out of control and . . .

In three more minutes Cardwell pulled up to the Southwest Gate, waved to the guard, and nosed his ancient Duster into its parking slot.

The grandfather clock in the Oval Office was chiming ten o'clock when Anders Martin ushered in a sullen Abner Hoffman.

Rattigan rose from his chair and shook the Vice President's hand, greeting him in a hearty tone.

"I'm glad to see you, Ab," he said. "I meant to call you yesterday, but things were moving so fast."

Hoffman said nothing. He took a seat when the President pointed to the sofa, and Rattigan, pressing a button on his telephone, summoned a mess boy from the little galley adjoining the Oval Office.

"I hope Karnow brought you up to date," Rattigan said. "Coffee?" He nodded to the Navy steward, who retreated to the galley.

"He brought me up to date," Hoffman said mildly. "I know more about Bolivia than I want to know."

Rattigan gave him a sharp, quizzical glance. "Well," he said, "I suppose it could be worse. From what we've heard today everything is quiet down there. I'm hoping this thing will blow over soon and we can bring those men home."

The steward brought a silver tray, set it on the round table between the two men, and poured two cups of coffee. The President handed Hoffman's up to him, then took up his own.

"I'm glad you're here, Abner. I've really wanted to get your thoughts on this whole business. What do you think, after all you've heard?"

"I think," said Hoffman, "that you and I should be perfectly frank with each other, Mr. President." He set down his coffee cup, from which he had not drunk. "You obviously didn't want my judgment enough to call me before you decided to send those troops.

"I think you could guess what my reaction would be," Hoffman continued. "Maybe that's why you didn't bother to call me."

"I'm sorry, Ab," Rattigan said.

"So why call me in now? Why bother to give me a fancy briefing in the Situation Room when it's too late for my opinion to count?"

"Because I need your help."

Hoffman looked puzzled.

"I have an assignment for you," Rattigan said carefully. He stood up and walked across the office toward the french doors, where he stood with his back to the Vice President. "That's why I asked you over here, Abner. I want you to go down there."

"You what?"

"I want you to go to La Paz," Rattigan said, turning to face him. "I want to make it unmistakably clear to the Bolivians and everybody else down there that we mean business. I want somebody to take a close look at things down there and report to me. I'd like you to go as soon as possible."

"Why me?"

"Because I can't go myself," Rattigan said. He turned to study the Vice President's reaction, but Hoffman stared at the floor, avoiding his gaze.

"Besides," said Rattigan, "I'd like to see you get a little more involved in the foreign side of things. I don't think the press exposure would hurt you at all."

Hoffman looked up, then threw back his large head and laughed.

"Lord," Hoffman said, rubbing his eyes. "I really do admire your gall. A little press exposure would be good for my image!" Suddenly he was serious. "Why can't we be frank, Mr. President? You don't give a damn about my image. You want to get me publicly committed to your policy down there. You want to tie me to the mast."

"As long as you're a member of this Administration, Abner, you're already tied to the mast," Rattigan said. "I'm not saying you can't have your private opinions. But . . ." His voice trailed off.

"But what, Mr. President?"

"I want this Administration to speak with one voice."

Hoffman stood up. "Then that voice, Mr. President, will have to be yours. I disagree with what you're doing. I think it's—"

"I know all that, Abner," Rattigan said. "But the OAS, we understand, will be passing a resolution pledging some five thousand South American troops to Bolivia. When those troops arrive in Bolivia next week, I want you to be on hand to greet them. You can talk to Brooks Healy about plans for the trip, and we'll—"

"I'm sorry, Mr. President, I can't do it."

Rattigan eyed Hoffman closely, but said nothing.

"There's nothing in the Constitution, Mr. President, that says I have to obey your orders. I don't see how I can keep my integrity and—"

"Abner," said Rattigan, "I didn't want to have to push you. I didn't want that. But today at four o'clock the press office is announcing that I've asked you to make that trip. If you're going to defy me, you'll have to do it in public."

Hoffman turned to stare back at the President, the shock in his eyes so great that Rattigan thought the Vice President would shout. But then his rage seemed to collapse visibly.

"Mr. President," Hoffman said wearily, "if that's what you want, you can make your announcement. I'm not going to get into a public brawl with you."

"Abner," said Rattigan, "I don't like putting this kind of pressure on you. But I've got to run this government. You understand that."

Hoffman said nothing.

"I wanted you to agree to this trip. I don't much like to squeeze people."

"I appreciate your consideration," Hoffman said bitterly.

"I'm sorry, Ab." The President shrugged slightly, dismissing Hoffman, and the older man walked out.

Late in the afternoon Triplitano called Cardwell with a message from the President.

"You'll probably hear this from him when things cool down," Trip said, "but meanwhile I deliver the bouquets."

Cardwell lifted his feet up onto his desk and smiled into the phone.

"You did a good job," said Trip. "He thought the speech said all the right things, and just the way he wanted to say them."

"Thank you, Trip."

"Don't thank me. I'm just delivering the message."

"Well, thanks for that."

"I think he's pretty high on you now. I hope you're ready to write some more speeches. He'll probably try to squeeze you dry."

"I wouldn't mind," Cardwell answered, but Trip had already hung up.

Cardwell left his office early to go home, just as the late fall dusk was falling. The street lights along Pennsylvania Avenue were already on; it was the height of the rush hour, and crowds of pedestrians drifted down the walk, bundled against the cold. He wondered how many of them had seen the President's speech, how many of them correctly judged the depth of this new crisis, how many cared at all.

He pulled out into the traffic. Triplitano's compliment glowed in his mind: *I think he's pretty high on you now.*

When he reached home, he found Nancy in the kitchen.

"I've been listening to the news," she said. "Do you think there's going to be a war or something?"

"I hope not." Then: "I wrote the President's speech last night. That's why I didn't get home. The President didn't like Leonhardt's draft, so all of a sudden he called on me."

"Hey, that's wonderful," she said.

She slipped into a chair to listen, and he told her the story, ending with the call today from Trip; the message from the President.

"So it looks as though I'm in favor," he said. "At least for a while."

He saw Nancy shaking her head from side to side, laughing a sort of desperate, mirthless laugh.

"What's the matter?"

"Oh, God, it's so funny," she said, but she looked as if she would cry.

"What?"

"I was going to ask you to quit." She didn't look at him. "To quit your job. I was going to try to persuade you to give it up and go back home. So we could—"

Cardwell stared back, waiting to hear her out.

"I thought about it all day," she said. "I'd decided it was the only way we could be happy. And now you come home, all excited." She shrugged hopelessly and tried to manage a smile. "I'm sorry," she said. "How selfish can I get?"

"I can't quit," he said. And then, unable to say more, he shrugged. "Let's have a drink."

In the dim study he poured two drinks, and pressed one into her hand.

"Nan," he said, "I can't just quit. You know that."

"I didn't mean right away," she said. "I was going to ask you to quit right after the election. There's nothing that requires you to stay another term."

He turned away from her to stare through the study window. "Look," he said, "let's not discuss it now."

"We've got to discuss it!" Her voice was tight, distorted. "Something is ruining us, and I don't know whose fault it is! I feel so selfish, so guilty. I feel angry all the time." She shook her head. "I've tried to like this place. I've tried to help you, and I just can't!"

She leaned forward, crying, and he let his hand rest tentatively upon her back. At his touch she straightened up to look at him.

"John," she said, "can I go home for a while?"

"We can go home for Christmas."

Deep in the night Cardwell wakened and sensed that Nancy was awake beside him.

"Nan? You awake?"

Without a word she moved against him and he embraced her, stretching his arms around her shoulders, shielding her.

"It's all right," he whispered. "It's all right."

When they made love he felt as if he were floating high above her. Then slowly he became aware that she moved, not with him, but in a fierce, desperate rhythm of her own, as if she aimed to seize her pleasure by her own will, in spite of him. Her frenzy made him feel a kind of dread; they *were* like strangers.

Then it was over, in a series of soft explosions. He followed her, feeling himself falling from his great height. When they had subsided, she lay quiet against him, and he knew that she was crying. He reached up in the darkness to feel her face.

"What's the matter, Nan? Why are you crying?"

"Because this is all we have. All we have left."

He drew away.

"I don't think so," he said. "I hope not."

She soon stopped crying and dropped toward sleep; he turned and moved away, leaving a wide dead space between them. What had gone wrong?

Sunday the Third

On Saturday, assured that all was still quiet in Bolivia, the President and his wife helicoptered to Camp David. When he awakened Sunday morning he felt, suddenly, almost cheerful, his mood lightened by the lovely comfort of the Aspen Lodge.

They took their breakfast before the great fireplace of the lodge, near a broad window that opened on a view of the Catoctin Mountains and the tree-filled valley below.

Rattigan sat staring down into the valley, relieved to be away from the heavy formality of the White House, while Lisa, in a quilted wrapper, read the *Times*.

Washington seemed a million miles away, and Bolivia, with all its troubles, might be on another planet. Yet he knew, gazing from his breakfast across the quiet hills, that he had not escaped. The telephone could ring at any moment: It could be Karnow or Healy, or someone else. . . .

"Aren't you going to read the paper?" Lisa asked.

"I was going to try not to, for once," Rattigan said. He was transfixed by the view. "What are they saying?"

"It's all about your speech."

For the past two days the press had carried mostly news, not comment: The soldiers had been followed to Bolivia by a small army of newsmen. But today the editorialists would take over, and the columnists. They had had time to consider the implications of the President's unexpected move. This was their day to speak.

"They aren't so bad," said Lisa, "except for the *Times*. The *Post* says you may have prevented a disaster; they're very fair. Jack Peale says you've proved at last that you do have a spine. The *Times* says the whole thing smacks of adventurism, and the columnists are pretty harsh. Do you want to read them?"

"Read me the *Times,*" he said. He closed his eyes, blocking out the peaceful view.

"This isn't the editorial. It's the Op Ed page." She rattled the pages slightly and began to read in a pleasant, neutral voice.

"'Among the people who were the earliest, the most active, and the most earnest supporters of Carl Rattigan,'" she read, "'there is today a sense of deep betrayal.'"

Rattigan sighed.

"'Betrayal is a strong word,'" she continued, "'but a valid one. For this is not a Johnson or a Nixon who has sent troop transports roaring off into the night on another exploit as world policemen.'"

She looked toward her husband quizzically, as if asking whether she should continue, and he nodded.

"'The citizens who helped Rattigan to victory never believed for a minute that Nixon or LBJ were their kind of men. Nor did they even fully trust John Kennedy, suspecting him to be a cold warrior at heart, though they loved his wit, his style, his *savoir-faire.*

"'But Rattigan was one of them. This they were led to believe by his conduct in the Senate and by his public statements through the years. But now, Bolivia—and betrayal on the single issue that his most committed supporters feel most deeply about: the application of U.S. force abroad.'"

"I'd like to tell him," Rattigan said tightly, "that three thousand men is considerably less than five hundred thousand. Let me see that."

She folded back the pages and passed them to him.

Reading the column, he felt his anger boiling up. They couldn't understand. They wouldn't. They made it sound as if he had *wanted* to send these troops!

The process had begun—the endless second-guessing, the mournful analyses, the solemn slogan-making—it would go on unabated in each day's papers. He had done the unpredictable, he knew, and in the eyes of the newspaper boys, especially the smart ones who affixed neat labels to politicians and Presidents, to act unpredictably was unforgivable.

He read on. "Sooner or later, it seems," the dean of the *Times* pundits wrote, "every President turns messianic, apparently feeling he must save the world."

"Just watch them," the President said to his wife. "Within a week they'll all be taking in each other's laundry. By Friday, at least three columnists will have used the word 'messianic.'"

"Why do you take it so hard?" she asked. "I've heard you say that outside New York and Washington, the columnists don't matter much."

"They don't matter *much,*" he said. "But they matter. They matter."

He rose, letting the paper fall onto the floor, and stood staring toward the window. But he no longer saw the placid mountain view. The world—in the pages of these papers—had followed him and robbed him of his peace.

"I swear, I'll never allow another newspaper in this place," he said bitterly. "And if one slips in, I swear I'll never read it."

Lisa nodded sympathetically but said nothing. It was a resolution he could never keep, she knew—like his resolution to avoid military commitments. And soon, when she rose from breakfast to go to dress, she noticed that the President had sunk onto the big sofa before the fireplace, and she smiled. He had pushed aside his breakfast tray and was avidly reading the Washington *Post.*

At home in Bethesda, John Cardwell, too, was observing the Sunday ritual of newspaper reading. He sat with his legs curled around the legs of a kitchen chair; the *Post* lay in a heap on the floor, the *Times* was still stacked neatly on the table.

Nancy moved about the sun-filled kitchen, removing breakfast dishes to the littered sink.

"Amazing," he said as he picked up the paper. "The *Times* looks like a special issue on Bolivia."

Sarah Tolman had made page 1 again, with a vivid description of scenes around La Paz: scores of jets from the United States lined up in readiness at the airport; the sudden appearance, in La Paz's narrow streets, of U. S. Army Jeeps and soldiers. Her long account continued on an inside page. He spread the section open on the table and continued reading it, but he found his mind wandering off into images of Sarah herself. How long had she been down there? Ten days? What timing!

Suddenly a headline on the inside page caught his eye: a boxed, double-column story in the neat gray format of the New York *Times*. It was a background story headed simply, "The Bolivia Speech."

His eyes left Sarah's story, and, almost holding his breath, he began to read. The story was a shrewd reporter's effort to trace the genesis of Rattigan's speech: the struggles in the State and Defense departments, the President's Thursday meeting. It was, for the most part, accurate.

A small subheading jumped at him.

"Hey, look at this."

As vivid as a blinking neon sign, the sight of his own name flashed out on the gray page.

"What?" said Nancy.

" 'Cardwell Emerges,' " he read aloud.

" 'The State Department paper became the basis for a speech draft by Fred Leonhardt, the chief presidential speechwriter, who is believed to have deep private reservations about U.S. involvement in Bolivia.

" 'Leonhardt's draft, according to informants, took a basically soft line, and was rejected by the President. A wholly new speech was then written by John Bolt Cardwell—' "

"Johnny!"

" '—a White House aide little known until now.' "

He let the paper fall forward for a moment, feeling a strange uneasiness. The President would probably be furious to see this account of backstage White House life.

"Here, let me see it," Nancy said. Her bitterness toward John temporarily subsided. She leaned forward and read aloud.

" 'Cardwell, thirty-four, a former newspaper publisher from Kentucky, was in charge of the President's aborted nonpolitical trip last week. Now, with his authorship of a major foreign policy address, there are those in the capital who view him as a new and potentially powerful voice in the White House.' "

"Aren't you excited?" Nancy said.

"Christ!" he said. "That's not the sort of thing that should be in the paper! Everybody will think I leaked it. I'd better call Trip." He headed for the den and dialed the White House operator. "Can you reach Mr. Triplitano at home?"

After a silence, Trip came onto the line. "How's the man in the news?" he said.

"A bit overwhelmed," Cardwell answered.

"If you can't stand the sight of your name in print," Trip said, "you shouldn't talk to reporters."

"You know I didn't leak that story!" Cardwell couldn't tell if Trip was joking.

"I know that," Trip said. "You're not that foolish, I hope."

"Well, who would do a thing like that? Who's responsible?"

"I don't know," Trip said carefully. "Maybe the President."

"Not on your life."

"Why not?" Trip asked. "He's the biggest leaker in the White House."

"Well, for one thing," Cardwell said, "he wouldn't want to look like a talking doll who's programmed by his speechwriters. He's probably calling for my scalp right now."

Trip laughed. "Jesus. Every White House staff man must think the President has a little black book for him! They think he sits around all day marking debits and credits for each one. Forget it. If he were upset you'd have heard from him by now."

"I hope you're right," said Cardwell.

"Look, John. He knows who leaked that story."

"Leonhardt?"

"Exactly. The man's covering his ass. He thinks the President has made a big mistake, and he wants to signal all his friends that he's not responsible."

"I can't believe he'd stick it to the boss that way."

"Well," said Trip, "to the people Fred cares most about, he comes off looking like a hero. They know he opposed sending the troops. He wrote a soft-line speech. He did his best."

"And to those same people," Cardwell said, "I look like some kind of warmonger?"

"Oh, no. You come off looking like a 'new and potentially powerful voice in the White House.' Isn't that the phrase?"

"Why don't you go to hell."

"I'm already on the way," said Triplitano. "I'll see you there tomorrow."

"If I still have a job tomorrow."

Triplitano laughed. "Look. He's got much more to worry over than you and Fred Leonhardt. He's probably sitting up at Camp David right now sweating his ass off about Bolivia: Suppose Chile isn't scared off? Suppose the Russians get involved? Suppose some GIs get killed? I'd say that seeing your name in the *Times* is way down on his list. I'll see you tomorrow."

When Cardwell hung up, his uncertainty had been transformed to satisfaction. "A new and potentially powerful voice in the White House." In Washington, he knew, the labels affixed by reporters could have powerful effect: "Mr. Cardwell, who is known to be close to the President . . ." In such words there was an element of self-fulfilling prophecy: If it is said that a man has real importance, then he becomes important: Sources feed him information, and reporters call to ask his opinions.

He almost smiled. Maybe this was good for Nancy. She had come here hoping to bask in his importance, and she'd been disappointed. But now . . .

Forcibly he stopped his fantasy. He walked back to the kitchen, eager to finish the *Times*.

Monday the Fourth

On Monday it rained, and the lights blazed in the Oval Office to counter the drizzling gloom outside. Karnow had spread two maps on the floor, and the President, seated in his favorite chair, leaned over them.

"So they're still building up?" asked Rattigan.

"It looks that way," Karnow replied. "But we can't pick up any intelligence about their plans. All we can do is wait and see."

"Our troops are here and here and here," said Karnow, pointing. "The carriers are here and here"—he indicated two locations off the coast of Chile—"and, of course, the planes are here." He pointed to La Paz.

"Suppose they tried more air strikes," Rattigan said.

"Our planes would be after them in five minutes."

Rattigan studied the maps. "The OAS contingents really go in Friday?" he asked.

"A few of them," Karnow said. "At least that's what we understand will be happening. The Vice President will be there Friday."

Rattigan nodded. "In our case, anything Chile might want to do would best be done before then—before more troops are likely to come in."

Karnow said nothing.

"Well?" said Rattigan.

"Well, I'd think so," Karnow said. "But we don't know their minds."

Rattigan rose and walked toward his desk. "It's funny, it's so quiet." He stood almost precisely at the center of the room, where the presidential seal was pressed into the rug. "I almost wish they'd do something, just to break the suspense."

Karnow nodded, lifting his maps and folding them.

"Do you know anything about sharks?" asked Rattigan.

"Sharks?" Karnow looked up.

"Years ago, I read a piece on sharks. It was by a man who had been attacked four times by sharks and lived." Rattigan came back to his chair and stood behind it. "I only remember one thing he wrote. When a shark is in the water, everything gets quiet. There's this eerie stillness, as if every other creature in the sea were waiting. The small fish all head for the bottom, and this deep calm falls. He said he noticed it all four times."

He eyed Karnow intently. "Well, I feel that same kind of stillness—"

Karnow smiled and shrugged. "I think," he said, "that you should try to think of yourself as the shark."

"I wish I could," said Rattigan. "I wish I could."

Before ten, Cardwell got a call from Chuck Ruter of the Newhouse newspaper chain. Cardwell knew Ruter slightly; he was abrasive, persistent, suspicious, cynical—in short, a superb reporter.

"How did you come to write that saber-rattling speech on Thursday night?" Ruter asked.

Cardwell sighed. "Well, Chuck, the President asked me to."

"That's all? That's your answer? What about the power struggle between you and Fred Leonhardt?"

"There isn't any power struggle," Cardwell said. "Look, Chuck. You guys refuse to understand how these things happen. You seem to think that speechwriters are ventriloquists and the President's the dummy. Leonhardt wrote one draft. The President wanted to change the emphasis; he asked me to try my hand, and so I did."

"Thereby emerging as a major figure in Rattigan's palace guard."

"That's bullshit and you know it."

Ruter, surprised by Cardwell's vehemence, laughed. "You're a lot more modest than some of your colleagues."

Cardwell said nothing.

"Okay, second question: Why has the great man suddenly taken to the iron fist?"

"I don't know what you mean."

"I've been going through the language of that speech," Ruter said, "and comparing it to some of his campaign rhetoric. It makes pretty interesting reading."

Cardwell said nothing.

"Listen to this," Ruter said. "From a speech in Detroit three years ago—two weeks before he got elected: 'Our foreign policy must be based on our interests, not the interests of other nations. To our allies, we can provide encouragement, moral support, and even money. But—unless we are willing to repeat the bitter lessons of the past—we must not be too eager to sell arms and send troops.' Do you remember that one?"

"Yes," said Cardwell. "I think I may have helped write it."

"Well, how can you square it with the Bolivian speech?"

"Well, first of all," said Cardwell, "Bolivia isn't Vietnam. It's in this hemisphere, and it's passably democratic. We've sent three thousand men, not five hundred thousand. They're not in combat. Repeat: not in combat."

"Not in combat—yet."

"And frankly, Chuck, I think it's not quite fair to pick a passage out of context like—"

"An old complaint," said Ruter. "Politicians used to say they'd been misquoted. Now they accuse reporters of taking them out of context."

"For God's sake, Chuck—"

"Anyway, you haven't answered my question. Has Rattigan changed his tune? Is he now for selling arms and sending troops? Is he giving us a brand-new policy?"

Cardwell wiped his forehead. *Who am I to speak for him like this?*

"I'm sorry, Chuck. Those are questions I can't answer."

"Well, somebody'd better answer," Ruter said. "Because everybody's asking. A President can't turn his back on every principle he campaigned on. At least he can't without having people ask some questions."

"Chuck," said Cardwell, "I'll just say two things: First, I don't think he's turned his back on any of his principles. And second, I hope you'll admit that what he's doing *may* be right."

"Of course he *may* be right," Ruter replied. "He may be the greatest President since Lincoln. But at this minute he just looks wildly inconsistent. And even being right won't help him; you guys have got to persuade people that he's right."

"Well," said Cardwell, "maybe I can start by trying to persuade you at lunch some day soon."

"Okay, I'll call you," Ruter said. "And, by the way—you didn't answer all my questions."

Cardwell laughed and hung up.

The Capitol at noon was virtually deserted, the chambers of the House and Senate empty. Most members were still at home for the weekend, and only a handful of tourists could be seen, walking slowly in the great rotunda, murmuring quietly among themselves, staring up into the vast hollow of the dome.

Abner Hoffman's ornate office just off the Senate floor was the only scene of intense activity. The Vice President, having summoned more than a dozen reporters to a meeting in his office, stood near the door, receiving them with his usual show of joviality.

"Murphy! Great to see you! Hope I didn't spoil your vacation. Don't tell me you reporters work when Congress is relaxing."

When the group was assembled, he swept them into his inner office, gesturing toward the few upholstered chairs arranged around his desk. A few reporters sat; most of them stood.

"Bob, come up here," said Hoffman.

A trim, well-dressed man with blond hair turning gray stepped to his side.

"Gentlemen," said Hoffman, "I think most of you know my friend Bob Johnson." They knew him well: He was a Washington physician famous for his suave manner, his staggering fees, and his roster of famous political patients.

"Since the announcement I have today is of a medical nature," Hoffman said, "I've asked Bob to take an hour away from his patients to join us here." The reporters exchanged glances, lifted eyebrows, frowned. Could this be serious?

"Mr. Vice President," said a correspondent standing near the desk, "is something wrong with you?"

Hoffman exploded into laughter. "Now, hold a minute. I'm doing fine, just fine. Bob, why not read your statement?"

The reporters lifted their notebooks.

"Let me begin," the doctor said, "by saying that the Vice President is in excellent health. If any of you wrote a story saying otherwise, you'd be wrong." He looked down to the sheet of paper in his hand, and the newsmen saw that he was nervous. He was not a politician; in the presence of curious reporters, he lost his easy calm.

"I have this statement," he said self-consciously.

"Okay, doctor, just read it," someone said.

" 'On Saturday morning,' " Johnson read, " 'the Vice President paid me a visit at my office. He told me that he was planning, at the President's request, to travel to La Paz, Bolivia, to meet with that nation's leaders and to pay his respects, on behalf of the United States, to Latin American troops arriving in that country.' "

The newsmen stood impatiently, pencils poised.

The doctor read on: " 'The Vice President asked me to check his medical records to be sure that his immunizations were up to date.

They were, so I took the occasion to administer a brief and routine examination. I found him to be in excellent condition for a man of his age and medical history.' "

The pencils paused again, and the writers glanced at one another.

" 'As you may know, however, the Vice President has a history of rheumatic heart disease occurring in childhood.' "

"I didn't know that," one reporter said.

"It's a matter of public record," Hoffman said. "It's nothing serious, really."

" 'Though little trace of that childhood illness is discernible,' " Johnson read, " 'and though the Vice President is in generally excellent health, I urged him not to travel to La Paz, which is situated at an altitude more than twelve thousand feet above sea level. It was my conviction' "— the doctor hesitated —" 'it *is* my conviction that for the Vice President to travel to such an altitude, without any period of acclimatization, might, in view of his history, involve unacceptable medical risks.' "

"Doctor, are you saying—"

"Let him finish," Abner Hoffman said.

" 'I therefore insisted that the Vice President cancel his plans, and he has reluctantly agreed. I must stress—' "

The reporters were suddenly excited.

"Doctor," said one, "can I interrupt for just—"

" 'I must stress,' " Johnson went on, " 'that this is a precautionary measure, which in no way reflects upon his general health or his ability to perform his duties. He is in excellent health.' "

"Is that the end?" Hands went up.

"Mr. Vice President, is this a postponement or a cancellation?"

"A cancellation, made reluctantly," Hoffman replied.

"Have you notified the President?"

"I have."

"When did you do that? On Saturday?"

"Well, no," said Hoffman slowly. "On Saturday I was still fighting the doctor pretty hard about this thing, and, as you know, the President was at Camp David. I conveyed the message to the White House this morning, and I assume he is aware of it now."

It was not true. Hoffman's note to the President, with a copy of the doctor's statement, was being delivered at this moment.

"What I'm getting at," said the reporter, "is why this announcement isn't being made at the White House. If this trip was initiated by the President, and if it was on his behalf, then why—"

Another reporter interrupted. "I'd like to get back to this medical thing, if we can. What exactly is the danger? I mean, if—"

"I'd prefer," said Dr. Johnson, "not to say 'danger.' There is a remote possibility."

"Of what?"

"There's a remote chance that a patient with a history of this kind—childhood rheumatic history—could suffer what we call hypoxia, due to extreme altitude, causing a sudden strain—"

"Hypoxia?"

"Oxygen deprivation. That kind of strain could lead to an acute coronary episode, or, more likely, acute congestive heart failure."

At these words Hoffman frowned. He wanted no stories about heart trouble; he wished the doctor would be more vague.

"I think the likelihood is slight," said Johnson smoothly. "But it is enough to make me recommend he cancel this trip."

"Doctor," said a reporter, "what are the Vice President's symptoms?"

Hoffman winced.

"He's asymptomatic now," Dr. Johnson said.

"He's what?"

"He has no symptoms."

Hoffman interrupted. "Gentlemen, we're going to give you copies of this statement. I think you'll remember the words 'precautionary measure.' "

"Mr. Vice President," Murphy Morrow asked, "why wouldn't you go to Bethesda or Walter Reed for this sort of checkup? Don't Vice Presidents get free medical care?"

"I happened to be in Bob's neighborhood and thought I'd stop by to get my shots if I needed them. That way I could be sore over the weekend—on my own time, and not the government's."

The newsmen laughed, and Hoffman smiled.

"Sir," said Baron of the *Post*, "who asked you to take this trip?"

"The President, on Friday."

"Were you looking forward to the assignment?"

"I'm always ready to serve the President," Hoffman said.

"But now, on your own initiative, you're canceling the trip?"

"No," said Hoffman, "not on my own initiative. On my doctor's."

"But you haven't discussed it with the President?"

Hoffman fought to keep control. "The President is a very busy man. Now, if you're trying to suggest that I'm evading this trip, let me set you straight right now—"

Hoffman's aide Warren Jasper, who had been standing on the fringe of the group, moved toward the outer office. The questions would be rough, but the old man was good, he could handle them. They had ducked the trip, successfully. And the best part of it was that Dr. Johnson's story was true: The medical facts were there; no one could accuse the doctor of fabricating an excuse. He was a good friend, of course, and he had been prompted. But it had worked.

Jasper sat down. It was near the morning deadline time for the afternoon papers: The meeting would end soon. Slowly a grin spread over his face.

Halfway through lunch in the staff mess, John Cardwell looked up and saw Fred Leonhardt entering the room. Leonhardt, trailing smoke from his large curved pipe, did not come directly to the round staff table where Cardwell, Triplitano, and a few others sat; he sauntered among the smaller tables, exchanging pleasantries with other White House staff men and their guests.

Cardwell turned back to his lunch and listened once again to the conversation at the table. There was an empty chair beside him. He knew Leonhardt would take it.

Two young economic aides from the EOB were disagreeing mildly.

"I know inflation hurts," said one. "But in an election year I'd rather have six points of inflation than six of unemployment."

Leonhardt reached the table. "Young economists!" he boomed. "The dollar is not what it was when you began your meal."

He sat down between Cardwell and Triplitano.

"Mr. Press Secretary! I see your tormentors have set you free to have a cup of soup. *Bon appetit.*"

"Hi, Fred," said Trip, unsmiling.

"And John Cardwell!"

Cardwell tried to smile in answer to Leonhardt's false heartiness.

"But why so glum? Your name is mentioned prominently in the press. You're powerful and famous. Surely that's cause for rejoicing? I'll make a toast!" Leonhardt reached for his water glass.

"Careful, Fred," said Triplitano. "That glass may have a leak."

Someone across the table chuckled; Cardwell wondered if the others caught the meaning of Trip's words. He looked at Leonhardt and thought he saw Fred's smile fade just a little.

"A toast," he said. "To the resident hawk in this otherwise placid aviary!"

There was some uncomfortable laughter. The men around the table had sensed the edge of bitterness in Leonhardt's voice.

"Not a hawk, Fred," Cardwell said. "More like a parrot."

The listeners laughed, relieved to hear Cardwell respond good-naturedly. Most of them, like Cardwell, were younger men, members of the "A group"—junior aides required to eat lunch early, then leave to make way for more senior men. When Leonhardt had come in, they had almost stopped their conversation in deference to him.

"The parrot," Leonhardt said. "A noble bird. An entertaining bird. But not a useful bird." He was no longer smiling. "You might say that the parrot is the least useful of all birds. He lacks originality. The parrot has no mind of its own."

Cardwell flushed. He had not wanted a confrontation, but it had come.

"Fred," he said, "if you're still sore about that speech, I wish you'd stop. The President *asked* me to rewrite your draft—I didn't volunteer. He's got this funny idea: He thinks *he* should make policy, not his speechwriters."

"Hear, hear," said Triplitano.

"It's not the speech that bothers me," said Leonhardt, backing off. "It's the policy. I'll admit that. Did you see the columns in the Sunday *Times?* Just what I expected."

"I saw the *Times,*" said Cardwell. "Fortunately, the country isn't run by editorial writers."

"Ultimately they do have great impact. Editorial writers, professors—they mold opinion, not the politicians."

"Well, Presidents bend opinion too," said Cardwell. "When the polls come in next Friday I'll let you see them, and you can judge his power against the *Times.*"

"There's always support in the first days of a crisis," said Leonhardt coldly. "I'm talking about the long haul."

"Well, in the long haul," said Cardwell, "there are things a President can do to win the people."

"Like what? Send more soldiers off? Make a few more jingoistic speeches?"

"Oh, Fred, dry up," said Trip. "You make it sound like this is World War III."

"Maybe not World War III," said Leonhardt, "but it's dangerous enough."

"Excuse me, sir." A waiter stepped up to the table and set down a telephone between Leonhardt and Gary Triplitano, nodding toward Trip. He lifted the receiver, and the men around the table stared at their plates, busying themselves with their food, straining to make it obvious that they were not eavesdropping.

"Yes, sir," said Trip. "No, I haven't seen it."

His tone told them the President had called.

"He did? He called the press in?"

Cardwell had finished his lunch. He got up to sign his check.

"Yes, sir," said Trip. "I'll be right up."

Triplitano hung up and folded his white napkin by his plate.

"Excuse me, gentlemen," he said. He had not yet finished eating, but he pushed his chair away. "I've got to go upstairs."

He joined Cardwell, and they left the mess.

"Hoffman again," Trip said when they reached the hall.

What's happening? Cardwell wondered, but Trip volunteered nothing, so he did not ask.

"By the way," said Trip, "I thought you held your end up pretty well in there with Fred."

"I'm trying to learn to use my elbows," Cardwell said.

Trip smiled. "Good man. When you've mastered use of the elbows, the next lesson is the appropriate application of the knee."

At Cardwell's door they parted, and Gary Triplitano rushed upstairs.

The President paced the Oval Office restlessly, waving Hoffman's memo, which he had just received, and a torn-off Associated Press bulletin.

"That no-good bastard," he said to Brooks Healy, returned from the OAS meeting. "That no-good bastard."

Triplitano slipped into the room and Rattigan looked up. "Have you seen this?" He slapped the wire copy lightly against his thigh.

"I stopped by the office," Trip replied. "We're already getting calls. They want to know why Hoffman announced it himself."

"Well, you can tell them that he announced it himself because his name will never again be mentioned by this Administration. He's out! He's pushed me too far!"

Triplitano glanced at Healy, who was sitting in one of the white sofas flanking the office fireplace.

"I was giving him a chance," Rattigan said. "Well, you see what his answer is. He gets his friendly neighborhood doctor to forbid the trip! I wish he'd at least had the guts to tell me to my face he wouldn't make that trip. I would have given him something to go to his doctor about!"

Triplitano joined Healy on the sofa, prepared to hear the President through his diatribe, knowing it would not be wise to say too much himself. Outside, beyond the thick bulletproof glass of the office windows, the rain fell steadily.

Rattigan flung the papers onto his desk.

"He's been trying to cut me up all over this town, with his little off-the-record sessions with reporters. My big mistake was in not slapping him down the first time he tried it."

"It just could be," Healy said mildly, "that Abner's doctor is telling the truth. I just can't believe he'd—"

Rattigan shook his head. He strode over and sank into the sofa facing them.

"It's all my fault, I guess," he said. "I should have known Abner would pull something. I should have known he wouldn't make this trip. He's too far gone. Every shred of trust I might have had in him is gone." He shook his head. "He knew we could never be close. But he could have tried to make it work. Now I'm going to shut him out so tight he'll think the door is nailed."

Healy frowned, wondering whether to speak. He leaned forward, then decided against it.

"Suppose I did let him sit in all the meetings," Rattigan said. "How could I trust him not to be out with reporters five minutes later? I'd be spending all my time trying to clean up after him. He'd have me looking like a damn fool."

"He's signaling publicly that he's against you on Bolivia," Trip said.

"It's not Bolivia. If it weren't this, he'd be onto something else. He really hates my guts."

"Mr. President," said Brooks Healy mildly, "I'm going to make a suggestion. You don't have to pay a particle of attention, but I feel obligated to make it."

Rattigan nodded glumly. "Okay, make it."

"Ignore Abner Hoffman."

Rattigan looked up sharply.

"Ignore him," Healy said. "Pay no attention. Pass this thing off as lightly as you can."

Rattigan shook his head, but Healy continued.

"Anything else you do will make it worse. Of course you're going to drop him from the ticket. But suppose you called him in and told him that. He'd figure he had nothing more to lose, and he'd just give you more trouble. The best you can do now is try to keep him quiet; try to avoid making a bad situation worse."

The President said nothing. Hoping that he was mellowing, Healy talked on.

"We shouldn't misinterpret Abner. He's really an old-fashioned isolationist. He really *is* upset about this business in Bolivia. But when it's over, he'll quiet down. Meanwhile, why give him what he wants—national attention—by *your* reaction?"

Rattigan gave Healy a skeptical look.

"Try to keep it cordial," Healy said. "Try to placate him until the troops come home. Then, as you move toward the convention, you can call him in, offer him a judgeship, and ask him to go quietly."

The President stood and walked toward his desk. Triplitano nodded, signaling him: I agree.

"That's all well and good," Rattigan said, "except for one thing." He turned to face Healy and Triplitano. "What if this thing doesn't just blow over? What if it goes on, and men start getting killed?"

"I'm hoping that won't happen," Healy said.

"But if it does?"

"If it does," said Healy softly, "you probably won't have time to worry about Abner Hoffman."

Rattigan stared through the glass-paned doors out to the Rose Garden, empty and gray in the winter rain. "All right," he said to Triplitano. "Hold all the questions on this thing until your briefing.

Then try to play it straight: We're sorry the Vice President can't go, but we understand completely. Act as though the whole thing is routine, and if you get any questions about a rift between us, remind them what I said a week or two ago."

Triplitano nodded.

"I have the fullest confidence in Hoffman, there is no rift. . . . We're sending Secretary Woodson to La Paz. I'll call him now and tell him."

He fell silent, staring once again through the glass doors. After a moment Healy and Triplitano realized that the time had come to go.

"Good afternoon, sir," Healy said.

"Thank you, Brooks."

They left by the door that led into the hall. When it swung shut, Rattigan stood for a moment in the silence, staring after them.

"That no-good bastard," he half whispered.

Wednesday the Sixth

Carl Rattigan required less sleep than other men, but when he slept, he slept soundly. He could will himself to sleep; could climb into bed or touch his head to the back of a chair and fall asleep in seconds. Other men—and Lisa Rattigan—marveled to see him, aboard a crowded plane or even in a motorcade, lean back, sink into sleep, then awaken minutes later, eager and refreshed.

But in the days that followed his dispatch of troops to Bolivia, he was keyed up and restless. Concerned about the safety of the troops, he could not will himself to sleep at night. He would lie in the darkness for an hour, then switch on the reading lamp beside his bed, scan memos and newspapers, call the Situation Room—then try to sleep again. Finally he would drift off—but not into the deep, enfolding sleep to which he was accustomed.

Even when he worked into the small hours, sleep would not come. Vague worries and imaginings crowded his mind; he learned, listening in the darkness, that the White House, like all old houses, had voices of its own, faint sighs and whispers, clocks and machinery groaning, as if the house itself were dreaming fitfully.

At least once each night he would call the Situation Room. Each time he called, the question he asked the clerk would be the same: "All quiet down there?"

"Everything's quiet, Mr. President."

He would awaken tired. His aides and visitors noticed that the President was snappish, irritable. Healy thought his outburst against Ab Hoffman was unlike him—extreme. But none of them suspected that he simply could not sleep.

On Wednesday night, one week after the troops went to La Paz, the President and Lisa watched a movie in the East Wing theater, dining from trays beside their easy chairs. Bored by the film, he tried to doze: He leaned back, closed his eyes, then shook his head. It was no use.

Afterward they walked, trailed by two agents, through the dim hall toward the elevator in the Mansion. Rattigan stopped off at the little Navy dispensary and said to Sorrel, "Don't come up tonight. I'm going to bed early."

"You're not sleeping, are you?" Lisa asked when they were back upstairs. "I saw a light under your door last night at 3:00 A.M."

"I'm getting enough sleep," he lied; "I woke up to do some reading."

He took a long, hot bath, and went to bed—ignoring, for the first time in many months, his nightly burden of memos and newspapers. At first he dozed: a thin, restless, unsatisfactory sleep.

But in an hour he was awake again. The clock beside his bed said 1:00 A.M. He called the Situation Room.

"Everything quiet?"

"Everything's quiet, sir."

He read, jotted some notes, tried to sleep again, and then, just before three, called downstairs again.

Things were still quiet: A good sign, he thought. Every day of quiet was a day earned, a day closer to the arrival of the first Latin troops on Friday. At three he fell asleep, and sank into the kind of sleep he had been missing: his old deep, steady, peaceful, floating sleep.

Hours later, at the first faint sound of the telephone beside his bed, Carl Rattigan was totally awake. He reached through the darkness for the small telephone with its faintly glowing dial, knowing that a call at such an hour could never be good news.

It was Sheldon Karnow. "Mr. President, I have some trouble to report."

He snapped on the lamp, squinting in the sudden light, and waited for Karnow to go on.

"We've got some movement in Chile: a heavy load of radio traffic, lots of aircraft in the air. I think they're moving troops."

Rattigan caught his breath. For days a line of U.S. ships, bristling with antennas, had hugged the coast of Chile, listening; a flock of eavesdropping airplanes had prowled above, just outside Chile's airspace. What had they learned?

"Can you get confirmation?" Rattigan asked.

"We're talking to La Paz now," Karnow said. "But it's all confused. We have reports of jets, and of helicopters following the railroad from Antofagasta toward La Paz."

"Jesus Christ." What he felt was dread.

"You think they'll hit La Paz?" Rattigan asked.

"No, I'd guess not. Their strength is in the south and the southeast, so I'd think they'd try to hit some smaller targets, drop some troops in where their chances are the best."

Rattigan said nothing. He swung his feet off the bed and sat upright, rubbing his chin with his free hand.

"Mr. President," Karnow said, "you have planes around La Paz and on the carriers. If you give the order you can have them in the air within five minutes."

It would mean flying U.S. warplanes over Chile, Rattigan knew. And it would mean shooting. "I can't do that," he said. "At least not until we've got some information."

"Well, we're talking—"

"Where are you now?" Rattigan asked.

"I'm still at home, but I can be down there in twenty minutes."

The clock beside the bed showed six-fifteen. It was still dark outside. "Okay, come on," he said. "I'll meet you in your office. Tell the Sit Room to keep me posted."

Though he had slept only three hours, he was alert. He cradled the receiver, then lifted it again.

"Good morning, sir," the operator said.

"Call Secretary Healy," he told her. "Tell him I need him at the White House right away. And give the same message to Secretary Woodson, Mr. Martin, and Mr. Triplitano."

She hesitated. "Mr. President," she said, "they're on their way. Mr. Karnow called them and they've—"

"That's good," he replied, and hung up.

He shaved quickly, half listening for the telephone and remembering, from last week's meeting, General Roundcastle's words: If you send troops, you've got to be willing to use them. . . .

And if you're going to use them, you've got to send enough. He had ignored Roundcastle, dismissed him as a quaint old warmonger. But this time, who'd been right? Three thousand troops around La Paz; they hadn't been enough.

He rubbed his face with a thick white towel and moved back to his room. The waiter returned, bearing a tray with a silver pot of coffee. Rattigan ignored him, searching in an antique chest for socks and underwear. The waiter moved to the windows, pulled open the heavy draperies, and left.

If you don't send enough, you'll have to send more. In the middle of his dressing, he reached for the phone.

"Operator? I want General Roundcastle at this meeting. If nobody's called him, can you reach him now?"

"We'll call him, sir."

Within ten minutes after Karnow's call, the President was dressed. He buttoned his coat and stepped into the hall. Already two agents were waiting, holding open the elevator door.

By noon the network news broadcasts were leading with a strange announcement from Santiago: The Government of Chile had indeed sent troops across the frontier into Bolivia. But this act, claimed Santiago, was not aggressive: The troops had been sent in response to a request from a new peoples' government in Bolivia—a "provisional government" headed by Roberto Aguila. Chile had launched a "program of assistance" to a "fraternal state."

The President and his advisers huddled until midafternoon. Then, at his afternoon briefing, Gary Triplitano read a tersely worded statement: In response to an act of "naked and shamcless aggression" by the regime in Chile, the United States was stepping up its efforts to help the legitimate Government of Bolivia to defend itself. Accordingly, the number of United States military personnel in Bolivia was being increased immediately from three thousand to twenty thousand. While the basic mission of the U.S. troops would remain unchanged, American military forces would be authorized to undertake "active defense missions" in support of Bolivian troops.

The reporters clamored for more facts. Would the United States reduce its troop commitment if more Latin American nations dispatched troops to Bolivia? What, precisely, was the mission of the U.S. troops? And what was the meaning of this strange new phrase: "active defense"? Did it mean the U.S. troops would take part in combat operations against Chilean forces?

Triplitano resolutely refused to go beyond the formal statement. Gamely he fended off the excited reporters' questions until finally, frustrated and under deadline pressure, they broke and ran for the telephones.

Monday the Eleventh

Four days later, it happened: A U.S. helicopter, lifting Bolivian troops into a firebase, was shot down. The American pilot and his crew of three were killed, and all the Bolivian troopers. There was a fire; the chopper burned.

"We're getting lots of shooting at these choppers," the Sit Room clerk said to the President when he gave him the news. "I'd say—"

Rattigan cut him off. "Call me if you have anything else."

"Sure thing, sir."

Rattigan closed his eyes and saw the chopper burning: a brief orange glare. He shook his head.

Four dead Americans. Lots of shooting. It had started.

Mondays were always quiet on the Hill; the agenda in both Houses was always light because it was hard to raise a quorum: Too many members were back in their states, stretching the weekend to include another day of rest or politicking.

Abner Hoffman convened the Senate, stayed on the platform for the chaplain's prayer, then turned the gavel over to Harris Paige, the junior senator from Idaho, and moved onto the floor.

A few senators stood in little clusters near the giant leather sofas around the walls.

Hoffman approached one group, which greeted him with handshakes and broad smiles; they were all his friends.

Burton Joy of Iowa pulled him into the circle.

"Abner, I hope to God you people know what you're doing, but it looks bad. I don't see how we can say they're not in combat when our men are getting killed."

The others nodded, and Abner Hoffman shrugged.

"The answer," he said, "is that they *are* in combat. I guess we'll have to settle down to that."

Back in his office off the Senate floor, Hoffman sank into his chair.

The first edition of the *Star* was on his desk: U.S. TROOPERS DIE IN LATIN FIGHTING.

He read the account, spreading the paper on the desk before him.

Alone in his great ornate office, he shook his head, then rubbed his face slowly with both hands.

It was sadness, not anger, that he felt now: the sadness of futility. He knew, reading of the soldiers' deaths, that something inevitable had begun. He had had no part in this decision, yet he would be held to account for it, he knew that. More men would die, he knew that too. And he was powerless to stop it.

Or was he?

He called Andy Martin at the White House.

"Andy, I'd like to see the President," he said. "As soon as possible —today."

Martin was the soul of courtesy. "Certainly, sir. Can I get back to you? I guess you know how hectic things are here."

"I'll be here until noon," Hoffman said. "I'm worried about these casualties. I think we're headed for . . . I just think he and I should have a talk," Hoffman said.

Within an hour, Martin called him back.

"Mr. Vice President, I'm sorry, can we put this off till tomorrow? Things are piling up, and he's already an hour behind. I'll tell you what—"

"Goddamn it, Andy, I can't believe—"

"I'm looking at my schedule, sir. I see you're down for the leadership breakfast Wednesday morning. Could it wait till then? There's some time right after, and—"

"Tell me something, Andy," Hoffman said. "Is he this busy, or just unwilling to see me? Are you telling me he's too busy to see the Vice President of the United States?"

"Sir," said Martin smoothly, placatingly, "I'm sure you know it isn't that. It's just—"

"I *don't* know that," Hoffman said coldly.

"—just that this day is so pushed full you'd probably be interrupted anyway. Can I make a suggestion? Dictate a memo and I'll shoot it in to him."

"Go to hell, Andy. I want to see him! I'm not some fifth-rate bureaucrat. I want to—"

"Mr. Vice President," Martin said, measuring his words, "I'm going to do my best. I'll keep trying, I can promise you that. Meanwhile, I'd suggest you send a memo in. I'll call you if I work it out."

"All right, Andy," Hoffman said. He was breathing hard. "I'll do that. And I'll wait for your call."

"Thank you, sir." Martin hung up, and the Vice President slammed down the receiver, knowing there would be no call.

Tuesday the Twelfth

Far to the south of La Paz the fighting raged, intense and bloody.

On Tuesday morning Sarah and Tony Jack, at Colonel Redwine's invitation, decided to skip the press briefing for American reporters. They drove, in Redwine's Army sedan, to the airstrip outside the city, to see the first big planes leave with U.S. wounded.

A row of tents and air-filled domes had been set up beside the strip: a field hospital, like a tiny city built almost overnight.

They drove past it, past the large planes that waited on the strip, down to a roped-off helicopter pad. One helicopter roared away, blowing clouds of reddish dust up from the ground, and another one dropped in. They were bringing the wounded—Bolivian and American—from their battles in the South.

The American boys wore coarse blue pajamas, standard Army issue. Some had rolled their sleeves up; she saw pale flesh, bandages, casts, tattoos. A plain-faced Army nurse, wearing a flight jacket and baggy fatigues, climbed up the ramp and disappeared into the plane.

"It's quite an aircraft," Redwine said. "It carries forty stretchers, plus the crew. It's like a flying hospital: oxygen, the whole works."

The last stretcher was moved aboard, the patient on it encased in white, invisible. A glucose bag swung over him, hooked to a metal rod.

"Burn case," Redwine said.

"It didn't last long, did it, Colonel?" Sarah said.

"What?"

"Our noncombat role."

Redwine shrugged. "Whoever thought it could? Those jokers up in Washington?"

"I believe they hoped it could," Sarah replied. "Some of them, at least."

"Well, that's just wishful thinking. You can't send people into a mess like this without someone getting hurt."

Sarah swung around and glared at Redwine. "You don't care, do you, Colonel? You don't feel a thing! You can come out here and watch all this and comment like a tour guide while they unload these boys who're all torn up! You can live quite comfortably with lying euphemisms like 'active defense.'"

"Miss Tolman, I am a military man," he said. "A professional military man. If you think I can see all this and never feel a thing, you're dead wrong. I saw this in Korea when I was twenty years old, I saw it in Vietnam, and now just as I'm about to retire, I'm seeing it again. And I can tell you, it makes me as sick to see it now as it did years ago."

He glared at her, but did not raise his voice.

"Long after you write your story and fly back to Washington, Miss Tolman, I'll still be here, watching them haul bodies off the choppers. And it will make me just as sick to watch it as you feel now. But I've learned just one thing. I've learned that it doesn't do any more good for me to cry over these men than for a doctor or a nurse to cry. We're professionals, Miss Tolman. That means we don't cry. We just try to get them out of here and home as fast as we know how. I hope you'll put that in your story. And I hope you'll call them men, not boys."

Back at the hotel for lunch, Tony ordered drinks while Sarah repaired her makeup.

"I'm sorry," she said, "I don't guess I exactly distinguished myself out there."

"Well," he said, "I am a little bit surprised. I can remember how you hated sitting around in Saigon. You were always ready to go roaring off to battle, the more blood the better. What's the matter?"

"I was ambitious then. I wanted to win a Pulitzer. It was an adventure for me—a way to prove myself. I was younger."

"You were also," Tony said, "the best-looking piece in Saigon. And you don't hurt the scenery in La Paz." He was grinning.

"Well, I've proven myself now," she said, continuing. "I won a prize. I guess I just don't want to do it all again. Or see it."

He reached across the table and touched her hand lightly before she moved it away.

"I thought Vietnam was awful," she said. "The whole time I was there, I saw the horror, and it affected me. But all the while I had this feeling—this faith—that it was some sort of lesson. I was convinced that we would come through it more sober, more restrained. Less likely to rush into other horrors."

She drank again, then shrugged.

"But here we are again."

"It's not the same at all," Tony said. "And you know it."

"Oh, it's basically the same," she said. "It's the same for those kids who're getting shot up. It's the same for the 'burn case.'" She was surprised at the bitterness in her own voice. "It's the *same,*" she said.

"You've been here three weeks," Tony said. "You could go home. The *Times* has other people here."

"It seems like twenty weeks," she said.

"How long were you planning to stay?"

"Not more than three weeks," she said. "Then everything started happening. I have this awful talent for being in the right place at just the right time." She sighed. "But the truth is I called the office Thursday after Chile moved in, and asked if I could stay the rest of the month."

"And they said yes."

"They said yes." She smiled a rueful smile, and Tony grinned. "I guess I'm like the old fire horse. I hear the bell and get restless."

"You really haven't changed a bit," said Tony.

Later, upstairs in her room, she uncovered her typewriter and sat down to write. The light outside her window told her it was after two o'clock; she knew that she must hurry to file in time to meet her evening deadline.

She would not file an account of the fighting; the wire services could cover that.

She sat still, her eyes closed, tilting her head back, waiting for an idea to drift in: a way to begin. Then she started to type.

She began this day's story with a scene that had burned itself into her mind: two helicopter crewmen, an hour away from battle, lifting gray zippered bags, heavy plastic body bags, into the hands of the litter bearers: the war dead going home.

Wednesday the Thirteenth

Throughout the President's Wednesday breakfast with the Democratic congressional leaders, Abner Hoffman sat quietly at his end of the table, answering politely when he was spoken to, then addressing himself once again to his breakfast plate. When the President passed out copies of some private poll results Cardwell had sent him —a version highlighting the most favorable facts—the Vice President studied it politely, then laid the paper forgotten by his plate.

It was a routine weekly meeting and it ended quickly. Rattigan walked his guests to the elevator nearby, bade them a cordial farewell, then returned to the family dining room where Hoffman waited, fingering a gold-chased spoon beside his plate. Hoffman rose, in a reflex courtesy, but the President motioned him back into his chair.

"Do you want to talk in the office, or would you like a second cup of coffee?" He was still taking Healy's advice.

"I'll take the coffee," Hoffman said.

Rattigan leaned over and shook the little bell beside his plate.

He waited while a waiter appeared to pour out the coffee, then spoke.

"Well, Abner," he said, "what's on your mind?"

"I'm getting questions about this business in Bolivia."

"What kind of questions?"

"I'm being asked to defend it, Mr. President."

Rattigan shrugged. "Defend it, then. You know why we're there."

"I'm not sure I do," Hoffman said coldly. "Furthermore, since you didn't ask for my advice, didn't ask me to your meetings—"

"I'm sorry, Abner," Rattigan broke in, not wanting to hear the complaints, "but things were moving quickly, and I just didn't think. . . ." He paused as if hearing the weakness of his words. Then, after a moment's thought, he said, "Why shouldn't I be frank? I knew what you would say, Abner. I've heard your arguments; so on that count there was no need to ask you."

"Beyond the formal reasons."

"Exactly." Rattigan stood up, leaving his bit of coffee still untouched, and walked across the room toward the yellow-curtained windows. "And frankly, Abner, I felt I couldn't trust you. I couldn't trust you not to call in the reporters and tell them your troubles—"

Hoffman interrupted. "If you're still angry about that—"

"I'm not angry, I'm just telling you the facts." Rattigan stood before the window, his back to Hoffman.

"If I had a mind to, Mr. President," Hoffman said slowly, "I could still talk to reporters—meeting or no meeting."

"I know," said Rattigan. "But you'd have less to tell them."

The draperies were drawn shut, closing off the view of the pickets outside on Pennsylvania Avenue. The President raised his hand as if to open them and look, then turned instead and looked at Hoffman.

"I was wrong, Abner. Certainly I should have had you in. All I can say is that I'm sorry. From now on you'll be consulted." He said it as though the case were closed; the matter finished. "You've got full access—to me, to Healy, to Karnow. If you have questions, ask them. If you have advice, tell me."

"And if I have doubts?"

"Tell me about them," Rattigan said. "I'll take them seriously." He turned again, and drew the curtains back and blinked as the dull glare of morning filled the room. "Hell," he said softly, "I have doubts myself."

The crowd was not too large, maybe a hundred. A cluster of Park Policemen stood talking near the curb, scarcely glancing at the marchers who circled slowly and quietly, causing no trouble. From his distant vantage point, he could not read the placards; could not tell if they were chanting.

"Look at that," he said. "I never thought I'd see a thing like that." Abruptly he drew the curtains shut and turned to Hoffman. "I wonder if they think I like sending troops? I wonder if they think I wanted this to happen?" He went back to the table, reached down for his cup, and drained it. "Come on, let's go," he said, heading for the door.

They took the elevator to the ground floor, met the phalanx of Secret Service men who waited in the hall, and walked, coatless in the cold, through the open colonnade to the President's office.

Hoffman did not sit down when they reached the Oval Office. "If this keeps up, you'll be in trouble," he said.

"*If* it keeps up," Rattigan said. He leaned over his desk, propping himself on outspread hands, and glanced at the notes and memos spread there by his secretaries. Then he looked up at Hoffman. "But if we can get a resolution from the OAS, troops will arrive from the Latin countries, and we can start pulling our units out."

"How long do you think that will take?"

"I don't know. I had thought I would have it by now. It could be days, maybe weeks. Maybe a month."

"Then I hope you're prepared to wake up every morning and see twice as many pickets outside your window as you saw today. Because the people won't sit still for long, I'll tell you that."

"The people support what I did by sixty-five per cent, according to the most accurate information we can get."

Hoffman shook his head. "You let this thing go on a month, then take a poll. You're in trouble now. Well, you'll be in worse trouble."

"All right, Abner," Rattigan said. "Then let's see if we can't prevent that. You're supposed to be a spokesman for this Administration. You get around. You can make a pretty good speech. Why don't you get out and help explain why we've—"

"Because I'm not going to put my head in the noose for a policy I oppose!" Hoffman almost shouted. Then he dropped his voice. "I want to turn this policy around, not crusade for it. Our boys are getting killed down there, and blood is on—"

"All right, that's enough! I don't need a casualty count from you!" The President was stung; his eyes blazed. "You're part of this Administration. And I wonder if you don't care less about the blood than your own political skin."

"I care about both, Mr. President," Hoffman said, fighting to control his anger. "I care about both."

"Then you'd better be on the team, Abner, because you're in this for better or for worse. If it gets bad for me, it's bad for you." He glared at Hoffman. "And even if it goes well for me, it could go badly for you."

"Is that some sort of threat?"

"It's advice. You should take it." He sat down and once again began to read the papers on his desk, but Hoffman did not move. He stood as if rooted to the floor, looking first at Rattigan, then down at the presidential seal in the center of the rug.

"Well," said Rattigan, "it's time to start the day."

For a moment Hoffman stared again at Rattigan. Then he turned to leave.

"Thank you, Abner," said the President. "I'll keep you posted."

When he was gone, Rattigan reached for his telephone and called Brooks Healy.

"Brooks," he said, "I'm putting you on Ab. He's yours from now on. I don't care what you say to him. I don't care how you persuade him. I just want you to keep him quiet."

Thursday the Fourteenth

The tables in the bar at Sarah's hotel in La Paz were small, their dark wood tops scarred and stained. During the day—particularly between noon and three o'clock, the hours of the siesta—the bar was usually filled with businessmen, rich Bolivians and their guests, chattering in Spanish and English. In the evening, as if by agreement, the Americans took over: reporters from the States down to cover the newest foreign crisis; embassy people in dark suits; a few Army and Air Force officers.

Now it was four-thirty—too late for the Bolivians and too early for the Amercans. She found an empty table against the wall and eased into the chair that face the entrance. When the lone bartender headed for her table, she waved him back; she would wait for Tony.

She was tired, weary of the ugliness, the futility, the sadness of this war. It would go on—how long, she couldn't guess—but she wanted to leave it, to pick up once again her Washington routine. She thought of those pleasantly gossipy lunches at Sans Souci, the probing interviews with high officials who talked more than they should because they were disarmed by her face and her warm, sympathetic voice. As a young girl she had worn her beauty carelessly; now she was not above using it as a subtle weapon. And why not? The politicians, the best ones, used their charm like actors, to gain the right effect. Why not—

She jumped when Tony touched her shoulder.

"You looked a thousand miles away."

"I was," she said. "At least a thousand."

"Well, come back for a minute. I've got news."

He summoned the bartender, ordered two manhattans, and turned to her again. "Press your fatigues. You're going to see some action."

"Tony, what have you been up to?"

"We leave tonight," he said. "I know a major down near Cochabamba, so I called him. He said they're going on those so-called active defense missions down there, so I got us on a chopper. Ten o'clock, at—hey, what's the matter?"

She shrugged. "I don't know. I'm just not up for it, I guess. I was sitting here before you came in, thinking about Washington. I'm not sure I want to go down there."

"Sarah, sweetheart, where's the old fight? I remember when you used to claw and scratch to get on board a chopper headed for the field."

"How long ago was that?"

"Sweetheart! Once a trouper, always—" Then, seeing that she was not smiling, he turned serious. "Look. This is a great opportunity. You'll be going back home soon. You've filed some great stuff in the past three weeks. Why not top it off with one good story from the field?"

She looked down at her drink, folding her hands about her glass, and Tony knew that she was weakening.

"We'll be back in twenty-four hours—that's a promise. You'll have some stuff that will stand their hair on end. You'll get a raise.

You'll be the toast of Washington: Sarah Tolman, fresh from combat—"

She was smiling. "Screw you," she said, and Tony knew that he was winning. He swung his glass up to his lips, took a long drink, and rolled his eyes.

"Remember how it used to be when you'd go to the field? 'Jesus, it's a girl!' You'd toss your hair and give those kids that sexy smile?"

"I was younger then," she said.

"Just wait and see," said Tony.

At six o'clock, as he climbed into the back seat of his limousine, Abner Hoffman said, "Let's drop by the Statler." An old-timer, he still called it by its former name.

Warren Jasper looked surprised. "I thought you wanted to go home."

"I do," said Hoffman. "I just want to stop by for a drink."

There was a convention of trial lawyers at the hotel, and many of them were friends and old allies of Ab Hoffman. He had turned down their invitation to address their final dinner, but he could not resist stopping by to say hello.

The big car headed up Seventeenth Street, moving heavily with the last wave of rush hour traffic. Then the driver turned right into K Street and gathered speed, and a minute later they pulled into the driveway of the hotel.

In the lobby a little knot of tourists recognized the Vice President.

"Hey, it's Hoffman!" someone said, and the Vice President smiled and waved. He walked quickly toward the lobby stairs, flanked by his phalanx of four agents, shielded from the tourists who wanted to shake his hand, ask him questions, collect his autograph.

They mounted the stairs and paused outside the ballroom door.

"I'll stay here twenty minutes," Hoffman said to Jasper. "Not a minute more."

The ballroom was a smoky hive of people, all pressing toward the three bars along one wall and around a long buffet set up in the center of the room. But when the Vice President entered and walked into the crowd, its focus changed. He was recognized; the word spread; people left the bars and the buffet and pressed toward him.

Flanked by his agents, followed by Jasper, Hoffman plunged into the throng, a smile lighting his face. He worked the crowd professionally, nodding, smiling, winking now and then at an old friend. Occasionally, shaking hands, he would bend confidentially to receive a whispered question from an admirer, smile, and then move on, following a path cleared for him by his agents.

"Mr. Vice President! Glad you could come!"

"I wouldn't miss it!" he would say, and flash his broad, ingratiating smile.

Jasper knew that it was automatic, that Hoffman's mind was somewhere else. His eyes, above his hearty smile, were fixed and distant.

"Abner, hello! This is a great surprise!" The association's president, an Oklahoman like Ab Hoffman, was an old friend, one of the few who could forget the formal title. "I'll take you around," he said, and fell into step with the Vice President.

In less than twenty minutes Hoffman, led by his old friend, had given almost every one of the conventioners a handshake, a wave, a shouted greeting. Then the party moved toward the door. Hoffman was joking with a little knot of middle-aged women—wives of delegates—who had attached themselves to him, delighted to be near a man so famous, eager to talk with him and to get some word to add to the stories they would tell back home. The ladies laughed. A few found scraps of paper and thrust them toward him, begging for autographs.

Hoffman frowned, then pulled out a pen.

"Where's your wife, Mr. Vice President?"

"She's at home, expecting me for dinner, and if you don't let me go I'll be in trouble." He smiled, scrawling autographs hurriedly.

"Mr. Vice President, what about this war? Is it serious?"

Hoffman looked up sharply. "You bet it's serious," he said. He searched their faces for his questioner, then found her: a tall, gray-haired woman with grave, dark eyes.

"I've got a son in service," she said.

"Well, you tell him I'm doing what I can to end it," Hoffman said. He put his pen away and pressed toward the door.

"How long will it take?" someone called from the group, and Hoffman shook his head.

"I can't say," he said. "I'm not the President, and I don't know his mind. He doesn't always ask my advice, and he doesn't tell me his plans." He was almost at the door, talking almost to himself, as if he were thinking out loud. "But I always tell him what I'm thinking, and I think we should end it soon." He stopped and smiled. "I must go, ladies," he said. "Good night, my friends."

Hoffman strode out in a flurry of applause. He did not notice, nor did Warren Jasper, that his words, spoken carelessly and off-the-cuff, had been caught by a slender, disheveled lady lost in the crowd, and that she had taken them down in her tidy, nervous script.

Neither of them knew that before he was halfway home, she would be back in the newsroom of the Washington *Post,* tapping out her story.

Back at his big house in Georgetown, the Vice President dined quietly with Libby Hoffman, listening genially as she told about her day, smiling as she passed on bits of gossip from her luncheon earlier with a group of Senate wives.

Over coffee Libby stared at him. "Are you all right? You seem preoccupied."

"Just tired, that's all," he said.

But after dinner, in his study, watching television as Libby sat nearby with her needlepoint, he could not concentrate. He tried to focus on the film, but yesterday's scene in the Oval Office came back to his mind.

He felt a growing resentment that the President should ignore his counsel, then insist upon his loyalty. It had been a week since the invasion; the OAS ambassadors had met for days with no result: no resolution, no commitment of troops to aid the cause, supposedly their cause, which Rattigan had rushed in to help. Hoffman frowned and shook his head. Libby, glancing up from her needlework, saw him shift in his big chair and yawn. Ten o'clock already.

There was a long, insistent ring from the white telephone on his desk nearby: the direct White House line.

"Abner?" It was the President. "I have the first edition of the *Post.*" He spoke in a low, controlled voice. "There's a story on the society page that I want you to hear."

Rattigan began to read, and Hoffman heard his words from the reception quoted back. Hoffman felt betrayed, then angry—why hadn't he seen the *Post*'s reporter? Didn't they know his words were casual, off-the-record? And he felt guilty, as though caught in some gross breach of etiquette—which, of course, was the case.

"Well, Abner, how about this?"

He could not exactly read Rattigan's tone, but Hoffman thought he heard sarcasm, and anger replaced his guilt.

"I'm sorry, Mr. President, I had no idea there was a reporter there," he answered coldly.

"You mean you said it?"

"Of course I said it."

"Well, please unsay it before the next edition." Rattigan's voice was crisp. "I don't care what you do. You can say you were misquoted, deny you were at the party, issue a clarifying statement—whatever you like, just so you do it quickly."

Hoffman felt the heat rush to his face. He took a deep breath, hoping his voice would not betray his anger.

"Mr. President, I wasn't speaking for the record. But I didn't say anything I regret."

There was a moment of silence.

"Get it changed, Ab," Rattigan said tightly. He hung up.

Libby greeted him with questioning eyes.

"The President," he said. And he told her, in a few words, about their meeting, about the *Post*'s story, and about Rattigan's angry call.

"What are you going to do?" she asked. "You can't say you were misquoted."

"I'm going to have a drink," he said, "and go to bed."

Long after midnight Tony and Sarah landed at a small airfield near Cochabamba. The pilot, a thin-faced warrant officer, steered their little plane off the runway, and they rolled up to a long, tin-roofed building.

Tony's friend, the major, was waiting beside his Jeep.

"Sarah," Tony said brightly, "this is Lane Hackney. Sarah Tolman, Lane."

The major stared at her without speaking and turned to Tony.

"You didn't tell me your friend was a lady."

For a moment Tony looked sheepish. He darted a glance toward Sarah.

"I don't see how we can accommodate a lady," Major Hackney started, but Tony broke in with a rush of words.

"I'll admit she looks like a lady, Lane. Lipstick and all that." Sarah was dressed in fatigues and a shapeless Army jacket. "But she's no lady. She's a tough old female reporter. Mean as hell. She tried to join the WACS but they wouldn't let her in—told her she was too mean and aggressive. So she's a reporter instead."

"Tony!" Sarah dropped her eyes, embarrassed, and Hackney, in spite of himself, smiled slightly.

"She won a Pulitzer in Vietnam," Tony said. "Reporting from combat."

"Is that right?" Hackney raised his eyebrows.

"It was a long time ago," Sarah said.

"Okay, let's go." The major helped them into the rear of the Jeep, took his seat beside the driver, and they roared off, out of the lighted area beside the airfield into the darkness.

It took them forty minutes to reach the little camp. When they arrived, Sarah was chilled from riding in the high mountain air. She was shivering, but when Hackney took her arm to help her from the Jeep, she stopped herself by force of will.

The building he led them to—a bunker, actually, sunk halfway into the ground and banked with dirt—was in the center of the camp, surrounded by similar buildings.

"Coffee?" he said, and nodded to his driver without waiting for their answer.

Sarah tapped the wall of the building.

"Corrugated tin," said Hackney. "A prefab job. The engineers dig a hole and then just drop them in. They built this camp in thirty-six hours."

She smiled, and Hackney returned her gaze with a smile—a half grin of hospitality mixed with frank male interest. He was a big man, about forty, with large hands, a strong neck, and close-cropped, blondish hair. An ex-football player, she judged—and a career soldier. She looked down: He wore a wedding band.

"We've got two hundred men in here," he said.

"And one woman," Tony laughed.

"Wait'll they see that," Hackney said.

Over coffee around the small table in the center of the bunker, he showed them maps.

"The idea," he said, "is to build a ring of camps around the city. We've got control of this whole valley"—he pointed, then ran his finger down the map—"from north to south. And they"—he moved his finger right and left—"are in the goddamn mountains."

She tried to imagine the scene marked by the map: Cochabamba, set in the green and fertile valley that snaked through the middle of the Andes, mountains higher than all others but the Himalayas. The city was at eleven thousand feet; on either side of the valley the steep bluffs rose almost vertically to cliff and plateaus beneath the mountains above, and some of the peaks reached seventeen thousand feet.

"There up there on these bluffs with God knows how many people. And artillery. If you'd been here earlier you could have heard the shelling like the Fourth of July."

Most shells, he told them, fell short of the city. They were aimed at the American and Bolivian garrisons that had sprung up in the area after the invasion. Were the bunkers safe?

"Safe enough," he said, then turned back to his map.

"When we got here, the Bolivians were just squatting down and taking it. So we're trying to teach them some tactics." He had the usual unconscious American assurance of superiority—not quite arrogance, Sarah figured, but likely to be misjudged by the proud Bolivians.

"There's not much you can do, really. We helicopter men into the hills and they patrol. If they meet the other side they'll call in air strikes." He looked up from his map, at Tony. "We haven't run into them yet. But if we found a crowd of them all together, we could wipe them out."

"And lose a lot of your men in the process." Tony had seen the tactics years before in Vietnam.

The major shrugged and waved his right hand, gesturing toward the silent bunkers outside in the camp. "My group don't mind. I've got the meanest bastards in the Army."

Sarah had laid her notebook by her cup. Hearing the phrase, she jotted it down, and Hackney gave her a quick glance of suspicion, then looked away. He was ill at ease with her: a man accustomed to a man's world. She wondered about his wife. Where was she? The Southwest, Sarah guessed. The major's voice had a flat southwestern sound: maybe Texas.

"When do your men go out?" Tony asked.

"At 6:00 A.M."

"I'd like to see it," Tony said, and Hackney nodded.

Sarah checked her watch: it was two-fifteen. Suddenly she was tired.

"Less than four hours," she said. "Can't we get some sleep before we go?"

"Lady," the major said, looking sharply up, amazed, "nobody said a thing about you going."

"Let her go," said Tony.

Hackney set his jaw. "You can get a perfectly good story here."

"If you don't let her go, she'll find someone who will," Tony said. "Hell, she'll go up there by herself."

Until now she had had no desire to join troops in action. That had been long ago, she thought. She would have preferred to stay back in La Paz. But Hackney's manner challenged her, stirred a rebellion in her, made her long to prove herself again.

"Come on, Lane," said Tony. "She'll be okay, I promise."

Sarah knew it would be best to let Tony do her pleading.

"Come on, Lane. It's only a patrol. You said you hadn't found them yet."

"Okay," the major said. "She can go just for the ride. But she'll have to stay aboard the chopper."

The major's driver led them to a pair of empty bunkers. Inside hers, Sarah found a sleeping bag rolled on a wide, shelf-like bunk. Without undressing she turned out the bunker's light and crawled into the bag.

For what seemed a long time she lay in the darkness listening. There was no sound, except for the faint drone of a mobile generator —a rough hum that soon became part of the silence. She felt cold; she tugged her jacket close around her neck, and drew her knees up in the sleeping bag. Eventually she fell asleep.

Friday the Fifteenth

She was awakened by the sound of helicopters coming in—a harsh, vibrating roar that seemed to shake the earth. It was five-thirty. Sarah left the sleeping bag lying open on her low bunk, laced the heavy boots she had been issued in La Paz, and left the bunker.

The cold air shocked her awake. She stood blinking in the heavy morning fog, shivering. Where were the mountains? The fog obscured everything beyond the bunkers nearest hers.

She looked to her left and saw Tony Jack emerging from the fog.

"They're having trouble landing," he shouted through the roar. Then he was beside her. "They're swinging a light up through the fog and talking them in by radio. We won't be able to leave until the fog lifts."

Tony, eager to be off, had risen early. He was clean-shaven. "Lane sent me to get you. He says you can wash up in his bunker; his driver'll give you coffee."

Fifteen minutes later she stood with Tony and Major Hackney in the clearing beyond the bunkers: a makeshift heliport. She had tied her hair back tightly off her face and rolled it into a secure little knot: her "combat hairdo," Tony told the major.

The choppers, waiting for the fog to lift, had killed their engines. But the air was filled with voices, with the rattle of equipment. Two platoons of infantry would make the trip: two troopship helicopters guarded by two gunships. She heard the soldiers forming in the fog across the clearing: shouts; young voices.

Hackney introduced them to a lanky captain, Philip Nearson, who would lead the operation.

"Jesus Christ, a woman!" She could tell by his voice that he was a New Yorker.

"She's just going for the ride, Phil," Hackney said. "She won't be getting off."

They drew helmets and flak vests from a shed nearby, then walked with the two officers toward the helicopters. The fog was lifting; she could see the slender rotors of one helicopter through the gloom; they seemed too frail to lift the heavy ships.

A boy's voice cut through the fog. "Hey, Grant, there's gonna be a woman on our chopper."

"Shee-it, man."

Men were jostling, moving toward the choppers. She heard the spatter of an engine.

"Watch out for the blast," Hackney yelled, and she felt the rush of wind, saw the dust dance up around her feet.

Nearson, the young captain, took her elbow, boosted her aboard, and Tony followed. They found seats near the front and strapped themselves in.

Sarah patted her jacket pocket, checking for her notebook, then looked about. There were twenty men aboard, maybe more, their faces almost identical beneath their helmets. They were in full gear: packs, which caused their bodies to pitch forward as they sat, and rifles held loosely between their knees. All of them were looking at her, staring. Sarah closed her eyes.

She felt the ship lift off, swinging slightly from side to side as it rose. The sound was a high whine—then, as they gained altitude, a steady, almost reassuring roar, punctuated by the frantic chatter of the rotors.

She opened her eyes. They had stopped staring. Most of the men sat with eyes closed, their heads pushed forward by their helmets. They were not asleep, she knew; simply finding privacy by closing their eyes.

Tony, beside her, tinkered with a camera; Nearson glanced at her, then looked away. They climbed, higher and higher, above the moving fog, northward up the valley. She searched, looking through the wide-open door, for Cochabamba, but saw nothing; the city lay below them. She caught, now and then, glimpses of the mountains, incredibly high and silent. They seemed to Sarah incapable of harboring danger—so calm, so richly covered with trees and greenery. Then she looked about the tense interior of the helicopter, saw the rifles once again, and felt the cold like a hand laid on her neck. She turned up her collar, closed her eyes, and almost dropped off, lulled by the steady roar.

Suddenly—she didn't know how long she had been drowsing—she felt the helicopter drop downward, felt an inward sinking lurch, as if she were in an elevator plunging down, out of control.

She started awake: They were landing. She saw through the open door a rocky landscape, a flat, graveled plain, then trees, stretching thick and heavy up a hillside. They were in foothills—high, but not as high as the great mountains beyond.

The pilot dropped the craft slowly, easily. She saw the ground; sunlight playing off a rocky mica formation. It was clear below; the fog was gone.

Nearson leaned forward and shouted back to her.

"Stay on the chopper when we land. When everybody's out, you can go up with the pilot and he'll fly you around."

She nodded, then glanced toward the door, feeling tense.

They touched the ground; the blast leveled brush in the clearing, sent small rocks and debris flying. Quickly the men crowded toward the door, holding their rifles near their chests, and jumped.

Still strapped in, she watched them: They ran, crouched near the ground, toward the trees. Sarah leaned forward and unfastened her belt.

Tony and Nearson stood. As they passed her, Tony looked down and raised his eyebrows. She winked in reply, and Tony grinned.

Half the men were off, then Tony, then Nearson. She edged forward on the ledgelike seat. When the last man jumped, she left her seat, lunged for the door—then stopped: She felt an upward lurch; the ship was lifting off; it had already left the ground.

Sarah hurled herself out, fell a full eight feet, and lay breathless on the rocky ground. Then she started up and ran scambling for the trees.

"Goddamn it!" Nearson saw her. "I told you not to leave that chopper!"

She reached the trees and stood defiantly before him.

"I'm calling back that chopper, and I'm going to put you on it!"

"You are not!" Sarah shouted. "I wouldn't think of going back. I've been on a thousand trips like this, and I won't be left behind!"

"Atta girl," said Tony.

"I'm sending you back," said Nearson. "Radio!" he shouted.

"I will not go," she said, and she whipped out her notebook. "I have a story to write, and I will not be prevented—"

Tony put his hand on Nearson's shoulder. "Let her stay," he said. "She has more guts than fifteen men. I know her. Let her stay."

Nearson, tight-lipped, glared at her, and Sarah glowered back.

"All right," he said tightly. "Get over in those trees and let's get organized." The captain's face was red. She smiled.

"Yes, sir, Captain!" she trilled, snapping a salute, and she headed for the trees.

"A woman!" she heard a trooper say. "A woman! Shee-it, man."

By nine o'clock they were walking in a loose double column, with Sarah and Tony near the center. They had found what seemed to be a natural path or trail leading up from the flat place where they had landed into the wooded hills.

No one talked; there was only the clank and rattle of equipment as the men walked; the sound of boots scattering small rocks; an occasional low curse when someone stumbled.

Once when the column stopped, Sarah removed the notebook from her jacket and wrote, "Nothing so far. Completely quiet. Beautiful." She had not expected to enjoy herself, but she was struck by what she saw: trees so heavy they nearly blotted out the light; occasional shafts of sunlight pouring down through a fissure in the trees. She wondered what these men were thinking, whether they were aware of all these splendid sights.

They walked an hour in silence, climbing up into the heavy forest, always on the strangely perfect trail. It was almost a path, yet Sarah was convinced—by the quiet, by the beauty—that they were in a place where no other people had ever been.

Two or three times Tony raised his camera to record some scene along the way: a scene looking up the trail, framed by a line of helmets; the pattern of the marchers as they climbed—the line of men arrayed as if they were on a stairway.

Sarah's mind floated off. She was contented; she almost hummed.

"Hey, look at this."

The soldiers closest to Nearson huddled about him: Sarah peered forward, straining to see, and Nearson pointed down toward something just beside their path.

"Somebody's been in here," he said softly.

It was a sort of hut, fashioned of bent-over saplings, covered with broken branches. Sarah followed Tony forward, her notebook ready.

Then Nearson said what the others had noticed also: "See those branches? They're still green."

She felt a chill, then caught herself and jotted down a few lines: the time, Nearson's name and rank. Then: "After an hour or two, found a sort of nest." There was no mistaking it; the ground beneath the arched saplings was scuffed and rubbed. One person, perhaps two, could have rested here.

They walked on, cautiously now. The silence, Sarah noticed, took on a sort of tension, as if all of them, like her, had suddenly realized, *this is serious.*

After two hundred yards, someone shouted from the head of the column; a young trooper, the point man, came back and spoke to Nearson.

"Let's go," the captain said. Quickly they moved forward—up the trail into a flat place, a clearing entirely shaded by the trees.

It was a campsite. A soldier found the spot where a fire had burned, covered over now with loose-thrown dirt. Nearson leaned over the spot, extended his hand: "They were here last night. . . ."

He waved, ordering his men into a circle around the outside of the clearing. Soon he was on the radio, reporting in a low, calm voice what they had found. His message was received without comment.

"Okay, let's wait here," Nearson said when he was finished. He spent a moment bent in conversation with a sergeant, then sent two soldiers scrambling up the trail.

Tony offered her a cigarette.

"Glad you came?"

She smiled weakly. "Ask me later."

"This is the stuff great stories are made of," Tony said.

She made no reply.

The scouts came back; they had seen nothing. The column took up its march again.

This time they walked more slowly and quietly, scanning the trees and brush on either side. After a time Sarah realized that she was listening so intensely—listening for anything—that her head had begun to hurt. She tried to relax and she allowed her mind to wander.

Suddenly, to the rear, there was a shout, a sputter of rifle fire, then silence.

They scattered from the path and dove for the ground.

"Medic!" someone shouted.

"I got him, Captain. Over yonder." The voice came from the rear.

A medic moved back through the column; Sarah and Tony followed.

She wrote the trooper's name in her notebook: Samuels. He was a young black man with a broad face and enormous eyes. Blood was spreading in a slowly growing blot across the chest of his fatigues.

"I saw him stick his face out and I shot him," Samuels said.

They heard Nearson on the radio, reporting to the camp. "We got one of theirs, and we have one man wounded." Then, to no one in particular: "Now they know we're here."

"I shot him dead," said Samuels to the medic. Then, "Man, how come I'm shaking?"

"You're okay."

"Man, I'm shivering," Samuels said. "Look how I'm shivering." Then he died.

"Litter!" the medic called.

"Give me your position," said the radio voice from their outpost miles below, and Sarah heard the captain murmuring his reply.

She was frightened. "Tony," she whispered, "how many do you think there are?"

"I don't know. I hope only that one."

The soldiers swung out into a tight circle, facing outward, finding shelter beneath trees and bushes. Sarah and Tony crawled along beside the path to rejoin Nearson.

"Well, ma'am," the captain asked her tonelessly, "how do you like your job?"

"I wouldn't miss this for anything," she said defiantly. But she was trembling, and she knew Nearson would notice.

"This is a bad spot," he said. "If anybody else is up there, they can fire right down that hill."

They waited, crouched against a large tree, for fifteen minutes.

then half an hour. After several minutes more of silence, Sarah opened her notebook and began to write.

She had filled the page when she heard the sound: a dull concussion. She recognized the sound.

"Jesus, grenade!" someone shouted, and then she saw the flash, a hundred yards above them on the hill. Dirt flew up and scattered, followed by a genie-puff of smoke; before the echo died she heard shouts and more rifle fire.

"Stay down!" said Nearson, and he flung himself against her.

Sarah struggled to break free. From three spots nearby she heard calls for the medics; she could see two soldiers lying near the path, knocked back from their positions by rifle fire; they seemed to be dead.

"Tony?"

"I'm okay."

The din grew louder: The soldiers were firing back up the hill, scrambling from tree to tree to gain protection.

Nearson, moving cautiously, took up his radio and spoke into it, in a voice unnaturally low and calm. He was calling for an air strike.

"Five minutes," came the reply.

"That may be too long," he said.

"They'll never be able to see with all those trees," Tony said.

They waited minutes, listening to the shouts and rifle bursts.

Nearson looked up. "Where the hell is that gunship?"

Immediately they heard its roar, and he answered himself: "Here it comes."

He listened for a moment, then fired a white smoke flare to guide the gunship to the hillside.

In a moment the chopper clattered into the airspace just above them. Six fifty-caliber machine guns, three from each side of the ship, poured out a stream of bullets into the trees above the trail. Four automatic cannons augmented the barrage, blasting chunks of rock high into the air in random patterns, as the shells traced lines across the hill above them.

A third sound joined the cannon blasts: the whoosh of rockets discharged from chutes beneath the runners of the gunship. Sarah could see whole areas of the hill chewed up as if worked over by earth-moving machinery.

"Look up there," Nearson shouted, pointing to the sky.

Through the trees she saw helicopters: troop-carrying craft.

Nearson was on his radio again.

She saw more gunships, circling into position to increase the fusillade. The noise was like a hundred thunderstorms.

"We're going to pull out," Nearson said. "The ships will give us cover. They say there's a big clearing up this trail."

The noise was unbearable: rockets, cannon shells, machine-gun bursts.

Suddenly she saw Nearson wave and men were all about her, scrambling, darting, running toward the clearing up the trail. Several carried wounded soldiers piggyback as they ran.

Nearson pushed Sarah. "Go ahead!"

She began to sprint; she could not see the clearing. She felt as though she were running in slow motion. She ran fifteen yards, stumbling and panting. Then, just ahead, she saw an object bounce into her path.

"Grenade!" someone shouted.

It moved toward her in slow motion, rolling on the path. She could see its square-cut grooves and indentations, like giant scales.

"Move!"

She veered off to the right, half diving to the ground as it exploded.

I'm all right, she thought. She was vaguely aware that Tony had dived behind her.

"Tony? Are you okay?"

After a silence she heard his voice. "I'm not sure," he said. "I don't know."

Then Nearson was beside her.

"I'm all right," she said. "I didn't get hit."

Nearson stared down at her. "You're not hit bad," he told her, "but you're hit."

She looked down at her right arm and saw blood creeping down her sleeve. Nearson took out a handkerchief and tied a snug tourniquet below her shoulder. Then she fainted.

When she came to, the helicopter had landed back at the camp; bearers were lifting the dead and wounded off. She felt a sudden rush of nausea.

As she was lifted off and loaded onto a litter, she saw Nearson and Major Hackney staring down at her.

"Am I all right?" she said.

"You're all right," Nearson said. "You'll have a little scar, but it's up high. You can even wear short sleeves."

She started up and felt, with her left hand, for her notebook.

"Take it easy," Hackney said. "You've lost a little blood."

"How about Tony?" she said, settling back. "Where is he?"

Nearson looked down at her, then at the major, and she knew what he would say.

"I'm sorry," Nearson said.

Brooks Healy, summoned to the Mansion for a late lunch with the President, stepped off the elevator into the West Hall to find Lisa Rattigan waiting for him.

"Lisa, it's good to see you." He kissed her lightly on the cheek. "Will you be joining us?"

"No," she said. "I wanted to talk to you before he comes over." She led him into the sitting room nearby, to the long sofa beneath the fan-shaped window. She sat down and filled two small goblets with sherry from a decanter on the table.

"I'm worried about Carl," she said.

Healy took the glass she offered, but said nothing.

"I've seen him go through a lot," she said, "and I think I understand him—as much as any woman can understand a man."

She looked at him as though uncertain whether to continue, and he nodded, encouraging her.

"I never ask him questions," she continued. "I never have—I mean about his work, about politics. Not even when he's worried and I want to help. But he's always known I'll listen when he wants to talk. And sometimes he unburdens himself, complains—says all the things he's not allowed to say to other people. I'm his escape valve."

She waved her hand. "But all through this latest business he's been so silent, so depressed. The other night I asked two couples over—old friends, the Dick Wheelers, Bob and Julie Arnold. These are people he loves: witty; they take his mind off business, talk about old times. I'd warned them when I called that there was just one rule: no mention of Bolivia; not a word."

She sipped her sherry.

"Usually on evenings like this he's able to forget his worries. But all through dinner he just sat there, barely talking—only enough to answer questions. He didn't smile twice. Of course, the party just died; it was over by ten o'clock—"

Brooks Healy raised his hand. "Lisa, you can't blame him if he's preoccupied. My God, he's—"

"Brooks, stop it, please. I know it sounds petty and trivial, but I know *him*. He's in the grip of this thing and he's depressed. He doesn't know what's going to happen. Men are getting killed. Now he wakes up in the morning and sees pickets in the street—probably the same people who voted for him in the last election. For the first time in his life, he's afraid."

Healy nodded sympathetically. "I know these are terrible days. But he's pretty strong, don't you think?"

She smiled—a slight, wan smile. "The other night I woke up and saw the light beneath his door. It was three o'clock. I went into his room and he was reading." She looked past Healy, remembering the scene. " 'Carl,' I said, 'you've got to get some sleep.' I got into his bed and made him turn out the light. Then I dozed off. Later I woke up again and I could tell that he was still awake, lying there in the dark. I said, 'Carl, are you all right?' and do you know what he said?"

Healy stared at her.

"He said, 'Every morning when I go to the office there's a piece of paper on my desk. It tells me how many nineteen-year-old boys were killed while I was sleeping.' " She shook her head.

Healy stood up and turned away from her. "God knows," he said, "I brood about them too."

"When do you think it will be over?" She asked the question with a hint of challenge in her voice.

"I don't know. Soon, I hope." Healy sat down again, leaning forward to toy with his sherry glass. "If things go well, it could all be over soon. We could have most of our troops home by the first of the year."

"And if things don't go well?"

"I don't know. It could go on for a long time. But there's no use worrying about what *might* happen. We've got enough problems without—"

They heard the elevator doors roll back. The President walked into the room.

"Brooks." He sounded tired. "I'm sorry to keep you waiting."

They shook hands, and Rattigan kissed Lisa.

"What is this, a tryst?"

"I was warning Brooks," Lisa said, smiling. "If he doesn't keep you out of trouble, I'm going to fire him."

"She means it, Brooks." Rattigan smiled, but Healy thought he looked tired—his eyes were flat and strained.

The telephone beside the sofa rang. Rattigan reached for it, and Lisa, waving, started out of the room. Brooks Healy followed her.

"I know there isn't much you can do," she said, almost whispering, "but for God's sake, help him to get out of this."

"I'll try."

"By Christmas—promise?"

He smiled, shrugged in a gesture of futility—and Lisa walked off down the hall.

Over lunch Brooks Healy briefed the President on the OAS talks, which still dragged on.

Listening, Rattigan dawdled at his food, and stopped eating once or twice to rub his face with both hands, wearily.

"We could get a resolution in a minute—unanimously—if it were just a matter of censuring the Chileans," Healy said. "But we don't want a resolution without a troop commitment. That would be words without action, and it would hurt more than it would help."

Rattigan nodded. "So what do you predict?"

"I don't know. They all seem to be waiting for somebody else to make the first move."

A waiter cleared the dishes and served coffee. Rattigan pushed his steaming cup away, rose, and walked to a window. He parted the curtain slightly; the pickets were still there.

"We've offered some rather substantial incentives," Healy said. "But most of them are scared. They're afraid they'll unhinge the left wing in their countries—afraid they'll set off demonstrations, riots—"

"We risked that!" Rattigan's voice almost echoed in the still room. "Will you tell me why we should take risks and why they shouldn't?"

Healy said nothing; he knew the question was rhetorical—that silence was the best reply.

"Brooks, listen to me." Rattigan circled back around the table and took his chair again. "Today is Friday. I want something to announce by Sunday: a troop commitment from the OAS. I don't care how big or small—I want it." He spread his hands on the bare mahogany table and leaned toward Healy. "I want you to call in each one of those ambassadors, one by one, today and tomorrow. Every one. Give them one short message to send back home, and tell them you want a reply before they meet on Sunday. You can tell them that, if no troops are pledged by Sunday, the United States will begin a drastic reappraisal of our programs of assistance—all of them. You can tell them that we are contemplating major revisions in all programs of aid to countries in this hemisphere, and that we are prepared to make substantial reductions. And you can tell them that if they have any questions about the meaning of your statement, they can come to see me. I'll be here."

"Mr. President . . ." Healy spoke slowly, "I just want to point out that that's a short-run tactic. It'll probably work. But the long-run cost, in terms of—"

"Long-run cost!" Rattigan almost shouted. "What about the long-run cost of our being down there, taking casualties while these bastards temporize? Don't talk to me about long-run costs! I'm really tired of all this talk! Now kindly get out there and call them in!"

"All right, sir."

Healy simply stared at the President. Rattigan returned his gaze, but the anger faded from his eyes.

"I'm sorry, Brooks. I know you don't like to play the game this way. It makes it difficult for you. But I want that resolution; I want those troops."

"I know," Healy said softly.

"I can't let this go on, with our troops and Paraguay's the only ones in there. Paraguay! My God—a dictatorship! Carl Rattigan in bed with Badillo!" He shook his head, then stood up, signaling Healy that their meeting was over. Healy stood too.

"Brooks, one more thing." He looked down, and Healy sensed that the President somehow wanted to avoid his eyes. "I'm not going to make policy on the basis of domestic politics." He hesitated. "But I can't ignore the fact that this next year is an election year."

"Yes, sir."

Rattigan looked up. "That's the last time you'll hear me mention that."

Healy nodded, and the two men walked together into the hall. At the elevator they shook hands.

"By the way," Rattigan said, "have you talked to Ab yet?"

"Not yet."

"Give him a call. He's talking to reporters again. Did you see the story in the *Post?*"

Healy nodded.

"I lost my temper when I saw it. I called him and told him to retract. I don't know what he did—or whether he did anything at all. But I want to keep him quiet until this thing blows over. Give him a call; invite him for a drink. Try to make him feel important. He likes you."

"Mr. President," Healy said, "I don't know what I'm supposed to be—the hatchet man or the friendly family doctor."

"You're the friendly family hatchet man," Rattigan said.

When Healy had gone, the President walked back into the empty dining room, crossed to the windows, and peered out, holding back the curtain. Then he dropped it, took a deep breath, and went back into the hall.

Cold winter sunlight shone through the fan-shaped window. It was three o'clock. He stood before the window, studying the scene: a patch of lawn, green despite the winter cold; the gray mass of the Executive Office Building, all columns and balconies and intricate shadows.

He longed to try to take a nap, but there were appointments scheduled for the afternoon; his desk was piled with letters, papers, intelligence reports. And even if he tried, he knew he could not sleep.

He felt a sudden desire for a drink, but shook his head. It was something Rattigan never did. In the Senate he had enjoyed a civilized drink in midafternoon, but as President it was out of the question. It was one of the little disciplines he observed. He sat down in the wing chair, rubbed his face again with both hands, then leaned forward.

The usher answered his ring almost instantly.

"I'd like a drink," he said. "Scotch and water, lots of ice."

Just before five o'clock John Cardwell walked up to Triplitano's office, delivering an advance copy of the latest Gallup poll. The loss of American lives in Bolivia had caused another dip; barely 50 per cent of the people now held a favorable opinion of Rattigan's leadership.

Triplitano, brandishing a big cigar, scanned the figures, then puffed a cloud of smoke. "In the good old days, Friday was a nice day. Now it's the day we get the polls and the weekly casualty list."

"Read the memo," Cardwell said. "I'm not sparing him. This is serious."

"You know me," said Trip. "I don't mind the truth. I just hope you won't rub it in too hard."

He offered a cigar, but Cardwell shook his head.

"John, what do you think of all this?" Trip leaned back in his chair. His expression was casual, but Cardwell knew he wanted a serious reply.

"I don't know, Trip. I guess he had no choice. I guess he did just what he had to do. But I don't like what it's doing to him."

"You mean personally?"

"I mean politically." He pointed to the poll, lying on Trip's desk.

"Suppose he goes in deep, really gets in trouble down there. What would you do?"

"We've talked about that before, and I told you," Cardwell said.

"You wrote campaign speeches about peace. Would you stay?"

Cardwell nodded yes.

"That's still the answer?"

"Yes."

"Why?"

He hesitated. Then: "Because I believe in him. I trust him."

Trip said nothing. He stared at Cardwell.

"He's been good to me," Cardwell added.

"Even if he ends up taking us right into the soup?"

"I try to be an optimist about that."

Triplitano leaned forward and swept the air with his cigar. "Well, prepare to be busy, because he likes you. He trusts you. And when he likes somebody, woe be unto that body."

Trip's secretary walked in and laid a clipboard on his desk: the latest wire-service bulletins. Idly, he flipped through the torn-off paper.

"Jesus, look at this."

Cardwell leaned toward the desk.

"Some guy got killed down there, and Sarah Tolman's been hurt."

Hurt! Hearing her name, Cardwell felt the blood rush from his face.

"Is it serious?" His own voice sounded far away.

"No, but Jesus, what was she *doing* down there? They were really out in the boondocks."

Cardwell's impulse was to grab the clipboard from Triplitano's hands. Instead he walked around the desk and read over Trip's shoulder.

"Miss Tolman, who was only slightly wounded, had been in the country since November 21. She was flown immediately to La Paz for evacuation to the United States."

"She's a hell of a girl," Trip said. "You know her?"

"Very well."

They talked for a moment more, but Cardwell was not listening. He excused himself, leaving the poll with Trip, and went back to his office, feeling an unexpected anger. How could she be so foolish? Take such risks?

Several times during the afternoon he sent Dot Orme to check the ticker for more news of Sarah. There was nothing. He watched the evening news: still nothing.

Finally, at seven-thirty, he went home.

That evening the Senate, meeting late, passed a war-powers resolution approving the President's dispatch of troops to Bolivia. The vote was grudging: not the landslide that the House had given Rattigan. But as the President said to Lisa when he got the news: "It's enough. We have to take what we can get, don't we?"

Saturday the Sixteenth

Sarah's room at Walter Reed Hospital was one of those reserved for high-ranking officers or dignitaries. It was large, private, and handsomely furnished.

She was awakened before dawn by the throbbing in her shoulder, then frightened for a moment by the strangeness of the place. Then she remembered: the hospital. It had been only twenty-four hours, but already Bolivia seemed a long time ago, the memories fuzzy and indistinct. Was it the drugs? By force of will she dredged up the scenes of the past day: the woods high over Cochabamba; a grenade; Tony Jack's strangely flat last words: "I don't know." Impossible. She had slept, escaping the pain and memory through most of the flight back to La Paz. Redwine had been there to see her off, all dignity and sympathy, their clash at the airfield seemingly forgotten. Now *she* was one of the wounded, carried gently on a litter from helicopter to ambulance to transport plane. Redwine promised to send her clothes, her typewriter—all the gear at her hotel—back to Washington.

Tony! She started awake again, stabbed by the memory. She must write his wife—no, call her. Where did she live? And his children. She heard footfalls outside her room, the nurses making rounds before the change of shifts.

The transport plane had had no windows. All through the long flight home she had tried to sleep, fighting pain, nausea, claustrophobia. Most of the others on the flight—youngsters, wounded worse than she—had slept, too. The Army nurses, girls, in baggy fatigues, had moved up and down between shelf-like litters, holding cigarettes for some of the young men, carrying blankets, offering small cups of lukewarm coffee. Once Sarah saw a nurse kneeling by a litter, holding a hypodermic syringe. Watching, she held her breath: If the plane should lurch . . . Expertly the nurse administered the shot, patted her patient lightly on the shoulder, and moved back down the row of litters.

They had landed at Andrews in the small hours after midnight. She remembered only relief at being home, and her sleepiness. And now . . .

There was a soft knock at her door.

"Come in."

It was a doctor, vaguely Spanish-looking. He wore a white smock over his uniform and carried a clipboard.

"You're the reporter—Tolman?

She nodded.

He checked her pulse, scribbled something on his chart, then turned to leave. At the door, he said, "You can go home tomorrow. If it hurts, the nurse can give you something."

She nodded again. Soon she fell asleep.

At noon she awakened, starved and crying from the pain.

The nurse who answered her call gave her a shot and pointed to the flowers—two vases, one filled with spring flowers and the other with roses.

The small one had a handwritten card: *"John and Nancy Cardwell."* She had never met his wife. She smiled and closed her eyes, then leaned forward and picked up the second card: a heavy, almost square envelope with lettering that said only, "Miss Tolman."

The card, deeply engraved in cursive script, read, *"The President."* Not, *"The President and Mrs. Rattigan."* Simply—The President. A lovely gesture. Who had told him? She was touched and flattered—surely it was official and not personal—but somehow she was weighed down by it too, as if it imposed some burden or obligation upon her.

There were two telegrams—one from her office and one, full of worry, from her parents in New York. They would be frantic. She would call to reassure them. After lunch.

The drug spread warmly through her body. She fought sleep. A tray was brought: chopped steak, a salad, milk. She devoured it all, then settled back to sleep.

"Miss Tolman?" It was the nurse lieutenant. "You had a phone call."

"Thank you. Did they—"

"It was the White House," the young nurse added eagerly. "They left the number."

She knew the number. She struggled to dial with her left hand; the nurse took over, dialed, then handed her the phone and reluctantly left.

She wondered who was calling. John Cardwell, perhaps. Or Triplitano.

"Miss Tolman? The President was calling."

She caught her breath. There was a silence, then a clicking noise.

"Sarah? This is Carl Rattigan."

"Mr. President." The title seemed strange to her.

"We've been a little worried about you."

"It's nothing, really. I'll be back at work on Monday."

"Don't you dare think of it. Take some sick leave. The *Times* can well afford it." He was trying to be jovial, she knew. "Why don't you take a rest and then drop in to see me—give me a firsthand report?"

She deflected his invitation: "Oh, Mr.—" She found it strange to use the title—"I'm so confused right now, I'm afraid I'd just waste your time."

"Now, you know that's not—"

"You can get more from my stories. Do you ever see them?"

"Of course," he said. There was an awkward hesitation—as if he had meant to say more, then decided against it. Then, "You're very influential."

She wanted the conversation to be over. The flowers—thank him for the flowers.

He accepted her thanks smoothly, then changed the subject. "I don't think I've ever seen you at a press conference. Don't you have a pass?"

"That's not my beat," she lied. Actually the *Times* gave her free rein, and he knew it.

He laughed. "Well, take it easy. And try not to be so damned brave next time."

"I'll try." And it was over.

The nurse came in—had she been listening outside? Sarah turned away, not wanting to meet the girl's frankly curious stare, not wanting to talk to her. Sarah raised a hand, shielding her eyes.

"Are you all right?" the nurse looked at her sharply.

"I'm fine, thank you."

"If it hurts I can give you a shot."

"Really, I'm fine."

The nurse looked at her, then walked out, and Sarah dropped her hand. She had not wanted the girl to see her crying.

On ordinary Saturdays Lisa Rattigan was able to coax the President away from the Oval Office by midafternoon. When they were fortunate he could rush off to spend the night and Sunday at Camp David; in busier times she would schedule a movie, a game of bridge with old friends—anything to punctuate his work week with some relaxation.

Today, she knew, he would work late. She told the kitchen to prepare a supper of soup and sandwiches, so they could eat whenever he returned to the Mansion. Then she busied herself inspecting the rooms downstairs.

Arlene Sprague and her staff had been busy through the week, dressing the house for Christmas. The columns in the lobby were garlanded with ropes of evergreen, and the crèche—a Neapolitan wood carver's fantasy—had been set up in the East Room.

She walked from room to room, hearing her footsteps resound on the hardwood floors. When they were filled with people, she loved these rooms. But when they were empty, peopled only by guards and cleaning crews, they had the vast, forlorn silence of an empty theater.

She walked into the Blue Room, the oval chamber at the center of the house. Its ornate chandelier had been removed, and two men on ladders were hanging decorations on the tree. When they saw her below, they both looked startled; they were decorators called in from outside, and they had never before seen her in person.

"Don't stop!" she waved and smiled. "Just passing through." The two men smiled, waved back to her, and resumed their work.

Christmas. The coming holiday did nothing to relieve her spirits. The hard knot of anxiety inside her would not go away. She was determined to show a face of strength; to encourage her husband, at least try to be his solace and confidante. But *she* had no confidante; the fact made her feel drained and lonely.

She circled back toward the elevator, passing the lobby guard and smiling.

The decorations were perfect, and yet they gave her little satisfaction. They were for other people: the flocks of tourists who poured through the house each day; the congressmen and dignitaries who would throng the house next week for two preholiday receptions.

She pressed the elevator button, stepped into the well-lighted cubicle, and rode upstairs, making a mental note to call Arlene and praise the decorations.

The upstairs quarters had no decorations—only a few vases filled with greenery. She had asked the staff to keep it simple, to confine their decorating to the state rooms. She gave them no reason, but upstairs she knew Christmas finery would have a cruel meaning—reminding her husband that this Christmas he had little to celebrate.

Her job was to protect him, and she was good at it. It was her talent, one of the qualities that had made the elegant First Lady a minor legend even before her husband sought the presidency.

"She understands him so well," their friends would say. "She knows him better than he knows himself." And in a sense it was true.

So skillful was she at shielding him that at least once she had, she was convinced, saved him from himself—from a misstep, a folly that would have cost him his career.

Lisa stepped into the West Hall, circled it once, and sat down. A servant had left the *Star* on the low table; she picked it up, then idly set it down, in no mood for reading.

Theirs had been a good marriage. Not a perfect one, but good and durable. She had seen too many couples ruined by the pressures in Washington, their lives and careers hurled out of control. She remembered the words of a canny old southern senator, a lifelong bachelor: "Three things can ruin a man in this town. The first is money. The second is power. The third is women."

Her husband could not be tempted by money—he had inherited. Power had come to him easily enough; he had not found it necessary to make too many compromises. He was able, he was tough, he was attractive.

She picked the paper up again, and scanned the headline: PEACE VIGIL STARTS TONIGHT. Her mind strayed backward: women.

There had been a problem. When she had learned about it she had pushed aside the emotions wives are supposed to feel: no shock, no rage, no agony of betrayal. She simply told him what she knew, and then reminded him—as calmly and unemotionally as possible—what it could mean to his career. And she had taken another bold step to see that it would end. He had already begun his drive toward the presidency; both knew that he could not afford a scandal. So it had ended, and without scandal. How long had it been? An age. By now he had surely forgotten it, dismissed it from his mind. . . .

She read the headline again, scanned the story below, then laid aside the paper and walked into the dining room nearby as if pulled by a magnet.

Pennsylvania Avenue below was filled with traffic—Christmas shoppers flocking to the downtown stores. The sidewalk just beyond the high fence was empty, already cordoned off. But across the avenue there was a growing crowd; Lafayette Park was filling with people: the vigilkeepers. She saw a line of park policemen, stretching down the curb, each wearing a black greatcoat and black gloves.

Trees and cars partially obscured her view so that she could not see their faces. The crowd would be tremendous; she knew that already the park was half full, and it was only four o'clock. Most of them were young—probably students out of college for the holidays. They stood in quiet groups, greeting one another as the crowd swelled. There were few signs, but she knew the banners would appear. And there were older people, women bundled heavily against the cold; numbers of clergymen in stiff white collars.

She left the dining room. There was a telephone beside the sofa in the hall.

"The chief usher, please."

She drummed her fingers lightly, waiting for his answer.

"Mr. Carson? Lisa Rattigan." She spoke firmly, with a hint of command in her voice. "I want to close the upstairs dining room for a while. And the family dining room downstairs."

There was the briefest silence, then: "Certainly, madam." She could picture Mr. Carson writing on a notepad as she talked.

"We'll take our meals in the West Hall or in the Yellow Oval Room. If the President has guests for lunch, you can set up a table behind a screen in the State Dining Room."

"Of course," he said. But there was a trace of puzzlement in his voice.

"There's no need to say anything about this. If you get any questions, just say we're having some work done on the floors."

"Of course." He paused. "And, how long would you say this will—"

"Until I tell you."

"Oh, yes, ma'am. Certainly." His voice brightened. "You can depend on us. In fact, we may have some work that needs to be done in those two rooms. I'll check and—"

"Thank you, Mr. Carson." She could count on him.

When she hung up she walked back into the dining room. She stood just inside the doorway, studying the scenic wallpaper that gave the room its special character: hills and forests and waterfalls—some ancient artist's fantasy of early America. In the foreground, soldiers of the Revolution had been painted in, tiny figures standing in stiff formal clusters. But despite their uniforms and weapons, the setting was quiet, pastoral, rivers and green valleys, blue sky.

She was tempted to go back to the window; to study once again the crowd that was gathering in the park, but she did not.

Carl was too busy and distracted to notice where he took his meals. He would ask no questions, she knew, about her attempts to make his life more bearable. And yet she found herself half-wishing that he would. . . .

It was almost six o'clock. She left the dining room, switching off the lighted chandelier and closing the door firmly as she left.

Monday the Eighteenth

With Christmas approaching, Washington's rush hour became an all-day affair. Cars choked the downtown streets, and at every intersection policemen, clad in overcoats and bright orange vests, struggled to keep the traffic moving: only a week until Christmas.

The motorists who clogged Pennsylvania Avenue scarcely noticed, in their eagerness to reach the downtown stores, the peace vigil being kept in Lafayette Square. The vigilkeepers, most of them students and clergymen, their faces red with cold, had hoisted a large banner, lettered in blue: PEACE ON EARTH. They huddled, two hundred strong, beneath the banner. Occasionally someone in the group would raise his voice in song and the demonstrators would join in, caroling for the passersby.

No one paid much attention. Washington had been hardened by years of protest marches, vigils, and demonstrations. The vigilkeepers were earnest, quiet, well-behaved.

The park policemen assigned to the demonstration thought themselves lucky. This was easy duty. They tried to keep a proper official distance, but occasionally they would fall into conversation with the demonstrators. And when they were offered steaming paper cups of coffee by the vigilkeepers, the policemen, almost numb with cold, usually accepted. Hell, why not?

Today, however, the policemen were a little tense and edgy. According to the morning *Post,* this was the day that the President would leave the White House to lead a brief ceremony on the Ellipse: the lighting of the nation's Christmas tree. A leader of the Christmas vigil—a youthful clergyman—had told the press, "We'll be there too." At noon, an extra twenty park policemen came on duty at the square. They formed a line along the sidewalk between the vigilkeepers and the avenue.

And today, when a young man in a ski parka offered coffee to one of the officers, the policeman shook his head.

"Thanks, but no thanks," he said.

In the Oval Office, Anders Martin laid the clipping on the President's desk.

"I've seen it," Rattigan said.

"If you like, sir, you can speak from your office and light the tree from here. The networks can handle it easily enough, and that way—"

"That way I won't have to face a demonstration."

Martin said nothing.

"No," said Rattigan. "I'm going down there." His voice was final. "The worst thing would be to duck it."

"All right, sir," said Martin, frowning. He added, as he left for his own office, "We're laying on lots of agents and park police."

"Why? Hasn't this crowd been peaceful?"

"They have been until now."

"Then why are you so excited? Maybe they'll like what I have to say. I'll be giving them good news. Hell, maybe they'll even cheer."

"I hope so, sir," said Martin, and he left the room.

Downstairs, Dot Orme answered her telephone, then buzzed Cardwell. "It's Sarah Tolman. Can you talk to her?" Cardwell grabbed the phone.

"Sarah?" He assumed that she was calling from the hospital. "How're you feeling?"

"I'm freezing. I'm calling from the Northwest Gate. I thought you might be free for lunch, so I made a reservation for two."

"I'll be right up." Eagerly he got into his coat and left the office, calling over his shoulder as he went, "I'll be at Sans Souci."

In the restaurant he helped her off with her coat, steered her to a table along the wall, and ordered bloody marys.

"Do you see them staring?" he said as the waiter left. "Half the people in this room know you on sight, and the other half are asking, 'Who's the beauty with her arm in a sling?' "

She smiled.

"It's such a nuisance. People say, 'How'd you hurt your arm?,' and I feel foolish answering, 'I have a shrapnel wound.' It's so unfeminine. Maybe I should tell them I fell out of bed."

"Are you all right, really? I'm surprised you're out so soon."

"John, dear, I'm fine."

Their drinks arrived. He raised his glass to hers. She drank, then lowered her eyes reflectively. "Actually it seems a long time ago. Three days ago I was in Bolivia. That's no time, yet now it seems remote. I keep forgetting I was there—repressing it, I guess. And then I look down and see this"— she shrugged, indicating the sling —"and it all comes back."

Cardwell said nothing.

"I was excited when I went down there," she said. "Now I'd like to forget that it exists."

He nodded. "I know someone else who feels that way."

"How is he?" Sarah asked.

"Worried. Unhappy. But I think he's convinced himself that what he did was right."

Cardwell signaled a waiter. They ordered lunch, then turned back to their drinks. When he looked up he saw she had turned even more somber.

"How can he be so sure he's right?" she asked.

"I don't know. You'd have to talk to him. Maybe he'd say that what he did wasn't 'right,' but simply 'least wrong.' He was forced. He tried not to get involved. What he finally did was unavoidable, Sarah."

She made no reply and he continued, speaking almost as much to convince himself as to convince Sarah.

"What could he do? He got a plea for help from an ally. There's the Rio treaty. And the ally is deserving—it's a legitimate government, elected. Far more democratic than some of its neighbors. And it was clear-cut. There was an attack followed by a virtual invasion. He tried to keep out—but there was no way. He was confronted. . . ."

He saw that she was looking remote, tuned-out.

"You're not listening," he said.

"I'm sorry, John. Suddenly what you were saying was so—so abstract, and I was back there."

"Why don't you talk about it?" he said gently.

So all through lunch Sarah, her dark eyes sharp as she remembered, told him what she had seen. She poured out in a rush of words the story of her meeting with Roberto Aguila, the fearsome revolutionary whom she had found intelligent and gentle. She told of standing on the airstrip near La Paz, watching as the dead and wounded were loaded off helicopters to be ferried home—blood and bandages, frightened faces—and the slim gray plastic bags. She recalled the words of Samuels, the black trooper: "Man, how come I'm shaking?" He had died. And Tony.

As she finished, Cardwell saw that her eyes were glistening.

"How can he know he's right?" she said. "He sits up here four thousand miles away and makes decisions based on reasons of state:

treaties, agreements, prestige. Does he consider those dead boys? Does he have the slightest notion of what it's like down there?"

"Of course he does," said Cardwell. But Sarah shook her head.

"How does he decide how many deaths it's worth? Is it worth fifty? Five hundred? Five thousand?"

"So far," he said, trying to check her, "there've been many fewer than those numbers killed. How many? Twenty? Thirty at the outside?"

"In two weeks' time," she said. Sarah stared at him. "You're awfully cool," she said. "Are you that convinced he's right?"

"I don't know," Cardwell said. "I don't know if he's right. I was beginning to think so, but I don't know. The compromise I've made with myself is this: He's the President. I'm a speechwriter, a political type, a pollwatcher. He's entitled to my help in taking his case—whatever it may be—to the people. As long as I can't decide it on the merits, I'll go along and help him."

Sarah was quiet for a moment. "Ve only did vot der leader ordered," she said softly.

Cardwell looked up as if he had been slapped.

"I'm sorry," she said. "But what you said seemed such an easy way out."

"Sarah. Surely you'll at least admit that he *may* be right. That the reasons of state—the so-called abstractions—may still be compelling reasons."

"I know," she said. "When I'm in Washington—when I'm in a room like this"—she gestured toward the chandelier in the richly appointed restaurant—"then it's easy to think he's right. In a place like this, you can talk about a thousand deaths a year and remember that fifty times as many die in automobile crashes. It seems a price that can be paid. I could almost even think that way in the bar of my hotel down in La Paz."

Her voice was husky. "But then I think of the moment when they took us off that helicopter. We'd left a few hours before, and Tony was alive. They were all alive. And then . . ." Her voice trailed off, and Cardwell gazed at her, not knowing what to say.

"I don't know what to think," she said. "I know he may be right. But I know that even if he's right, he's wrong too. Terribly wrong. Does that make sense?"

"Yes, it makes sense," he said. Then, hoping the subject somehow could be changed, he said nothing. They ate in silence.

After a while, he said, "This is a strange town. The best people, the smartest ones, are always the most sensitive ones, and they're all doubters. The only people who hold their positions with certainty, the zealots, are all third-rate or worse. The zealous generals who want to drop the bomb. The zealous liberals who think that if we smile and say our prayers we can have peace.

"But anyone who thinks straight has to have doubts. And the final irony is that the zealots—the third-raters—have the edge. They're certain; they're convinced. The doubters are partly crippled—self-crippled. They're always saying 'On the other hand . . .' And that cripples them."

Sarah looked directly at him. "And you? Have you resolved your doubts?"

"I wish I had," he answered. "But all I've done is try to set some limits on my doubts."

"So you've resolved to resolve your doubts, is that it?"

They laughed together, relieved to find some pretext for lightness.

A waiter brought them coffee, then moved away.

From the corner of his eye Cardwell saw a familiar figure moving across the crowded restaurant: Fred Leonhardt. He was moving toward them, drink in hand, smiling and waving to Sarah.

"Well," said Leonhardt, "how's the Rover Girl?" He bent to kiss her cheek.

"I'm fine, Fred. Just glad to be back."

"And in such company!" Leonhardt boomed, nodding toward Cardwell. "When you left, Sarah, he was little more than "a White House source." Now he's a 'highly placed source.' Or maybe even 'a source close to the President.' "

"Cut it out, Fred," Cardwell said, trying to sound cordial.

But Leonhardt bored in deeper. "John's the fair-haired boy these days," he said to Sarah. "He serves up that good, red-blooded rhetoric you've been hearing."

"Really?" Sarah, sensing the tension between them, tried to seem neutral and disinterested. Cardwell said nothing. What Leonhardt was doing was unforgivable: White House staff men did not bicker among themselves in public places, least of all this one. He wondered who else in the restaurant had heard.

"How about it, friend?" said Leonhardt. "Did you write the speech he's giving tonight?"

"As a matter of fact, Fred, yes."

"Well, don't hold back on us. What'll he say? Is he going to light the big tree with a flame thrower? Will he show up with a knife between his teeth?"

Cardwell glared, determined not to answer. Leonhardt shrugged and turned to Sarah.

"Sarah, it's good to see you. Can we have lunch some day? I think us doves are entitled to equal time."

"Of course," she said. When he had gone she said, "Poor Fred. Sometimes he's such an awful fool."

"He's no fool," Cardwell said, still flushed with anger. "He knows what he's doing. He was letting it be known just where he stands—popping off in here in front of a dozen reporters."

Outside they stood in the sharp wind while Sarah struggled to button her coat with one hand. Then they walked toward Pennyslvania Avenue, dodging crowds of hurrying passersby.

"What about this speech?" she asked, all sharp reporter again. She was always on the job.

"It's not what Fred implied," he said. "In fact, it's quite the opposite."

"Do you want to tell me more?"

"No, but if you'll meet me at five o'clock, I'll take you to hear it."

"I'd love to," she said.

"Come to the Southwest Gate. I'll meet you there."

"I'll be there."

They parted at the corner of Seventeenth and Pennsylvania, and Cardwell walked back to the White House in the cold.

By five-fifteen, when Cardwell and Sarah reached the Ellipse, darkness had fallen, and a chilly wind was sweeping up from the Potomac.

They walked quickly, bending to shield their faces from the wind, and took their places on the fringes of the crowd.

"Do you want to get up closer? I can take you to the press section."

"No, let's stay here," Sarah said.

They were a long way back, about a hundred yards from the brightly lighted stage, where a chorus was already singing carols, filling the time before the President's arrival. The voices, overamplified by loudspeakers, cut the air with a harsh metallic edge.

Cardwell looked past the high dark shadow of the Christmas tree, waiting to be lighted, to the Washington Monument, then back to the shifting crowd. Even in the dark he could estimate its size: about three thousand, many of them families with children. No signs of trouble. But when he and Sarah had walked down from the Southwest Gate, he had noticed an unusual number of policemen: park policemen in their black uniforms trimmed with gold; city police, many of them on small white motor scooters, lining the curb near the Ellipse.

"God rest ye merry, gentlemen,
Let nothing you dismay—"

Cardwell became aware of a stirring in the crowd; television lights blinked on, starkly white. The Marine Band, seated before the floodlit platform, interrupted the choir's singing with a fanfare. The President's car was here.

"There he is!"

The singing trailed off raggedly, the band swept into "Hail to the Chief," and the crowd burst into applause.

Rattigan appeared, followed by Lisa in an orange coat. He was shaking hands with dignitaries on the platform.

"John!" Sarah touched his elbow, nodding to her right. He saw a knot of youths near the rear edge of the crowd. They were not clapping.

"We've got a ringside seat," he said.

More applause.

"Mr. Mayor, Chairman Roseman"—effortlessly, Rattigan ticked off the dignitaries' names—"once again we gather to light the Christmas tree and to launch another observance of the Pageant of Peace. . . ."

Cardwell closed his eyes, listening. The President was reading quickly, moving routinely through the ceremonial portion of the speech.

Then Cardwell remembered. He reached into his pocket and pulled out a copy of the text, an advance copy he'd brought from Triplitano's office to give to Sarah.

Rattigan's voice boomed out across the crowd.

"We cannot forget, this evening," Rattigan said, "that the world's peace has been shattered. American soldiers are on duty tonight in Bolivia seeking to re-establish peace and stability in that beleaguered country, seeking to prevent the tragic situation there from growing into—"

Suddenly, without warning, the chanting started.

"Peace on Earth!"

The youths at the crowd's edge numbered no more than fifty, but they were chanting loudly. "Shut up back there!" someone shouted from the crowd, and Cardwell thought: Oh, God. No brawls, please.

"I wish that I could announce tonight," said Rattigan, ignoring the commotion, "that they are flying home, their mission completed. But I cannot. I can only repeat what I said when I dispatched those troops: They will stay in Bolivia—"

"Peace on Earth!"

"—as long as necessary. But they will stay no longer than necessary."

"Peace on Earth!"

"Indeed," shouted Rattigan, "the day of their return may have been hastened by an action taken this afternoon—"

"Peace on Earth!"

"—by several nations of the Organization of American States."

Flashbulbs were popping near the chanters.

"A majority of those nations have agreed," Rattigan read on, "to join the United States in action to defend Bolivia against aggression. They have voted to dispatch troops to join our troops in a common effort. They have ratified, by their vote today, the judgment I reluctantly made twelve days ago: that the cause of peace—"

"Peace on Earth!"

"This is awful," Sarah said.

"—can only be served"—Rattigan's voice was raspy and harsh, without its customary warmth and fullness. He was angry. "—by a resolute, determined answer to aggression."

These were the words Rattigan had hoped would please his listeners. The United States was no longer acting alone in Bolivia. Yet the words were lost. The chanters, Cardwell knew, could not have heard the President's announcement. And the crowd, restless and distracted, scarcely noticed what the President was saying.

Rattigan spoke on, words about peace and the holiday approaching, but his words were drowned.

"I take great pleasure"— Cardwell, though he could scarcely hear the words, knew that the President was nearing the end —"in lighting, once again, the nation's Christmas tree, a symbol of faith, good will, and our steadfast hope for peace."

Rattigan pressed the switch. A sea of flashbulbs popped and the great tree came to life, sixty feet of brightly-colored lights against the black sky. Seeing it, Cardwell felt a small wave of relief—as if its light could somehow change, erase what had just happened.

But the crowd, upset by the demonstration, had started to break up even before the President stopped speaking.

Cardwell shook his head. A disaster.

People were scattering. The President, not even waiting for the benediction, was hustled off the crowded platform by the agents. The choir struck up again, singing desperately, and then it was over.

"Let's go," said Cardwell.

"No, let's wait a minute," Sarah said. "I want to see if they arrest them."

Reporters flocked to the spot where the demonstrators stood.

But there were no arrests.

The youths, who had stood huddled together even after the crowd broke up, left off their chanting and began to walk, moving through the remnants of the crowd. It was over.

"Let's go have a drink," said Cardwell.

There was a quiet bar in the Hay-Adams, the staid hotel overlooking Lafayette Square.

Tonight, even at the cocktail hour, it was half deserted.

Cardwell helped Sarah off with her coat, carefully remembering her arm.

They took a corner table. The waiter, seeing that they were cold, suggested hot mulled wine. They nodded.

"I'm sorry," Sarah told him. "I know how rough that was for you."

He shook his head. "The roughest part," he said, "is that no one heard it. He was telling them that this OAS move takes some of the pressure off. Those Latin troops will put the heat on Chile, and that could bring the whole thing to an end. It's no longer a matter of old Uncle Sam acting virtually alone." He shook his head again. "But nobody was listening."

"Nobody was listening," she said gently. "And none of them will listen until he says what they want to hear, that he's bringing those troops home. All of them. That's what they've got to hear."

Their drinks arrived, the two mugs sending up clouds of spicy steam. They toasted, and after a few sips Cardwell felt warmer, almost cheerful.

"Well," he said, "I guess it could have been worse. It didn't last a minute. It was off-camera. And there was no rough stuff—no fighting, no arrests."

"Your kind of demonstrators, huh?"

"I won't go that far."

But Sarah was serious. "Somebody around this town," she said, "once stated a law: If a situation can get worse, it will get worse."

"Tolman's Law?" He tried to smile.

"No, I'm serious. This may not have been so bad. But it will get worse. Unless he turns around and—"

"It's a lousy law," said Cardwell. "And I want to change the subject."

So they talked of other things, careful not to return to what had happened on the Ellipse. While she talked, he half listened, nodding now and then, gazing always at her gravely perfect face: her large dark eyes and wide, expressive mouth. And while she talked, he was thinking. She is beautiful. Why is she alone?

He asked her interviewer's questions: about her life, her crazy love of danger, her choice of a newspaper career.

Much later Cardwell looked at his watch and was amazed: more than an hour had passed.

"I'm sorry," he said, "I've got to go." Nancy, he knew, would call him at the office, wondering about his plans. "Can I drop you anywhere?"

"No, thanks. I'm going just a few blocks to the office, and I need the exercise."

"You're not working. Not with that arm?"

"Not really. I just want to see some friends—and see if I can type with one hand."

They went out into the cold.

On the curving driveway leading to the sidewalk, Sarah, walking ahead of Cardwell, missed a step. She flailed her free arm, fell helplessly, and Cardwell caught her.

"Are you all right?"

He let her rest against him.

"I'm fine. I just went toppling. Bad balance with one arm."

He caught her scent again, the rich perfume that he identified only with Sarah—musky and oriental.

He let her go.

"Let's keep in touch," she called as she walked off up Sixteenth Street. "Thanks for the drink."

Cardwell stared after her for a moment, then walked back toward the White House, skirting the edge of Lafayette Park, where the peace vigil was still in progress. In the distance he could hear a carol.

He went straight to his car and drove home, still feeling the warm imprint of Sarah's body against his chest.

Alone in his office, thinking of Rattigan's plight, Abner Hoffman smiled. He felt not the slightest bit of sympathy for Rattigan: only the hope, which had been building in his mind for many days, that he would not be linked in the press or in the public mind to Carl Rattigan's blunders. He must let it be known, in small ways and large, that Rattigan's policy was not *his* policy; that Rattigan had made decisions without the counsel or agreement of his Vice President. He must signal his independence—soon, before the situation in Bolivia worsened.

He swung his great chair back to face his desk, stretched, then raised his heavy frame out of the chair. Time to go home.

The agents in the hall stood when he appeared.

"Mr. Vice President."

"Gentlemen! The stores are open late. Take me home and you'll still have time to do some Christmas shopping."

They fell in behind him, following him down the hall toward the elevator, the ground-floor exit, and his big car.

As the Vice President's car pulled onto Pennsylvania Avenue, turning left, he looked out and saw the crowd in Lafeyette Park. The student vigil. They were gathered, two hundred strong, near their long white-and-blue banner: PEACE ON EARTH.

Hoffman leaned forward. "Let's turn around. I want to go over there." He pointed.

His driver, with a slightly puzzled raising of the eyebrows, swung the limousine sharply in a U turn.

In a moment the car stopped along the curb at Lafayette Park, and Hoffman emerged, smiling his brightest smile.

He shook hands first with the policemen who stood shivering in the cold.

"Officer? Abner Hoffman. Good to see you." And, in answer to their startled looks: "I was just on my way home and thought I'd stop to say hello."

The vigilkeepers recognized him instantly.

"It's Hoffman!" someone shouted. Hoffman smiled and waved.

Someone began the chant: "Peace on Earth! Peace on Earth!" But it was ragged and weak; most of the demonstrators were too stunned and curious to join in. Hoffman moved across the sidewalk and plunged into the crowd, pumping hands and smiling, working the crowd as if they were a welcoming committee of voters along an airport fence.

"Good evening. Abner Hoffman. Just thought I'd drop over to say hello and Merry Christmas."

He was at his folksiest, grinning and at ease.

"I know you young folks must be cold. How do you stand it? Good evening. I'm Abner Hoffman." He moved among them, murmuring and smiling. The Secret Service agents followed him, their faces blank, impassive.

Toward the middle of the line, Hoffman raised his voice, eager to be heard by all of them.

"I certainly admire your spirit," he called out. "I really do."

A clergyman, one of the leaders, stepped forward.

"Mr. Vice President, we're not sure what this is," he started.

Hoffman beamed and shook his hand; but the clergyman continued, his Adam's apple working nervously above his stiff white collar.

"I mean—did somebody send you out here? Is this—is this a put-up job?"

"Yeah, what is this?" someone shouted. "Peace on Earth!" someone else shouted, trying to set up the chant. But the sound died.

Hoffman raised his hand for silence.

"I can tell you why I'm here," he said calmly, still smiling. "I was on my way home, and I—"

"Does Rattigan know you're here?" someone yelled.

"No," Hoffman said sharply. "I'm on my own. The President doesn't clear everything he does with me—and I don't clear everything I do with the President."

He paused, letting the words sink in.

"The President has his views; and I have mine."

"How about Bolivia?" someone called out.

Hoffman shook his head. "No, no speeches. I just want to say that I admire what you're doing. I hope it has a good effect. And I think it will—if you stay with it long enough."

He had already begun moving down the line of demonstrators once again, heading back toward his car. En route, he shook a few more hands. As he started into his car, there was a scattering of applause from the crowd. Hoffman straightened up, waved right and left, then ducked into the car.

He relaxed in the big back seat, and his car sped toward Georgetown.

Suddenly he felt free. It was a good feeling.

Wednesday the Twentieth

Brooks Healy arrived fifteen minutes early at the Metropolitan Club on Wednesday and took the elevator directly to the top-floor dining room. He avoided the lounge on the second floor with its dark walls, its great leather chairs, and its air of slightly stuffy camaraderie: He wanted to be waiting when Abner Hoffman arrived for lunch.

Healy stepped off the elevator, nodded to the dining room captain, and chose a table in a quiet corner of the vast and lofty room. It was after one o'clock; the dining room was almost full, but the other men were finishing their lunch. He and Abner, Healy guessed, could have a quiet conversation.

Brooks Healy was normally an assured man, but today he was particularly confident, for he understood an axiom of political life in Washington: A Vice President has no power.

Healy, not a cruel man, turned that thought gently over in his mind as he studied his menu. Carl Rattigan had chosen him to deal with Hoffman because he had finesse, could handle it delicately without causing Hoffman too serious a loss of face.

Even though Hoffman was above him in the official hierarchy, Healy held all the power; he spoke directly for the President. But he would speak softly.

He looked up to see Abner Hoffman coming toward him, a giant, rather shambling man, almost swaying as he walked among the tables. He was early, too.

"Mr. Vice President." Healy rose, offering his hand.

"Hello, Brooks." Hoffman shook hands, sank into his chair, and glanced around the room, nodding to friends he saw as he studied the surroundings.

"I'm sorry to make you change your luncheon plans," Healy began, "but—"

"No problem, Brooks," Hoffman interrupted, waving his hand as if in forgiveness. "I know you must be doing the Lord's work."

They chatted as they waited, the usual trivial talk of men who are marking time, who know that their small talk must soon give way to serious matters. They talked, guardedly but pleasantly enough, about the weather, their Christmas plans, half a dozen other topics of no consequence.

Halfway through lunch, Hoffman laid down his fork. "Well, Brooks," he said, "do you want to tell me why we're having lunch together? Should someone else be here? He asked you to see me, didn't he?"

"Yes, Ab, he did." Healy was grateful to Hoffman for being so direct. Now it would be easy. And because they were in such a public spot, surrounded by acquaintances, there would be no scene.

"He called me this morning. He saw in the *Post* that you're speaking tomorrow at the Press Club. He said you haven't submitted a text for him to see. Frankly, he's a bit worried."

"That I'll denounce him?"

Healy ignored the thrust. "He's worried because he thinks it's important, while we're in the middle of an international crisis, that the government speak with one voice."

Hoffman reached into his pocket, pulled out a big cigar and lit it, sending a curl of smoke toward the high ceiling. He puffed contentedly, turning the cigar to get an even ash.

"He'd like to see your speech, Ab. The advance text."

"I don't have a text," Hoffman said. "I'm going to speak as the spirit moves me, off the cuff, extemporaneous." He puffed again on his cigar. "A good old Oklahoma stump speech, Brooks, before the National Press Club. No speechwriters, just divine inspiration, like an Oklahoma preacher."

Healy smiled politely, but his voice was serious.

"Ab, he knows how you feel about what he's decided—about the troops. He knows you disagree with him, and he understands that."

"He does?" Hoffman's tone was broad, almost mocking.

"But this is an exceptionally difficult moment. I don't have to tell you that the Chileans are watching. They're watching our every move, probing to see if we show any weakness. If they should read that you—"

"Bullshit."

"I mean it, Abner. You could prolong this thing if you're not careful. You could—"

"Bullshit." Hoffman leaned toward Healy. "Why don't you cut out the phony diplomatic rigamarole? He's not just concerned about Chile. He's worried about his political image. He doesn't want to be embarrassed. He sent you over here to threaten me, didn't he?"

"No, Abner." Healy shook his head, and Hoffman settled back in his chair, shifting his bulky frame and puffing stubbornly at his cigar. "He knows your position," Healy went on. "He knows you're not going out of your way to support him publicly. But he wants you to keep your disagreement *private,* between the two of you. I don't think that's unreasonable."

"He wants to muzzle me, is that it?"

"He wants you to promise that you'll keep it private. No public statements. No public brawl."

"And if not? If I refuse?"

Hoffman was making it difficult, challenging him directly.

"Brooks, Brooks, old friend. Cut out the bullshit. You're here to threaten me. Don't be such a gentleman about it. He's going to scratch me off the ticket. Isn't that it?"

"I think I can say," Healy went on, "that as far as your place on the ticket is concerned, it's a sure thing. You're on. Assuming, of course, that there's no unpleasantness. No public squabbling over policy. He won't break up a good team."

"The carrot instead of the stick, Brooks?"

Healy ignored him and continued, speaking slowly. "I think you know what that means for the future, Ab. You'd be in line for the nomination the next time around. And you'd probably have his support. He thinks you're—"

Hoffman laughed: a big, body-shaking laugh that came from deep within him. Then he laid his cigar aside, rubbed his eyes, and shook his head, still grinning.

"Brooks," he said, "if you can believe that kind of hogwash, I don't want you negotiating with the Russians!" He laughed again. "You think he'd support me? He hates my guts! He's letting *you* give me all these assurances so *he* won't have to honor them! Good old Carl!"

A waiter, seeing that they were ignoring their food, took their plates away and brought them coffee.

"I'm sorry, Ab," said Healy. "I'm sorry you feel this way but—"

"Suppose I refuse to keep my mouth shut. Suppose I tell the Press Club just exactly what I think. Suppose I don't make the pledge of silence that you're asking. He'd dump me."

"You said it," Healy answered. "Not me. I think you know the result."

"And you didn't come to threaten me?" Hoffman's resistance was far stronger than Healy had expected. He would have to use some muscle after all.

"Ab, excuse me for being candid," he said, "but I'm not sure you've got much choice. I don't want to give you an elementary civics lesson; you know the system. The Vice President just doesn't go about making policy on his own. He's on the President's team, and the President is captain of the team. If you openly crossed him, you'd be violating every precept of political tradition."

He eyed the Vice President seriously.

"Also, you don't have any power to act, even if you do denounce his policy. It would be self-destructive. You'd be crossing the President in a time of trouble. You'd be read out of the party. The country would react. You'd be the villain."

He paused, studying Hoffman's face for his reaction, but he saw none.

"You don't have any cards, Ab," Healy said softly. "You just don't have any cards." He'd not wanted to be so blunt, but Hoffman had forced his hand. Well, it couldn't be helped. Maybe candor was the best, even the kindest, tactic.

Hoffman toyed with his cigar. He said nothing for a moment. Then he began speaking, quietly and slowly.

"Brooks, who's the ranking authority in the vice presidency right now? It isn't you. You're a nice fellow. You may be a fine Secretary of State. But you don't know any more about this office than a bird knows about a bull. And it isn't him, either." Hoffman waved his cigar, now, over his shoulder in the direction of the White House. "He's President. He's smart and shrewd and handsome, but he's no expert on my office."

His voice went even quieter. "I'm the expert. I'm the expert because I'm the Vice President. Not you, and not him."

"Ab, I understand that. But—"

"Now, you just hold on. I've learned something about my office in these past three years. Lord knows, there's not much else to do when you're Carl Rattigan's errand boy." He shrugged, as if to say it didn't matter.

"What I've learned is this: The Vice President has no power—*if he thinks about his future!*" He flourished his cigar, and his voice rose. "But if he just drives that from his mind, why, it's a miracle! He can stop being the President's errand boy. Just like that! And do you know what he becomes when he disregards his future?"

Healy shifted uneasily in his chair.

"He becomes," Hoffman said, *"the second most powerful man in America."*

Hoffman let the phrase hang echoing between them. Then he continued. "Everything you say may be correct, Brooks. *If* I think of my future. If I cross the President, he can make it difficult for me with the party. He can certainly drop me from the ticket next year. And he can try, probably with some success, to make me look bad to the public as a whole. But Brooks, all that stuff matters only if I care about my future."

The dining room by now was nearly empty. Hoffman leaned forward and smashed his cigar into the ashtray.

"But if I don't give a damn about my future, none of that counts! I'm still the Vice President! Now, I'm going to tell you one other thing that I've learned about this job.

"The vice presidency is a joke to everyone in Washington. When I was on the Hill, I thought it was a joke too. But 99 per cent of the people don't live in Washington. They live in Cleveland, Ohio, where I made a speech last week. They live in Savannah, Georgia, where I spoke three weeks ago. And they live in Minneapolis, where I gave a speech the next day. In three years in this job I've traveled half a million miles. I've given two hundred speeches outside of Washington. And nobody out there treated the vice presidency like a joke. They all thought I was No. 2 in this government of ours, No. 2 in the country. They treated me with great respect."

He leaned back, palms flat on the table, and stared at Healy.

"Great respect, Brooks. So this is what you can tell the President: You tell Carl Rattigan that he can't hold the future over me for just one simple reason—I've chosen not to think about the future. I think he's making a major, tragic mistake. I think that you, Brooks, are helping him make that mistake. And I'm going to speak my mind about it! This little speech tomorrow is just a beginning. Just a little toe-dipping, to let you boys know that I mean business. And the American people are going to listen to me, Brooks! They're going to see me on television. They'll see my picture on the cover of *Time,* and they'll read what I've got to say. And if they agree with me, maybe I can help turn you fellows around. Maybe I can't—but maybe I can."

Healy sat stunned.

"You know," said Hoffman, sitting forward again, "the President doesn't have as much power as he thinks he has. What can he do to me? Call me a scoundrel? Drop me from the ticket? Why, my old Senate seat is opening up in Oklahoma three years from now. Even if Carl gets re-elected with some other fellow on the ticket, do you think he can stop me from winning back my seat? I'd campaign up and down that state. I'd campaign on the slogan, 'He had the guts to stand up to the President.' Not that I was right or wrong, but *that I had the guts*. And I'd *win*."

After a long silence, Healy shook his head. "Ab, I'm sorry you feel the way you do. I'm truly sorry. But if you make that speech . . ." He hesitated, wondering if he should show *his* anger, whether he should tell him that he was undermining a good man and an important cause, that Rattigan was right and that he, Hoffman, was dead wrong, however convinced he was to the contrary. But it was no use. At this point, anger would only end his usefulness as honest broker between these two strong men. And, Healy believed, there would be further need for such a broker before much more time would pass.

"It's late," said Hoffman, rising. "Thanks for lunch." As if nothing had happened.

"No hard feelings?" Healy rose to shake hands.

"No hard feelings, Brooks. Please believe that." And he was gone, shambling out as easily as he had entered.

For a few minutes after he had signed his check, Healy remained at his table, trying to gather his thoughts. He had come here expecting to work his way with a few gentle strokes. But abruptly he had been turned around, and by a country politician.

It was two-thirty, late. He rose, walked out of the dining room to the elevator, and descended to the ground floor of the club.

He had come here feeling that he and the President had all the cards. Now, as he stepped into his long, black limousine, he wondered if he and Carl Rattigan had any of the cards.

Thursday the Twenty-first

Less than two hours after Abner Hoffman's luncheon speech to the National Press Club on Thursday, the Washington *Star* was on the newsstands with a banner headline—V.P., PRESIDENT CLASH—and a subheadline beneath: Hoffman Reveals Opposition to Bolivian Venture.

At the White House, secretaries congregated around the news tickers, tearing off stories about the Vice President's speech for the President's aides to read. The press lounge filled with reporters, gossiping eagerly about the speech, waiting impatiently for Gary Triplitano's afternoon briefing. What would the White House say?

John Cardwell took a call from Sarah Tolman.

"What do you think of this development?" she asked.

"It's incredible." He had the wire service stories spread before him on his desk.

"Well, I know this puts the President in a difficult position, and I'm sorry for that. But as a reporter, I have to tell you it's the best thing that's happened in this town in years. God, it's fascinating!"

"Were you there?"

"You know, I almost never go to the Press Club; it's not my favorite place. But I'd been away so long—I wanted to see people. And I had this funny feeling that Hoffman would be worth hearing. Ever since that off-the-record session at his house in November, I've had the feeling that sooner or later he'd get it out in the open—this thing with the President."

"Well, he's certainly done that, hasn't he?"

"It was a strange speech, really. He just rambled on. People were in a holiday mood. They weren't expecting anything serious. He told some of his Oklahoma stories, kept it light and funny; had everybody laughing. Then at the end, boom: He turned serious for five minutes, as if it were all an afterthought."

"Don't be fooled," said Cardwell. "He knew what he was doing."

"Of course he did! He's really a master. Even though people think he's some sort of country bumpkin."

"That's to his advantage, and he knows it."

It was in the last five minutes of his speech that Hoffman had dropped the phrases that made clear his disagreement with the President, the phrases that made the headlines: "'Dispatch of Troops a Tragic Blunder,' Hoffman says"; "President Faces Rising Tide of Opposition."

"What you've read in those stories," Sarah said, "comes mostly from the question-and-answer session after the speech. You should have seen it: People had settled back for a lightweight, funny speech, and suddenly they were bolt upright, scrambling for their question cards and scribbling furiously. Abner looked so calm and innocent—he must have enjoyed every minute of it."

One question, read to the Vice President by Pete Wellfleet, the Press Club president, put the issue squarely: "Do you realize that your remarks today could mean the end of your political career?"

Abner Hoffman, speaking slowly, had answered, nodding, "I know that. But it might do something else. It might bring about some changes in a policy that I believe is wrong—dead wrong. And that's more important to me now."

Before he finished, an Associated Press reporter ran from the Press Club ballroom toward the telephones, followed by Reuters and the UPI.

"I've never seen anything like it," Sarah said. "Suddenly it was over. We were all left wondering whether we had really heard it, and Abner strode out, surrounded by his Secret Service agents."

"Sounds like a great piece of theater," Cardwell said. He tried to suppress his feeling of grudging admiration for Ab Hoffman: The old bastard—he had style. And guts. "Are you going to write about it?"

"You bet I am," said Sarah. "Do you want to make a statement—as a 'highly placed source in the White House'?"

"I'd better not."

"All right, you've missed your chance. I'll call somebody else." And she hung up.

His next call was from Anders Martin.

"John, I'm calling every member of the staff. The President doesn't want any staff member to comment to the press, on or off the record, about the Vice President's remarks."

"Andy, how's he taking it?"

There was a brief silence. Then: "He's mad as hell."

Gary Triplitano started his briefing thirty minutes early to accommodate the large crowd of reporters that had gathered during the afternoon.

Television cameras and lights had been set up. He cleared his throat and stared into the lights.

"I have no formal statement. I'll take your questions."

Fifty hands went up.

"Trip, will the President reply to the attack that the Vice President made on him today? Will he have any statement?"

"No, he won't have a statement."

"Well, can you describe his reaction?"

A few reporters laughed. Trip ignored them. He answered carefully, referring unobtrusively to a typed page on the podium before him.

"The President, of course, regrets that the Vice President has seen fit to use a public forum to express his disagreement with the President. He values advice and opinion from all his advisers, and he respects that advice even when it is in disagreement with his decisions. But the President feels strongly that such matters should be a matter of confidence between the Commander-in-Chief and his advisers. He feels that when one of his advisers breaches that confidence, the national interest is not well served and the effectiveness of that adviser, necessarily, is lessened."

The words were bland, devoid of color, bureaucratic. The reporters scribbled dutifully, eager for Trip to finish so they could resume their questions.

"The President," Trip continued, "acknowledges the Vice President's right to his opinion and convictions. But he wants it to be clear that the Vice President's remarks reflect a personal, not an Administration, viewpoint. The President, in his constitutional role as Chief Executive and Commander-in-Chief, will continue to make decisions based on what he believes to be the best interests of the American people; he will be swayed by no other considerations."

The hands went up again.

"Trip, you used the phrase, 'a breach of confidence,' or something similar. Is the President saying he can't trust the Vice President?"

"I won't comment on that."

"Trip, two questions. The Vice President is elected like the President. Does the President consider him no more than 'one of his advisers'?"

"I'm sorry, but—"

"I'm not finished. Part two: You say, 'the effectiveness of that adviser, necessarily, is lessened.' Does that mean Abner's had it?"

The crowd of reporters guffawed, and Triplitano, despite himself, broke into a grin. When he recovered himself he said, "Gentlemen, I'm not going beyond my statement. You'll have to make your own interpretations."

"Trip, does the President plan any rebuttal of the Vice President's speech today, or any kind of retaliation?"

"On the first part, I have no information," Trip replied. "And on the second part, the answer is an absolute, categorical no."

Gamely, persistently, the reporters sought answers that went beyond Trip's statement. But he was adamant. The briefing ended quickly, and the reporters raced to their telephones and cameras. Even without help from the press secretary, they could read between the lines: The President was furious. He was making it clear—though in the politest language—that henceforth, Ab Hoffman would be considered "less effective"—and that the President would not be budged by Hoffman's public pressure.

It was, as Sarah had said, one of the best Washington stories in years. The reporters phoned in their stories; the broadcast men, caught in the blue-white glare of floodlights, filmed their reports. When they had finished, they stayed at the White House, eager to see if anything more would happen; they gathered in tight clusters to discuss, over and over again, the day's developments. And over and over, they spun variations of one question: How did Carl Rattigan really react—and what would he really do?

When he was about to leave his Oval Office to return to the Mansion, the President called Anders Martin in.

"I don't want you to say anything to anybody," he told Martin, "but I want Abner off the list, and I want you to take care of it."

"Sir?"

"I want him off the list—I don't want to see him over here. I don't want to see him at parties, dinners, meetings, anything."

Without any question, Martin scribbled a note on the clipboard he always carried. Then he looked up at the President.

"How about Cabinet meetings? How do you want to handle that?"

"I don't want to handle it. You handle it. Just don't notify him, I suppose."

"Thank you, sir. I'll take care of it."

When Martin had gone, Rattigan spun slowly around in his great swivel chair to face the tall windows behind his desk.

It was dark outside; he could see nothing but his own reflection in the polished window glass.

He was not angry any more. The rage and anger he had felt earlier, reading the news accounts of Hoffman's speech, were gone. Now he felt almost no emotion. There was no need to denounce or attack or humiliate Ab Hoffman. He would simply freeze him out, ignore him.

Actually, he had no choice. How could he trust Hoffman? How could he admit Hoffman to the inner councils, trust him with secrets, when the man had openly announced his disloyalty? Why give him material for another hostile speech? Just let him rave. Let him complain, pop off, make speeches—until he realizes it will do him no good, that no one listens, that this sort of pressure doesn't work. And meanwhile, cut him off—isolate him; freeze him out. There was nothing else to do.

He heard Sheila Roundtree enter, and he swung around. She was carrying a stack of letters.

"Just leave them on the table," he told her. "I'll sign that stuff tomorrow. I'm going home."

Sheila buzzed, and his agents appeared to escort him back to the Mansion.

"Good night, Mr. President." She tried to sound cheerful.

Back in her office she opened one of the french doors and stood in the cold air, watching the President walk through the colonnade, flanked by his agents. It was a ritual she often observed at the end of the day. What did he look like, walking slowly, surrounded as he was? Like—a prisoner. She shook her head, then closed the door.

Nancy Cardwell, freshly coiffed and gowned, turned toward her husband as he drove.

"Why are we invited to this party? Do you know her?"

"I met her at that dinner for Badillo. She was at my table."

On this night, the party to which invitations were most coveted was one to be given by Annette Michaelson at her great house on Kalorama Road. It was an annual affair; many years before, Mrs. Michaelson had thrown the first one to mark the birthday of her husband, Oscar. His friends, the great and famous of the capital, had come, enjoyed themselves—and the party had become a Washington tradition. Now, even though Oscar Michaelson had been dead for more than twenty years, the tradition was maintained.

They drove down Massachusetts Avenue. Nan said suddenly, "You're always so quiet now."

"I'm sorry. I was thinking about Hoffman."

It was true. They talked less and less these days. The growing distance between them troubled Cardwell when he thought about it, but the problem seemed beyond them both. Earlier tonight, dressing for the party, he had talked excitedly about the day's events, sketching the growing cleavage between the President and his Vice President, until he realized that Nancy was only half attentive, preoccupied with her preparations for the evening. Finally, feeling rebuffed, he had gone silent.

The Michaelson house was a Norman castle, built of sandstone and granite, set well back from the street. It was enormous, too big for Annette Michaelson and her staff of servants. When she died it would probably become an embassy residence, like so many of the houses on her street. They parked and walked in the cold, past half a dozen Cabinet limousines, up to Annette's house.

"Mr. Cardwell! This is your wife?" Mrs. Michaelson herself, in a gold caftan, was at the door. "Do come in, and try to find someone who isn't talking about that awful speech today. I'm afraid it's the only topic tonight, but isn't it exciting? Someone, do take their coats." They heard a babble of voices, laughter, orchestra music. "When I see Abner I'm going to scold him, Mr. Cardwell," she said brightly. "I've known him for years. But don't you think it's crude, his carping like this? Like a couple having a spat at a party."

Deftly she waved them farther inside, toward a great drawing room that was filled with people.

The crowd spilled through the tall glass doors at the end of the room into a tent that had been set up to enclose the terrace.

"How old do you think she is?" Nancy asked.

"Seventy. I don't know."

"She beautiful, don't you think?"

There were at least three hundred people at the party. Cardwell saw Cabinet officers, Supreme Court justices, senators—all friends of Annette Michaelson's: busy men, Cardwell suspected, who professed a hatred of big, crowded parties—but who were enjoying this one.

The party went late and the crowd stayed, lured by the prospect of the buffet supper to be served at midnight. And Cardwell learned that Annette Michaelson had been right; there was only one topic: Abner Hoffman's speech. Why had Abner done it? He was a brilliant man, a shrewd man. How could he so forget himself—let his frustrations burst through this way? The duty of Vice Presidents is to suffer in silence, isn't it?

Once, scanning the crowd as he listened to more talk of Hoffman's indiscretion, Cardwell saw Sarah Tolman. She was standing near the tall doors that led into the ballroom-tent. She wore a bright orange sari, which set off her dark hair and her rich olive skin. Her injured arm was caught up in a sling made of the same bright fabric: a touch of glamor. She was talking to a tall man whom Cardwell didn't know: Were they together? He saw her touch the tall man's sleeve, tilt her head back, and laugh.

Later, after the midnight supper, there was dancing. The crowd began to wane, and Cardwell suddenly felt tired.

He found Nancy in the tent, finishing a dance with a young man he did not know. The music ended; Cardwell shook hands with her partner and exchanged perfunctory pleasantries; then he and Nancy were alone.

"Come on, let's go," he said. "It's getting late."

"Late? It's barely past midnight!" Her face was glowing.

"Nan, I've got to work tomorrow."

"We never go anywhere. And then, when we do, you—"

"Nan, I don't want to argue."

"I want to stay. I'm having fun. For a change!"

Abruptly he turned to walk away. Nancy followed him.

"Are you going to leave me here?" she said.

"I'm going to find a quiet spot somewhere. When you finish playing belle of the ball, we can go home."

Back inside the house he climbed the broad stairs in the center hall, eager to escape the music and the crowd, suddenly weary of seeing the same faces; weary of the endless introductions, smiles, handshakes, small talk, repetitive political chitchat.

There was an open door near the top of the stairs; he caught a glimpse of bookshelves and dark wood paneling, warmed by lamplight. The music and the voices downstairs seemed remote and far away.

He stepped inside.

The room, he realized, was Oscar Michaelson's study: filled with his books and pictures, left here even though their owner had been dead for years. There was a round table in one corner, covered with dark velvet, crowded with photographs in silver frames: Michaelson with Truman, Michaelson with Kennedy. A letter from Eisenhower that began, "Dear Oscar—"

"He was a great man, wasn't he?"

"Sarah!" He recognized her voice before he turned and saw her.

"I'm not a very good dancer with this damned arm, so I found a place to hide." She was sitting in a large chair, holding a leather album open in her lap.

"It's amazing—what a life he had. Someone told me that every President from Truman on offered him a Cabinet post—and he refused them all. He thought his advice would be worth more if he were independent—if he could tell the President what he thought without risking his job."

Cardwell said nothing.

"You get a real sense of his personality, don't you? Here, look at this." She leaned forward toward the low table before her chair and lifted the lid of a vermeil cigar box. There was an engraved inscription. Cardwell leaned forward as Sarah read aloud: "'Two roads diverged in a yellow wood. . . . I took the one less traveled by, and that has made all the difference.' Given in love and admiration to Oscar Michaelson by his wife, Annette. December 1956.'"

"That's nice."

"It's so touching, and rather formal. And she didn't say just 'love,' but 'love and admiration.' Think of that, after so many years of marriage. I almost cried."

He had sunk onto the arm of the big chair where Sarah sat, and was leaning forward, reading with her. Now she lowered the lid gently, leaned back, and returned the album to the tabletop. He caught the clean scent of her hair and sensed, leaning toward her, that she was uncomfortable.

"I met your wife," she said. "She's very lovely."

Abruptly he stood up.

"She seemed to be enjoying the party."

"Yes, that's one thing she does enjoy."

He felt as if he were standing in a shrine: a shrine not only to the memory of Michaelson, the rich Washington lawyer, but to the woman he had married—the remarkable Annette, still full of life and energy even though she was a widow now, and in her seventies. Love and admiration.

"It's funny," Sarah's voice almost startled him. "I envy people like your wife. She seems so—so untouched."

"What do you mean?"

"I have the impression she's never had to struggle. The things I had to learn came naturally to her. The right clothes, the right things to say. She's shy, but she has a sort of assurance."

You, he thought: How could you envy her?

"My parents were never rich. Never poor, but never rich. My mother worked, and I went to college on a scholarship. I did well. I've always done well." Sarah fished in her evening bag for a cigarette, then rose and came toward him, needing his help to light it. "But there's something in me that can't help envying people like her. All her advantages."

He found a lighter among the picture frames and leaned toward Sarah, watching her face as she bent toward the flame. She inhaled, then sighed.

"I guess there's no way to overcome things like that," she said.

He frowned at Sarah.

"I can't believe you could envy anybody. With all you have."

In the silence he could hear the music down below, insistently lively. There was less noise, however. Fewer voices. The party was almost over.

"With all I have." She half smiled. "Every night I go home to a dark apartment. Every night I—" She stopped, and Cardwell felt someone behind him in the doorway. He turned.

It was Nancy.

"I think it's ending. Are you ready?" She nodded toward Sarah.

"I've been ready," he said. And they went downstairs, the three of them.

At the door they looked for Mrs. Michaelson, but she was somewhere else.

Cardwell helped Sarah with her coat; then he and Nancy saw her to her car. She had come to the party alone.

Nancy said nothing until they were almost halfway home. Then:

"Why did you go upstairs?"

"Because I was tired of the party."

"I mean with her."

"I didn't go up with her. She was already there."

Silence. He turned right at Wisconsin Avenue and they rode past the Washington Cathedral, its spires lighted against the winter night. There was a Christmas tree on the cathedral lawn. Strange. He had no feeling that Christmas was approaching.

"You know her, though."

"Know who?"

"Sarah Tolman."

"Of course I know her. Everybody knows her, for God's sake. She's a reporter. She's well known enough. She's somebody you talk to on the phone or meet at lunch. Everybody knows her."

Why should he have to justify his friendship with Sarah? There was no reason, yet he felt vaguely guilty. A stoplight blinked on; he braked the car and turned to look at Nancy. She was staring straight ahead.

"Look. I have no idea what you're thinking, but it's ridiculous.

Sarah Tolman has a million professional acquaintances, of whom I am one."

"But you find her attractive."

"I find her interesting."

They crossed the district line into Maryland, and he drove home by habit, not thinking about the route he took. Once they left Wisconsin Avenue there was almost no traffic. Soon they were home. He switched the car off and turned off the lights.

Though it was dark, he could see her silhouetted against the light from their house.

"Nan, what's the matter?"

"I don't know! I'm trying. I'm trying to be the kind of person you want me to be, but I just can't." She turned to face him, then looked down again and shook her head. "I'd like to be—interesting. I really would. I'd like to be one of those women who finds Washington fascinating and is interested in all the political things. But I can't."

"Look, its all right." He knew that he should reassure her, so he put his arm about her.

"It's not all right! I feel as if I'm losing you, and I don't know what to do."

He moved toward her, tilted her head up, and kissed her lightly. He wanted to feel something—but there was nothing, and he felt guilty.

"It's all right," he said. "A lot has been happening. We're going home Saturday. We'll have ten days together, no distractions. Okay?"

"I really need to go home." The thought of it was enough; he felt her relax beneath his hand.

They went inside.

Later, sound asleep, she drew herself up into a childlike crouch and pressed against him, her head seeking the hollow of his arm. He moved, put his arm loosely about her, and lay awake for a long time, wondering what had gone wrong.

Friday the Twenty-second

There was an avalanche of comment in the press about the split in the Administration.

As usual, Cardwell thought that Sarah had written with the most understanding. She wrote, in Friday's *Times,* with intuition that surprised him, about the two strong men whose private disagreement had so suddenly become a public feud.

She saw the split as an inevitable occurrence—not only the result of differences about policy, but also a clash of personalities. She detailed Abner Hoffman's long frustration, his growing sense of impotence.

"Now they are in conflict," Sarah wrote, "not only because of their differences, but also because of their similarities. Each is strong, each brilliant, each shrewd and proud, each greatly ambitious. And each is determined to prevail."

Cardwell, his feet propped on his office desk, read on to the end:

"The political marriage of Carl Rattigan and Abner Hoffman was, from the beginning, a marriage of convenience. It was in many ways a brilliant match. But, like many such marriages, it was sustained by necessity, not by affection or respect. And like so many others, this marriage of convenience has proven not strong enough to survive a crisis."

Returning to his office after lunch, Cardwell encountered Triplitano.

"Well, buddy?" Trip cuffed his shoulder. "What do you think?"

"I think Abner Hoffman has balls of iron."

Trip laughed, then nodded. "He certainly knows how to seize the initiative. They've already asked him to be on 'Meet the Press.' He'll probably get a *Time* cover, the whole treatment."

"How's the boss?"

"Sulking in his tent. A bad case of wounded pride and dignity. But I'm not worried. Actually it could have a good effect. He's been looking for a way to jettison Abner, and now he's got it, handed to him on a silver platter."

"Is he going to strike back?"

"Not publicly. The idea is to maintain his dignity, be presidential, say nothing. Just give Abner plenty of rope. He'll come over as strident and disloyal, and our man will get the sympathy."

Cardwell shook his head. "I think you're wrong."

"Why?"

"You said it yourself: Hoffman has the initiative. Every minute that he has center stage—every minute the President is silent—is a point gained for Hoffman and lost for us. He can't let Hoffman attack him publicly without answering. He's got to answer."

"If he does that, he just lends dignity to Hoffman. He turns a one-night story into a big deal."

"I think you're wrong."

"He's the President, John. He can't get down in the gutter with Abner Hoffman. No dignity, man."

"Dignity, hell. Dignity comes from strength, and if he just lets Hoffman go on hitting him he won't look very strong. I mean it. The worst thing he can do in this case is to wrap himself in the dignity of his office. He's being attacked."

Triplitano shrugged. "If you feel so strongly, why not send him up a memo?"

"I think I will."

"But don't just tell him to fight back. Tell him how. Tell him what to do. Give him some ideas to play with."

"Okay, I will."

Triplitano waved and moved off down the hall, toward the staff mess, and Cardwell went back to his office.

Warren Jasper strode into the Vice President's office carrying an open box of letters, cards, and telegrams. Behind him, in the outer office, bags of mail were stacked. He had asked the mailroom to send it all upstairs: He wanted Hoffman to see it—the sheer volume of it.

"Can you believe it?" Jasper set the box on Hoffman's desk.

"How much of it is hostile?" Hoffman stood and reached into the box, pulling out a sheaf of telegrams.

"Less than a third," said Jasper. "We're getting three kinds of mail: thousands from people who agree with you, a few from people who think you're a dangerous character, and a good many that say, 'I disagree with you, but I admire your courage!' "

"How much mail?"

"More than five thousand telegrams since yesterday. The letters started coming in at noon."

"We should buy stock in Western Union." Hoffman stroked his chin. He was trying to appear unimpressed. But soon, swayed by Jasper's enthusiasm, he broke into a grin. "I guess I struck a nerve." He unfolded one of the telegrams, read it, then tossed it back into the box and seized another. "I want to give them all a personal reply. My signature. If these people care enough to write, they should hear from me."

Jasper nodded and walked out, and Hoffman settled into his big chair to read more telegrams.

He was both touched and awed. He had not suspected that his words, spoken to a few hundred reporters in Washington, could reach so far, touch people so deeply. The public—there were millions of them out there, and they were listening to him, reacting to his words, writing to him.

Reading the telegrams, Abner Hoffman felt like the head of a vast, silent, unseen family. And he felt suddenly close to them—protective. They cared about him. They were depending on him. They took him seriously.

He knew, for the first time, really, what real power was, the kind of power the President had: power to command network time, to enter the homes of these silent millions—speak to them, and draw such a response. There were employees downstairs, a score of them perhaps, whose only job was handling Rattigan's mail. Incredible.

"Warren!" He was grinning now.

"Yes, sir?"

"Bring me some more of these things. I want to read them all!"

Bustling about their bedroom, preparing for the flight to Louisville, Nancy Cardwell caught herself whistling. For days—for the past month—she had felt rocky, near the edge of tears. Now she was cheerful.

From her closet she scooped up an armload of dresses, heaped them across the bed, and began removing the hangers.

Was it the old childhood excitement of Christmas that she felt, or simply joy to be going home? The latter, she suspected. She wanted, needed, the comfort of her family—their appreciation. She wanted the luxury of being loved simply because she was herself.

Her husband could not give her that. She sensed—in his distance, his coolness, his air of preoccupation—that he was disappointed in her: that his love for her was not freely given, but conditional. He wanted her to be something she was not.

She frowned. Then, tenderly, carefully, she began folding the dresses, lifting the neat packages she made into the open cases.

Why should she pretend any longer? She did not resent his job—only that it left him no room in his thoughts for her. She would save some anecdote, some bit of family news for him—and then, telling him, she would notice that he was not listening. He would nod, murmur as though he were listening—but his eyes were far away.

The dresses filled one suitcase. Best not to stuff them in too tightly. She snapped the lid shut and stood back, feeling already a sense of accomplishment.

Home. There would be parties, reunions with old friends, gatherings where she knew—and was known by—everyone present.

At parties in Washington there was a certain desperation in the air—desperation to be clever, to be well informed, to meet the most important person in the room. It was so—artificial. She hated it. And the people were all strangers, transients.

She hated it. But John, unfortunately, thrived on it: He loved the endless talk of politics, the large gatherings of strangers, the obsession with what the President did, what the Vice President said.

Nancy felt her resentment rising and turned her thoughts deliberately toward more cheerful things: Christmas at home.

From a bureau drawer she took more clothes—underthings, nightgowns—more than she needed for a ten-day stay. She moved to the bed and began folding them, laying them neatly in the second open suitcase.

Home. She was whistling again, soundlessly.

She heard the telephone.

The den. She walked down the hall toward the sound. It was growing dark outside, but she did not switch on the light.

"Nan?"

"Oh, hi. I was just packing."

She drew in her breath and held it, waiting.

"I was wondering if we could postpone the trip a day or two. I may have to stay here as late as Christmas Eve."

Don't say anything. Let him explain.

"Are you there?"

"Yes, I'm here." Tonelessly.

"I'm working on a speech. An answer to Hoffman. I just feel I shouldn't leave until I know how it works out."

"A speech."

"For the President. It's not long, but I want to—"

"When does he make it?"

"I don't know if he will make it. He may not make it. But I'm urging him to do it, and I want to stay here and argue for it."

She said nothing.

"Dot says she can get us on a plane on Sunday, late."

Why should she pretend? Why play the dutiful, long-suffering wife when she was no good in that role? She wanted to go home.

"I'm going home," she said. "You can come on Sunday if you like. Or you can stay here. Do what you like. But I'm packing, and I'm going home tomorrow."

There was a silence.

"All right," he said softly. "Suit yourself."

"I can't suit you, so I intend to suit myself."

"I'm sorry, Nan."

"You can take me to the airport in the morning."

Back in the bedroom, she felt bitterness give way to a sense of triumph. She almost threw her clothes into the bags; slammed the lids shut, hefted them off one bed onto the floor; shoved them together in a neat row by the door. She left the fourth bag empty—for his things. He could pack for himself. How could she know what he would need, or when he would come? Let him do it.

When she finished, she was whistling again. Loudly now.

Saturday the Twenty-third

The next morning at the airport, Cardwell and Nancy waited silently until her flight was called, then kissed good-bye: coolly, out of habit, almost mechanically.

"I'll be home tomorow, I promise," Cardwell said.

Nan's mind, he saw, was already somewhere else: at home in Louisville.

He spent the day in his office, polishing the short speech he would urge Rattigan to make. Dot Orme had gone home for Christmas. He called a typist from the correspondence pool, worked until dark, and sent the finished draft off to the Mansion.

He drove home satisfied. His arguments were so strong, so persuasive, that no one would fail to see their force and logic. The President would make the speech.

The house was dark and empty. He switched on lights in every room, dined on beer and leftover chicken in the kitchen, then went to the bedroom.

His empty suitcase stood at the foot of their bed like a challenge—a reproach. He spent fifteen minutes packing, then walked barefoot to the kitchen for another beer.

Nancy's unhappiness hung over the house like a vapor. He wandered to the study and tried to read. No good. He tossed the magazine lightly across the room, stood up, and sat down again.

Other women gave their husbands support, encouragement, approval. He thought of Annette Michaelson: ". . . in love and admiration." Automatically Sarah's face flashed into his mind, leaning toward him as he lit her cigarette.

By now Nan had been at home for hours. He thought of calling, then looked at the clock: No. She would be somewhere with her family—a dance, a party.

He left the den and walked from room to room, switching off the lamps. Ten o'clock. He went back to their room, stripped to his shorts, and went to bed.

Midnight.

The telephone.

He stumbled to the study, muttering sleepily.

The operator's voice, too bright, too wide-awake:

"Mr. Cardwell? The President."

Only after they exchanged their pleasantries did his mind fix and focus. Rattigan was talking.

"I think it's a damned good speech. It certainly says what I'd like to say."

"Thank you, sir. I—"

"I'm just not sure I'd better use it now. I think Abner will talk himself out of breath, and I'd rather he do it without my help."

Cardwell said nothing.

"You know you're the only person advising me to talk back to Abner. You know that?"

"Trip told me that."

"The only one."

I'm right, too, Cardwell said to himself.

"The others tell me I should just give Abner enough rope. But you—"

"I'm afraid he'll use the rope on you."

Rattigan laughed.

"Well, we'll see. I just wanted to thank you. I'm going to hold this speech. I can use it any time. But I'm going to sit tight now. I don't want to give Abner any more headlines. But if you feel I'm wrong, I appreciate your telling me."

"I will, sir," Cardwell said. "And I'll start by sticking by my memo and that speech."

"Are you staying here for Christmas?"

"I'm sorry, no. I'm—"

"Call me when you come back. I want to see you."

The line went dead.

Sunday the Twenty-fourth

Cardwell flew home on Christmas Eve, to stay with Nancy and her family. In their big house in Anchorage, outside Louisville, he felt a stranger. Her parents treated him politely, even warmly. But in their eyes he always saw a question: *Are you making her unhappy—our daughter, whom we love?* Here in the house of her childhood she was theirs, not his.

On Christmas Day it snowed: tiny weak flakes that rode the wind, then disappeared when they touched the ground. Cardwell and Nancy drove to his parents' house in Louisville for dinner: a long, quiet ritual with just the four of them. The women listened while their husbands talked of politics, of the President, of Hoffman, of the crisis in Bolivia. He told his parents about his work: the trip he had planned for Rattigan in November; the television speech about Bolivia, written on short notice; his weekly memos analyzing the opinion polls. His mother nodded, fascinated, proud of her son; Nancy seemed far away.

After dinner they went into the study, drawn by its warm fire and the lighted tree. His mother poured coffee, and suddenly his father rose.

"Let's take a walk."

"Your father's finally taken up exercise in his dotage," his mother said.

"No, I just want to get outside."

Outside, he let his father set the pace, down the wide street with its bare trees. Snow blew around them and disappeared.

"I get the impression," his father said, "that you're doing some good work up there."

"It's getting interesting," Cardwell said. "It's not just speeches now. I'm getting involved in the political side of things."

"The President's noticed you."

"I think he likes me. I'm not sure why."

"He likes you because you're smart and you can be trusted, and there are too few men like that." He was speaking not from pride, but from his experience with politicians. "Too many of the smart ones are killed up with ambition; they don't know a damned thing about personal loyalty. And too often the men who are most loyal are the least able; all they have to offer is loyalty, and that's not enough."

Cardwell nodded. They walked in silence until they reached a corner. Then his father stared at him.

"So you're happy? You like it?"

"It's exciting. I always found it exciting—you know, watching it. Now I find it exciting to be involved."

"I know."

"A couple of times he's called me, about a speech or something, and suddenly, right in the middle of our conversation I get this feeling: 'My God, I'm talking to the President.' I keep wondering when I'll lose that feeling."

"I hope you don't." His father smiled. "It's a nice feeling."

They were talking, Cardwell realized, not as father and son, but as two men who had shared a similar experience. His father, as an editor and publisher, had been sought out for his advice and friendship by governors, senators. His closest friends were men in public life. Since boyhood Cardwell had viewed his father with respect—even a touch of awe: He was a powerful man. But there was a certain distance between them. They had almost never talked intimately as father and son, much less as friends. Now there was something shared between them; they could be friends. Cardwell studied his father's face as they walked. He was sixty, gray, and balding, but there was authority in his face. He knew his own worth. The eyes, the high cheekbones, Cardwell recognized as his own, and he thought: Is this my face, thirty years from now?

They reached another corner and turned back.

"I'm proud of you," his father said. "Your mother and I are mighty proud of you." Father to son again.

Cardwell said nothing, and his father noticed the silence.

"Well, how about it? Are you proud of yourself? Is it what you want?"

More silence.

"You said you find it exciting. You didn't say you find it fulfilling."

"I don't know," Cardwell said. "Things happen so fast I don't have time to think about them." He looked at his father. "Do I seem unhappy?"

"There's something wrong. You're preoccupied, distracted. You didn't smile twice at dinner, and you didn't even seem to notice Nancy. I could tell your mother was upset."

"Maybe I'm just tired."

"Maybe so."

He did not want to answer questions—perhaps because he did not know the answers. But suddenly he was talking: about the Bolivia crisis, Hoffman's defection, his own occasional doubts. He told about the night he wrote the television speech.

"I wrote a speech defending his decision without knowing what I thought. It just had to be done, and I did it. If I'd stopped to think about it I might have disagreed. I keep thinking: If I weren't in the White House, if I were on the outside looking in, I'd probably be against Rattigan now."

His father nodded.

"Now I'm giving him political advice about how to deal with Hoffman, how to fight back, how to defend himself—and for all I know, Hoffman may be right! What do I know about it? The President may have made the mistake of the century."

"Yes, he may have."

"So what am I supposed to do?"

"Defend the President."

Cardwell raised his eyebrows.

"Help him. Help him fight Hoffman if that's what he wants to do."

They had reached the broad walkway that led up to the house. But instead of turning into it, they walked on up the street.

"Give yourself more credit," his father said, looking at him. "Your instinct tells you to stand by the President, doesn't it?"

"Yes."

"Then trust that instinct."

"Why?"

"Because it's a loyal, generous instinct. Does that sound old-fashioned?"

Cardwell nodded, but his father talked on.

"You could agonize all year about the rightness of the thing—about whether what he did was right or wrong—and you'd never find the answer. What makes you think you could? Don't you think the President wonders, himself? Don't you think he's uncertain, too?"

"I know he is."

"Then who are you to be so pure?"

"I know, Dad, but—"

"I've seen so many men like him. Not Presidents, but men like him, governors. They never know. They're forced to make decisions —spend millions of dollars, fire somebody, do something unpopular, raise taxes, risk the next election. They do it; they have to. Sometimes they're right, sometimes not. And they very seldom know—really know—whether they're right. And if they're so damned sure, they're usually fooling themselves. But they do it. And then they're all alone with the consequences.

"And Presidents. I guess it's worse for them." He looked at Cardwell. "I never knew a President the way you know this one, but I've met a couple, and I've studied them all. And every one, as far as I could tell, was a troubled man. Every one was frustrated by how little good he could do and frightened by how much harm he could do. I don't know that for certain, but—"

He broke off, and the two of them walked on, looking at the pavement.

"Hell, we've all got doubts," his father said. "I have my doubts. If it had all been left to me, I might never have sent those troops. But he's done it. He's given his reasons. Now all we can do is wait and see. Meanwhile, he deserves a hearing. He deserves your loyalty."

"I tried that argument on a friend at lunch," Cardwell said, "and I was told that men were dying, that I was using the same arguments that Hitler's henchmen used."

"Your friend is a fool," his father said bitterly, "if he can't see the difference—"

"It's a she." He thought of Sarah.

"Well, she, then. There's a moral difference between Carl Rattigan and Adolph Hitler, and if she can't see that, she's blind." His father stopped walking and stared at him. "Is that what worries you? That you're a Nazi? Come on, son."

"What worries me is that I may be wrong."

As if on a signal, they turned and began walking home again. It was midafternoon; the sky was going dull. Cardwell noticed that the snowflakes, growing larger, clung to his topcoat now.

"You may be wrong," his father said. "The President may be wrong. I suspect he's considered all that and he's willing to take the risk. Well, you take that risk with him. If your instincts tell you to help him—if you aren't convinced that he's dead wrong, then, by God, take that risk! Help the man! If you're wrong, then accept responsibility for being wrong. But he may be right. And if he is, you'll have the satisfaction of having been loyal to him. So help the man, and don't paralyze yourself wondering if you're right or wrong!"

Cardwell, surprised by his father's vehemence, merely nodded, and they turned up the walk toward the house.

"You know, I hate those bastards," his father said.

"What bastards?"

"You know, the pure ones. The ones who're guided by principle above all else. There's something cold and ungenerous about them. They don't know a goddamned thing about human loyalty, for all their principles. They think the population is divided up into heroes and villains, and it isn't. It just isn't."

He saw that his father was staring straight ahead again, and he wondered what the old man was remembering.

They climbed the broad steps and reached the door.

"I'm sorry it's so cold," his father said. "This walk should have lasted twice as long."

Cardwell smiled. "I enjoyed it, too."

"That's not what I mean. It's not the job that's bothering you most, is it? There's something else."

His father, he knew, had sensed the distance between his son and Nancy.

"It's none of my business, but if you want to talk about it—"

They had never been close; Cardwell had never troubled his busy father with questions or asked him for advice. And now, too late, his father was intruding upon his life with questions and advice.

"Some other time, Dad," Cardwell said. He meant never.

They went inside.

When they returned to Nancy's house, her mother was waiting with the message.

"You had a call from the White House. We tried to reach you, but you'd—"

It was Triplitano who had called.

"Merry Christmas, buddy. You having a good holiday?"

"Great," Cardwell said. "We needed the rest."

There was a silence. Then, "Have you seen the New York *Times?*"

"No, I'm sorry. That's one of the things I came down here to avoid."

"Well, a lot is happening. There's a full-page ad in the *Times*. Peace on Earth and all that." He paused. "It praises Hoffman's courage, calls on the President to bring the troops home, and promises support to Hoffman in his heroic effort to change the President's mind."

"I don't understand," Cardwell said. "What's the big deal?"

He heard Triplitano sigh. "The ad," Trip said, "was signed by twenty of the biggest money raisers on the East Coast. They were responsible for raising about two million dollars in the last campaign. Rattigan supporters to a man."

Cardwell whistled.

"There's a coupon at the bottom soliciting contributions," Trip said.

"And the President's fit to be tied."

"If Santa Claus walked in the door, he'd punch him in the nose. He's furious. He told me that every one of his advisers was a damn fool except you—that he should have blasted Hoffman two minutes after that Press Club speech. Now he wants to make that speech you wrote."

Cardwell smiled.

"Buddy," Trip said, "how soon can you get back up here?"

"Back to Washington?"

"You're No. 1 in his book now. He may call you himself. He wants you to write the State of the Union speech."

"I thought that was almost done."

"It was. Leonhardt was doing it, but he took enough time off to send a memo to the boss suggesting that we take some troops out of Bolivia. He suggested that Hoffman might be right. Now Leonhardt's in the doghouse, and anything he's touched is poison. Including the State of the Union draft."

"I don't know," Cardwell said. "I'll have to make some plans and call you back."

"You know how important this is."

"Of course, I—"

"I mean the State of the Union. Hoffman will be sitting on the dais. It's going to be a rather awkward moment for our man."

The State of the Union. The thought hit Cardwell like a chill. He would have less than two weeks to work. Two weeks of days and nights.

"Trip, I'll have to make some plans. I'll get back to you."

"All right. Let me know. We'll send a car to meet your plane."

For a moment after hanging up, he stood beside the phone. Then he turned and saw Nancy in the doorway.

"Same old story?" she said.

"I'm afraid so."

"What are you going to do?"

"I don't know. Go back, I guess. Tonight, or in the morning."

Abruptly she turned and walked into the broad hall, toward the stairs. He followed her. Halfway up, she whirled to face him.

"They just won't leave you alone, will they?" she cried.

"Nancy, for God's sake, not so loud."

"I don't care if they hear! They know how miserable I am." She rushed up the stairs toward their room, but Cardwell did not follow.

"Do they know how miserable I am?" he called after her.

She turned, caught by the sharpness in his voice.

"Where are you going?" He was heading down the stairs.

"Out!" He slammed the door.

He did not know where he would go when he started to drive. He steered automatically, through the neoned outskirts of Louisville, past stores and service stations blinking with garish Christmas lights, through fine old neighborhoods with large houses and occasional outdoor Christmas trees. Within half an hour he had reached his parents' house.

His father poured their drinks, and they sank into big chairs in the study. The fire was dying, and the Christmas tree had been turned off.

"I knew something was wrong," his father said. "She scarcely said a word at lunch today. She seemed unhappy. That's why I mentioned it today."

Cardwell said nothing.

"Your mother and I talked about it when you had gone. We figured there was nothing we could do, not knowing the situation."

"I know it's not all her fault," Cardwell said. "But I don't know what I've been doing wrong." And slowly, hesitantly, he began to talk: about his work—the late nights, the missed dinners, the long hours away from home; about Nancy's dislike for Washington, her growing resentment of his work.

While he talked, his father stared at the dark Christmas tree. Once, when the old man got up to refill their glasses, he leaned down to light it and the tree winked on, incongruously cheerful.

"So there you have it," Cardwell said. "Maybe I'm doing something wrong. But she's not giving anything. No support, no encouragement. Not anything."

"What are you giving her?"

Cardwell, stung by the question, hesitated. "Everything," he said. "All the usual things."

"And that's not enough."

"I'm doing important work, work that matters to me and to other people. Should I drop it all?"

"Have you thought of doing that?"

"Why should I?"

"To make her happy."

"I never noticed that you gave up a day of work to devote to home and family."

His father said nothing, and Cardwell instantly regretted his remark.

"You're right," his father said. "I was like you. I never would have dreamed of it. And now I have a few regrets."

"Did mother ever complain about your work?"

"No. The question never came up. If she ever had an unhappy day, she's never told me yet. We've been lucky."

"Then what do you regret?"

"For one thing, that you and I were never close."

Cardwell could not speak. He stared at the floor, then looked back at his father.

"Why don't you come back home?" the old man said softly.

Cardwell gazed at him.

"Today you were telling me to help the President."

"I don't mean come back right now. After a decent interval. After the election."

"And be your assistant?" He had to say it.

"I won't be here forever. I may retire."

Cardwell shook his head. "I'm sorry, but I can't do that. I just don't think it would give me—what I want now."

"Which is?"

He hesitated. "I don't know. Happiness, I guess."

"That's no answer. All of us want that. What would it take to make you happy? Money? Prestige? Another wife? What is it that you want?"

Abruptly, to conceal his hesitation, Cardwell flung his answer into the silence:

"Power," he said. "Most people would be uncomfortable saying that word, but I'll use it. I like the feeling of running things, of influencing events. And that's what I want to do."

"Power? Up there? In the White House?"

"Yes."

His father shook his head.

"Is that so bad?" Cardwell asked. "You've had—" He could not say the word. "You've had—influence."

"Of course, it's not so bad. It's not bad at all. But you'd better learn one thing: If you want power, you can't have it where you are. Not in the White House."

Cardwell started to reply, but his father raised his hand.

"You can have your name in the paper. You can have a nice office. You can ride in Air Force One. But that's not power. It's proximity to power. You don't get power by working for someone else, not even the President. You get it by working for yourself."

Cardwell shook his head, but his father continued.

"Come back home. Run this newspaper. If that doesn't give you what you want, you can run for mayor. Run for Congress."

No one could understand. He had come to his father seeking solace—seeking that fleeting sense he had felt earlier on their walk, that they were friends. Instead, the old man was lecturing him as if he were a boy.

Tired of the lecture, Cardwell stood up.

"I'm sorry, Dad. That's not what I want. Not now."

Silently they walked to the front door. He had not worn a coat; the draft when he opened the door made him shiver.

His father followed him onto the porch and laid his hand on Cardwell's shoulder.

"I know what I say sounds like clichés," he said as they stood in the cold, "but I've reached the age when I realize that things I once thought were just clichés are actually very true.

"One of them is that a man can't do what he wants to do. He must do what he must—his duty, as boring as that sounds." He hesitated. "And part of your duty is to make her happy."

Cardwell could hardly hear him, he spoke so low.

"Dad, I know that. But I have a duty up there too. In Washington."

"You do," his father said. "I hope you can find a way to do them both. For your own sake." He hesitated. "I only wish that there was something I could—"

Cardwell clasped his father's hand.

"Dad, go on in, it's cold," he said. He bounded down the steps, surprised at the huskiness he had heard in his own voice.

When he returned he found Nancy in their room and wondered if she had been there since he left.

"You go on back tomorrow," she said. There was no anger in her voice. "I'm going to stay here for a while."

"Until New Year's?"

"No, longer than that."

He was quiet.

"I want to do some thinking," Nancy said.

"I think we should both do some thinking."

"I just don't feel I'd have that much to go home to. You'll be working day and night, and—"

"It would be that different here?"

"I have my family. I have lots of friends I want to see."

He shook his head.

"I'm proud of you," she said. "I'm proud of all the things you're doing. But I can't live that way. At least not for a while."

"So you're just giving up."

"Please, I want to stay here for a while. I want to see what happens."

He felt a little angry, nothing more. He had no sense of a crisis or break between them, only a sense that they had lost touch, lost contact. What should he feel? A great emptiness? Maybe that would come later. And maybe not.

At midnight he called Triplitano.

There was a plane to Washington at ten in the morning. He would be on it.

A White House car would meet him.

Wednesday the Twenty-seventh

Rather than have his big car block the narrow Georgetown street, Brooks Healy told his driver to come back in an hour. It was two days after Christmas; colored lights glowed in the windows along the street.

He climbed the high front steps of Abner Hoffman's house, struck the brass knocker several times, and waited in the cold winter dusk.

The Vice President himself answered the door.

"Brooks, how are you? I'm glad you could come." Cordially he took Healy's coat and led him into the empty living room. "Can you keep yourself company for a minute? I have some people with me in the study. We're just finishing up."

He disappeared, not even offering Healy a drink to pass the time, and Healy sat down, trying to suppress his annoyance.

This time their meeting would be different. Healy had no illusions now about the Vice President's powerlessness. Hoffman had suddenly made himself a power, made his name one to be reckoned with. And this time Hoffman had arranged their meeting; he had summoned Healy with an invitation for a cocktail in the afternoon. "I have something I want you to tell the President," he had said. Healy had instantly accepted.

Now Healy sat waiting in the stately drawing room of Hoffman's house as darkness fell outside. He crossed his legs, uncrossed them, stood, and surveyed the room: high ceilings, damask draperies, antiques. The furnishings bespoke quiet good taste, a certain wealth; they belied Abner Hoffman's folksy Oklahoma image. But didn't everybody know that it was just an image? Healy sat down, irritated that he had been kept waiting even five minutes. Had Hoffman planned this—to keep him waiting like an errand boy? Was it his way of showing his new power, his—

The study door flew open and Hoffman emerged.

"Brooks, come on out here for a moment and say hello to some old friends."

Healy walked into the hall.

"Brooks, you know Nathan Wein? Wells Read?"

Healy didn't need to hear their names. "Of course," he said. And he thought: money. They had been two of Carl Rattigan's biggest backers in the last campaign: Read, the older man, a patriarch of Wall Street; Wein, still under forty, a builder of conglomerates with a genius for fund-raising. Three years before, at one cocktail party in his New York apartment, Wein had raised two hundred thousand dollars for Rattigan.

Now both men seemed ill-at-ease.

"How are the tigers of Wall Street?" Healy asked, smiling deliberately.

"Holding on," said Read, and Wein nodded. "It's a nervous time, as you can guess. You know, the—"

"The war," Wein said.

"I know," said Healy.

There was an awkward silence.

"Well, it was good seeing you both," Healy said. He extended his hand, freeing the visitors from any obligation to make further conversation.

When they had said their good-byes, Hoffman led Healy into his paneled study and poured the drinks.

"You know why they were here, Brooks?"

"I have a feeling you wanted me to see them."

"They want me to make a run, Brooks. Against the President."

Healy almost flinched. But he said nothing.

"They say they'll raise the money. All I need. All I have to do is give the word, enter a couple of primaries." He looked at Healy, eager for some reaction. "They feel that strongly—about what Carl is doing to this country."

Healy only stared back.

"You're surprised?" said Hoffman.

"Yes, I'm surprised, Ab," Healy said. "And disappointed. Disappointed that you could even consider such a thing. You told them you'll do it?"

Now it was Hoffman who made no reply.

"Abner, believe me. I'm speaking as a citizen. If you did such a thing you'd knock this country into a cocked hat."

"Or save it."

"Nonsense. You'd set off a battle that would prove nothing and solve nothing. But think of the precedent you'd be setting. You'd make the vice presidency a shooting blind for ambitious politicians. Every future President would have to fear his Vice President, and the presidency wouldn't be worth twenty cents."

"Don't you think I've thought of all that?"

"I hope you have. And I hope you've considered the fact that this could ruin you. Not just defeat you. Ruin you."

"I don't think he could do it," Hoffman said simply.

Then: "They told me they could raise a million dollars, Brooks. They know enough people who're opposed to what Carl's doing that they'll—"

"So what did you tell them, Abner?"

"I told them I didn't really want to do it."

Healy's eyes widened in surprise.

"That's not what you expected me to say?"

"Frankly, no."

"Well, it's true. I told them I didn't want to split the Democratic Party. I told them I didn't like the prospect of dividing the country so sharply, spending so much money in a fight like this. I told them I'd rather use other methods to persuade the President—"

"Abner, can I tell him that?"

"Tell him what?"

"That you're not going to make a race against him."

Hoffman smiled. "Is he so worried?"

"He's concerned about what you might do next. He thinks your Press Club speech was a disaster for the country."

The Vice President was grinning. "And I guess that peace ad in the papers didn't reassure him much. The one praising my courage and urging me to speak out some more."

"What do you want me to tell him, Abner?"

"Don't you think it's interesting? How all of a sudden these liberal millionaires and students and peace groups are interested in me? A country boy from Oklahoma?"

Healy sighed. "Mr. Vice President, you have something you want me to tell the President. Tell me what it is."

Hoffman's smile faded. "Tell him," he said, "that I don't want to fight him. I don't want to run against him." He paused. "And tell him he can prevent it."

"He can—"

"All he has to do is take those troops out of there. Bring them home. Go on television and announce that he's decided to bring them home."

"While you acknowledge the cheers of the crowd for persuading him to do it? Abner, there's a word for that, and it's—"

"You can call it what you want to. I call it saving lives."

"The word is blackmail."

"Shall I bring up what you offered me if I wouldn't speak my mind to the Press Club? Shall we talk about blackmail, Brooks? Let's not waste time."

Healy glared at the Vice President. "I don't think he'll be interested," he said.

"That's not for you to say, is it, Brooks? You're just the go-between. Actually, I think he may be interested."

Healy moved toward the door. "Is that all, Abner?"

"Tell him I'd like to know his answer by tomorrow afternoon. I've got to make my plans." He opened the door into the hall, and they moved toward the front door. "And tell him I'd like to see him. We shouldn't have to deal through a middleman."

"Abner, I hope you know I consider this a distasteful job."

"I'm sorry, Brooks." He retrieved Healy's coat from the hall closet, and the two men shook hands gravely.

Outside in the cold, Healy looked up and down the street. He had not been an hour; his driver was not back.

He swore—then saw his big limousine parked in the shadows half a block away. He hunched his shoulders and walked quickly up the street.

His driver jumped when Healy opened the door. "Oh, Mr. Secretary. Ready to go home?"

"No," Healy said, "not yet. Let's go to the White House."

Cardwell, working late in his office, heard a knock at his door.

It was the basement guard.

"Sir, your car's outside."

"Thank you, Sergeant. I'll be right out."

Funny, he thought, how easily I take to it. A White House car.

The day before, the driver who had met his plane had said to him, "Well, I guess we'll be coming for you every day."

"Excuse me?" Cardwell had been puzzled.

"We'll be coming for you every day. We've got your name on the list for portal-to-portal service."

Portal-to-portal service. A car outside his house each morning and a car to ferry him home each night. It was one of the perquisites reserved for the President's first-ranking assistants. What did it mean? Cardwell wasn't sure. But this morning there had been a car. And now, this evening.

He pulled on his topcoat and left the office, nodding to the guard as he walked out to the car.

"Home, sir?"

"Yes, please," Cardwell told the driver, and settled into the rear seat of the trim sedan.

He was tired. In twenty-four hours he had plunged into the mountain of documents from which the State of the Union speech must be prepared. The sheer size of the job oppressed him, almost overwhelmed his excitement at having been tapped for the job.

And Leonhardt. The man's resentment, his bitterness, left Cardwell with a feeling of regret and half guilt.

Cardwell had gone, after meeting briefly with Triplitano, to Leonhardt's office—to arrange for the transfer of the State of the Union paperwork, to relieve Leonhardt of his duty.

Leonhardt had greeted him with bitter challenge in his voice.

"Do you want to take the papers, or are you taking over my office in the bargain?"

"Fred, I'm sorry about this. You know it wasn't my idea."

"But it's an idea you like. The young hotshot moving in."

Cardwell had laughed, it was so ridiculous. "Do I seem so ruthless?"

"No, quite the contrary. You're very polite and self-effacing. A perfect gentleman. That's why you're so effective."

Leonhardt pointed to the stack of folders; Cardwell began sifting through them while Leonhardt watched him, saying nothing, sucking insistently on his unlighted pipe.

Then Leonhardt spoke. "Look, I'm busy. Why don't you go back to your office and I'll have that stuff sent down."

"Well," Cardwell said, "I'd hoped we could talk about it. I know I'll be relying on the work you've done."

"Don't," Leonhardt said. "If he sees the slightest resemblance between your version and mine, he'll be after you. And once you're on the President's little list . . ."

"Thank you, Fred."

Leonhardt said nothing until he reached the door. Then: "You know he's a little bit paranoid, don't you, John?"

"Oh, Fred, come on."

"No, I mean it. He really is. He's a little bit off his perch. I wrote him a memo outlining some alternatives that would get us out of this mess down there, and he simply blew his top. Now I'm the enemy. He doesn't want to hear my name, much less any disagreement with his policy. If that's not paranoid, what is?"

"Fred, he's not paranoid. He's just mad as hell at you," Cardwell had said.

When he said it, Leonhardt had not replied. He simply stared at Cardwell, a curious pop-eyed stare of surprise and anger, clenching his pipe more tightly between his teeth. And Cardwell had left.

Poor old Fred. A brilliant man, but a bit of a fool. Cardwell leaned back with his eyes closed, remembering the scene.

The car, deftly piloted by the White House driver, moved quickly toward Bethesda, past houses and buildings still decked with Christmas lights.

He thought of Nancy. He had been tempted to call her, to announce that he was safely back in Washington, and to tell her about the White House car. But no. Stubbornly he had decided to let her make the first move. She would grow bored and miss him. She would call.

His briefcase was on the seat beside him, filled with papers. He opened it, snapped on the reading lamp above the rear seat, and tried to read. It was one of the things he had seen often in Washington when he had stopped his old car for a red light: a sleek black limousine waiting in traffic; in the rear seat, an official barely visible, reading. Now he was one of them. But it was no use. He felt self-conscious. He put the papers back into the case and snapped it shut.

When they reached his house the driver said affably, "All dark. The wife away?"

"She's still at home for Christmas," Cardwell said. And he added, almost defensively, "She'll be back in a few days."

But would she?

He thanked the driver and walked up to the dark house, clutching his briefcase.

The President's first reaction upon hearing Brooks Healy's report was simply to stare at Healy: a long, uncomprehending gaze. Then the President sighed, shook his head, and sat down.

"The blackmailing bastard," he said.

They were in the Yellow Oval Room. Healy had arrived while the President and Lisa Rattigan were at dinner. One glance at Healy's face told them that something was seriously wrong: Lisa, with a gracious nod to Healy, had excused the President, promising him a warm meal later.

"He wants to see you," Healy said. "He doesn't much like dealing with you through me, and I can't say I blame him."

"That bastard." Rattigan stared into the fire before the sofa where he sat. Then he looked at Healy, "Why should I see him?"

"For one thing, you may be able to convince him how much harm he's doing. He scarcely listens to me."

Rattigan waved his hand, dismissing the thought.

"And for another, if you boycott Abner very long, he'll make capital of it in the press."

"How?"

"I don't know. Somehow. He's a very clever man." Healy sat down in a gold-upholstered chair, stood up, then sat down again. "In any case, I think you should try to reason with him."

"Reason with him!" The President stood up. "Brooks, can't you see? Abner's past reasoning with. He wants my job. He wants me out of here. Do you think reasoning with him would do some good?"

"He said he really doesn't want to run against you. He wants to convince you to change your mind. To bring the troops home."

"And make him a goddamn hero? The man who turned the President around? I'd rather fight it out."

"So you won't see him."

"Brooks, if I thought that talking to Abner would do the slightest good, I'd see him. I'd go to him—I wouldn't make him come to me! But it's no use. He wants to be President. That's his idea, and once a man is taken over by that idea, nothing short of defeat will stop him."

Caught up by what he was saying, the President turned and walked toward the windows that overlooked the South Lawn. Then, seeing that the draperies were drawn, that there was no view, he turned back to face Healy.

"All this stuff about a deal. He doesn't mean it. He knows I'd never accept a thing like that. Never! He's already decided to run. Now he's just building up a case. He'll be able to claim that he was forced to run—that he had no choice."

"Then why not call his bluff?"

"What do you mean?"

"Take out a few of the troops. Then, if he runs—"

Rattigan's eyes went hard.

"You know I can't do that. Not just to stop Abner."

After a moment Healy nodded. "I know," he said softly. "I'm sorry I said it."

A silence fell between the two men, the sort of silence that falls between two friends who know there is nothing to be said. They stared into the fire for a long minute, listening to its busy crackling.

"Brooks?"

"Yes, sir?"

"What do you think will happen?"

"If he runs in the primaries?"

"Yes."

"I think you'll beat him."

"I know I will."

"But I think it's a disaster anyway. That such a thing could even happen. I told him that."

"I know."

Another silence.

"When do you think he'll announce?" Rattigan said.

"I don't know. Soon, I'd think."

The fire leaped and subsided, then flared up again.

"By the time he stands up to announce," Rattigan said, "I want everyone to know that Abner Hoffman tried to blackmail me."

Healy only nodded.

"Everyone. I want them to know that Abner Hoffman tried to blackmail me."

There was a white telephone on an antique desk across the room. The President pointed toward it.

"All right," he said to Healy, "call him. Tell him I said 'No deal.'"

Healy stood up. "This is final?"

"Absolutely."

"You know what it means?"

"Of course I do. Where are you going?" Healy was walking toward the door.

"I thought I'd go in person."

Rattigan laughed. "Always the diplomat."

When Healy was in the hall, Rattigan called him back.

"Brooks? I want you to tell him one more thing."

Healy raised his eyebrows.

"Tell Abner I hate him."

"Mr. President, I—"

"Tell him I hate him. Not for what he's trying to do to me, but for what he's doing to the country."

For a moment Healy stared at the President, as if uncertain how to reply.

"Tell him I said that."

Healy nodded and was gone.

Later, taking his dinner from a tray in the West Hall, the President told Lisa in a few words what had happened.

She listened, unbelieving at first, then moved onto the sofa beside him while he finished eating.

"When will he announce?" she asked.

"I don't know. In a few days, I'd guess."

She winced, filled with pain at the prospect, and said nothing more, busying herself with mail and reading while he went to his room to call his close friends and advisers.

What could she do? She felt a sudden urge to go to Abner Hoffman herself: to beg, implore him not to do this thing. But she suppressed that wild impulse.

When it was time for bed she went into his room and climbed into bed with him, to give what solace she could by being near.

"Darling, are you too upset?"

"I try to be a fatalist," he said. "Just take things as they come. Now, don't you worry." His voice was strained, heavy.

She lay awake until she heard him breathing regularly, then fell asleep herself.

Sometime before dawn Lisa awakened. He was not beside her.

"Carl?"

She found him in the Yellow Oval Room, staring out across the South Lawn toward the monuments.

"Carl?" She touched his elbow.

"That bastard," he said huskily. "Do you see what he's done?"

"Come back to bed."

"Suppose I wanted to pull those troops out. Suppose that sometime in the next two months things started going better. I couldn't bring them home!"

Futilely she tugged at his sleeve.

"If I pulled them out people would swear it was political, that I was doing it to win votes. To get Abner off my back." He shook his head. "That bastard."

"Try to get some sleep," she said, pulling him toward his room. "Try to get some sleep."

On Friday, the White House received the latest weekly casualty figures from the Pentagon: fifteen Americans killed or missing in action; sixty-two wounded. They were the highest casualties suffered so far in what the protesters' signs now called Rattigan's War.

JANUARY

Near the Precipice

Monday the First

At noon on New Year's Day, Abner Hoffman stepped before a battery of television cameras in the Senate Caucus Room.

The reporters who had been summoned to cover the event did not grumble, though they had to work through the holiday. Rumors had been floating for three days that Hoffman would run against the President; the newsmen, having caught the scent of drama, were restless, excited, eager for the conference to begin.

"There he is," someone called, and Hoffman, with his wife, his two married daughters, their husbands and children, came through a tall door. Bright lights warmed the room, and Hoffman struggled toward the platform: smiling, waving, blinking into a hundred cameras.

He went directly to the podium.

"In this historic room," he said, reading from a text taped to the lectern, "John F. Kennedy announced his candidacy for the highest office in the land."

A score of microphones around the lectern caught his words. "Here, too, his brother Robert announced his candidacy"—he paused—"and began his unfinished effort to put his country on a new road: the road toward lasting peace."

From the rear of the Caucus Room, where Hoffman's staff and friends were gathered, there was a spatter of applause, but he read on.

"I am here for a similar reason today"—his voice rose and quickened—"to announce my candidacy for the office of the President of the United—"

Before he could end the phrase, the cheering drowned him out. His friends, family, and staff—a crowd of at least two hundred—rose in a standing ovation.

Sarah Tolman, from her seat in the press section near the podium, surveyed the crowd in the ornate room, waited for the cheers to die, and jotted phrases on a small pad. Hoffman, she noted, was superbly turned out: pale blue shirt, dark gray suit, a blue and red tie. He was not a handsome man, but he looked solid, strong, trustworthy. Did he look presidential? Almost, she thought. Almost.

"My fellow citizens, this is the first day of a year that may well point the direction for America through all the remaining years of this century.

"Our nation is faced with a crucial decision: whether to embark again upon a series of bloody, far-flung wars that can bring only tragedy abroad and dissension at home; or whether, alternatively, to put some limits upon our ambitions and concentrate upon building a better land at home.

"That choice, I believe, should be made by the American people—not by one man. And that is why I am in this race!"

Again there was a drumfire of applause.

"I know there is no precedent," he said, "for a Vice President to challenge the President for their party's nomination. For that reason, I have made my decision reluctantly and prayerfully.

"But I must do it—"

More applause.

"—not for reasons of personal ambition, but because events compelled me. For the President—" Hoffman's voice slowed and he spoke darkly "—the President seems dead set on a course of action directly opposite from what he promised this nation three years ago."

Hoffman, pointing a finger directly into the camera, stared into the eyes of several million television viewers. His voice carried the weight of genuine outrage barely suppressed.

"I have worked closely with the President for many years. I have had, and I still have, the highest regard for him and for the office he holds.

"But I am convinced that he has made a major mistake in the matter of Bolivia. And I am convinced that this mistake, if it is not corrected, could lead to a national and global tragedy."

He paused.

"And so, my fellow citizens, I shall take my case directly to the people. I am going to run for the office of the presidency—to get our nation back on the right road."

The final wave of cheers rose and subsided.

"I'll take your questions," Abner Hoffman said.

"Mr. Vice President," the UPI man asked, "Can you tell us what primaries you'll be entering? What your plans are for the campaign?"

"Well, to begin with, New Hampshire. And frankly, we haven't decided about others. I guess we'll have an announcement down the road—"

At the White House, the President and Lisa Rattigan watched in the west hall upstairs.

"I can't understand," she said when Hoffman had finished his prepared remarks, "how anyone could be impressed by such a—"

Rattigan pressed a finger to his lips.

"New Hampshire," he said after the first reporter's question.

"He's so false," Lisa said. "So transparently false. It's just ambition, nothing else. Don't you think everyone will see it?"

"No," said the President, staring at the screen. "He's doing a good job. He's doing a damn fine job."

It was the tribute of one professional to another.

"When does the campaign start?" The Vice President repeated a newsman's question and broke into a grin. "It starts right now."

There was applause.

"I'm going to New Hampshire tomorrow, and you're all invited. Bring your fur parkas and your boots. They tell me it's snowing up there, but that won't stop us!"

His press conference was over. Hoffman, smiling, strode into the crowd, shaking hands with newsmen and supporters, smiling for the cameras, beckoning to his wife and family to join him for more pictures.

When it was over, the President rose abruptly and snapped off the set. Lisa rose too and met him in the center of the room.

Instinctively she reached out, encircling him tightly with her arms.

"I want to help you," she said, pressing her head against his chest. "Carl, what can I say?"

He held her too, for a long moment, not replying.

"What can I do?"

"Just what you're doing," he said hoarsely. "That's enough."

At five o'clock, unnoticed by reporters and only barely noted by passersby, the Vice President's limousine swept through the Southwest Gate. A guard waved it by and swung the big gates shut; the car circled the South Drive and drove up to the Diplomatic Entrance.

The President, earlier in the afternoon, had called his new rival to an off-the-record meeting.

They met, the two of them, in the Treaty Room on the Mansion's second floor.

"Abner? Good afternoon." The President did not get up from his place at the large table in the center of the room, and he made no offer to shake hands. "Can I get you a drink?"

"No, thank you." Hoffman stood uncomfortably at the end of the long leather-topped table until Rattigan pointed to one of the chairs beside the table.

"I thought you were very effective today."

"Thank you, Mr. President." Hoffman sat down.

"I thought you did a good job of—expressing yourself," Rattigan said.

"Thank you."

"You could have attacked me personally, and you didn't. I suppose I should thank you for that."

"I don't want to get personal," Hoffman said. "I want to fight this one on the issues. There won't be any personal attacks from me."

"I appreciate that." Rattigan's tone was neutral, without an edge of bitterness, but Hoffman wondered if the President was mocking him.

An awkward silence followed. It lasted until the Vice President felt compelled to speak.

"I'm interested to know why you called me here. I thought you didn't want to see me."

"I thought we should lay some ground rules," Rattigan said, "for your campaign. Come to some points of understanding."

"A good idea. How about 'No personal attacks' as rule No. 1?"

"Fine." Rattigan nodded. "I'm calling a Cabinet meeting for Wednesday. I'm going to tell them that if any Cabinet officer wants to campaign for either of us, he should resign first. That's rule No. 2."

Hoffman nodded agreement. "I'd like to be at that meeting," he said.

The President stared at him. "Suit yourself," he said.

Another uncomfortable silence. The two men sat staring down the table at one another, beneath the huge Victorian chandelier that dominated the room.

"Well," said Hoffman, rising from his chair, "I guess we can't think of any more rules."

"Can't you, Abner?"

The Vice President extended his hand, but the President did not stand, so he withdrew it. "We're leaving early in the morning for New Hampshire," he said, moving toward the door. "I'd guess I'd better go."

"Abner."

"Mr. President, I'm sorry it's come to this, I really am," Hoffman blurted. "But I don't see how it could have ended any other—"

"Abner," said Rattigan, "there was one thing you didn't mention on television today."

Hoffman had reached the door. He stopped.

"Your resignation," Rattigan said.

On the table before the President lay a manila folder.

"Abner, I want you to resign." Rattigan shoved the folder a few inches in Hoffman's direction.

"Here's a letter you can sign. I've saved you the trouble of dictating it yourself." He flipped the folder open; the letter was one paragraph long, neatly typed on vice presidential stationery.

Hoffman scarcely glanced at it. "If I were planning to resign, Mr. President, I could write my own letter."

"Sign it, Abner."

"I'm sorry. There's not a chance."

"Do you think I'm going to let you run up and down the country denouncing me while you're still in my Administration?"

"Mr. President, I was elected. *Elected*. By the same people who—"

"Do you think they elected you to take pot shots at the President?

Hell, no, they didn't!" Rattigan stood up, glaring at Hoffman. "I can't let you use your office this way, Abner. I can't do it."

"Mr. President," Hoffman said softly, "you can't do anything about it."

For a long moment Rattigan stared at Hoffman. Then he sighed and sank into his chair.

"You took an oath, Abner."

"An oath to obey you?"

" 'To defend the Constitution against all enemies, foreign and domestic,' remember?"

"And who chooses the enemies, Mr. President? Carl Rattigan, all by himself?" Hoffman smiled derisively.

"Abner," Rattigan said, "I'm going to chew you up and spit you out. I mean it. Not because you're trying to bring me down, but because what you're doing could ruin this country."

"That's mighty interesting." Hoffman smiled. "How you identify this country's welfare with yours."

"Get out of here."

Hoffman turned.

"Abner? One more thing." Rattigan's voice was still tight with anger. "Are you planning to tell the press about this?"

"I thought I might."

"I'd appreciate it if you didn't."

Hoffman said nothing.

"And if you do"—Rattigan pointed a finger—"I'll have to deny it. I'll say you're lying. It'll be your word against mine."

"Good-bye, Mr. President," Hoffman walked out.

"Good-bye, Abner," the President called after him. "I'll see you Wednesday."

Tuesday the Second

Not one prominent New Hampshire Democrat turned out to greet Ab Hoffman on his trip to Concord—not even a lowly state legislator.

But when Hoffman emerged from the old granite Capitol where he had filed his candidacy, he faced a throng of two hundred people, most of them young. A few held handmade signs: LEAD US TO PEACE.

Hoffman beamed. Cameras were clicking. He smiled at Libby Hoffman, then left her side to shake some hands.

"I'm not here to make a speech," the Vice President said jovially. But the reporters glanced knowingly at one another: He would not pass up this opportunity.

"Starting today," said Hoffman, "I'm going up and down New Hampshire. Between now and March 5, I'm going to speak to the people." He paused, then added: "*All* the people."

The youngsters cheered, and Sarah Tolman, standing in the group of reporters, wrote in her notebook: "Crowd spontaneous, enthusiastic. If an advance man planned this, he's a good one."

Now Hoffman's voice went slow and serious. The crowd, sensing his shift of mood, grew quieter.

"In the seven days between Christmas and New Year's Day," he said, "fifteen young Americans died in Bolivia. Fifteen." He eyed his listeners gravely. "Those are the newest figures released by the Pentagon. Fifteen young men who will never see another Christmas, another New Year's Day."

His craggy face was a mask of fatherly concern.

"I say that is a senseless waste of life."

He shook his head.

"I say it must stop."

Sarah looked up at the crowd. They were with him: rapt. Some were nodding.

"With your help, it will stop." Suddenly he smiled. "So now let's get to work!"

"Mr. Vice President," a reporter shouted, "what percentage of the vote would you consider a victory?" Warren Jasper, riding the press plane up, had told them 40 per cent would be a victory—enough to embarrass Rattigan.

Now Hoffman only grinned.

"Fifty-one per cent," he said. Then he stopped grinning. "I'm in this race to win."

His young followers shouted, and Sarah wrote in her notebook: *This man is serious.*

When the White House press corps trooped into the briefing room for their late-morning session with Triplitano, they sensed a surprise in the works. Trip was not waiting at the lectern, as was his habit. A Signal Corpsman was on the podium, fussing with a recorder. An omen?

The President walked in, and instantly those reporters who were seated leaped to their feet. Rattigan waved them back into their seats.

"Gentlemen, good morning. And ladies." Rattigan was smiling slightly. "I'll take your questions."

There was a moment's silence. Then Murphy Morrow was on his feet. "Mr. President, is this on the record?"

Rattigan nodded.

"We're interested, sir, in your reaction to the Vice President's announcement."

"I was surprised," Rattigan said. There was an explosion of laughter, which the President joined.

It was the President's first press conference in weeks, and he had been asked the question he wanted to hear.

"I'm sorry the Vice President has chosen the course he's taking," Rattigan said. He was serious now. The reporters bent to their notebooks, pencils flying. "Not for personal reasons; I think the people, ultimately, will understand the reasons for this government's decision to share in the defense of Bolivia, and support that decision.

"I regret the Vice President's decision for other reasons. I think it raises some dangerous possibilities. I'll mention two."

He was speaking easily, forcefully. The reporters wrote furiously, struggling to keep up.

"First, there is the possibility that other governments may misinterpret us. They may assume that because there is a disagreement between the President and the Vice President, that the government is weakened—that we will be weak or unpredictable or indecisive."

He paused.

"That is not the case. As President and Commander-in-Chief, I am responsible for the decisions of this government. Those decisions are going forward. Our policies are firm, and we are not making any twists or turns.

"But the Vice President has made it more difficult for us to get that important fact across. In fact, his actions may very well prolong this war. And so I think what he is doing is not good for the country."

"Mr. President?" A reporter was on his feet, but the President had not finished.

"Second, there's the danger that the Vice President, caught up in the business of a primary campaign, will not be able to fulfill his obligations as Vice President, as the second-ranking official in the government."

A couple of the older, more cynical reporters glanced at each other with raised eyebrows. How could Rattigan talk with a straight face about Hoffman's importance in the government? Hadn't he held Abner down from the beginning? Suppressed him? Barred him from any real responsibility?

The President continued.

"This isn't simply a matter of time spent away from Washington. There has to be an atmosphere of trust between any President and his Vice President. I'm afraid the Vice President's actions diminish that. They raise a question of whether discussions held in confidence may be used for political advantage."

Rattigan paused as if searching for a word. Then he shrugged slightly and pointed to another reporter who had raised his hand.

"Mr. President, in this connection, we've heard reports that you want the Vice President to resign his office, and that you've applied some pressure. Is this true, sir?"

"I don't think," said Rattigan, "that anything I could do could force the Vice President to resign if he weren't willing to do so. He's an elected official." They did not notice, so intent were they on catching every word, that he had sidestepped the question.

"Have you discussed this matter with him, sir?"

Rattigan smiled. "I understand the Vice President is busy in New Hampshire. I don't think he has time for discussions with me, do you?"

The reporters laughed. He had sidestepped again, successfully.

"But let me be frank. I think the Vice President is doing violence to our system of government. I look upon his decision to use his office in this way as a challenge, not so much to me as to our form of government."

"Oh, boy," one reporter whispered to a colleague, "will you listen to this?"

"Mr. President, about your plans. The filing deadline for the New Hampshire primary is January 5. That's Friday. Are you planning a trip this week?"

Rattigan joined their laughter.

"No," he said.

"Will you prevent your supporters from entering your name on the ballot?"

"No," he said.

"Are you planning to campaign actively?" another reporter asked.

Rattigan hesitated.

"I don't want to answer that," he said. "I have no plans at present. I have, as you know, enough to keep me busy here. I think the best course would be to do my job as well as I know how. That's what I intend to do."

"Mr. President, are you saying that you're going to stay out of New England so the Vice President won't have a target? Are you not going to campaign?"

"I didn't say that."

"Sir—"

"I said I wanted to defer a discussion of my plans until a later date."

He pointed to an upraised hand in the rear of the briefing room.

"Sir, can you tell us when you might have an announcement of your plans?"

"Next week," Rattigan said. And Triplitano, sitting near him, had the distinct impression that the President was surprised by his own answer. Trip leaned forward, curious.

"I'll have some things to say about my plans on several matters next Thursday night," Rattigan said.

"State of the Union?" one reporter whispered to his cohorts.

"I'll be going to the Hill next Thursday," he continued, "to address the Congress. Until then—"

The reporters scribbled busily.

"Until then, I won't have anything to say about my plans."

Gene Taylor of UPI, glancing at his watch and sensing that there would be no more news, stood up and shouted, "Thank you, Mr. President!" and the press conference ended.

Back in the Oval Office, Triplitano pointed his thumbs toward the ceiling.

"That was perfect, Mr. President. Just perfect."

"Thank you, Trip." Rattigan smiled.

"One thing, sir: What are you going to tell them Thursday night?"

"In the State of the Union? I don't know."

Trip's mouth dropped open.

"I don't know." The President shook his head. "I just heard myself self say that. I don't know whether I should go up there and campaign or not. I just don't know."

"Well, sir, you have a week to think about it."

"And you." Rattigan smiled, then frowned. "You and your friend Cardwell."

Triplitano rose to leave.

"Give him a call," said Rattigan. "Tell him I want to see him in the morning."

Wednesday the Third

"I'm impressed," Dot said as she handed him the note.

"Don't be," Cardwell said. But he smiled at her.

The note was from Anders Martin. "The President would like you to attend the Cabinet Meeting at noon, then join him afterward for luncheon in his office." It confirmed what Trip had told him the night before: The President wants to see you. Stand by.

Cardwell checked his watch: ten-thirty.

A Cabinet meeting. He had attended one or two and found them boring. What, after all, did the Secretary of Agriculture have to say to the Secretary of Defense? The meetings were mere formalities, opportunities for the President to make a few announcements, to give his Cabinet officers a sense of contact with the busy President.

It was an honor, nonetheless, to be invited. No more than ten of the White House Staff usually came to the meetings, and they were clearly the front-liners: Martin, Triplitano, Karnow. . . .

And the meeting would have a touch of drama. Ab Hoffman, Trip had told him, would be present. What would the President say?

Cardwell glanced at his watch again; he tried to organize the poll results for his meeting with the President, jotted some notes, and grew more impatient. Trip would be there for lunch, too. Good.

At eleven-fifty Cardwell went upstairs.

He walked past the Oval Office. The door was closed, and an agent sat outside; that meant the President was in his office. Cardwell passed the office that adjoined the Cabinet Room. The door was open; he waved to Sheila Roundtree.

Only two Cabinet members had arrived: Healy of State and Jenkins of Interior. They were chatting with Triplitano, who had just come from his morning briefing.

Cardwell joined them.

"Gentlemen, you know John Cardwell, don't you?" Trip said. "He's mangling all your programs for the State of the Union speech."

They smiled and shook hands.

"Will the Vice President be here?" Jenkins asked.

Trip and Healy nodded, and sure enough, just before twelve, Ab Hoffman swept in. The conversation ceased.

"Gentlemen," he boomed. "And Trip, how are you?"

"Morning, sir. You know John Cardwell, of the President's staff?"

They shook hands, and Hoffman moved about the room, cheerily greeting his colleagues as they arrived.

Why all the smiles? Cardwell wondered. Isn't he the enemy? Why not just treat him civilly? Why all the excess warmth? Then he understood: They're nervous. He's making it easier for them.

Then they heard the heavy door click open. Without looking, they knew that Rattigan had entered from his secretary's office.

Normally the President stopped to shake hands and banter with his Cabinet officers. Today he strode briskly by the group nearest the door, passed quickly behind Hoffman's back, and went to his large chair at the center of the table.

"I'm glad you could all get here," Rattigan began. "What I have to say won't take long, but I wanted you to hear it face to face."

Rattigan looked around the table. Cardwell noticed that his glance slowed for a fraction of a second as he focused on Abner Hoffman, who was seated directly across the table from him. The President was tense, preoccupied. Hoffman's face was open and amicable, as if this were a routine meeting.

"This is an unprecedented political situation we're facing now," Rattigan said. "Never before in American history have we had a Vice President actively campaigning against a sitting President. Ab has his reasons for this; I guess the newspapers have pretty well expressed what his feelings are."

The President took out his glasses and put them on.

"I thought there were some things that should be said to the Cabinet about all this before it goes much farther. Basically it's this: This government must keep moving. It can't be crippled because we have an intramural political fight on our hands. And that's not all."

Rattigan reached forward and fingered a pencil on the table before him.

"It's just as important that this government not *look* as though it's handcuffed and caught up in bickering. That would undo all the work this Administration has tried to do in the past three years, and it would be unfair to the public.

"So I want to lay down a couple of rules to see that we don't jeopardize what we've built. The first is this: I don't want any man in this Cabinet participating in political campaigns. Not for the Vice President and not for me. Politics is out of bounds—at least until next fall."

Cardwell studied the faces of the men at the table. They were grave, listening intently.

Rattigan half smiled. "I know some of you fellows believe your own press clippings about what political wizards you are. But you'll have to resist temptation. The more involved you get in trying to play political games, the worse you'll be at running your departments. There's not a man at this table who was picked because he was a good politician. But I do think you're an excellent group of Cabinet officers, and I want it to stay that way."

Cardwell saw Brooks Healy, seated on the President's right, nod slightly, as if agreeing silently, and he wondered: Is this warning meant for him, too? Healy, the President's friend and confidant? He suspected not.

"I don't want to see any stories coming out that things are going undone in the Interior Department because the Secretary is out playing politics."

Jenkins, the Interior Secretary, looked nervously from side to side, then back at the President.

Rattigan paused, surveyed the table, and spoke almost mournfully.

"There's another thought I'd better express also. I want to say it now so that every man here understands it clearly." He looked around the table. "This is the President's Cabinet. That's elementary, but I want you all to think carefully about it. It's the President's Cabinet, not the Vice President's, and that's the way it will be as long as I'm the President.

"I know all of you want more money for more programs. I know some of you may be tempted to work with the Vice President—to let him surface your requests in his campaign. So I'll give fair warning: This is the President's Cabinet.

"You don't have to agree with everything I say or do. You don't. If you don't like what's happening in Bolivia, I can't change your minds. But I expect you to keep your disagreement a private matter between us and go on running your department—or get out. I'm not going to hold a grudge against any man who comes to me and says, 'You're wrong and I want out.' But I am not going to let politics undermine the unity of this government. So you're either on this team —or off it."

He stopped, rolling the pencil in his right hand.

"That's all I've got," he murmured. "If no one has anything to add, that's it."

There was a moment's silence. Abner Hoffman cleared his throat and shifted in his chair.

"I want to endorse all we've just heard," he said. "A man appointed by the President owes his loyalty to the President." He smiled. "And he's right about another thing. You're a hell of a Cabinet, but not much as politicians."

Their laughter shattered the tension. Even Rattigan smiled. But when the laughter died he rose and walked out of the room, trailed by Anders Martin. The meeting had lasted less than ten minutes.

Cardwell and Triplitano followed the President to the Oval Office. He stood at this desk for a moment, looking down at some paper there, then motioned them into seats on the sofas near the fireplace.

Cardwell surveyed the room. The winter sunlight that streamed into the room emphasized its cathedral calm: pale walls, stately high windows, the seal woven into the handsome carpet. Behind the President's broad, cluttered desk four flags stood along the wall, strung with battle streamers: the trappings of office. Who would want to give them up?

"It's not going to work," said Rattigan, "what I was talking about in there. It can't work. Those are good men, but they're human beings. They're going to be pulled and tugged every way." His voice was flat. "It's just no good."

A waiter came in with a silver tray: sandwiches and a pot of coffee. The President watched absently as the waiter set the tray before them and poured three cups of coffee.

"What if I call a meeting of the National Security Council?" Rattigan continued. "Ab's a statutory member. I have to let him in. Could I talk about the situation in Bolivia?"

"The enemy within the gates," Trip said softly.

"Suppose we deal with some secret information in that meeting?

Ab's running against me. How could he help but benefit from it?" He reached for his coffee cup, then sat back again.

"Ab's made a big mistake. A hell of a mistake." He sighed. "He's going to tear up this government. And that's what I hate."

Cardwell and Triplitano reached for their sandwiches, not knowing what to say; they busied themselves eating for a minute while Rattigan sat back watching them.

"I'm confused by these poll results," he said after a moment. "Do you want to talk about them?"

"Yes, sir." Cardwell removed from his portfolio a chart that he had made with inch-high figures drawn in black:

The President	45 %
The Vice President	31 %
Undecided	24 %

"Is that all voters nationwide?" asked Rattigan.

"No, sir. Registered Democrats only, polled by telephone."

"That many Democrats are undecided?"

"I can't explain it. It's as if they want to support you both, but don't know what to do."

"Goddamn Abner," Rattigan said softly. He looked toward Triplitano, then back at Cardwell. Then, with a shrug, the President said, "So what does this poll mean?"

"Not much right now. But let's not fool ourselves. Only half the voters are Democrats. Even in a Democratic primary not all of them vote—not even a majority. If 75 per cent of Hoffman's Democrats turned out to vote and only half of yours turned out, and the undecided split evenly, then it's a 50–50 tie. And if a sitting President has half of his own party against him—"

Cardwell hesitated.

"Then the President loses," Rattigan said. "A handful of voters can turn him out."

"I'm afraid so."

"Well," said Trip, "that's putting the situation in the bleakest terms. The fact is, you're way ahead."

Rattigan ignored him.

"What do you think I should do?" he said to Cardwell.

"I think you should fight like hell, beginning right now."

The President reached for his coffee cup, half-drained it, then set it down.

"You mean start campaigning—in New England?"

"You should get the State of the Union speech behind you first. I know you're reluctant to talk about politics in that speech, but I don't see how you can avoid it." I think you've got to keep him from gaining in the polls—in New Hampshire and in the country. You've got to dominate the news, keep before the public, simply overwhelm Hoffman before he gets off the ground."

The President nodded and was silent for a time. Then his face seemed to brighten.

"I have some plans I haven't told you about," he said. "I think I can do all that without getting in a slugging match with Abner. I think I can beat Abner without setting foot in New Hampshire." And for the next half hour, the President leaned toward Cardwell and outlined the plan he would unveil at the Capitol the next week.

Friday the Fifth

On Friday, afternoon newspapers across the nation front-paged a brief story about Carl Rattigan: The President had confirmed, in a terse but courteous letter to the New Hampshire Secretary of State, that he would be a candidate for re-election. He would allow his supporters to enter his name on the New Hampshire primary ballot. But he left unanswered the question that now fascinated reporters and political enthusiasts: Would he come to New England to answer Abner Hoffman's challenge? Would he come to New Hampshire as a candidate? Storm through the snowy, steepled little towns to meet the people and defend his record? He gave no hint.

Late in the afternoon, Cardwell sat in his office, staring out across West Executive Avenue toward the Executive Office Building, watching it go gray with the winter twilight.

He was alone. Dot had gone home, after sending out thirty copies of the latest draft of the State of the Union speech. By midday tomorrow the copies would be back, each covered with scrawled comments from high government officials, and he would begin another draft. But for now, he could relax.

He swiveled his chair around to face his desk, rubbed both hands down his face, and looked at Nancy's letter. It lay open on the desk before him, two pale blue pages covered with her prim schoolgirl script.

"I've done a lot of thinking since you went back," she had written, "and the more I think the more I realize how unalike we really are."

He had planned to call her today.

But when her letter came in the afternoon's batch of mail, and he read it, he had decided not to call—not yet. He needed time to think about what he would say.

"Now," she had written, "I'm trying to decide whether I think it could ever be much different for us. I had hoped you would settle that question for me—that you'd say something or do something to make me think that things would change. But maybe that's too much to hope. So I'm still trying to figure it out."

He had been staying late at the office nights—calling later and later for his White House car—because he didn't like returning to the empty house. And mornings, leaving the house when he saw his driver waiting, he would snap on a lamp or two on his way out. He told himself it was a precaution against prowlers, but he knew better: He hated coming home to find the house in darkness.

He had called her one time in these ten days, but their conversation had been strange: all impersonal small talk. He had not told her, because he found it difficult to talk about his feelings, what it was like for him: that he had realized in her absence how he had grown used to her. He found it difficult each night, tired as he was, to fall asleep in their wide, empty bed; he missed her familiar shape beside him and the regular rise and fall of her breathing. And sometimes he would awaken in the small hours, feeling a sharp-pointed sensation of desire, only to remember that he was alone.

But was it Nan he missed, or simply the comfort of having someone near? The very question made him feel guilty—and he remembered his father's words: You have a duty to make her happy.

"I think I still love you," she had written. "But I honestly can't guess what you feel for me. I've been thinking about it a lot, and I just can't guess."

What did he feel? Affection, certainly. Desire. He cared for her, missed her. Couldn't she see that?

"I think I still love you. But I'm not sure I can still live with you. Does that sound too confused?"

No more confused than he felt. He had read her letter several times, and every time, arriving at this point, he felt a rush of anger, disappointment—and surprise at Nancy's determination.

"There's only one thing I'm not confused about: that I should stay at home until we sort things out. I think I can get some substitute teaching work down here. Not at Country Day, but in the public school. And as far as I can tell you're busier than ever; you have less time than ever for personal problems. So I've decided just to wait and think some more, and see what your reaction is. . . ."

He found some stationery in the desk drawer, fished it out, and picked up his pen. He sat staring for a full minute at the blank white paper, then crumpled it and reached for his telephone.

"Operator?" He gave the White House operator the number in Louisville and sat waiting.

"It's ringing, sir," she said after a moment.

Then, not knowing what he might say to Nancy, he said, "Operator, let's cancel it." Abruptly he hung up and sat staring at the phone.

It was early—six o'clock—but he felt hungry. He dialed Triplitano's office, hoping to lure him to a restaurant for a drink or two, but there was no answer.

He called the *Times* bureau.

"Miss Tolman? She's in New Hampshire, sir. Can I—"

He left his name, hung up, grabbed his coat, and walked to the steak house on Seventeenth Street, next to Sans Souci, where he had a long dinner, all alone, reading a newspaper.

Sunday the Seventh

On Sunday morning the President received, with his morning mail, a letter from Fred Leonhardt: his resignation. For "personal reasons," Leonhardt wrote, he had decided to leave the staff. The letter was correct enough, phrased with all the routine pleasantries: "the great honor of serving you"; "with deep regret." Leonhardt had made his resignation effective in two weeks.

Rattigan sighed. Fred was gone now, bitter and angry. He would surely talk to the press. There would be a flap: HIGH AIDE QUITS IN PROTEST. A few days' excitement, a few days of embarrassment for the President. The columns, he knew, would accuse him of intolerance—of refusing to hear opposing views from his own counselors. PRESIDENT'S ISOLATION GROWS. And wouldn't they be right? He shook his head. The bastards. They could never understand. He couldn't keep a man like Fred Leonhardt; he could not have, at the heart of his official family, an aide whose loyalty and devotion he could not absolutely trust.

But why not?

Because there was no time left to debate the issues with his own staff. He had made his decision. He was challenged now by his own Vice President. Now it was time to choose up sides, to get moving—

Leonhardt. What would he tell the press?

With a heavy sigh the President picked up a stack of folders. There was one thick one with a red tag affixed to it: Cardwell's latest draft of the State of the Union speech. The President opened it.

Thank God the speech was coming soon. It would knock this business off the front pages; Leonhardt's departure would seem small stuff indeed, against the news that would be coming soon.

He thought of the reporters, notebooks poised, avid for news, hounding him, giving exposure to every rumor, every hairline crack in the Administration's façade, gossiping endlessly among themselves, seizing upon every problem, every setback for the President, and magnifying it.

The bastards—they could never understand.

Cardwell was in his office when Sarah called late on Sunday afternoon.

"You left a message with my office Friday?"

Hearing her voice, he smiled. "How'd you know to call me at my office?"

"I know your type."

"I was trying to lure you out for a drink when I called on Friday," he told her.

"Wonderful. Does the invitation still hold? I have a million things to tell you."

They agreed to meet at a place Sarah suggested: a little restaurant on Connecticut Avenue, not far from her apartment on Macomb Street.

He had driven himself to the office today. Now he raced the old Duster through the empty streets, enjoying the sensation of driving after two weeks as a passenger in White House cars.

Sarah was waiting when he reached the restaurant.

"Rumor hath," she said when they had ordered drinks, "that you're writing the State of the Union."

"Rumor hath it right."

"Would you like to give an off-the-record preview?"

He laughed. "Not on your life. Tell me about New Hampshire."

"I can't tell you my secrets if you won't tell me yours."

He smiled, turning aside her challenge. "I've been reading your stories. You seem to be the only one who thinks that Hoffman has a chance."

"Of course he has a chance. He's not just running a symbolic race to influence the President. He's running to win."

"Sarah, why? Because he's ambitious, or because he really opposes the President on principle?"

"Because he's ambitious. *And* because he opposes the President on principle. Who can tell where one stops and the other begins?"

Cardwell frowned.

"It's the same with your man," Sarah said. "He thinks that because he's threatened, the country's threatened."

He smiled and she continued.

"That's what makes it so fascinating, to me at least. Every politician believes the country's welfare depends on his own victory in the next election. And they're not cynical. They really believe it."

They finished their drinks, and he ordered two more. Sarah, encouraged by his interest, told stories of her week with Hoffman in New England.

"And his crowds are getting bigger?" Cardwell said when she paused.

"Bigger every day. It's funny. There's very little frenzy. None of the usual campaign noise, except from the young people. But the crowds come. And they listen. They're starting to take him seriously."

"He's winning votes?"

"Not many. Not now. But he's got eight weeks to campaign." She toyed with her glass, staring downward, then looked at him. "What about your man? When does he go up there?"

"He may not go."

"John, how could he be so foolish? He has to go!"

"I think he has some other plans."

"But not to campaign at all?"

"He's a resourceful man, Sarah. He has his own ideas."

"To be announced in the State of the Union speech?"

"Exactly."

Sarah refused another drink, and he suggested dinner.

"I couldn't," Sarah said. "Don't you have to be at home?"

"No," he said. Then he added, "Nancy's not here." He felt he must explain. "She wanted to stay at home for a while, so I came back alone."

He saw that Sarah was unsure how to reply.

"I think we're separated," he said bleakly.

"I'm sorry. I truly am."

"I haven't told anybody. You're the first person I've told that to."

Sarah, seeing that he wanted to talk, nodded sympathetically.

"I didn't think she'd stay. I thought she'd come on back. But then she wrote this week." He shrugged. "She's staying."

"Let's do have dinner," Sarah said.

And so Cardwell found himself telling Sarah, through dinner and several cups of coffee, about his problems with Nancy. He knew, seeing her as she listened gravely, nodding occasionally, that he shouldn't tell so much, but he went on. She was the only person, since his meeting with his father on Christmas night, whom he had told. And he sensed, even though she said little, that she understood all he was saying.

When he finished he shrugged almost helplessly, and they sat silent for a long time.

"So, who's to blame?" he said after a while, to break the silence.

Sarah shook her head. "Why should anyone be blamed? It's not her fault that she can't stand this life. And it's not your fault that you love it—find it necessary. I think it must be terribly sad and lonely for both of you. But why should you feel guilty, either one?"

"I feel guilty that I don't feel guilty," Cardwell said. "I just feel numb. Ever since that night in Louisville I've been waiting to feel some great emotion, and I haven't. It worries me."

"I know," she nodded.

"I keep wondering if I've lost my capacity to feel things. I used to have it."

"I think nature has this merciful device that keeps us going," Sarah said. "People in battle or in big disasters go into a kind of daze. They don't feel pain; they're numb—but they function. Maybe it's the same when something happens in your personal life. It's not that you can't feel—of course you can. But you have to keep on going."

"You sound as if you've been through it too."

"Battles and disasters," Sarah said. "I'm a reporter."

"I mean a separation." He looked directly at her, and Sarah looked away.

When she met his eyes again, she shook her head. "Not a separation," she said. "An end. If it had been a separation there would have been some hope, I guess. I could have fooled myself But this—" She trailed off, half embarrassed.

"You can tell me, if you like."

"Another time, perhaps." She smiled. "I'm supposed to hear your story, not tell you mine."

He paid the check and they left.

"Can I drive you home?" he asked.

"I'm just around the corner."

"Then I'll walk you home."

She lived on a narrow tree-lined street just off Connecticut Avenue near the zoo: a dead-end lane flanked by low brick apartment buildings. They walked in silence. Cardwell was fascinated by what Sarah had said; she had almost given him a glimpse into her unknown life, and he was eager to see more. He had known her always to be friendly, intelligent, wholly self-possessed—but little more. Now she had revealed that she was capable of emotions he had not seen before: separation, hurt, resignation.

"How do you handle it?" he asked abruptly as they walked.

"What?"

"Being alone."

"I know it sounds corny, but I try to keep busy," she said, and he knew she would say no more.

Her apartment was in the last brick building on the street, on the ground floor.

At her door she turned to thank him. Before she could speak he leaned forward and kissed her tentatively, then trapped her in his arms.

It was a long moment before she pushed him gently away.

"Why did you do that?" She was flushed, fumbling for her key.

"Why did you let me?"

"I don't know." After two tries she made the key turn, and her door swung open.

"Can I come in?" He glanced past her, eager to see the place where she lived, as if the objects around her could tell the story she had declined to tell.

"I think you'd better go."

"Why? Because I might do something I'd regret?"

"No, because I might."

He almost smiled, but he saw that she was serious.

"When can I see you?"

"I'm going to New England tomorrow," Sarah said.

"You'll be back for the State of the Union?"

She hesitated, then nodded.

"Then I'll see you Thursday. After the speech."

He turned and left before she could answer. And once outside, he almost ran the two blocks to his car.

Thursday the Eleventh

Late on the afternoon of the State of the Union speech, Cardwell called Sarah Tolman's office.

"I'm sorry," said the voice in the *Times* bureau, "Miss Tolman is with the Vice President's campaign."

"Can I leave a message? Tell her I'd like to take her to dinner after the speech tonight. The name is Cardwell. C-A-R-D—"

"I'll leave a note, sir."

He began reading his final draft of the State of the Union speech again, wondering if the President would order more changes. He had come to the White House early, expecting to spend the day making last-minute revisions. But there had been no word. What was the President doing?

The telephone rang: Triplitano. "Have you got a final draft?"

"I haven't heard a word," Cardwell replied. "I sent my last draft up to him last night and haven't heard a word since then. I thought I'd hear by lunch, but I haven't."

"Don't worry. My guess is that you won't hear anything. He likes to spend a day alone with it. He probably figures he's squeezed you dry by now, so he'll make his own changes."

"Then I'll relax." But Cardwell was nervous.

For two weeks, as succeeding drafts of the address had flown back and forth, Cardwell had come increasingly to think of the speech as his: his words, his thoughts. But now the speech was Rattigan's. The

President was shaping and turning Cardwell's ideas in his own way. There was nothing more to do.

It was three hours before the speech, but already he was beginning to feel the sensation akin to stage fright that overtook him when the President made a speech Cardwell had written.

He called Sarah's office again. She had not come in. Cardwell hung up, cursed silently, then brightened: He could look for her at the Capitol tonight. She would be there. He would seek her out.

He read his copy of the speech for the hundredth time, read it again, glanced at the clock, then swung his chair around to face the window. It was snowing outside; the flakes were clinging to the cars parked on West Executive.

A motorcade of White House cars would take him and the staff to the Capitol to hear the speech. They would have seats, as they had had in years past, among the senators and congressmen on the packed House floor. Seats at ringside.

Dot buzzed. "Arlene Sprague called. You're invited to a small buffet supper upstairs after the speech. Just the President and Mrs. R., some staff, and a few friends. I told her you'd come."

"I may have other plans."

"It's all right. It's very informal and spur-of-the-moment. She said if you can't come, you won't be missed."

He let Dot go home, then tried to occupy himself with the *Star*. But he kept checking his watch.

At seven-thirty an usher knocked on the President's door.

He straightened his tie, took the black speech binder from its place on his bed, and walked into the hall.

Lisa was waiting, smiling, dressed in a bright blue suit, her face made up a bit more vividly than usual, for the cameras.

She smiled and touched his arm. "Are you nervous?"

"No, not very."

"I like the speech," she said.

"I think this one is going to put Abner on the run," he said as they took the elevator down.

Triplitano and Martin were waiting in the Diplomatic Reception Room. They helped the President and Lisa Rattigan into their coats, and the four of them went outside into the swirling snow. They climbed into the long, black presidential limousine, and it swung off toward the Capitol, followed by a car filled with Secret Service agents, flanked by motorcycle-riding officers.

The intersections were blocked off along the the big car's route; policemen waved them by. No one talked. Lisa Rattigan gazed out at the streets, at the snow that lay heavier now, shining beneath the streetlights.

The President was reading the speech one last hurried time. Lisa turned back and watched him for a moment. As he read, she noticed, he was clenching and unclenching his right fist—rhythmically, unconsciously—like a man preparing for a fight.

In the crowded, ornate hallway outside the House chamber, Cardwell saw her.

"Sarah!"

"John, how are you?" She turned, smiling, and waited for him to press through the crowd toward her. "I read the advance text. Where's that big news you promised?"

"It's not in your text, but it's in his," he said. "Did you get my call? Can you meet me for dinner after the speech?"

"I'll be working till midnight," she said. "I've got to file a story."

"How about after that?"

He saw the flicker of uncertainty in her eyes.

"Are you boycotting me, Sarah?"

She dropped her eyes.

"Look," he said. "I'm sorry about the other day. I—"

"Don't apologize. I understand."

The crowd pressed about them. He moved her away from the elevator doors, into a corner of the wide hall.

"John," she said, "I'm not upset about that. I was even flattered. But I don't want to do anything to jeopardize a friendship."

"Okay, we're friends. Can you have dinner tomorrow?"

"I'll be back in New Hampshire. I've been going back and forth."

The elevator doors rolled open, and she pulled away.

"Soon, then," he called as she stepped aboard.

"Soon."

The doors closed; he lost her and moved along with the pushing crowd toward the chamber of the House.

Abner Hoffman was already in his seat, to the right of the Speaker above the marble dais. In the last moments before the President's entrance, Hoffman was waving to friends on the floor, smiling jovially. He seemed unconcerned.

Cardwell heard a stirring in the gallery and looked up: Lisa Rattigan had entered. There was a quick burst of applause as she sat down, followed by the wives of several aides. Libby Hoffman was not among her guests; Cardwell surmised that she was seated somewhere else—in the family gallery, perhaps.

All nine of the justices of the Supreme Court were seated in the front row, in their robes. The President's Cabinet secretaries were seated near them, with Brooks Healy on the aisle, first among equals. And up above, looking directly down upon the dais, the reporters were crowded into their section of the gallery—White House regulars wedged in among the Capitol Hill veterans, working together tonight as on no other night.

"Mistah Speakah!" It was the doorkeeper's annual moment of glory. "The President of the United States!"

And Rattigan swept in and walked down the center aisle, flanked by an honor guard of portly senators and congressmen.

It was an entrance that cried out for music, for "Hail to the Chief." But there was no music—only the rolling thunder of applause as Carl Rattigan, smiling, made his way to the dais, nodding right and left, stopping once to reach out and shake hands with an aging senator.

Cardwell stood to join in the ovation, and he saw the black book Rattigan carried: the speech text. He thought he saw Rattigan as he turned to mount the platform, meet his eyes and nod slightly—or was it his imagination?

Abner Hoffman was standing by the Speaker, applauding with the crowd, slowly and rhythmically—not so slowly that an opponent could say that he was snubbing the President, but slowly enough to fall short of enthusiasm.

Rattigan reached the Speaker, gave him a warm handshake and a smile, and Cardwell now could almost feel the question of the crowd: What will he do now? Greet Hoffman—or turn away?

Rattigan was a master. Seeing Hoffman, he seemed almost surprised: Why Abner, my good friend, what are you doing here? The President smiled, grabbed the Vice President's hand, and turned slightly to face the cameras: Let's show them we're gentlemen; friends despite our differences.

Hoffman, surprised by the warmth of the greeting, responded with his own broad smile, and the crowd roared, relieved and happy. They cheered again when the President nodded to Hoffman and turned toward the lectern, and stood clapping until Rattigan laid the black book down and raised his hand, first acknowledging the applause, then signaling for silence.

The Speaker introduced him, and Rattigan, stopping another effort at applause, began his speech.

"Mr. President," he said, "Mr. Speaker, members of the House and Senate, distinguished guests, my fellow citizens."

Cardwell relaxed a little, and the President slid into the speech.

"The Constitution requires that the President shall, from time to time, give to the Congress 'information of the state of the Union, and recommend to their consideration such measures as he shall judge necessary and expedient.' I am doing that this evening. But I am also taking the liberty, as have many Chief Executives before me, of speaking directly to the people of the United States. For the problems that we Americans face this evening cannot be solved only by the Congress or only by the President. The problems confronting us can be dealt with only when and if the people of the United States fully understand what the issues really are."

Rattigan's voice was forceful, confident. His audience had settled into a rapt silence. Cardwell, listening, half smiled; he knew the speech almost by heart.

"The first hurdle to understanding things as they are," Rattigan said, "is the notion that we can put our problems in separate pigeonholes, to be dealt with separately. It is false doctrine, I believe, to hold that America has two sets of problems, one labeled 'domestic,' and the other 'international.' America has, in this tiny, crowded world, only one set of problems. Some of them are domestic problems with worldwide impact. Others are foreign problems that directly affect our lives at home.

"Tonight I want to discuss them all—the whole range of problems that confront us, and to ask, in Lincoln's words, 'Where we have gone, and whither we are tending.'"

Cardwell's eyes moved around the upper gallery and stopped on Lisa Rattigan. She was leaning forward, her eyes fixed on the President, the picture of devoted attention.

"Three years ago," Rattigan said, "we came to office and found on the national agenda a backlog of unfinished business—"

This was an election year. And so the President could be forgiven if he spent some time praising the achievements of his own Administration. Cardwell shifted in his seat.

"Tonight," Rattigan disclaimed, "I can report to you that we have cleared away much of that unfinished business."

As the President catalogued his Administration's successes, Cardwell watched for the reaction. Democrats applauded lustily; Republicans politely, but with restraint.

Where was Sarah? Cardwell looked up, craning to see her, catch her eye. But he could only get a partial glimpse of her; she was absorbed, following the President closely on her copy of the text, jotting notes, underlining.

The President was doing well; there were frequent bursts of applause, mostly from the Democratic side of the aisle, as he unveiled his program. Once or twice, Cardwell noticed, Abner Hoffman joined in the applause. But for the most part he sat unmoving, listening gravely and attentively, his face a solid, impassive mask.

Now the President moved into a new section of the speech, and there was an audible flutter of page-turning up above: All of the press, and many of the officials in the gallery, had copies of the speech.

"The challenges we face at home are of our own making," Rattigan said, slowing his pace. "Those we confront abroad are not. Events we cannot predict or control force us to act. Often we must act almost against our will; we must make hard decisions we would rather avoid.

"But act we must; decide we must. For the—"

There was a weak effort at applause. It quickly died, and he went on.

"For the consequences of inaction, we have learned, can often lead to tragedy in a world where the strong and ambitious still prey upon the weak. Action, to be sure, causes danger and difficulty. But inaction can bring disaster."

A few partisans cheered, but for the most part the crowd was silent.

"In Bolivia tonight," Rattigan said, "twenty thousand American troops are manning battle stations."

His voice was calm, confident, unapologetic.

"Those men are there at my command."

Total silence.

"Why did I send them there? Not because I wanted to. Not because I take lightly the use of armed force by the United States. Not because I was unaware of the consequences of my decision and the dangers it entailed."

Rattigan leaned forward, speaking with absolute conviction, pointing one finger upward for emphasis.

"I sent those troops because there was no other honorable choice."

There was a brief explosion of applause—very brief—which Cardwell joined. He looked again at Hoffman on the dais; the Vice President was sitting with his arms folded.

"The peaceful nation of Bolivia was invaded," Rattigan said, his voice rising. "The invaders chose not to call it that. They claimed, piously and cynically, that their purpose was to assist in the 'liberation' of Bolivia.

"From whom were the Bolivians to be liberated—themselves?"

Mixed laughter and applause.

"Bolivia was, until this act of aggression, at peace with its neighbors.

"Its government was legitimate—fairly and freely elected by the people.

"Its government, though not without its flaws and difficulties, was struggling earnestly to be responsive to its peoples' needs, to govern by standards that—though they might not be ours exactly—were democratic standards.

"Bolivia is a poor nation and a weak one," Rattigan said. He paused for a long moment.

Then he added: "And Bolivia is in our hemisphere—our neighbor.

"Could we, in the face of all these facts, refuse to join a coalition of allies in her defense? Could we honorably deny our help? *I say we could not!*"

Real applause now. Cardwell sighed, relaxed a little. The President was doing well.

"There are those," the President said, "who sincerely believe that we should have stood aside; that we should have delayed sending troops until international bodies had met and acted; that we should play the role, in this conflict, not of a partisan but of a peacemaker.

"I respect the sincerity of their view. I considered it carefully—and I rejected it.

"Why? These were my reasons—"

As Rattigan explained his decision once again, Cardwell felt a surge of sympathy and admiration for the President—and pride at his own efforts in the President's behalf. *If words have meaning,* he thought, *this should convince them.*

But he knew that words were not enough. No words—not even the most eloquent words—could decide the issue; for Hoffman, after all, was driven by ambition as well as principle. The clash between them would be—already was—not only a clash of principles but also of personalities, of strong men who by now hated one another.

"It is not a secret to anyone in this chamber," Rattigan said, "that the Vice President disagrees with me. Because he disagrees—and for other reasons of his own—he has chosen to make his own campaign for the presidency."

All eyes now were on Hoffman; he shifted heavily in his big chair behind the President, but his face registered no emotion, only careful attention to Rattigan's words.

"My friends and fellow citizens, I shall be frank. I deplore the Vice President's decision. Not because he disagrees with me, for that is his right—but because he has chosen to divide our government at the top, to precipitate a constitutional crises without precedent in our history."

There was a cold silence in the great chamber. Cardwell thought he saw Hoffman frown slightly.

"I would prefer it—for constitutional rather than personal reasons—if the Vice President had resigned his office before launching his campaign. But he has made his decision, and the people will soon make theirs.

"I hope that while their decision is pending"—here Rattigan lowered his voice—"there will be no mistakes about one thing: This government will govern; it will function."

There was a scattering of applause, then silence.

"This nation, of course, has always thrived on controversy and on criticism. But we must not allow it to be crippled by either. This government, specifically the executive departments and the armed services, must continue to function in an orderly and effective way even while criticism and controversy go on. There are those who feel that this unprecedented political challenge to the President threatens the efficiency of the Executive Branch of the government. Let me assure you tonight that this is not the case. This government will run, and it will run smoothly. Politics and political campaigning will not cripple this government; I guarantee that."

That, Cardwell knew, was an applause line—and the applause came: the loudest and the longest of the evening.

"And so," Rattigan said when the applause died, "in an effort to keep partisan political activity at a minimum, certainly this far in advance of a national election, I hope to curtail my own political activity. Should I decide to run for re-election, I will hope to do so without campaigning actively in any primary contests. The job of the President is a full-time job, particularly in difficult times like these. I do not believe that my campaigning in a series of party primaries can help me perform my duties as Chief Executive."

Now the applause was loud—but not so loud as the buzz of comment that Rattigan's announcement touched off.

That's a mistake, Cardwell thought. The President had been adamant on this point; he did not want to dignify Hoffman's campaign by appearing opposite him; Rattigan wanted to remain above the battle—but could he?

Cardwell braced himself for the final portion of the speech.

"The most important of those duties," Rattigan said, "is the quest for peace.

"I have said that American troops will remain in Bolivia as long as they are needed.

"And I have emphasized that they will stay *no longer* than they are needed.

"All of us, whatever our feelings about the wisdom of this involvement, want to see it end.

"With that in mind, I have agreed, with the heads of state of other nations in the hemisphere, to meet next week in Punta del Este, Uruguay, to review our progress, co-ordinate our policy concerning the conflict in Bolivia, and seek a way toward peace."

With the last word the applause broke out again—a steady, sustained roar. Cardwell looked at Hoffman; he had joined in the applause—halfheartedly, Cardwell thought—and his brow was furrowed.

"Upon completion of our sessions in Punta del Este, I will take advantage of invitations I have received from our South American allies to pay them brief visits on my way home."

Cardwell leaned forward, searched the press gallery, and saw Sarah. She was writing hurriedly, trying to catch every word.

On the podium Rattigan acknowledged the applause with an upraised hand. A smile turned up the corners of the President's mouth, and Cardwell knew what he was smiling about. *The crafty bastard,* Cardwell thought, and he smiled too. *Maybe he won't have to campaign after all. At least not in New Hampshire.*

"These then, my fellow citizens, are the goals I believe we must move toward," Rattigan said: "A continuing ability to shape the world in which we live—without creating chaos among ourselves; an unending effort to move ahead at home, providing ever greater opportunities for Americans to live more fulfilling lives. I believe we can do these things. I know we can do them, if we seek to understand the roots of our problems—and if we unite to solve them.

"What is at stake, my friends, is freedom—at home and in the world. And if we are not willing to defend freedom in the world, we may someday not have it at home. Nor . . . deserve it."

There was a momentary silence, a sharp crash of applause, and the noise swelled as the crowd rose to cheer the President.

Cardwell looked up and found Sarah gazing down at him. He did not smile, and she did not. She only nodded slowly and looked at him as if to say, *Good work.*

Sarah and the other reporters, Cardwell knew, would be the first to catch the real meaning of the President's speech—and of the trip next week. The speech and the trip were signals that the President was taking the initiative, that he had begun his counterattack against Abner Hoffman.

Cardwell went alone to the late supper at the Mansion. It was a quiet, happy, informal affair, held in the upstairs private rooms of the White House. About forty people—Cabinet officers, senior staff members, friends of the President—circulated in the West Hall and the upstairs dining room.

Cardwell did not join the cluster of well-wishers who crowded around Rattigan. What could he say? Could he congratulate the President on his excellent speech—a speech he, Cardwell, had largely written?

In the dining room—the handsome chamber with its antique scenic wallpaper—Cardwell encountered Triplitano in the buffet line.

Trip squeezed his arm. "Great job, John. Were you watching Hoffman? He was getting green there toward the end."

"I thought he kept a pretty good poker face," Cardwell said.

"Pretty good, but far from perfect. I could see some pain there, near the end. Old Ab was thinking about his campaign from here on out: He'll be slogging through snowdrifts in Nashua, New Hampshire, while our man is at the summit. Ab'll be talking to the Kiwanis Club in Keene while the President's on the networks."

"I hope so," Cardwell said. And in this happy setting, in the warm afterglow of the President's forceful performance at the Capitol, he could almost share Trip's optimism.

The table, glittering with candles and silver, was laden with food: Crab Imperial in gleaming chafing dishes; ham, turkey, several salads. They took their plates out into the West Hall, where a television set had been placed so the guests could watch the coverage of the speech.

Cardwell watched and listened, fascinated, almost neglecting to eat. The panel of network reporters and their guests—these brains, these pundits—they were discussing his speech, his creation; sifting its contents, debating its meaning, pondering its significance.

He grinned in sheer amazed pleasure. Trip noticed his reaction.

"A nice feeling, isn't it?"

"It sure is."

"Don't let it go to your head."

Before he could reply, Cardwell saw Trip stand up and move away, carrying his plate and napkin. The President, Cardwell saw, had beckoned to Triplitano; he was standing near the tall door that led into his bedroom, waiting for his press secretary to join him for a moment of private discussion.

Cardwell watched until they disappeared and the door had closed. And suddenly he remembered Trip's words of several weeks ago about power and influence in the White House: *Around this place, it's not effort that counts in the long run. It's closeness. It's who talks to the President when he gets up in the morning and when he goes to bed at night. It's the ones he trusts the most, depends on the most: the guys he calls when he's got a problem. There can only be a few like that. . . .*

Trip, with the breezy, informal manner that disguised his keen politician's instinct—he was one of that tiny few.

The party swirled about Cardwell; he was oblivious to it. He dawdled over his food, at once too tired and too keyed up to eat. He tried to follow the earnest newsmen's comments on the speech. But his mind wandered back to the scene in the great chamber tonight: Rattigan's moment—the President smiling, raising one hand high to acknowledge the applause—and Hoffman: impassive, heavy-lidded, applauding slowly, dutifully, almost reluctantly.

"John?" It was Triplitano. He had come back into the hall. "Can you join us for a minute?"

Cardwell laid his plate down and followed Trip into the President's room.

Rattigan sat in a large wing chair by the fireplace. He was wearing his glasses now, staring at Abner Hoffman's flickering image on a television set.

"Well, it was a forceful speech," Hoffman was saying. "The President certainly made the best case he could for his position."

The President touched a remote switch by his chair and the set went dead.

"John, thank you," he said, rising from his chair. "You did a great job. I think we're on the road now. I think we've got Abner on the run. Have you started getting your shots?"

"Shots?" Cardwell was puzzled.

"I want you to go on this trip. Leonhardt's gone now. I'd like you to take over. You can help me with speeches on the plane."

"Thank you, sir. I'd like that."

After a few moments of small talk, Trip indicated with a nod that they should go. Cardwell thanked the President, shook hands, and followed Trip into the hall.

"It sounds like a great junket," Cardwell said.

"Great junket!" Trip, the veteran, laughed aloud. "You'll have to get five shots in a week. Meanwhile you'll be writing a dozen speeches, plus arrival-and-departure statements." He laughed again. "You know what you'll get from this trip? Airsickness, writer's cramp, and a sore tail."

Friday the Nineteenth

Eight days later, Air Force One roared off from Andrews, leaving frozen Washington behind for Uruguay. The great plane gathered speed, cutting upward through a layer of cold gray clouds. They would fly in sunlight, miles above the weather.

In his rear compartment, the President worked alone, wearing a blue bathrobe over casual clothes, puffing on a big cigar. For now, he felt good—relaxed. The summit would be exhausting, to be sure, and damned difficult: These Latins—all of them, it seemed—were long-winded, obstinate, explosive, incapable of really pulling together.

But he would try to push them—use a little muscle if necessary. He knew the pressure points, the little vulnerabilities, the precious channels of American aid and trade he could use as instruments of persuasion.

Four days from now, when the meetings would be over and he

would begin his series of state visits to their capitals, he hoped to have all that he wanted: an agreement by the Latins to put their troops in Bolivia under a unified command—a touchy, tricky question involving the Latins' sovereignty as well as vanity; a commitment of considerably more Latin troops to the war effort—which Rattigan would be willing to finance quietly with U.S. dollars; a program of postwar regional development for the entire continent—including Chile, whose participation would be angrily opposed by the rightists, like Badillo of Paraguay.

It would be difficult, exhausting. But Rattigan was optimistic. He relished the challenge of the summit and the change it offered from his routine back in Washington. And he liked the contrast it would offer to Abner Hoffman's tawdry little sideshow in New England.

Up forward in the staff section, Cardwell was relaxing. For him the pressure was off now that the trip was under way. He had spent the past week cutting, shaping, polishing the speeches—transforming the State Department's stilted, wooden phrases into words more human, more informal, more suited to the President's own style. Many of the drafts would be rewritten once again as the trip progressed—as ideas occurred to the President. But for now, the heat was off.

Cardwell pressed close to the window by his seat and stared out. Occasionally now there were breaks in the clouds, and he could see, miles below, the vast, bottle-green Atlantic.

The sound of the big jets was a steady, lulling roar, the sound of power.

Power. What better demonstration of it could there be than this trip of the President's? The power of the United States to create great events: a summit conference with all its built-in drama.

The low drone of the jets relaxed him toward sleep. He loosened his tie, took off his shoes, and removed the armrests from the three-across row of seats he occupied. From the overhead rack he took a pillow and sky-blue blanket woven with "Air Force One" and the presidential seal. Soon he was asleep. He slept through a brief refueling stop and through another steep climb into the southern sky. Then, two hours later, he felt a hand on his shoulder.

"Out of the sack, pal."

It was Trip.

"The boss wants to see you."

"Later," Cardwell yawned. Then he sat up and straightened his tie. "What's up?"

"The President has had a busy day aloft. He consulted with the Secretary of State and his trusted aide, Mr. Karnow. He then consulted at length with his trusted aide, Mr. Triplitano. He had lunch and a long nap. Now he wants you. That's all I know."

Cardwell ran a comb through his hair, tucked in his shirt flap, and followed Trip down the narrow aisle to the office compartment in the rear section.

Rattigan, in robe and slippers, was dictating to Sheila Roundtree.

"Oh, good. Come in. Sheila, that's all." She disappeared.

"I like this airport speech," Rattigan said. "I made a couple of changes, and they've put it on cards."

"Good, sir."

"Are you all set for the others?"

"We've got a draft prepared for every one," he answered. "And plenty of time and manpower if we need to change them. We're in good shape."

"Well, good, because I've got a job for you."

He pointed again at Cardwell. "You'll have a White House phone in your room at Punta. I want you to use it. I want a briefing paper twice a day on press reactions back in the States."

Cardwell nodded.

"I'll be busy, but I'll read them. I want to know how I'm doing—and how Abner's doing."

"Right, sir." Cardwell picked up a small tablet from the President's desk-table and jotted on it.

"I'll tell you what I think," Rattigan said. "I think Abner'll lose big in New Hampshire. I think I can win without campaigning."

Cardwell wasn't so sure, but he said nothing.

"I think the State of the Union wounded Abner and this trip will finish him off—knock him out of the headlines." He thrust his cigar forward in a jabbing gesture. "That's what I *think*. But I want to see how it's going. So keep me posted. Especially on the New Hampshire media."

Back in the staff section, Cardwell and Trip ordered bloody marys from the blue-coated steward.

"It's a funny operation," Cardwell said. "We fly four thousand miles to issue a communiqué that was written back in Washington.

The reporters fly four thousand miles so they can send it back to Washington. I fly four thousand miles so I can call Washington to find out what the reporters are saying. It's a little crazy, when you think about it."

"Try not to think about it," Trip said with a grin.

But Cardwell could not help thinking about it. When he had finished his drink and Trip had gone, he sat staring out of the window by his seat, reflecting on the trip.

What was the true purpose of the trip—diplomacy, or domestic politics? Not even Rattigan, Cardwell suspected, could answer that one. Rattigan's motives and purposes were all blurred, blended, indistinct.

The drink made Cardwell feel warm and drowsy. He nodded, slept, then, much later, started awake: The big plane had started descending.

He saw turrets of clouds off on the horizon. Directly below the plane the water, vast and dark, glittered in the late afternoon sun. He could see the shadow of the plane riding on the ocean below.

Suddenly the shadow disappeared, melding into a heavy gray-green mass below: land, stretching ahead as far as he could see: They were over Uruguay.

They circled the airport for fifteen minutes, allowing the three press planes a chance to land first so the reporters could be on hand to record the President's arrival and hear his statement.

He emerged, blue-suited, smiling, waving to the airport throng. Lisa, in bright red, walked slightly behind him down the airplane steps.

A band blared fanfares. The throng cheered, then cheered again. Rattigan shook hands with the Latin Presidents who had arrived before him. The big jet's engines faded and died; the national anthems of Uruguay and the United States were played; Rattigan stood at attention for his twenty-one-gun salute; a thousand cameras clicked, flags waved, schoolchildren dutifully cheered; another President had arrived.

Looking for a spot where he could stand during Rattigan's short speech, Cardwell walked near the roped-off press section.

"John, how are you?" It was Sarah Tolman. "Are you running this show?" She was smiling, glowing, friendly, her dark hair blowing in the breeze that swept the airstrip.

"No," he said. "Actually I won't have much to do at all. I'm just along for the ride."

"You're too modest. The jungle tom-toms tell me you handled all the speeches."

"That's right, but they're all done. Do you want to have that dinner you promised me? Tonight?"

"I'm working. How about tomorrow? Trip told us there's a monumental bash planned for the press tomorrow night. After that?"

He nodded and waved, then turned his attention to the podium near the foot of the airplane steps.

Rattigan's speech was short, simple, and optimistic, briefly stating the goal of the conference: unity among the hemisphere nations.

When it was over, the crowd scattered, and a fleet of limousines whisked the six Presidents off toward the city. Trip stayed behind to brief the press, and Cardwell listened.

"You have a lid," Trip shouted, using the same microphone the President had used, "until seven o'clock tomorrow morning."

The reporters groaned.

"That's when the host-country Minister of Information, Mr. Fernandez, will give you an agenda briefing."

They groaned again. But they were obviously enjoying themselves, caught up in the drama of the summit, looking forward to a few days in a new country, glad to be in a spot where there was sun instead of snow.

When it was over, the reporters pushed toward their bus. Trip joined him, and they walked toward a waiting staff car.

"Well, buddy, so far, so good," Trip said. "Traveling with the President has its advantages: no baggage to carry, no passport check, no customs, no waiting for cabs. And these bastards in the press are mesmerized. They love these trips. In twenty minutes they'll all be drunk and playing with the *señoritas.*"

Cardwell smiled and nodded, but he wasn't really listening. He was following Sarah with his eyes as she walked toward the press bus with her colleagues. The scarf she wore was blowing in the wind, and her long, dark hair was lifting, moving as she walked.

Beautiful, he thought.

She was writing as she walked, holding a small pad in one hand and writing with the other, only half looking where she walked. For a brief moment Cardwell was afraid she might stumble. Then he remembered: She's a veteran at this. She even managed to make it seem graceful, walking and writing all at once, with her hair blowing behind her. Beautiful.

Saturday the Twentieth

On Saturday, the first full day of the summit meeting, the sun, intense and clear, warmed Punta del Este's gentle curve of beach, inviting visitors to come and relax. But on this weekend the main attraction of the sleepy resort was not the sunny beachfront, nor the rolling, glittering surf, but the gathering of the six Presidents in the ballroom of the Hotel La Playa.

When the participants were gathered and in their places—the Presidents, their aides, interpreters, messengers, and technicians—photographers were invited in. They were allowed two minutes to capture the scene for the world to see: the chief participants sitting stiffly, formally around the table, each with a clean notepad in place before him and crystal pitcher of water nearby. It was a scene that disclosed nothing: not a shred of useful information. Their pictures taken, the cameramen were herded out and the ballroom doors swung shut.

Carl Rattigan, sitting in his heavy chair at the big doughnut-shaped table, tried to be patient.

The President, accustomed to doing things quickly, informally, American-style, chafed under the requirements of formal diplomacy. He disliked the long and elaborate opening statements, the lengthy translations, the exaggerated deference with which it was necessary to treat the various Latin chiefs.

Let's get down to business, he thought, as the President of Uruguay, a stocky, balding man in a blue double-breasted suit, reached the midpoint of his opening speech.

"And so, my esteemed colleagues of the Americas, we gather at the summit—not merely to plan how we shall react to fate, but also to master and direct it—"

Rattigan shifted in his seat. The opening statements would take until noon; he would speak last—briefly and simply, merely outlining the objectives he felt the meeting should achieve.

He shook his head, trying to listen to the interpreter. He jotted a note or two from the Uruguayan speech: "proceed cautiously . . ."; "remember the limitations imposed by history . . ."

Unconsciously Rattigan shifted from taking notes to doodling aimlessly on the pad before him.

Let's get down to business, he thought again. Already he was tired.

Toward the end of the morning Sheldon Karnow leaned forward from his place behind the President and pushed a folded note toward Rattigan. "YOU CAN PERCEIVE A THEME IN ALL THIS," Karnow had written. "THEY ARE TELLING US WHY THEY *CANNOT ACT.*"

Rattigan read it, nodded, then carefully, methodically shredded Karnow's note.

It was true. Almost all of the other five had spoken by now. Each had stressed the difficulties he faced in his own country: left-wing opposition, tight budgets, open sympathy for the Chileans, inadequate resources in troops and materiel. Each had made it clear that he deplored the barely disguised aggression of Chile, that he supported a strong and vigorous response to that aggression. Each had paid stirring tribute to the principle of regional co-operation. Then came the *buts:* the qualifications, equivocations, pleading of special difficulty . . .

Only Badillo, the crusty old dictator from Paraguay, was an exception. He had called for an all-out effort by all the allies against renegade Chile. He had talked of blockades, bombing, embargoes. And he had met, when he finished his long statement and sat down, polite applause, then chilly silence.

Karnow pushed Rattigan another folded note: "YOU'RE GOING TO HAVE TO USE A LITTLE MUSCLE."

Rattigan nodded, then lifted his ballpoint pen and wrote, "I KNOW." He was prepared, in the afternoon meetings with the individual chiefs of state—the so-called "bilaterals"—to badger, threaten, wheedle, and cajole.

He passed the note back to Karnow.

A burst of applause: The fifth President was winding up, and it was Rattigan's turn now. He flipped open the black binder before him, rose, and began to speak.

"My fellow Presidents and distinguished colleagues," he began, "it has been a long morning, so I will be brief."

It really didn't matter what he said here. The results of this summit, if there were to be any, would come not from pretty speeches in the plenary sessions, but from the little private chats.

He could be savage if he had to be. And now it seemed that he might have to use, as Karnow put it, *a little muscle.*

It was eight-thirty when Cardwell and Sarah Tolman walked into the ballroom of the Hotel Reposa, where the press were quartered.

The party was in full swing, and they could see that Trip's prediction of a bash was no understatement. There were three hundred people in the room—reporters from all over South America and the United States, with a scattering of Europeans, Asians, and a black journalist from Nigeria. All of them seemed to be talking at once: a haze of cigar and cigarette smoke floated upward toward the chandeliers.

A waiter passed; Cardwell took two drinks from his tray, handed one to Sarah, and they drifted into the crowd.

"John, how are you?" It was Triplitano, playing host, even though the party was being staged by the Government of Uruguay. "And Sarah!"

"Hi, Trip." Sarah extended her hand and Cardwell watched, admiring her. She was beautiful, dressed in a long flame-colored dress with a flowing skirt. And she was perfectly assured: a woman accustomed to the company of men—used to their admiration.

"My sources tell me," Triplitano said, "that your dispatch was front-paged in the *Times* today. And they tell me that it was the best damn story of any filed so far."

"I like your sources," Sarah laughed.

"He's marvelous," Sarah said when Trip was gone. And then: "I wonder who told him about my story."

"I did," Cardwell said.

"You!"

"I'm monitoring the press for the duration of the trip." He smiled. "And I have you under especially careful scrutiny."

"I really do like his sources," Sarah said.

Later, near the long buffet table that ran across one end of the ballroom, Sarah introduced him to a tall, gray-templed Englishman.

"An old, old friend, John," Sarah said. "Peter Lillykreb, the London *Telegraph*."

Cardwell recognized the name: He was a pundit of international reputation—and boundless pomposity. They shook hands.

"Peter and I were in Vietnam together," she explained. "Since then we see each other only at summit meetings."

"And state funerals," Lillykreb said, smiling slightly.

"John is with the President," Sarah said.

"Oh?" Cardwell could almost see the antennae quivering. "What is it that you do?"

"A bit of everything," Cardwell said. "Some political work, and—"

"Foreign policy?"

"Speeches, sometimes." Lillykreb's sudden fascination bothered him.

"Oh, speeches, quite. Well, I've read a few of those. Fascinating documents." Lillykreb was tall, with a deeply suntanned face and a high, beaked nose. He talked as if calling down from a great height.

"Would I be wrong," he asked, in a tone that suggested the impossibility of being wrong, "in saying that your President has reverted in Bolivia to the foreign policy of militarism and moralism?"

"Yes," Cardwell said gently. "I think you would be wrong."

"The policy of Eisenhower and Dulles? White hats vs. black hats?"

Cardwell said nothing. He did not want to argue with one of Sarah's friends.

"I entitled my last piece on this subject," Lillykreb said, "'Rattigan's Retreat from Realism.' What do you think of that?"

"I like the alliteration," Cardwell said. But he knew that soon he must defend the President; Lillykreb would bait him until he did. "I prefer the word 'morality' to 'moralism,'" Cardwell said. "I think it's more accurate."

Lillykreb looked at Cardwell as if there were a fly on Cardwell's nose. "Dear Sarah, your friend has all the appealing naïveté of most Americans. So appealing—and so dangerous for the rest of the world."

Sarah was about to make a light, conciliatory reply, but Cardwell interrupted.

"Who's naïve and dangerous?" He was speaking rather loudly. A couple of American reporters, heading for the buffet, stopped to listen. "Who was naïve when Germany invaded Czechoslovakia? If you'd done what Rattigan is doing now, we might have avoided World War II. If you'd—"

"My dear boy, please. No history lessons. That was my war, my generation. Now: Are you saying that in this re-enactment of ancient history, Chile is Nazi Germany? That Chile aims at conquering the world?"

"Did the Italians aim at conquering the world by conquering Ethiopia? Maybe if you'd stopped them—"

"Ancient history," Lillykreb said curtly. Then, with a suggestion of a smile: "Italy was allied with Germany back in those days. Who are Chile's allies?"

"That's a good question," Cardwell said.

"Moscow, perhaps? Peking?" Lillykreb was smiling.

"I suspect both of them are not totally indifferent to all that's going on."

"Dominoes, eh?" Lillykreb said contemptuously. "Incredible that anyone in a high position could be so naïve!"

"John, could you get me a fresh drink?" Sarah laid a hand on his arm, but Cardwell ignored her.

"Mr. Lillykreb, I'm sorry if I offend you by my ignorance. But you know, I'm at a loss: I just don't know from whom we Americans should take advice."

"From us British," the older man said with a faint, half-mocking smile.

"You British," Cardwell said, "have been a fifth-rate power with a fifth-rate economy ever since World War II. If it weren't for our generosity you'd have sunk into the ocean."

"John, please!" Sarah said.

"And Europe! They've been soaking their own continent in blood for a thousand years, and now, after we've been protecting them for a generation, they feel entitled to give us advice on foreign policy. There must be better places to get advice."

"Who are 'they'?" Lillykreb asked faintly, but Cardwell didn't stop.

"It makes me tired," Cardwell said. "Ever since World War II you people have been protected by what you're scorning now—a moralistic foreign policy; white hats vs. black hats."

"And you're in the white hat, of course?"

"You're damned right. Or in the light gray hat. And Chile is in a dark gray hat. Very dark gray."

"And Moscow, and Peking?"

"Dark gray."

"And you believe that your country stands for all that is right and good and virtuous?"

"*Much* that is right and good and virtuous. I believe that the American Revolution was the real revolution in this world, and it's been accepted that way all over the globe—by the people, if not by journalists."

"My dear young man—"

"What are we going to say to a country like Bolivia, that's struggling to make its way decently in the world? 'Sorry, you're not in our vital interest, and we can't bother about morality'? Give our regards to the wolves?"

"Mr. Cardwell, I think you are a very zealous and a very ignorant young man."

"That may be," Cardwell said tightly, "but I'm not cynical." He turned to Sarah. "I think we'd better go to dinner. I hope I didn't offend you, Mr. Lillykreb."

"Not at all. In fact, you enlightened me. I know something now about the men around your President."

Walking toward the exit through the crowd, Cardwell felt his face burning—not from the heat of his exchange with the British journalist, but because he realized suddenly that Lillykreb would have the last word: He would write a column—probably datelined Punta del Este—about the zeal and ignorance of the President's advisers. Well: Screw him.

"I'm sorry if I embarrassed you," he said to Sarah.

"Not at all." She smiled. "I thought you held up your end rather well. And you look rather cute when you get mad. Like a little boy about to fight. I guess I should have told you that Peter is an old, old friend—and a pompous ass sometimes."

He smiled, put his arm lightly about her waist, and they walked out of the hotel onto the beachfront promenade.

They found a dark and quiet restaurant not too far away, asked for a table near the rear of the room, and ordered drinks.

"They're like any other group of people," Sarah said. "Some are brilliant and some are fools. Peter is a bit of both. He's awfully arrogant, but he writes beautifully, and personally he can be very sweet. He was in—"

"I don't want to talk about him." Sarah gave him a startled look.

"I'm sorry," he said gently. "I'm just tired of shop talk. I don't even know whether I really believe all the things I said to him. I just got irritated, he was so smug." He traced a pattern with his fingertip on the linen tablecloth. "I'd rather talk about something inconsequential."

Wordlessly, Sarah nodded, and Cardwell felt a surge of gratitude.

They ordered dinner and ate quietly, conversing occasionally about nothing much, until Cardwell looked at her intently.

"Are you happy?"

She looked startled. "Why, yes, I mean—why do you ask?"

"I wondered if it was enough for you, being the reigning queen of the press corps."

"You're wondering why I never married."

"Yes."

"Sooner or later every man I meet asks me that question." She dropped her eyes and studied the table. "When I was younger I wasn't really interested. I was starting a career. I wanted to travel, be a success."

He leaned forward, listening.

"Then I just stopped picturing myself as a wife and mother, I suppose." She looked up and smiled, half embarrassed.

"But there have been men. You told me once . . ."

"Of course."

"And you wish you'd married?"

She hesitated, then looked down again. "It's a long story," she said slowly. "I didn't. Now I guess I don't expect to."

He saw that she wanted to let it drop, so he asked nothing more.

They refused dessert; Cardwell asked the waiter for the check, and they left the little restaurant a few minutes after midnight.

Outside, on the promenade, he put his arm about her, and they walked slowly back toward her hotel. The light and noise of the resort had faded, and they could hear the dull roar of the waves down on the beach. It was getting colder.

Halfway back, they stopped to lean against the railing of the broad walkway and listen to the ocean. After a moment, Sarah straightened up, and Cardwell, taking her lightly by the shoulders, kissed her. He felt her hesitate, then relax. When they parted, she leaned her head on his shoulder for a moment, then looked at him levelly.

"You're missing your wife," she said.

He stared at her.

"It's all right," Sarah said. "I understand. You can tell the truth. We're both adults."

"All right," he said. "It's not that I miss her. I don't, that much. I miss having an anchor point. A place where I belong. It's not a comfortable feeling."

"I know."

"I don't think we have anything left between us, at least not much. But you get used to having somebody to share things with, even if you're not happy together."

They started to walk again. Sarah slipped her hand through his arm and walked with her eyes down, as if searching for something to say.

"You asked if I miss not being married. Well, that's what I miss. No matter how exciting the life is, no matter how absorbed I get, I want to share it. Sometimes when I write a story, I pretend I'm writing a letter to someone." She hesitated. "A man. My husband, I suppose. I describe everything for him."

He stopped, seized her, and kissed her again.

"It's one o'clock," she said hoarsely. "We'd better go."

They walked back to her hotel, holding one another as the breeze from the ocean turned colder, feeling suddenly despite the hard day and night they had both gone through, as if the day were just beginning.

As they entered her hotel they disengaged, each instinctively on guard against careless eyes, gossip, scrutiny; each had too much to lose.

The ornate marble lobby was empty, except for a drunken Paraguayan journalist who sat on a broad couch, staring blankly into space.

Near the elevator she suddenly took his hand. And upstairs, in the hall, he kissed her as she tried to turn the key in her room door. She made a move to stop him but he held her tightly, until finally she ran one hand roughly across the back of his neck and through his hair.

He stretched his arm behind her to reach the doorknob; then he turned the key and led her inside.

Later he awakened in the unfamiliar darkness, groggy, uncertain where he was. Then he stirred slightly, felt Sarah's body against him, and he knew. They had fallen asleep in a loose embrace; now he could feel Sarah's bare back against his chest.

What time? He thought of reaching through the darkness for his watch but couldn't remember where it was, so he lay still, careful not to awaken Sarah.

Sarah. So different from Nancy: larger, slower, easier. Nancy in her lovemaking was quick, urgent, as if she were afraid her pleasure would not come unless she hurried it. There was in Sarah no such desperation; she was confident, almost languorous; sure of herself. And afterward, floating together, they had talked—easily, intimately: something he seldom did with Nancy.

Nancy's body was angles, Sarah's curves. Nancy's voice was thin, narrow, plaintive; Sarah's low, confidential, touched with something sad. When he talked to Nancy he always felt, just beneath the planes and angles of her body, something hard and complaining: tears about to happen. In Sarah he was aware of something rich and bottomless: her satisfaction with herself.

She moved, and her weight was suddenly uncomfortable against his arm. Gently he pulled it from beneath her head and moved away from her; gave her space, felt suddenly cool where she had been against him.

Then slowly, satisfied, he fell back to sleep.

Much later he started awake again, raised his head and saw Sarah, wrapped in a bathrobe, sitting with her back to him, staring out the window at the gray dawn that was coming up over the ocean. She was smoking; her cigarette glowed in the half light.

"Sarah?" He reached out and touched her somewhere near the small of her back. She moved away but said nothing and he heard her exhale, a long sigh. She had been crying.

"I'd like to think this didn't happen," she said.

"Why?"

"It wasn't supposed to happen. Can we just make believe it didn't happen?"

"No!" Angrily he flung back the covers and scrambled across the bed to sit beside her, forgetting that he was naked. "No, we can't forget it."

"I didn't say forget it," she said gently. But she leaned away when he put his hand on her shoulder. "But I can't see anything in this, for you or me." She stopped, then went on. "There's no way we can justify—"

"Justify! For once in my life I'd like to do something I didn't have to justify. Just once!" He found his shorts beside the bed, stood up, and pulled them on. "I'm tired of justifying, explaining, giving reasons. Justify my job to my wife. Justify the President to everybody. Justify, justify!" He saw the startled, stricken look in Sarah's eyes and pointed a finger at her. "And for God's sake, don't you cry!"

For a second she stared at him, then collapsed in laughter. "You look like a little boy again," she said, and she fell back onto the bed, still laughing.

He leaned over her and kissed her. "No justifications. Promise?"

"I promise. For the time being."

Cardwell walked across the room, fell in beside her, and buried his face in her long hair. He coaxed her gently out of her robe and they made love again, having freed themselves from the need to justify, explain, give reasons.

Afterward they lay together for a long time, saying nothing, staring together at the sun in the window, watching idly as the breeze stirred in the curtains.

Cardwell felt happy—really happy—for the first time in many weeks.

Sunday the Twenty-first

Gary Triplitano, at his Sunday afternoon briefing for the American press, found the reporters wary and restless.

"Trip," one correspondent asked, "have you just postponed the briefing by Sheldon Karnow, or is it canceled altogether?"

"Neither," Trip said, and there was a groan from the reporters. "There was never any briefing formally scheduled, so how could it be postponed or canceled?"

Already rumors were flying around Punta del Este that the summit was in trouble. The reporters were alert, sniffing the air, suspicious. And nothing in Trip's performance at the briefing cooled their suspicions. He was noticeably evasive. Where was Karnow with the communiqué? Why was it being delayed? What did Triplitano take them for—idiots?

The press secretary, uncharacteristically nervous and shifty-eyed, denied vehemently that anything untoward was happening. And that, in the curiously topsy-turvy world of the White House and the White House press corps, was a certain signal that something was happening.

Carl Rattigan, exhausted, tense, and angry, lay at the end of the day on a portable massage table in his hotel suite, accepting a pummeling from Sorrel, the young Navy medic.

The President, stripped and wrapped in a towel, seemed to be asleep. But he was listening closely to Sheldon Karnow, who sat in a chair against the wall, speaking in his usual precise, no-nonsense tone.

"Mr. President," Karnow said, "I would urge you to extend these meetings one more day if I thought it would do some good. But I think you've got all you can get from them."

"Which is damn little," Rattigan groaned.

"I think we can characterize the outcome as a partial success," Karnow went on. "A qualified success."

The President raised his head to look at Karnow. "We can characterize it any way we please. The press will characterize it as a partial failure." He lowered his head. "The bastards. Well, I'm not going to delay it," Rattigan said. "I know you're right. I'll sign the damned communiqué, empty as it is."

"It's not entirely empty. I think we can live with it."

"When do you brief the press?"

"I'm not sure. I guess Trip will call them together after dinner."

"Well, do the best you can," Rattigan said bleakly, and he waved a hand, dismissing his aide.

For a while after Karnow had gone, Rattigan lay drifting, listening to the methodical slap-slap of Sorrel's hands: trying to relax.

The meetings had not gone well. The Latin Presidents, prisoners of ancient, petty rivalries among their countries, could agree on almost nothing. They were willing to condemn Chile's aggression sternly, to deplore the invasion of Bolivia. But when it came to specifics, there was almost no agreement.

A unified command for the hemisphere troops based in Bolivia? The whole discussion of the question had been a brawl. Rattigan had proposed that a Latin general, not one from the United States, head the allied command; Rattigan wanted to avoid charges of Big Brotherism. But half of the Presidents were unwilling to take the political risk of providing a commander; of the other half, each was unwilling to see the honor go to some other country. And so there was a feeble compromise: An "Allied Defense Committee" would be set up to meet periodically in various Latin capitals to "oversee" the conduct of the war.

Remembering this empty agreement, Rattigan growled in anger and frustration. It had gone this way on every question. And the result was mostly empty words.

Well, Karnow was a good briefer: glib, convincing, articulate. If anyone could make the communiqué sound good to the press, Karnow could do it. Nothing to do now but hope for the best.

"You want to sleep a while, sir?" Sorrel asked.

"Thank you, I think I will."

Sorrel covered him with a giant towel, then a blanket, leaving only the President's face exposed, then disappeared, and Rattigan, eager to escape his disappointment, dropped off to sleep.

Just before the dinner hour Cardwell left his hotel and walked down the beachfront promenade to Sarah's.

He looked about the lobby, carefully scanning the room to see if he was observed by anyone he knew, then took the elevator to her floor.

She answered his knock.

"Hard day?" she asked when they had kissed.

"Not hard at all," he said, loosening his tie. "This trip is a reward for good work in the past, I think. I really don't have that much to do."

"How is it going?"

"You mean the meetings?"

"We're getting rumors that something's gone awry. Trip had a terrible briefing this afternoon. He—"

Cardwell crossed the room and embraced her, laughing, pinning her arms to her sides.

"It's going well for me," he said. "And that's all I care about right now. I didn't come here to talk business."

With his face buried in her dark hair he pushed her slightly backward and they fell together, laughing, onto the bed. He snapped off the lamp.

Later Sarah sat propped against her pillows in the darkness, and he lay beside her, studying her face in the occasional glow of her cigarette.

"I wish you were going to be on the rest of the trip," he said.

"I can't. I've got to get back and cover the campaign." She didn't mention Hoffman's name.

"I don't want you to think—" He hesitated.

"Yes?"

"I don't want you to think that this was just a lark." He inclined his head to study her expression, but could not see her in the dark. "That this was just because we were a long way from home."

Sarah said nothing.

"Can I—see you in Washington?"

"Of course," she said. "Whatever you want."

"Wait a minute. Don't you have any feelings in the matter?"

"Of course I do."

"But you don't want to get hurt—again." He was probing, trying to divine something of her past.

"Please. I don't want to talk about that."

Feeling a sudden distance opening between them, he reached for her. Lightly he traced a line with his right hand down her neck, across her shoulder, across the smooth curve of her body.

"Sarah?"

She didn't answer.

"You remember I said I thought I'd lost my capacity to feel anything? That wasn't true."

She stubbed out her cigarette, and Cardwell, as she leaned back, pulled her down into his arms.

"I feel—more than I've felt in a long time," he whispered.

Sarah lay still in his embrace for an instant, then struggled free and pressed a finger to his lips.

"Remember? You said no justifications, no explanations. You're breaking the rules. Please. Don't say anything." And she kissed him, to keep him from replying.

Monday the Twenty-second

The next morning nothing remained except the closing ceremony: Rattigan stood with the other Presidents on the steps of the hotel; they posed for pictures; each made a simple statement praising the meetings and endorsing the previous day's communiqué. Then, with handshakes all around, the summit was over, and Rattigan's wild race began.

For the President and his entourage, the next four days became a blur: Montevideo, Asuncion, Brasilia. Lima, Bogota, Caracas. They felt themselves moving across Latin America at double speed: from airport to airport, motorcade to city square, city square to presidential palace, palace to hotel.

Always in their ears there was noise: jets roaring, bands playing, loudspeakers whining and echoing, people cheering. And somehow amid the noise and the frenzied movement from capital to capital the disappointingly mixed results of the summit meeting were almost forgotten.

On Wednesday, as Air Force One began to descend toward Bogota, Brooks Healy smiled at the President and said with satisfaction: "By the time we get back to Washington, hardly anybody will remember that damned communiqué. They'll all have confetti in their hair."

Rattigan smiled and said nothing. But by the next day, as he and Lisa climbed up the plane's ramp after their stop in Caracas, he knew that Healy, as usual, was right: The reporters were impressed; maybe, after all, the trip would be perceived as a success.

Rattigan slept the whole way back to Washington: across the Caribbean, over Florida, and up the Eastern Seaboard, with the sound of cheering and brass bands ringing in his ears.

There was no band playing when Air Force One landed at Andrews Air Force Base shortly after eight on Thursday evening; no crowd to cheer the President's homecoming; no little girl in a starched white pinafore to present a welcoming bouquet—and no Vice President to greet the returning President.

The plane trundled off the runway to the edge of the airfield against a stiff wind from the north. The President, bundled against the cold and accompanied only by Lisa, Brooks Healy, and Triplitano, hurried down the ramp toward his waiting helicopter. The crowd of staff members waited in the cold to get their baggage, then scurried toward the line of White House cars that had pulled up near the plane.

Home at last.

Cardwell, exhausted, slumped against the back seat of his White House car.

"Home, sir?"

"You bet." He had tried to sleep on the last leg of the trip, but most of the passengers in the staff section were celebrating the end of their long ordeal with scotch, champagne, and songs—loud ones. Now he let his head fall backward.

Home at last.

Home. Suddenly he opened his eyes and sat up, straight, thinking of his empty house in Bethesda. Empty and dark.

"Driver? Can you take me to the White House instead? I'd like to catch up on my mail."

"Whatever you say, sir." His driver shrugged, then checked his watch. Nine o'clock. What's with these guys? Back home after a killer of a trip, and he wants to check his mail? Don't these guys ever get enough? "Whatever you say," he said. And he headed the black sedan toward the city.

Back at the White House, the President and Lisa persuaded Brooks Healy to stay for a late dinner after their arrival in Washington. They ate from trays in the Yellow Oval Room, before a cheery fire.

When dinner was over, Lisa excused herself and left to go to bed.

"I've got to leave myself," Healy said, still on his feet after she walked out.

"No, stay," said Rattigan. He was stretched full length on the sofa before the fire, scanning the last in the stack of the week's newspapers he had been reading.

Healy sat down.

"The coverage is great," Rattigan said, shoving a paper toward Healy.

Healy nodded. Accounts of the President's trip had dominated the front pages, pushed the stories of Hoffman's campaign into secondary spots in all the papers.

"Well, you've buried Abner," Healy said. "What do you plan to do next?"

The President didn't answer. He was staring into the fire. Healy watched him silently.

"I could *feel* the crowd in Caracas this afternoon," Rattigan said after a time. "Not just see it. I could feel it. Tired as I was." He straightened up, swung his feet to the floor, and looked at Healy. "I guess it had been building up, day after day. All those people in all those cities, all those cheering crowds. Then today it hit me: They're my constituents. Does that sound odd?"

"I don't think so." Healy understood.

"They didn't vote for me. They didn't elect me. Hell, most of them can't even speak my language. But they depend on me, on us. And they know it. They care what we do."

"I know."

"It really hit me, seeing them today. I felt responsible to them. Is that presumptuous? Arrogant?"

"I don't think so," Healy said gently.

The two men were silent for a time. Then Rattigan spoke.

"Brooks? Do you think it's right? What I'm doing? Do you think I'm right?"

"Yes, sir, I do. Beyond a doubt."

"Then I have to ruin Abner, don't I? Really whip him. Humiliate him."

"Just defeat him, Mr. President. By a good, wide margin." He pointed to the stack of newspapers. "And I'd say you're on your way."

Alone in the tomblike silence of his office, Cardwell spent an hour scanning the past week's newspapers.

Dot had arranged them in neat stacks, day by day: the *Times,* the *Post,* the *Star,* the *Sun,* the *Trib,* the *Monitor,* the Denver *Post,* the Los Angeles *Times.* And most important, the New Hampshire dailies:

CHEERING THRONGS MOB RATTIGAN.
RATTIGAN REASSURES LATINS.
MEETINGS A DISAPPOINTMENT, BUT TOUR A TRIUMPH.

He read on and on.

It was almost eleven when he looked up from the newspapers and turned toward the in box on his desk. Dot had piled it high with letters, memos, papers. Among them, he knew, would be the poll results: neat rows of figures, submitted by a private telephone pollster, reflecting the daily impact of Rattigan's trip. Polls of all voters. Polls of Democrats only. Polls from across the country. Polls from New Hampshire.

He reached toward the box, then hesitated. It was late. He could feel his weariness in every muscle. Tomorrow would be soon enough.

He dialed Sarah's number, and smiled when he heard her voice.

"Hi. I'm home. Why don't you invite me for a drink?"

"At this hour?" Then she laughed. "All right. Why don't you come and have a drink?"

"I've really missed you, Sarah."

"Then hurry."

He pulled his coat on and walked with his suitcase out onto Pennsylvania Avenue, where he hailed a cab and gave the driver the Macomb Street address.

For the first part of the trip up Connecticut Avenue, he watched the traffic; peered out at the few pedestrians on the street. Then he leaned back, smiled, and breathed a sigh of pleasure and fatigue. No empty house tonight.

Thursday the Twenty-fifth

The next morning, when they came out of her apartment building into the morning cold, Cardwell and Sarah walked hand-in-hand the single block up Macomb Street to Connecticut Avenue.

"Let's share a cab," he said. But Sarah shook her head.

"We famous Washington figures must be discreet about our indiscretions," she said, smiling. Before he could reply she pulled her hand from his, hailed a cab, and was gone.

It was five minutes before he saw another empty taxi. He hailed it, climbed in, and saw on the seat beside him a discarded copy of the *Post.*

RATTIGAN RETURNS FROM SUMMIT.

Cardwell smiled and picked it up.

CHEERED BY THOUSANDS IN TWO CAPITALS.

The story was essentially the same as those he had read the night before; only the datelines were new. He read a paragraph or two, then laid the newspaper aside and studied the traffic, the bare trees along the avenue, the people hurrying down the sidewalks, bent forward against the cold.

And Cardwell thought of Sarah: conjured up her face, her rich, dark hair, freed from its ribbon, falling heavily around her shoulders; her grave eyes.

"I've really missed you," she had said simply when she opened her apartment door. And she had treated him as though her apartment, with its litter of books and papers, its cluttered kitchen, was somehow his, not hers; as if he had always lived there; as if they belonged together.

She had known instinctively that he didn't want to talk about the trip. And so, after two drinks and an hour of comfortable silence, she had led him to bed.

"Hey, Mac, this is it."

"Excuse me?"

"The Northwest Gate. You want to go through?"

"No, this is fine."

Cardwell tipped the driver, nodded to the guard on duty at the gate, and walked up the long driveway in the cold, still thinking of Sarah.

On this morning after his homecoming, the President slept late. He awakened at eight-thirty, told the White House switchboard to hold his calls, then rang for coffee and the morning papers.

Lisa joined him for breakfast as he was scanning the headlines, propped up on pillows in his high bed.

"How's the conquering hero?"

He looked up and smiled. "Ready to do some more conquering."

"Tired?"

"Not really." He laid his paper down. "You know, it's funny, all those people. It's as if they were giving me their energy, not taking mine. I feel all charged up. As if I could do anything."

An expression of puzzlement crossed her face as she poured her coffee, but Rattigan didn't notice; he had returned to his reading. When she finished her coffee, she touched his hand.

"Hard day today?" she asked.

"No, easy. No appointments."

"Then why don't we go to Camp David?"

"Good idea. We've earned it."

When she had gone he reread the front pages once again, reliving, as he read, the past four days, hearing the thunder of the crowds.

Smiling, he settled back and let the papers slide off the bed onto the floor.

¡Viva el Presidente Rattigan! He could hear the shouts, almost feel the pressure of the crowds as they leaned toward the slow-rolling limousine.

That their cheers had been in Spanish, not in English, hardly occurred to him.

He shifted on his pillows, relaxing.

From now on it would be easy. The surge had begun—he could feel it.

And Abner Hoffman, charging so frantically across the frozen landscape of New Hampshire—Abner seemed a threat no longer, only an annoyance.

By ten o'clock even Sarah was far from Cardwell's mind. His desk was awash with charts and papers.

At eleven he dialed Triplitano. But the press secretary was tied up: The morning briefing was in progress.

Trip called back at one o'clock. "Were you calling to congratulate me on the good stories? They're all my work, you know."

"Trip, I think we need to see the President."

"The President is on his way to Camp David for a long weekend. He just took off, and I'm going out and get drunk. Can it wait till Monday?"

"I don't think so. I've been reading some new polls."

Trip hesitated a moment. "What do you want to tell him, John? Good news or bad?"

"I want to tell him that unless he gets his ass up to New Hampshire right away, Abner Hoffman is going to beat him. Bad."

"You're kidding."

"I mean it, Trip. I can show you the figures."

There was a long silence. Then Triplitano said, "Stay by your phone. I'll get back to you."

In fifteen minutes Triplitano called: "He wants to hear your story. We'll go up by chopper. Be on the South Lawn at eight forty-five tomorrow morning."

Friday the Twenty-sixth

The three of them—the President, Cardwell, and Triplitano—ate a late breakfast in the quiet Aspen Lodge at Camp David. Then they strode into the living room, where Cardwell opened his briefcase and spread his papers on the low table before the sofa.

He told the President bluntly about the polls.

"I've got lots of numbers, Mr. President, and we can talk about them all. But what they mean is this: Nationally, you're doing fine. You're fifteen points ahead of Hoffman nationwide. In New Hampshire, you're in trouble. You're only five points ahead of Hoffman."

"Why?" Rattigan's voice was toneless.

"Because he's up there campaigning and you aren't. They seem to like his nerve."

"Show me the numbers." Rattigan reached into a shirt pocket for his heavy horn-rimmed glasses and leaned forward.

"This is Gallup, all Democrats nationwide: the President, 52 points; Hoffman, 37; undecided, 11 per cent. The State of the Union speech gave you a boost, and the summit trip helped, too."

"But in New Hampshire?"

Cardwell pointed to a second chart. "This is also a poll of Democrats only: the President, 43 per cent; Hoffman, 38; undecided, 19."

"Is this a public poll?"

"No, sir. Private."

"But it will leak out soon."

"I don't know. I hope not. In any case, it means—"

"I know what it means." Rattigan took off his glasses, laid them on the table, and rubbed his face with both hands. "I know what it means."

"I think you should consider going to New Hampshire."

"I *have* considered it," Rattigan said dryly. "And I decided I didn't want to campaign up there if I could avoid it."

Triplitano spoke. "John, it's five weeks before the vote. Don't you think he could hold off awhile?"

Cardwell shrugged. "I don't know. But if this trend continues, it will get harder to deal with as time goes by."

As Cardwell spoke the President had seemed only half listening, staring down at the papers spread on the table. Now he rose, shaking his head as if to dismiss Cardwell's suggestion, and walked to the window, which looked out into the woods.

"I left the chance open that I'd go up there," he said. "I said in the State of the Union that I would *hope* not to campaign. But I left the possibility open." He stared for a long moment at the cold landscape outside: trees etched in vertical strokes of gray. Then he turned to face them.

"Why do you think I didn't want to go up there?"

Neither Cardwell nor Triplitano replied.

"Why?" the President repeated.

"I don't know, Mr. President," Cardwell said.

"Because to go up there would legitimize what Ab is doing. Can't you see that?" He turned back to the big window and spoke to the cold glass. "As long as he campaigned without an answer from me, it was as though he wasn't a candidate at all. But the minute I fly up there—the minute I start campaigning, the minute I start answering his charges—I make Ab a real candidate, a real threat." He shook his head impatiently. "I didn't want to *accept his challenge*. Because to accept his challenge would be admitting that I accepted what he was doing to the system. It would be like saying I approve, somehow."

Rattigan took a deep breath and exhaled heavily. "But Ab has the numbers." He turned to face them, looking as if he had awakened from a dream. "He has people taking polls up there, too, doesn't he?"

"I suspect he does," Cardwell replied.

"Goddamn the polls," Rattigan said bleakly, shaking his head. "Goddamn the polls."

Triplitano, glancing at a ship's clock on the wall across the room, saw that the two hours they had been promised were almost gone. He stood up. "Mr. President, do you want us to do anything when we go back? Make any plans?"

"No!" Rattigan fairly shouted. Then he pointed to the papers: Cardwell's polls. "I want to study these. I want to think about it. I'll see you Monday."

Their interview was over. Cardwell and Triplitano were driven on a golf cart to the helicopter pad nearby for the short flight back to Washington.

Neither of the two aides spoke until the trip was almost over. Triplitano studied a newspaper, letting each section fall onto the floor beside his seat when he had finished it. Cardwell stared down at the bare landscape rushing by, until the broad Potomac came into view.

"What do you think he'll do?" he said to Triplitano.

"I don't know."

"He doesn't have five weeks, you know. Not really."

"I know. I was just trying to ease his mind."

The helicopter swept along the curve of the river, over the city, then banked leftward, down toward the White House lawn.

"It's like everything else," Triplitano said suddenly.

"What?"

"You try to avoid a decision. Try to put it off. And then something happens that makes the decision for you. Forces you, you know?"

"I know," Cardwell said.

They waited in their seats until the rotors died, then left the helicopter.

Cardwell had parked his car on the curving driveway nearby. He shook hands with Triplitano, who walked off toward his office with a casual wave.

Cardwell waited by his car until the chopper left, climbing on its own noisy blast of wind until it hung a hundred feet above the lawn. Then it lurched off, clearing the trees that fringed the South Lawn, climbing past the Ellipse, shrinking as it receded into the gray sky beyond the river.

Sunday the Twenty-eighth

The Vice President returned to Washington on Sunday to appear on "Meet the Press."

"Mr. Vice President, how is the campaign going?"

"Very well, I think. I'm encouraged. Our crowds are getting larger every day, and I think people are listening to what I have to say. I think they're responding."

"Do you have plans to enter other primaries? To make this a nationwide campaign?"

"I think we'll concentrate on New Hampshire for the moment. But we're laying the groundwork for the other primaries, studying the laws and filing deadlines. And if the result is halfway favorable in New Hampshire, we'll have a nationwide campaign."

Hoffman handled the questions with the affable ease of a professional. He leaned forward almost casually, resting his folded arms on the desk edge as he fielded the questions, smiling genially at each of his inquisitors. But behind his smile lay a plan, a purpose: He had come to this studio on Nebraska Avenue not just to answer questions, but also to advance his campaign. He suspected—no, he knew—that the President would be watching. So Abner Hoffman waited for a question that would give him an opportunity—a question that would help him launch the newest missile in his war with Rattigan, a missile aimed squarely at Hoffman's reluctant opponent.

His opportunity came early in the program.

"Mr. Vice President, other Vice Presidents have differed with their Presidents, but they've managed to settle their quarrels in private. Did your differences with the President go so deep, really? Or is the real problem a personality clash between the two of you?"

"Mr. Steuben, I have the highest respect for the President," Hoffman said. "But our differences were just too wide to paper over. I believe the President betrayed his pledges to the people by choosing to be a warmonger instead of peacemaker. I felt his decision to send troops to Bolivia shouldn't go without a public challenge. That's why I'm in the race."

"And that is the only reason?"

"No. The President at this moment is contemplating steps that could plunge us more deeply into war. I think my candidacy puts me in a position to discourage or prevent those steps."

"Can you be more specific?"

"I'm talking about plans for an invasion of Chile by the United States."

In the Aspen Lodge the President reached for the telephone without turning away from his television set.

"Get Secretary Woodson," he said tightly.

Hoffman, on the screen, was still talking. "Yes," he said, "I'm saying that the President and his planners in the Pentagon are seriously considering that step, and I can document it."

"Jim?" The President had no time for pleasantries. "What the hell is going on? Are you watching Hoffman? Is he out of his goddamned mind?"

Hoffman's gray image on the screen talked on: "The President is trying to impose decisions like this one without public scrutiny, without public debate, and without public consent. I want to prevent that."

"Jim," said Rattigan. "I want you to call me back as soon as you know where this thing could have come from. Meanwhile, call the wire services—now, through the White House switchboard—and issue a denial. Tell Brooks Healy to issue a denial through all our embassies. You call him."

Rattigan hung up, still staring at Hoffman's image on the screen, and muttered once again: "He's out of his goddamned mind."

Rattigan sat through the final minutes of the program like a man hypnotized, his eyes fixed on Abner Hoffman in an expression of disbelief. When the interview ended, the President rose, snapped off the set, and stood before it, slowly punching the air with his fist, in a reflex gesture of combat.

Within an hour, the Secretary of Defense had issued a statement to the networks and wire services: Contingency plans, he explained, were different from *plans*. The fact that the United States might consider the remote possibility of invading a hostile nation did not mean that such a step was actually *planned;* the Vice President was in error.

But they all knew—Rattigan, Woodson, the White House men—that the damage done by Hoffman's wild accusation was well-nigh irreparable. Try as they might, they could never wholly undo it.

Late in the afternoon, as Cardwell sat reading in his study, he received a call from Triplitano.

"Listen carefully," Trip said. "If this gets leaked, the boss will know where to look, because you and I are the only ones he's told so far."

Cardwell felt his breath quickening.

"Get out your old Corona," Trip said, "and start writing an announcement. He wants to use it on Wednesday—after we spike these crazy stories about invading Chile. He'll go to New Hampshire Friday. Can you have a draft tomorrow afternoon?"

"Sure thing. When did you talk to him?"

"I just hung up. He's rarin' to go. He wanted to go to New Hampshire tomorrow."

"We convinced him, huh?" Cardwell was smiling.

"No," Trip said. "We didn't convince him. Ab Hoffman convinced him." And he hung up.

Wednesday the Thirty-first

Rattigan's announcement on Wednesday was short, bare of rhetoric, almost perfunctory: He would, starting with the coming weekend, make a series of campaign visits to New Hampshire. He hoped to visit most of the major towns and cities of the state between now and the primary. Details of his campaign plans would be announced as time went on.

"As you know," he concluded, scarcely looking into the camera, "I had hoped that it would not be necessary to take time away from my duties to campaign this early in the year. But I have decided that the dangers posed by recent irresponsible distortions of my positions, by factual misrepresentations and unchecked rumors are simply too great to be ignored. At a time when American troops are committed abroad, when both human lives and the national interest are at stake, we cannot afford to have misunderstandings about the intentions of the United States Government or the President. I will use my opportunities to speak in New Hampshire to clear up those misunderstandings and to prevent others."

In the Oval Office afterward, Rattigan took only a few telephone calls—from old, close friends and the more venerable political figures who called to wish him well.

Several times during the afternoon Triplitano came in to deliver wire-service copy with accounts of the President's statement and the political reaction to it. Each time, Rattigan would give the stories a hasty, cursory reading, then let them slide to the floor beside his chair.

When Sheila Roundtree entered the office with a stack of incoming telegrams and a folder of letters to be signed, he showed no interest. He waved toward the long table behind his desk.

"Just leave them there. I'll get to them later."

His secretary stood for a moment studying him. He was slumped in his big chair, his head propped on one hand. He looked tired—as if he were at the final exhausted moment of his campaign, not its beginning.

When Trip came in again, Rattigan sat up straight.

"Have you got anything from Abner?"

"Excuse me, sir?"

"Any reaction. I was wondering if Ab had made a statement."

"No, sir, I don't think so. He'd be the first person they'd ask for a statement, so he must be lying low, refusing comment."

"Oh no, he'll make a statement." Rattigan let Triplitano lay the wire-service stories on the desk before him, but he did not glance down. "Let me know when you've got something from Abner."

The President, of course, was right: Abner Hoffman, who was in Washington, issued a one-paragraph statement at two o'clock. He was delighted, his statement said, that the President saw fit, finally, to discuss the issues publicly in New Hampshire. The Vice President felt that, if his own past month of campaigning in New Hampshire had influenced the President to enter the race, he had made a positive contribution to the public dialogue.

An hour after Warren Jasper had dictated Hoffman's statement to the wire services, the Vice President ushered five trusted reporters into his big office in the Capitol. He poured drinks for them himself, from a large cut-glass decanter.

"Gentlemen," Hoffman said. "What you'll get from me today is not for attribution except to 'sources high in the Vice President's campaign.' You understand?"

His guests nodded affirmation.

"I thought you might like to know the real reason for the President's announcement this morning," Hoffman said. And as he spoke, he passed a singly typewritten page to each reporter. "This poll," he said, "shows me running roughly even with the President. Now, gentlemen"—he picked up his glass, gestured as if to make a toast, then took a swallow—"I'll take your question."

Cardwell stopped by Trip's office at the end of the day.

"Did you see this? Trip held up a copy of the Washington *Star*'s final edition. "Looks like Ab has his own pollsters."

Cardwell read the story. "Old Abner doesn't miss a trick."

He dropped the paper onto Trip's desktop. "He leaked this to take the shine off the President's announcement."

"Yes," said Trip, "but that's okay. It makes our man hate Ab a little more, and that's good. He started hating Ab—really hating him—last Sunday. He hates him more tonight. That's good. He's a better fighter when he hates a guy."

"Well, he'd better be good, because he has a real fight on his hands."

"Ab's polls are right?"

"Allowing for a little self-serving exaggeration, I'd say yes, as far as I can tell."

"Son-of-a-bitch."

They had a drink from Trip's desk-drawer bottle, but neither man said much. Each was preoccupied with his own thoughts about the President's dilemma. And each was thinking, not of this day's events nor of the next two days, but of the weekend and the coming month—of the snow, the crowds, the noisy buses loaded with jostling reporters; of banners and posters and of microphones that wouldn't work; of headlines and opinion polls. Of the campaign; of New Hampshire.

FEBRUARY

Running Scared

Friday the Second

They left for Manchester early on Friday: the President and Lisa, a brace of White House aides and security men on Air Force One, followed by a crowded press plane. The advance men had done their work well: When the plane touched down, the airport fence that held the crowd away from Air Force One was a solid wall of people that stretched a hundred yards, ten deep. Triplitano's aides were already spreading the local police chief's crowd estimate through the press section: "in excess of ten thousand." Ten thousand schoolchildren, union members, sign-waving housewives—and scarcely a hostile sign in sight.

The front exit of the presidential plane disgorged its crowd of staff aides, Secret Service men, and hangers-on, and a little band of photographers and dignitaries gathered at the front of the rearmost ramp —the presidential exit. After a long pause there was a flash of movement in the open door; a tentative cheer, then a roar as the President and Lisa Rattigan, in a red, fur-collared coat, stepped waving down the airplane ramp.

Lisa Rattigan's cheeks were as red as her coat. She was more than a little frightened by these mob scenes, though she endured them dutifully and with an unfailing smile. She reached out toward the hundreds of outstretched hands, touching them lightly rather than shaking them; nodding and smiling. But she glanced occasionally from side to side, as if seeking reassurance from her protective circle of Secret Service agents. And she kept a certain distance from the airport fence—only a few feet, but enough to give her safety from the pushing, shoving crowd who reached for her.

Carl Rattigan showed no such caution. He gave himself to the clawing crowd, pressed right up to the low fence, grabbed as eagerly for the outstretched hands of the spectators as they grabbed for his. He ignored his guard of agents; he seemed almost willing, at some moments, to vault the little fence that separated him from his admirers, and give himself over fully to the mob. And he showed no eagerness to be bound to six minutes of handshaking; he moved slowly down the fence, soaking up the energy and noise of the crowd.

By the end of this long day, he knew, he would be exhausted, bone-weary. His hands would be scratched and raw from hours of contact with hundreds of reaching hands—and, despite repeated antiseptic baths and application of ointments from a Navy medic, his hands would be swollen and patched with Band-Aids.

But the deepest part of him was indifferent to the pain and tiredness. He needed the contact with these crowds as other men need sleep or nourishment; as actors need applause. As surely as it drained his body, compaigning fed his soul, his ego—whatever one calls that deeper thing that lives in a man's body. Lisa couldn't understand that. Most of his staff men couldn't. The medical people, those mechanics of the body, couldn't understand it. Only other men like him—other politicians—could.

He had not sought this campaign. He had resisted it. But now he was in it. What the hell? He loved it. He plunged down the airport fence, clutching the hands that clutched at him. Away from home, he suddenly felt at home. He was happy. He was on his way.

Hours later, just before the President's final stop of the afternoon, in Concord, Cardwell spotted Sarah climbing from the press bus, her notebook in hand.

He left his place near the head of the stopped motorcade and ran to join her as the reporters rushed to their roped-off section near the podium.

"I thought you were traveling with the other side," he said.

"I travel with both sides," Sarah said. She turned her face up, then realized they couldn't kiss in public. "I came aboard in Manchester."

"How do we compare with Abner's show?"

"He's Clyde Beatty, one ring and a tent on the outskirts of town. You're the Ringling Brothers at Madison Square Garden."

"We're that impressive, huh?"

"But don't sell Abner short. He has guts. These people respect that. And he's come a long way."

"He certainly has." Abruptly Cardwell caught her elbow and stopped her in the midst of the hurrying crowd of reporters. "Where are you staying?"

"At the Holiday Inn in Manchester, with the White House press."

"Can we have dinner?"

"I'd love it. Where?"

"In your room. Let's be discreet about our indiscretions. I'll bring hamburgers." With a wave, he hurried off.

Later, when he came to her room, they made love wordlessly. Sarah's ease—the slowness and languor he had remembered—were not there now. They had been apart how long—only a week? A week, for Sarah, of hotel rooms, restaurant meals, and rushing for deadlines. She seemed eager, almost impatient.

Afterward, propped against pillows, they talked.

"You've arrived, haven't you?" Her voice was gently teasing.

"I don't know what you mean."

"You're running things. You and Trip. I watching you today—riding in the lead staff car. Walking up to the President and whispering little things in his ear."

"You have a shrewd eye, don't you, Sarah?"

"Pretty soon you'll be riding in his car. And your name will be in all the papers. The reporters will be asking Trip for your 'exact title.' So you've arrived."

"I guess you're right."

"Oh, come on, where's your enthusiasm? Are you going to tell me that it's all empty? That all your striving has been for naught? That it's lonely at the top? Are you going to say you'd trade it all for—"

"You won a Pulitzer Prize before you were thirty years old. How was it for you? Wasn't there anything you would have traded it for?"

"Of course," she said, and her smile faded a little. "I would have traded it. Only I could never decide for what."

"Let's not have a serious conversation," he said. He reached for her and pulled her back into an embrace.

They made a feast of hamburgers, beer, and coffee. Then after some desultory conversation about the campaign, they made love again, unhurriedly this time. Cardwell was reminded of the first night for them, in Punta del Este: Sarah's little room with the sound of the surf outside; the gray dawn; Sarah's cigarette glowing in the half light of the morning.

They fell asleep, still embracing, by ten o'clock.

At midnight the telephone by Sarah's bed rang them awake. Sarah reached for it.

"Hello. Trip? What time is it? What's wrong?"

Cardwell sat up and snapped the lamp on.

"John? I don't know." She hesitated, looking to Cardwell for directions. "We had dinner earlier, but I don't know—"

Cardwell took the phone. "It's okay, Trip. We're having a late dinner. How did you know where to—"

"I have the intuition of a housemother," Trip said. "But don't worry. Your secrets are safe with me. Can you get over to the President's suite in fifteen minutes?"

"What time is it?"

"Five after twelve."

"What does he want?"

"Not he. She. The First Lady. He's sound asleep. She called to summon you and me. She says it's urgent."

"Okay, I'll see you. Fifteen minutes." He was already reaching for his clothes when he hung up.

"Sarah, I'm sorry."

"It's all right. Trip and I are old friends."

"I hope I didn't make you feel—you know, awkward."

"I don't feel that way," she said. But when he had dressed and he leaned to kiss her cheek, he felt it burning.

The President's entourage had taken over most of the Sheraton-Wayfarer, near Manchester.

An agent outside the President's suite jotted their names in his logbook, then admitted them.

Lisa Rattigan was waiting for them, standing in the middle of the living room, her hand extended. To Cardwell she seemed smaller, less vivid than the woman he was accustomed to seeing at the President's side. She was wearing a beige dressing gown and holding an unlighted cigarette.

"Gentlemen. Do fix yourselves a drink."

Trip spoke for the two of them. "No, thank you. What can we do for you?"

She took a lighter from the coffee table and had raised it before Cardwell could move to help her.

"You can do one thing," she said, releasing a cloud of cigarette smoke in a long sigh. "You can stop killing my husband."

Cardwell shot a glance toward Trip, who neither answered nor changed expression.

"He made nine stops today," Lisa went on. "He almost lost his voice. His hands are scratched to pieces. He had an off-the-record dinner with contributors tonight, when he could hardly hold his head up. Then he came back to this."

From her place near the center of the room she pointed to a desk in the corner. It was piled with papers: memos, letters, reports.

"This was the first day, Lisa," Trip said gently. "He had to start off with a bang."

"Tomorrow's just as bad. And Sunday. Do you think he can keep this up five weeks? You're running things, aren't you? Do you think *you* can keep it up five weeks? Put some limits on it, Trip. Nothing before ten in the morning and nothing after nine at night. Please. I'm asking you."

"Lisa, he loves to campaign. He wants to pack as much in as he can. You know him as well as—"

"This is different." She sank into a chair across from the sofa where they sat. "Tonight he had to have a *shot* to go to sleep, he was so keyed up. He was exhausted, but he couldn't sleep, so he asked for a shot. That's unlike him." She snubbed out her cigarette and leaned toward them. "Trip, promise me."

"I'll do what I can."

"And you, Mr. Cardwell?"

"Mrs. Rattigan, I—"

"You're the one who got him into this, with all your polls."

"I gave him the information, if that's what you mean."

"The bad news, I know. But you pushed him a little, too, didn't you? To come up here?"

Cardwell hesitated.

"It's all right," she said. "I don't mind. But give him some good news, too, can you do that? He needs it so much." She gestured toward the littered desk. "Some goods news to go with the casualty reports."

Trip stood up. "Lisa, I'm sorry. I promise we'll do what we can."

She stood. "I mean it, Trip. This thing is killing him. I can tell how many men are dying down there by looking at his face. And this thing with Hoffman." She shook her head. "He used to love politics —the game, the competition. But it's all beyond politics now. He hates him so."

They were walking toward the door. Cardwell fell into step beside them.

At the door, Trip touched her elbow gently. "There's not much we can do about tomorrow or the next day. They're loaded up. But next week—" He shrugged. "I promise."

"Nothing before ten or after nine?"

"I promise."

Suddenly she raised both hands toward her face. Then, just as suddenly, composing herself, she lowered them and looked at Cardwell.

"I'm sorry, Mr. Cardwell, you don't know me. My husband likes you and trusts you, so I will too. And I want you to understand me. I'm not a campaigner. It's not natural for me—the crowds, the noise —all this manufactured frenzy. I don't campaign with him because I like to." She looked up at him intently. "I do it to be close to him. To protect him. Save him, if I have to. And if I fail at that, then nothing else matters very much, does it?"

"Of course not." He could say no more.

She smiled, and suddenly Cardwell saw once again the vibrant woman he had missed earlier. "Thank you, gentlemen," she said, and they were gone.

Later, on their way back to the corridor where their rooms were, Trip broke the silence. "He'll never know she did that. She waited until he was asleep to call us in."

"That's what they call a perfect political wife, isn't it? The way she guards him."

"That and more. More than you'll ever know."

They came to Trip's door.

"Good night, buddy," Trip said. "Be careful."

"Good night, Trip."

On the way to his own room Cardwell thought of returning to Sarah, but it was late. She was probably asleep. So he turned his key in his own lock and fell exhausted into bed without undressing.

Tuesday the Sixth

The President stayed in New Hampshire through the weekend and into the week, hurling himself across the state as if he were determined to meet every voter, shake every outstretched hand, shout his campaign rhetoric from the town-hall steps of even the smallest village.

He campaigned by car, bus, helicopter, and light plane. His caravan, with its tons of cameras, microphones, flags, and recording equipment, its legion of reporters and Secret Service men, swung wildly, tirelessly, from town to town.

Between appearances, Rattigan, though he was already hoarse, recorded radio and television spots. He met with campaign contributors and newspaper publishers, reciting over and over, in an earnest, gravelly voice, the theme statement of his campaign: "This is more than just another political campaign. This is a challenge to our constitutional system. It's that serious." He was determined to paint Ab Hoffman not only as an ambitious political spoiler, but also as a threat to the Republic.

On helicopter jaunts from one town to another he invited members of the local press aboard to interview him. He displayed an impressive knowledge of their towns, their local problems, their needs—knowledge devoured from memos he had ordered up from government experts in Washington.

He grew tired, hoarse, irritable. But he plunged on. Arriving at the site of another rally, staring out of his car at another excited crowd, he would arrange his weary face into a smile, inhale a new draught of energy, and push himself out toward them, shedding his fatigue like an outworn skin.

At the tag end of each day he would fall aching into bed, almost too tired to sleep. Lisa worried, reminded Triplitano of his promise to scale down the campaign schedule, and did her best to sustain and comfort her exhausted husband.

And as the week wore on, the crowds grew—and grew more friendly. The newspapers crowded their front pages with pictures and stories of the President's campaign. The little state seemed surprised and flattered that he would show them such attention, enliven their long winter with the organized madness of a presidential campaign.

He grew more tired. But on Tuesday, after five full days of campaigning, he turned to Trip and said, "I think it's turning."

Thursday the Eighth

While the President campaigned, Cardwell stayed behind in Manchester to study the figures. Alone in his motel room, the charts and papers spread across his bed and on a nearby table, he paced and pondered and jotted notes. Twice he made lengthy telephone calls—one to a pollster in New York and another to a political statistician in Boston; he questioned them closely about the figures, then made more notes.

At three o'clock on Thursday he sat down and typed out a memo to the President:

"Depending on which poll you believe," he wrote, "you are either eight or ten points ahead of the Vice President in New Hampshire.

"Our pollsters urge me to be cautious in interpreting these data.

We are talking about very thin margins of difference, and all polls, especially those taken by telephone in the heat of a campaign, must allow for error.

"Notwithstanding all these warnings, however, we can be pleased about these results. They show that your decision to campaign in New Hampshire was a good one; your efforts are having an impact on the voters; you are making progress.

"There remains a very large percentage of undecided voters—a mass of puzzled, troubled, uncertain people who number in the tens of thousands. They are the big question mark—the great hope and danger for your candidacy. If I am right in assuming that voters favorable to the Vice President are a hard mass of rather deeply committed citizens, and that our chances thus are small of winning defections away from Hoffman, then the undecided voter becomes the key to the outcome in New Hampshire."

When he had delivered the memo to Sheila Roundtree downstairs, he returned to his room, cleared away the charts and papers, and lay out on the bed, smiling a private, self-satisfied smile.

The undecided: He stopped smiling when he tried to visualize them. Who were they? Where were they? They did not come to rallies, did not cheer, did not join parades. He pictured them as stolid figures, sitting squarely in almost-empty rooms, watching the television news. They had no faces.

Thinking about them, he fell asleep.

The telephone awakened him. It was Dot Orme in Washington.

"Hey, there's a big story on the ticker about you. It's in the *Star,* too, with a picture of you whispering in the President's ear."

"Read it to me."

"'YOUNG AIDE EMERGES AS POWER IN RATTIGAN CAMPAIGN.' How does that sound?"

"Read the story."

"'A young political assistant, hitherto a background figure in Carl Rattigan's entourage, has emerged as a powerful figure in the President's New Hampshire campaign.

"'He is John B. Cardwell, thirty-four, son of a Kentucky newspaper publisher, and a White House speechwriter for the past three years.

" 'Though prominent New Hampshire political figures ostensibly head the President's campaign staff, observers have concluded that Cardwell and presidential press secretary Gary Triplitano are the *de facto* chairmen of the campaign.

" 'Triplitano, the President's personal and political spokesman, is a familiar public figure. But Cardwell has emerged only recently as a political adviser, chief speechwriter, and public-opinion analyst to the Chief Executive. Reporters have noticed that Cardwell, since accompanying Mr. Rattigan to last month's hemisphere summit conference in Uruguay, has been seen increasingly at the President's side.' "

At the President's side.

" 'Cardwell, a Brown University graduate and former columnist for the newspaper published by his father, shuns the limelight. But insiders know him to be a tireless worker with a fascination for the mechanics of political power.' "

Dot continued, but Cardwell only half listened. He was thinking now of Sarah, picturing her gently mocking face. She had predicted this: "You've arrived, haven't you?" He smiled, remembering.

"Dot?" He interrupted her. "Can you send me a copy of that story?"

"Is it true? Are you really running the campaign?"

"I don't know," he said. "I don't know who's running it."

Much later, Cardwell sat alone in the motel restaurant, finishing his dinner, when Triplitano strode in, scanned the room, and joined him.

"How'd it go today, Trip?"

Triplitano jerked his thumbs up and grinned. "We're getting a few demonstrators on the fringes of the crowds, but it's no big problem. He's clicking."

"Have you seen my memo?"

"I have, and so has he. It was waiting when we came in. He read it aloud to us, and we all gave a big cheer. You were exactly right, Johnny, about coming here. It was the right thing to do."

Cardwell shrugged. "It was the only thing to do."

"He's seen that AP story, too," Trip said, grinning. "Who's your press agent?"

"I don't have one, Trip. Didn't you read the story? I 'shun the limelight.' "

"It's all right. The boss is pleased. He wants to see you, as soon as things calm down, to talk about the undecideds. Meanwhile he wants you to leak the news about the polls."

"Wants *me* to leak it? You're the press secretary."

"Orders are orders. You're the big expert. You have credibility."

Cardwell laughed.

"One more thing," Trip said. "He wants you to move up here—set up shop for the duration. You can go home this weekend—get your clothes. You can move your secretary up here, anything you want. It's all paid for."

"Jesus."

"He wants to spend more time up here. He wants poll results every day if he can get them. He wants you to background the press, give him advice about what to do next, and stay in behind the local campaign people."

Cardwell stared at Trip, surprised, and Trip stood up.

"Congratulations, man. You've surfaced. Let me know if I can help."

Cardwell stood too, and they walked together out of the half-empty restaurant.

While they waited for the elevator, Trip turned to him.

"Are you going to leak the polls to the New York *Times*?"

"I thought I might."

"To Sarah Tolman?"

"She's with the *Times,* Trip."

"What's with you two?"

"We're good friends," Cardwell said curtly.

"How about Nan? Are you two on the outs?"

"We're having some problems. I'd rather not talk about—"

The elevator doors rolled back, and Trip waved Cardwell on.

"Look," Trip said when the doors slid shut. "What you do in your spare time is none of my business. But what gets in the papers about this Administration *is* my business. Sarah Tolman is a top reporter for the most influential paper in the country. And you, a married man, are one of the President's highest-ranking aides, or so I read in the press. Do you read my point?"

"I said we were good friends, Trip, and I meant that."

The elevator stopped. Trip followed Cardwell into the hall and touched his elbow.

"John, the fact that you're in the public eye is only one reason to be careful with Sarah."

"I won't ask you what you mean by that."

"Just be careful, old friend. Be careful."

Trip sauntered off, and Cardwell, his face burning, watched him disappear down the hall.

When he telephoned Sarah from his room, the residue of guilt from his lie to Triplitano still clogged his throat.

"Are you all right? You sound depressed," she said.

"I'm okay. Just tired."

"Me, too. Exhausted."

"I hope you're not too tired for a late drink."

They met in the dim bar of Sarah's motel. A half-dozen reporters were drinking and joking at the long bar, which ran down one wall; cigarette smoke climbed drowsily upward and hung beneath the ceiling.

He steered her to a table in the corner farthest from the bar.

"How'd it go today?" he asked automatically.

"He's doing well. His crowds are big. He's trying hard, not just going through the paces, and the response is good."

As she talked he slipped a copy of his memo to the President from his breast pocket and laid it on the table.

"It's a very professional campaign, John. You should be proud. The buses leave on time, the local politicians say all the right things, the bands are nice. The advance men are the best I've ever seen. Trip keeps the press bus happy. But I'm—" She saw the folded memo and reached for it. "Is this for me?"

"I'm being conspiratorial," he said. "That's scientific confirmation of how well the bands and advance men are doing their jobs."

Avidly Sarah unfolded the memo and began to read. "Oh, by the way," she said, "I read tonight how well you're doing your job."

He smiled, but Sarah had returned to the memo and its two pages of numbers. He let her read slowly, watching as she jotted notes on the margins of the memo.

"Duly noted," she said after a minute. "Can I have a drink now?"

He signaled the barman, ordered scotch for the two of them, and turned back to Sarah. "You don't seem too interested."

"Of course I'm interested, I'm just not surprised. I could feel it happening out on the road. He's a great campaigner. It's not surprising that he's making headway. But John"—she narrowed her eyes—"when is he going to *say* something?"

"Say something?"

"About the war. That's what this campaign is about, isn't it?"

"Sarah, of course. The campaign is *about* the war in Bolivia. There's no denying that. Whether he should talk about it is another question." She folded the memo and slipped it into her handbag as the barman brought their drinks. "He's doing well. Why complicate things?"

"That's the most incredible statement I've ever heard," Sarah said.

"I doubt that, in your business."

"How long do you think he can depend on flags and bands and advance men? Almost everywhere he speaks there's a little group of pickets holding up signs. At some point he's got to see them. He's *got*—"

"Sarah, forgive me, but I don't want to sit here arguing politics with you. It seems too strange. All the while we sit here talking shop I'm thinking, 'This is crazy.' It's as if we use shop talk to keep from talking about more important things. It's a dodge to keep us from talking about ourselves."

"I know."

"We run up against it, and then we run away. You run away."

"I know."

"Can I come up to your room?"

"John, I'm—"

"Don't tell me you're working. Don't tell me you're tired. We need to talk, Sarah."

She was nodding, her eyes cast down.

"I don't want to make love to you," he said softly. "We use that to keep from talking, too."

He saw she was crying.

"I want you to make love to me," she whispered. Then she stood up and was gone, leaving her drink untouched on the table.

He stopped to pay the check and finish his own drink. Then he left the smoky bar, taking with him the key Sarah had left on the table.

He found her sitting on the bed, brushing her dark hair. Her tears had blurred her makeup, but she had stopped crying.

"Sarah?"

She pulled him down onto the bed, letting the brush fall onto the floor; pulling, as she kissed him, at his tie and shirt buttons.

"Wait a minute," he whispered.

He took over: He undressed himself, then leaned across the bed and undressed Sarah, who helped him, never opening her eyes. When she was naked against the pillows, she turned her face toward the wall as if to avoid the light, and pulled him down again.

He left the lamp on, deliberately: He wanted to see her face. And through it all she lay inert, her face averted, as if she were being violated, until at the end she pinioned him and shook them both with her involuntary trembling.

While she was still rigid beneath him he pressed his face into her hair.

"Sarah, I love you."

She collapsed beneath him, but he did not move his face.

"I never knew what it was before, but I mean it. I love you."

Gently she pushed him away so she could see him.

"Is that what you wanted to talk about?"

"Yes."

"I thought we agreed there'd be no justifications, no commitments. No pledges about the future."

"I never agreed to that."

She looked away from him, to hide her eyes.

"I was afraid of this," she said.

"Afraid of what?"

"Afraid we'd let it go—too far."

"Too far! I'm in love with you, Sarah. Are you telling me you don't feel anything?"

"Of course I feel it. But I'm not sure, not certain. I'm fighting so hard. Can't you tell that?"

"You're not fighting it when we're in bed, are you? I'd say you're pretty enthusiastic then."

"Please, John. Don't make me miserable. If wanting you in bed means I'm in love, then I'm in love with you, God knows I am. But—"

"But?"

She held her head in her hands. "I want the sensations of being in love," she said slowly. "But none of the—"

"The other things."

"—the difficulties."

He touched her shoulder, but she shook herself away. "I don't want to ruin your marriage."

"Sarah, I'm afraid there wasn't that much left to ruin."

"And I don't want to face—all we'd have to face. The obstacles."

"What obstacles?"

She looked up at him abjectly, tears starting to course down her cheeks. "Ghosts," she said. And she began to cry.

"Sarah." He coaxed her into his arms and whispered into her hair. "I don't believe in ghosts." But she only cried harder, her body shaking against him.

After a moment he pushed her gently down beneath the covers and lay close to her, holding her as she cried. Then as she grew calmer he stroked her body softly with one hand, from the broad curve of her shoulder down to her thighs.

"Sarah, we don't have to think about those things. Just give it time. Don't ask questions yet. Let's just let it happen, see where it leads. Can we do that?"

He felt her hair against his face; she nodded yes.

"And if I say I love you, don't fight that. Just accept it. Like a gift. We can worry later, when we have more time." And he whispered to her hair: "I love you."

He had found the warm, smooth expanse of flesh beneath her navel. Now he rested his hand there, knowing it excited her.

"When you do that," she whispered, moving beneath his hand, "I forget—everything else."

"Me too," he said. "Me too."

"I had a horror of getting old. I was feeling old. And when you did that to me the first time I knew it was all right. I wasn't old.

When you woke up and found me crying that morning, it was because I was afraid it wouldn't last," she said. "You remember?"

"I remember," he said. "Try not to talk."

She moved her hand over his and pushed his hand downward. Then he covered her body with his, as if to shield her, and they made love again.

Friday the Ninth

In Manchester, Abner Hoffman was scheduled to appear on television at seven on Friday evening. Carl Rattigan, campaigning through the afternoon, had been shown the newspaper advertisements by Gary Triplitano.

"I want to watch it," the President had said. So his normal round of postcampaigning paperwork was postponed. When Rattigan returned exhausted to his suite in Manchester, he fell asleep on the massage table. Later, as he and Lisa ate an early dinner of sandwiches in front of the television set, he was tired and uncommunicative. But when Ab Hoffman's face appeared on the screen, Lisa saw her husband's eyes sharpen.

"The week's casualty figures from Bolivia were released today," Hoffman said, and he held up a sheet of paper. "Six United States soldiers dead, twenty-two wounded. I want to read to you the names and hometowns of the dead."

"You see what he's doing," Rattigan said tonelessly.

The Vice President, in his flat Oklahoma voice, read the names of the dead; their ages, ranks, towns:

"Bobby Lee Wilcox, age nineteen. Private first class. Eufaula, Alabama. Killed in action."

"He's going to tell them I'm a killer," Rattigan said bitterly.

"Ralph Warren Childs, age twenty-three. Second lieutenant—"

"Carl, you don't have to listen to this," Lisa said. But the President held up his hand to silence her.

Hoffman finished reading the list of war dead. "Each of these deaths," he said, "was an unnecessary death."

"That bastard." Rattigan leaned forward toward the television screen.

"When hostilities broke out in Bolivia," Hoffman went on, "the United States could have chosen the role of peacemaker, of honest broker." He paused and stared into the camera. "But the President chose another course of action. Thus he assumed responsibility for some tragic consequences. . . ."

"Because I had to, goddamn it!" Rattigan leaped to his feet, and Lisa moved toward the set.

"Carl, please—"

"Leave it on!"

"Now the President is campaigning in New Hampshire. He is telling the people of New Hampshire and the country that my candidacy is tantamount to a constitutional crisis: a dagger aimed at the heart of our political system."

"You're damned right!"

"That is not the issue. My candidacy poses no threat to our system —only a political threat to the President. It is the war that is the crisis and the real issue, and he created that issue."

"Oh, Jesus," Rattigan said, and he sank back into his chair. He picked up the white telephone beside his chair and told the Signal Corps operator, "Find Mr. Triplitano and tell him to call me." Then he hung up.

Hoffman was nearing the end of his speech. "My fellow citizens, let us not be misled about the real issue in this contest. Though the President may choose not to talk about it, the issue is there. It is the war.

"If you agree with the President that these young men died necessarily, then by all means vote for him. But do not be deceived about the meaning of your vote. Your vote will be interpreted, by your fellow citizens and by the press, not as a vote to save our political system from ambitious Vice Presidents—that is a small matter, after all —but as a vote for the war."

Rattigan waved a hand toward Hoffman. "This is coming from a man who promised to make no personal attacks. He's calling me a murderer."

"If you believe, as I do, that the President made a tragic choice last December, you can vote, on March 5, to save lives—"

Lisa snapped off the set as the telephone rang.

"Trip? How do you think I should respond to this?"

Lisa watched him as he listened.

"Say nothing! Like hell I'll say nothing! He's calling me a goddamn murderer!"

She listened for a moment, and she knew from the anger in his voice that he could not be calmed, distracted, turned aside from his zeal to justify himself. She went into the other room, closing the door behind her.

Cardwell did not watch the Vice President's broadcast. He was on a plane from Manchester to Washington.

He took a cab from National to the White House, studying as the taxi swept along the Potomac, the low, clean skyline of the capital. There was something familiar and reassuring about this cityscape: homelike and welcoming. He felt suddenly as if he had been away a long time—a month rather than only a week.

He dropped his bag in the office, then toured the halls of the West Wing. Without the President, without his top aides, without the reporters who usually crowded the press area, the place was empty, spiritless. The White House, the real White House, was in New Hampshire now. And though he had been back in the West Wing for only an hour, Cardwell was suddenly impatient for Sunday, when he would return to Manchester with his files, his secretary, his clothes and papers—to stay for the remainder of the primary campaign, working at the center of the action: running things.

After an hour he called a White House car to take him home. He read for most of the long rush-hour trip to the suburbs, looking up finally when he felt the driver nosing the black sedan into his driveway.

All the windows of Cardwell's house were aglow.

"Nancy!" he said to no one.

"Sir?"

"Nothing, driver. It looks as if my wife is home."

He refused the driver's help and carried his own bag to the doorstep, then let himself in with his key.

"Nancy!" he shouted. His chest felt hollow. What was she doing here?

"Nancy?"

He found her in the kitchen, opening cans for a solitary supper. She turned to him, surprised. "What are you doing here?"

"I'm just down till Sunday, picking up some things. How about you? When did you come?"

"Last night." She moved toward him and he kissed her tentatively, uncertain how he should behave.

"I got tired of living out of a suitcase. Tired of Mother and Dad. Tired of wondering whether you and I are separated or just on vacation, or what."

"Are you staying?"

"I don't know. Do you want me to?" There was an edge of challenge in her voice.

"Nan, please, I'm too tired for a big discussion. I was just—surprised to see you."

"Do you want to eat? I'm fixing soup and a sandwich."

"We could go out."

She shrugged. "No, it's almost done."

And so, unexpectedly, they were together again with no preparation for it: no dramatic scene, no cloudbursts of emotion, nothing, really, to say to one another. They resorted to the habitual phases of daily routine between husband and wife, almost as if they had not been apart.

"I read about you in the paper," she said as they sat down. "You're running the campaign?"

"I guess so. The President wants me to stay up there until the vote. I was coming to get my stuff. Dot's coming up, too."

"It's what you wanted."

"What?"

"Power, influence, all that. Aren't they what you wanted?"

"Nancy, I don't know. How can anybody say just what he wants?"

"Well," she said, "I'm proud of you. For doing so well."

He looked up at her, wondering if she was taunting him, hating his success. But she was looking directly back with an open, artless gaze.

"You're serious?"

"Of course I'm serious," she said.

While she cleaned up in the kitchen, Cardwell went to their bedroom to unpack his bag. He felt strangely disoriented—surprised by Nancy's presence and by her friendliness, as if he had been given some gift he wasn't sure he wanted.

Soon she came in and sat on the bed beside his open suitcase.

"You don't want to talk yet, do you?"

"Nancy, I—"

"It's all right. But can I talk? Can I explain?"

"Of course, sweetheart."

"The first few days after you left, I kept expecting you to call. I kept thinking that any minute the telephone would ring and you'd be calling to tell me you were sorry, that you'd treated me badly, that you'd neglected me. Then when you did call, we didn't really *talk*, did we?

"I had this fantasy all worked out in my head. A sort of script. You'd say, 'Nan, I want you to come to Washington. I don't want to be here without you.' "

"And what were you going to say?"

"I don't know. It's funny, your lines were the ones I had all planned, not mine. And then I realized it wasn't going to happen. You were busy writing the State of the Union speech. It was probably a relief to you not having me up here to complain. You were busy; you were happy. And right then I started growing up. That was when I wrote you that long letter. I began to realize that we might not get back together; that we might not be—meant for each other, or whatever you say." She shrugged. "It was the first time it had occurred to me."

"I thought your letter sounded—unlike you."

"More mature, you mean."

"I guess so."

"It was. Suddenly I was grown up. Mature. Realistic." She shook her head. "Only I realized I couldn't grow up until there was somebody who would let me *be* grown up. Do you understand?"

But before he could reply, she rushed on: "Mother and Dad still thought of me as their little girl, and they could never recover from that. So staying at home was no solution. Suddenly I wanted to come back to Washington, erase the past, start all over—show off the new me."

"But you didn't."

"You went off to South America, so there was nobody to show off to."

"But I came back."

She expelled a long sigh. "I guess I was still waiting for you to call. That was part of it. Part of me wanted you to beg me to come back."

"Nan, I'm sorry."

"No, let me finish. But another part of me realized you would have to change, too."

"So we come back to my sins."

"*You* were treating me like a child. You kept telling me to grow up, but you really just wanted me to be a good little girl. I had this feeling that something was happening to you—something bad. You kept reaching for power and influence and closeness to the President without ever asking what they could *do* to you. And you didn't want me to complain about it."

"You never did complain about it. It was always other things."

"That's because I didn't know!"

"But now you do."

"John, I'm sorry. I didn't come back to criticize you or blame you." She shrugged again, the old gesture of futility that always came before her tears. But now she didn't cry. "We always fight, don't we? Actually I came to tell you—that I love you. I called Dot. She said you were coming, and I grabbed a plane. I wanted to tell you, sweetheart."

"Nan, I'm sorry."

"I came to say I'm willing to give it a try again. If you are."

He stood stricken, saying nothing.

"All the time we'd been married I thought I loved you, but I'd just been *needing* you. You know?"

"I know."

"So now I'm back. To stay, if that's what you want."

When he did not answer, she looked up to see him rooted to the spot.

"Nan, I'm sorry. I'm trying to think about all this, and I'm exhausted."

"Then let's go to bed," she said in a voice that was curiously flat.

"Okay. I want to take a shower first."

Later, standing beneath the hot spray of the shower, he turned it higher, as if its sound and force could wash him clean of his confusion.

He was amazed by her strength, her equanimity. There was about her now something bottomless, almost like the strength that first attracted him to Sarah.

Thinking of Sarah he felt a sharp stab of guilt—and he could not tell what he felt guilty for.

He covered himself with soap, then moved again under the pelting spray of the shower.

Strange. When he had stayed with Sarah in her room that first night in Punta del Este he had felt no guilt, only freedom and release. Now, in his own house, preparing to go to bed with his own wife, he felt unfaithful: to Sarah.

He cursed, turned off the shower, reached for a towel, and rubbed himself dry with such force that his skin turned red. Slowly he climbed into pajamas, then stood staring at himself in the steaming mirror, knowing that he could not lie to Nancy; he must tell her.

She had dressed for bed, moved his half-empty suitcase to the floor, and was sitting lightly on the bed's edge, waiting for him.

He busied himself hanging his clothes in the closet, avoiding her eyes.

"Nan, I've got to go back up there Sunday. I won't be back for almost a month. Is this something we have to decide now? Maybe it would be better for you to go back home. At least until—"

"Is that what you really want to say?"

Cardwell didn't answer.

"Look at me," Nan said.

He turned.

"You're trying to tell me something. Look at me and tell me what it is."

He heard his own voice as if it were far away. "I'm saying—I think things have changed since we—" His voice trailed off.

"You have somebody else."

He only stared at her.

"Your reporter friend is up there. Sarah Tolman." She said it not as an accusation, but simply as a fact.

"Why would you think of her?"

He heard her give a weary little sigh.

"I've thought of her ever since I saw you together before Christmas. Upstairs together, at that party."

"There wasn't anything between us then."

"Then." She looked up at him. "But I could see the possibility. She was everything I wasn't. Or should I say she *is* everything I'm not? You found her interesting. You told me that."

He said nothing, and Nancy spoke: "Are you in love with her?"

"I think so. Nan, I'm sorry."

"Is she in love with you?"

"What is this, twenty questions?"

"You don't have to answer."

"I don't know! I don't know how she feels! This all just happened!" He was angry because she was so calm. "Do you think I could write an essay about it?"

"I only have one more question: Could you be married to her?"

"I don't know."

"What are you going to do?"

"That's all your questions." He turned, banging shut the closet door, and headed out.

"Stay here," she said. He stopped. "I want to talk about it." She seemed as detached, as remote as if she were talking about the lives of strangers. "Come sit down," she said, and dumbly he obeyed.

"It's funny," Nancy said. "A month ago, two months ago, this would have ruined me; I would have gone to pieces. But now I'm different. I can listen to all this and it hurts, because I still love you. But I can take it."

"You want me to ask why," he said bitterly. "All right. Because you've given your heart to God or something?"

"Because I know what I want. Two months ago I thought my

whole life depended on you. On your doing what I wanted you to, for me. Now I'm different. I love you. I want you, and I want to be married to you, if that's possible. But my life doesn't depend on you anymore. It depends—on me."

He was dumbstruck, struggling to follow what she was saying.

"And you," she said. "You don't really know what you want, do you? You think you do. But your whole life has been a string of accidents."

"I don't know what you mean."

"You went to your dad's newspaper because it was there, just waiting for you. You didn't really *decide,* did you? And then you married me—because I was there. Because I was pretty and almost rich and because we made a perfect couple, the bright young publisher-to-be and his lovely girl. A perfect couple."

"Because I loved you," he said. The next word—"then"—formed in his mind, but he did not say it.

"I think you did," she said. "But it was no *effort,* was it? It just happened. You didn't have to decide or choose or agonize. God knows, neither did I. We were so fortunate, so secure. So—taken care of."

She stared at him, challenging him. "And we came to Washington the same way. Another fortunate turn in the career of a bright young man. Another prize thrown at your feet, just to be picked up." She moved her hand in a sweeping gesture. "Bright young assistant in the White House. Loyal, quick, ambitious, presentable. Family connections; a pretty, empty-headed wife. A chance for power, fame, political success."

"Maybe those are things I want."

"Maybe. Maybe. Maybe they're things you *think* you want. Maybe they're things you won't like after you get them. But you don't really *know,* do you, sweetheart? You've just been sailing along."

"And maybe I want Sarah." He said it as a taunt, but she would not be goaded.

"Maybe," she said. "But you've got to decide. For once, you've got to choose."

He felt too stung to answer—too shaken by her calmness, her detachment.

"What do you want me to do?" he asked after a while.

"Go back up there and find out what you want. Tell me when you've come to some conclusion."

"You sound so cold-blooded."

"Far from cold-blooded," she said, and he saw that her eyes were filled with tears.

"I'll sleep in the other room," he said.

"No, stay here," she said. "We're still married." It was not a taunt as she said it: simply a fact.

For a long time after they went to bed they lay awake, aware of the distance between them, embarrassed at being so close, yet so far from one another.

"Nan?" he said after a long time, knowing she was awake. "Can I ask a question?"

"Sure."

"How can you love me if you don't need me?"

"I can't explain it," she said. "But that's the way I feel."

"And you'd want me back."

She stirred in bed and then sat up. "I'd want you back," she said. "But only if you change."

Then she said, "I'm going back to Louisville tomorrow. I'm doing some teaching, so I have a way to fill my time. When you've had time to do some thinking, when you've made up your mind, let me know." And gently she kissed him.

A long time later he fell asleep, feeling uncomfortably as if he were sleeping with a stranger, she seemed so new to him.

Saturday the Tenth

Carl Rattigan stared down from the helicopter as it lurched toward the ground and his scheduled morning rally.

The auditorium was like ten thousand or a hundred thousand others in America, a high school gymnasium—red brick, flat roof, bland and functional: the utilitarian architecture of democracy.

He was pondering what he would say to the two thousand citizens of Nashua who would be here to hear him. Depart from his bland, preprogrammed text? Answer Hoffman? Or try, against all temptation, to stay above the battle?

Before the rotors died he was out of his seat, pressing toward the door with Triplitano, Anders Martin, and his little band of Secret Service agents. Lisa was not there; she had stayed behind in Manchester.

There was a band, blaring noisily. Smile. Wave. A double line of gleaming state troopers, marking the route from the chopper to the gym. He moved down the line. Smile. Wave. Go with the text, or attack Abner? Hit him hard for that lousy broadcast? There was no way of knowing what to do until he met the crowd inside, listened to them with his politician's inner ear, tried to feel what they were feeling.

Inside now: a solid wall of noise. Another band, on cue from an advance man with a walkie-talkie, roared forth with "Hail to the Chief." He moved swiftly down the center aisle. The agents formed a seal around him, blocked him from the clutching, outstretched hands. He smiled and waved.

"Ladies and gentlemen," someone roared as he mounted the platform, "the President of the United States!" And Rattigan decided, as he faced the cheering mob so carefully brought to frenzy by his advance men, to throw away his text, to answer Hoffman, to lance the swelling boil of anger that Hoffman's broadcast had raised.

He looked out over the crowd and spread his arms, signaling for quiet. Then, smiling, he opened his speech text on the lectern; the tumult began to die, and the President aimed his voice toward the network cameras that were capturing the moment for the evening news.

"My friends"—he paused to sweep the great room with his eyes—"it's good to be in Nashua. Four years ago"—they stopped him with a cheer—"four years ago I campaigned here, and I met many of you then." He grinned, coaxing them, like a professional, to approve of him, to laugh. "We all look older now."

How simple it was, before a friendly crowd. Now he was off, speaking easily of previous visits to New Hampshire, of textile imports, of jobs; pausing almost imperceptibly now and then to encourage and receive their applause.

"But today"—here his voice darkened; he changed gears, switched the mood abruptly—"I want to talk about other things, about matters that are both political and personal. Serious matters.

"Last night, my opponent, the Vice President, made some serious accusations about me." Rattigan's eyes narrowed. "He called me, in effect, a murderer."

The word hung on the air, and then there was the reaction he wanted. "Nooo!" roared part of the crowd: an expression of denial, of disbelief. They were with him, these stocky union men and their solid wives.

"Before this campaign began," the President continued, "Mr. Hoffman pledged to me that he would not deal in personal attacks; that this campaign, already serious enough to strain our system, would not become an exercise in insults and slurs. I had hoped that we could debate our differences in—"

And then it came: a high, keening wail—a scream—from the rear of the crowd.

Rattigan faltered, hesitated. Someone was shouting in the crowd.

"Murderer!"

He was aware of movement in the rearmost section of the crowd. He saw the cameras swing away from him and toward the commotion, and then the cry came again: "Murderer!"

The young girls who were screaming had risen from their seats. Agents and members of the crowd were moving toward them. There was an explosion of shock as the girls raised plastic bags above their heads and drenched themselves in deep red blood: slaughterhouse blood, spreading garishly down their faces and onto their clothes.

"Ladies and gentlemen, let's relax," Rattigan said, and he tried to launch his speech again, searching frantically on the page before him for some paragraph to read, something to say.

"Murderer!" A dozen young men—college students, apparently—sprang up shouting in the crowd. Policemen rushed from the exits into the crowd; burly men in the audience headed toward the demonstrators.

The crowd set up a counterchant, a roar of rage and support for Rattigan: "GET THEM OUT! GET THEM OUT!" The demonstrators, no more than a dozen of them, were hauled out struggling by helmeted policemen and state troopers.

Then it was over. It had lasted no more than thirty seconds.

"My friends," said Rattigan, his voice trembling, "if anybody doubts that excess leads to excess; if anybody doubts that inflammatory words on television can lead to inflammatory acts, he need only look at this."

In his anger, he had done it: hung the demonstration squarely around Abner Hoffman's neck, blamed him for it. The reporters would not miss it: They would trumpet his accusation. Rattigan didn't care. He was too shaken, too full of rage.

He started to read from the prepared text, but his voice was unsure and reedy. The drama had exhausted the crowd, drained them; they were too restless, too distracted to listen well. Mechanically he read through the speech, faltering occasionally, trying to restore some rhythm to the speech. But it would not come; he droned through the speech, rattled, seeing in his mind's eye the little rank of screaming girls with blood-drenched hair.

And finally, mercifully, it was over. He accepted their applause, left the platform with his phalanx of aides and agents, swept out of a side door and back to the helicopter on the football field.

For a few moments, as the chopper swung and roared into the safety of the sky, the President said nothing. Then he pointed angrily to Anders Martin.

"I don't want another scene like that."

Martin said nothing.

"I don't care what we have to do, we can't have another scene like that. I don't care if we have to campaign in an armored truck. Do you hear me?"

"I hear you, sir," Andy Martin said.

No one else spoke, and the President, for the rest of the trip back to Manchester, said nothing.

That night the networks led their evening news broadcasts with accounts of the fiasco. And, by the strange alchemy of television, the scene in Nashua became even more hideous. Compressed and edited, accompanied by a newsman's portentous narration, the story made the screaming seem louder, the blood redder, the crowd angrier—and the President more ineffectual, more the helpless victim of events.

Cardwell, in Washington, watched the news, then called Gary Triplitano in Manchester.

"How's he reacting?" Cardwell asked.

"He wants to cancel open rallies. He wants all admission to indoor rallies to be by ticket. He's talking about cutting back his schedule and campaigning on TV." Trip shook his head.

"Andy Martin has been on the phone to advance men ever since we got back. He's telling them no demonstrators at tomorrow's stops."

"How the hell can he do anything about them?"

Triplitano grunted. "That's not my department."

"You know what he's thinking, don't you, John? He's sitting in his room thinking this would never have happened if he'd stayed in Washington."

"He *had* to go up there, Trip. He had to."

"Well, what are you going to tell him about disasters like this? Are you going to tell him to campaign in a tank? Have all demonstrators arrested and shot?"

"I'm thinking about it, Trip. I'll be back up there tomorrow, and we can think together."

Friday the Sixteenth

Something grim settled over the campaign: an air of tense control, of overplanning. The spirit of carnival that had enlivened the first week of Rattigan's campaign evaporated. The street crowds, once so spirited, so eager to shout and reach out for the President, now became silent onlookers, respectful and restrained.

Now when the President ventured out he was protected, hemmed in on all sides like a prisoner being led to the dock.

When he rode, he rode not in the open limousine, standing in the cold wind to wave and acknowledge the cheers of bystanders. Now the bubble top was in place on the great black car, and he rode in a warm, plastic-sealed cocoon.

Behind the scenes the word went out to campaign workers: no large outdoor events; admission to indoor speeches and rallies would be by ticket only.

Trusted party functionaries, controlled by Anders Martin and his advance men, would control the distribution of the tickets. And new phalanxes of guards, new legions of plainclothesmen and Secret Service agents would ring the halls, warily scanning the crowds, alert to the slightest unwanted movement.

The new grim atmosphere was reflected in Rattigan's face and voice—for he needed the electric charge that came from the crowds; he craved their cheers. And it was reflected in the headlines that came from the campaign:

SECURITY TIGHTENS IN WAKE OF DEMONSTRATIONS.
WRAPS GO ON IN RATTIGAN CAMPAIGN.

On Friday a crowd of loyalists gathered in Manchester for a fund-raising dinner to swell the President's primary campaign treasury. They came partly from New Hampshire and partly from Boston; from Providence; from New York and Washington; from Middleburg and Miami Beach.

They came, in black tie and furs and jewels, lured by the promise of proximity to the President and his elegant first lady, lured by the excitement of a hard-fought campaign; warmed by the enfolding satisfaction of being needed; they came, mixed briefly with the less gaudy gentry of New Hampshire, and added a touch of glitter to the gray-and-white cityscape of Manchester.

Triplitano and his staff positioned the press outside the Sheraton-Wayfarer's Convention Center so that the band of demonstrators in the parking lot would be outside camera range. And, for the most part, as the guests arrived to face the glare of floodlights, the demonstrators were subdued; they raised a din when they recognized Woodson, the Secretary of Defense, emerging from his limousine. And they jeered wildly, waving their signs, when finally Carl Rattigan's heavy car pulled up, ringed by motorcycle patrolmen and guarded by Secret Service men trotting in the snow.

They jeered, but Rattigan ignored them, disappearing with his guards into the building.

So the demonstrators waited, lowering their signs, blowing on their frozen hands, and stamping in the snow.

They knew their quarry would appear again.

Inside, Cardwell checked his ticket and found his place at a table near the front of the crowded ballroom, just beneath the long head table where the President would sit.

The others at his table were New Hampshire politicians and their wives—strangers to Cardwell.

He gave only his name when he introduced himself, not hinting of his connection with the President. And though he joined the dinner conversation enough to be polite, his eyes and mind ranged beyond the little world of his table: He was watching the President, studying his face, trying to divine the President's mood in the swirl and tumult of the evening.

Rattigan was smiling, rising often to reach across the table, offering his hand to the well-wishers who crowded, even during dinner, his table. There was no trace of preoccupation on his face, no hint of boredom or impatience. The President was enjoying himself, enjoying hugely this escape, however brief, from the hard routine of the campaign.

Lisa Rattigan was watching, too, from her place a few seats away from the President. And she, too, felt a surge of relief: This was good for him. He needed this evening—the closeness of uncritical friends and supporters; the warm cloud of approval in which they wrapped him; the testimonials, the outstretched hands.

She almost felt guilty for counting the glasses of champagne he drank. Usually, at gatherings like this, he let the waiter fill his glass a second time, then pushed his empty glass away and nodded "no" when more was offered. But tonight he was not so cautious—he was relaxing, letting go.

He ate heartily and let the waiters refill his glass without demurring. He waved his Secret Service men away from their stations in front of his place and let the crowd press in. He smiled and waved and felt the warmth of the champagne and the evening bringing a flush of pleasure to his face.

And when the time for speeches came, his euphoria infected the crowd; he set them laughing and cheering with his easy jokes, established a steady rhythm of statement and applause, felt their enthusiasm rolling over him almost as a physical sensation.

As he reached the conclusion of his brief speech, he held them rapt: "This is not just another contest for political office," he told his friends. "This is a campaign to protect the presidency from the most dangerous assault ever mounted against that office; a campaign to prevent future Presidents from being held hostage by their Vice Presidents."

Rattigan caught his listeners with his eyes.

"I want you to understand that, my friends and fellow Democrats. And I need your help—so that between now and March 5, every voter in New Hampshire will understand that, too."

He stepped back, finished, and the applause came—a long, steady, unanimous roar.

And then, quite suddenly, it was over. The lights went up, Rattigan's cordon of agents moved in, and the President was hustled out—through the cheering throng, through the crowded lobby, through the doors and into the bitter night toward his car; into the eyes of the field crews, whose floodlights cast a harsh glitter on the snow.

When they saw him, the crowd of demonstrators began to roar. Some of them set up a chant, one he had not heard before: "Killer Carl! Killer Carl!" The President's good humor evaporated; he stopped dead.

The cameras swung to pick up the crowd. Lisa felt an agent grab her elbow, push her toward the giant limousine; she caught a blur of lights, of waving signs, of state troopers joining hands to push back the crowd.

Then someone threw something. A demonstrator flung a rock, a snowball, something that struck the President's car with a harsh, shattering sound.

"Let's go!" an agent shouted—and the troopers moved, truncheons swinging, into the screaming crowd.

The big car started rolling off, crunching through the snow, gathering speed, moving away from the roiling mob of demonstrators and police. An agent had pushed Rattigan through the car door—but not before news cameras and microphones recording the fracas for tomorrow morning's news had caught this scene: Carl Rattigan, President of the United States, shouting to his tormentors, "Fuck you all!"

Sunday the Eighteenth

Abner Hoffman lost no time in reacting to the President's troubles.

At noon on Sunday, in a cold, tile-floored television studio in Manchester, the Vice President submitted to the last-minute ministrations of studio technicians. A pretty blonde dabbed pancake makeup on his chin; a bearded young man measured the distance from the camera to Hoffman and called for a floodlight to be moved. The interviewer, a lantern-jawed New Englander, smiled at Hoffman, and someone began to count; Hoffman cleared his throat and saw the camera light wink on.

"Our guest today," the interviewer said importantly, "is the Vice President of the United States, who for the past six weeks has been campaigning to unseat his onetime friend and political ally—"

While the interviewer spoke, Abner settled more heavily into his stage-set swivel chair, relaxed—but felt too the surge of energy and excitement that came to him at moments like this. He was ready, alert, hungry for the opportunity that was coming now.

"Mr. Vice President, how's it going? What's your feeling about the campaign as things stand now?"

"I think it's taken a sad turn, Bill. I hate to see—I think we all hate to see a President lose control, and that's what's happening." He shook his head slowly, in a perfect representation of regret, almost sympathy.

"You're saying the President has lost—"

"I'm not just speaking of the unfortunate incident on Friday night, the obscene remark. I don't want to exploit that. We all lose our tempers. The people of New Hampshire will make their own judgment about what the President did. . . ."

And then, ever so skillfully, he moved on. "When I say the President has lost control, I mean he's lost control of *events.*"

"You mean events abroad?"

"Abroad, yes, of course. But here at home too. Here in New Hampshire. I think it's a sad thing when a President can't travel among his own countrymen without creating disturbances wherever he goes. A sad thing when he has to become a prisoner . . . all these bodyguards."

He nodded sadly once again, then gave the camera a gaze of pure openness, pure seriousness, pure sincerity.

The interviewer pushed the questioning from one topic to another, but certain words, Abner knew, would echo in the minds of his viewers long after the program was over: *lost control . . . creating disturbances . . . obscene remark . . . a prisoner.*

Abner Hoffman, like every other politician, was an actor. He knew the power, not only of words, but also of the power of gesture and tone, and he had mastered them all. A few easterners and press people might think him a bit primitive, but he was actually the truest kind of sophisticate: one who knows precisely the value, the effect, of every gesture, however subtle.

This was easy. The hollow-faced interviewer, a bit awed by his guest, laid questions into Hoffman's lap shyly, deferentially, like a child offering small gifts.

"I'm not trying to divide the country," Hoffman said. "The President did that when he sent those boys down to Bolivia. I'm just trying to speak for all those Americans who are deeply concerned—"

All the old words, the old themes. His voice was the earnest, evangelical voice of a man who had sat years ago, in country revival meetings, wide-eyed as the preacher screamed about angels and damnation and the anti-Christ; but it was also the sober, measured voice of a man who had sat in Congress and in Cabinet meetings.

"I'm not ambitious for the presidency," he said. "I'm ambitious for peace!"

Soon it was over. The interviewer spoke his closing words, the camera lights winked off, and the hot studio lights were doused. Hoffman, sitting suddenly in shadow, sighed, mopped his broad forehead, and turned to search for Warren Jasper somewhere in the gang of technicians behind the cameras.

"How'd it go?" he asked.

"Great," said Jasper. "Great, just great."

And John Cardwell, sprawled on his hotel room bed amid a disorderly scattering of papers and memos, unconsciously echoed Jasper's words.

"Great," he said bitterly. And he rose, scattering more papers off the dull-red bedspread onto the floor, to snap off the television set. "Just great."

Cardwell had been studying, as he watched Hoffman's interview, the past week's polls: one, an in-depth study based on house-to-house interviews; and the other a quickie: a telephone survey to test reaction to Friday night's demonstration and the President's loss of temper.

Cardwell had been studying the polls, reading the numbers over and over, as if by rereading them he could somehow change them.

Because the news—the news that he must put into a memo to the President before the President returned to Washington on Monday—did not look good.

After two weeks of arduous campaigning, two wearying weeks of motorcades and rallies, two weeks of shouted speeches, two weeks of reaching for hands and votes, the President had gained ground—only to lose it. Hoffman was moving up again.

Cardwell circled the numbers from the house-to-house survey:

The President	47%
The Vice President	42%
Undecided	13%

What had done it? Cardwell shook his head. The demonstrators, certainly. And Hoffman—he was crafty, no doubt about it. But the worst part about it was this: Rattigan had done it to himself. Somehow, in three years of warm protection of the White House, Rattigan had lost a measure of his flexibility, his keen politician's sense of timing. He had been knocked off-balance—not reeling, but off-balance—and now it showed. Now, exposed as he was, he must recover—or lose.

Monday the Nineteenth

On Monday morning Carl Rattigan left New Hampshire to return to Washington for a few days: to rest, to review with his aides his domestic legislative program and, as Triplitano put it, to "act like a President instead of a candidate."

As the great airplane roared away from New England, rising through layers of dull gray clouds, the President tried to relax, to put New Hampshire and his troubled campaign behind him for a moment.

But before him on his fabric-covered work table was Cardwell's memo. The President had read it, circling the more discouraging numbers with his felt-tipped pen, laying the memo aside for a while, then reading it again.

Triplitano sat across from him, waiting for Rattigan to speak.

"I knew I never should have come up here," Rattigan said. He tapped the memo with his pen.

"Your polls went up the first week," Triplitano said.

Rattigan shrugged but said nothing. An Air Force steward in a pale blue blazer entered the compartment, poured coffee for the two men, and ducked out silently.

"You've got to find a way to handle those demonstrators. They're killing you," Trip said.

"I know," Rattigan said. "I know. And Abner's exploiting the whole thing to the hilt. Did you see him yesterday? All that sanctimonious crap about their patriotism? Their right to assemble? If they were blocking his car, do you think he'd defend them? Hell, no, he wouldn't. Old Ab would just as soon run over them as . . ."

Now it was Trip's turn to remain silent. There were times, he knew, when it was best to say nothing, to let his chief vent privately the anger he could not show in public.

"That bastard," Rattigan said. Then, seeing that Triplitano was indulging him, allowing him to talk on unchecked, he said, "I'm sorry."

Trip smiled. "It's all right, Mr. President. I agree with you. I'd like to bury him under a snowdrift and hold a rally on the site."

Rattigan smiled.

"I talked to Cardwell," Triplitano said. "He thinks he's got an idea on how to handle them."

"I'd like to run these last two weeks from Washington," Rattigan said. "Do some television from the White House to New Hampshire. High-level staff, above the battle—"

"They'll say you're running away from Hoffman," Triplitano said.

"Let them say it," Rattigan replied. But his voice held no conviction.

"I think you should wait to see what Cardwell suggests," Triplitano said. "Hold any decision until you hear from him."

"What he suggests? He's the one who screwed me up in the first place! I could have run the whole primary from the White House, stayed above the fray, but he came on with his goddamned polls and forced us in there."

"Mr. President," Triplitano said softly, "he didn't screw you up. Abner was chasing you all over the landscape, and you really had no choice. All Cardwell did was point that out."

"I know, I know," Rattigan said, silencing Triplitano with an upraised hand. He leaned toward Cardwell's memo, started to read it again, then stopped and began marking idly on it with the felt-tipped pen: a series of sharp, jagged, toothlike drawings across the upper margin.

He was tired. Not physically—he had always had bottomless energy—but tired nonetheless. Tired of fighting Abner. Tired of trying to speak above the clamor of the protestors. Tired of the endless motorcades, the cameras, the jostling crowds, the noise. Tired of the effort, the strain toward the end of every day to keep his hoarse voice from shrinking to a whisper.

Tired of being President? He wondered how many of his predecessors had felt this weariness. A man turns his whole life toward one end: works, schemes, campaigns, lies awake nights dreaming of the prize, aims himself like an arrow at just one goal, one target—only to find it not enough. Or too much.

Once he had loved it: loved the crowds, the confusion, loved even the bone-aching exhaustion at the end of a campaign day. But now—what was happening? That bastard Abner—he must love it; it's going his way now.

Rattigan sighed, and Trip looked up.

"Give Cardwell a call," Rattigan said. "Tell him to let me know what he wants me to do—as soon as possible."

"Yes, sir."

"Tell him I don't much want to spend the rest of the campaign in New Hampshire."

Triplitano nodded.

"And tell him"—Rattigan looked straight at Triplitano—"tell him I don't care whether I win on debating points or not. I don't care whether I convince the voters that I'm right and Abner's wrong." He reached down, folded Cardwell's memo, and chopped at it emphatically, using his hand like an ax. "I just want to destroy Ab Hoffman."

As soon as Triplitano reached the White House, he placed a call to Cardwell in Manchester.

"The boss wants your big ideas. Right away."

"I'm writing him a long memo now," Cardwell said.

"No time for that. He wants to see you. Can you come down right away?"

"I'll catch the next flight."

"I'll tell you what, sport. We're going to give you the first-class treatment. We're sending a JetStar up to get you. I'll have a car for you out at Andrews. Call me from there when you touch down, and we'll all be gathered to receive your wisdom."

Two hours later, Cardwell was airborne, the lone passenger in the little beige-upholstered cabin of the JetStar. He shut out the high whine of the engines and tried to concentrate on the half-finished memo he had spread on his lap. But he found himself remembering something Nancy had said on his last trip to Washington: *The things you think you want: Maybe they're things you won't like after you get them.*

He was at twenty-eight thousand feet in one of the presidential planes. A trim black sedan was waiting for him in Washington. He had access, at last, to the bright trappings of power—and yet he felt curiously neutral about it all.

And he had power now, or influence—whatever you call the golden coin that men fight to amass and spend in Washington. Yet he felt strangely inert. He felt none of the elation he had thought he would find near the pinnacle.

Funny how the signals came: the little signals of ascending status. Triplitano's call; the plane dispatched to New Hampshire for his convenience—these told him he had entered, at last, the little circle of the closest ones.

But somehow, knowing this gave him none of the joy he had expected to feel.

The car was waiting for him on the ramp, just as Trip had promised. The JetStar pulled right up to it, and in three minutes they were on the Suitland Parkway, speeding toward the city. His driver radioed the White House switchboard: "Tell Mr. Triplitano his party is fifteen minutes away."

All the trappings. But Nancy's words cut into his awareness: *Maybe they're things you won't like after you get them.*

They were waiting in the Oval Office: The President, Triplitano, and Brooks Healy, sitting on the comfortable sofas that flanked the fireplace.

"Trip tells me you can get me out of this mess you've got me in," Rattigan said, and Cardwell smiled. Then Rattigan turned serious. "Tell me what you think we should do."

"Well," Cardwell said, "I think we've got to do two things: First, we've got to redesign your campaign appearances so that most of them are unannounced. If you just walk down the street or go to a shopping center you can get all the people you need and all the coverage you want; the reporters have to follow you. That'll keep the demonstrators off guard."

Rattigan nodded, but he said nothing.

"I think you should do some really aggressive television," Cardwell said. "Saturate the state for the last ten days of the campaign."

"Defending the war?" Brooks Healy asked.

"Saying nothing about the war," Cardwell said. "That's Hoffman's issue. I'd aim my television right at Hoffman: Make him the issue, the villain. Force him onto the defensive for a change. That's what you did in the first days of the campaign, and it worked. Or started to work."

"We can have new spots ready to air in five days," Trip said. "All we have to do is buy the time."

"What all this ignores," Brooks Healy said, "is that this campaign is about the war."

"Of course it is," Cardwell said. "And we can't change that. But we can't talk about the war without getting defensive. It's too painful; people don't want to think about it. And it's too uncertain; nobody knows how it's going to turn out. The strategy has to be to prick Hoffman, to wound him, to make him bleed, and finally to discredit him with the voters. And we can't do that with a defensive issue like the war."

He looked to the President for some reaction, but saw none—not even a nod.

"That's it?" Triplitano said. "That's the big brainstorm?"

"That's it," Cardwell said, feeling abashed. "It's easy to say. The doing is the hard part."

No one spoke for a moment; they were looking to the President for his reaction.

"I like the television part," Rattigan said. "I like the thought of keeping Abner on the run. Of course, that's what we want to do." He hesitated for a moment. "But I don't like the idea of wandering around shopping centers trying to attract crowds."

"You don't have to attract crowds," Cardwell said quietly. "Just talk to the people you meet."

"I'm not running for sheriff," Rattigan grumbled. "I'm the President of the United States."

Cardwell said nothing.

"Frankly," the President said, "I'd hoped you were going to tell me a way I could handle this thing without spending so much time in New Hampshire." He looked at Healy and Triplitano as if he were seeking allies. "I could spend weekends up there—" And his voice trailed off.

Cardwell took a deep breath. "Mr. President," he said softly, "you can do what you think best. But I think you know you can't win with television spots alone. Not with Hoffman campaigning from daybreak until midnight at factory gates and on street corners, asking everybody why you're afraid to come. You've got to *be* there. You can't campaign by remote control."

He was amazed by his own fervor. He looked to Trip for reassurance, but Trip was staring at the carpet.

Abruptly Rattigan stood up. "Well, I'll think it over. Let me know where I can call you."

They were all standing now, and Cardwell's face was burning. *Don't call me,* the voice in his head said furiously, *I'll call you.*

In the hallway after they had left, Cardwell and Triplitano shook hands with Brooks Healy, then went into Trip's office.

"Score zero," Cardwell said gloomily.

"Don't be too sure," Triplitano said. "I think you were right about one thing: He knows he can't win without going up there and staying awhile. He knows that if he doesn't knock Abner out cold in New Hampshire, he'll have to chase Ab all over the country in other primaries. And how can he be President when he's doing that? He knows what he has to do. Only he doesn't want to do it. You want to go for supper? Big steaks? I'll buy."

Cardwell, feeling futile, refused.

"I'm going home," he said, and left.

But he did not go home. Nancy was still at home in Louisville and the empty house in Bethesda, with all its reminders of her, seemed an alien place to him. He decided to spend the night in town.

Without calling a car, he grabbed his suitcase and walked out of the West Wing and up Seventeenth Street toward the Mayflower.

After he had registered, Cardwell dialed the White House operator. "The President wanted to know where he could reach me," he told her. "I'm at the Mayflower, room 1023."

He showered, tried to take a nap, but could not sleep. Then, having second thoughts about spending the evening alone, he dialed Triplitano's office. Trip wasn't there.

Feeling bereft, Cardwell ate a solitary dinner in the dark-paneled restaurant downstairs, bought six magazines at the newsstand in the lobby, and returned to his little room.

He couldn't read. His mind was locked on the scene this afternoon in the Oval Office: Rattigan slumped on the heavy sofa, frowning at Cardwell's advice. *I'm not running for sheriff,* he had said. *I'm the President of the United States.*

No, you're not running for sheriff, Cardwell said now to himself. *But you'd better campaign as if you were.*

At ten o'clock the telephone beside his bed rang sharply.

"Mr. Cardwell? The President for you."

"John? Are you in town?"

"Yes, sir; I'm at the Mayflower."

"Well, get on back to Manchester tomorrow. Go ahead and plan a few days' campaigning for me up there. I'll come up on Thursday."

"Using my scenario? The unscheduled stops?"

"Using your scenario," Rattigan said. "I don't guess it can hurt to try.

"But get this straight: This is an experiment. If it doesn't work, I'm going to break it off."

"I think we can make it work."

"Okay. Call me when you have some plans." And with no good-bye, the President hung up.

We can make it work; we can make it work: the phrase set itself up like a chant in Cardwell's head. The restlessness he had felt earlier melted away; he was elated, eager for the morning to come, impatient to get back to New Hampshire.

And he was tired. Before eleven o'clock, he was asleep.

Thursday the Twenty-second

On Thursday the President returned to New Hampshire and plunged again into the campaign. His motorcade swung out of Manchester, northward up Interstate Highway 93, into the frozen, picturesque countryside.

Rattigan toured three shopping centers. He stopped at a little clapboard village hall and leaped out of his car to meet the startled old-timers who stood there gossiping in the cold. And once, while the reporters grumbled, the President ordered his caravan to a halt outside an elementary school as the children were leaving.

The motorcade turned back toward Manchester late in the afternoon, racing against darkness. Triplitano, riding on the press bus now, tried to reassure the angry reporters: Yes, they would get back in time to file their stories. He was sorry there had not been a firmer schedule, but the President wanted to campaign in an impromptu, informal way. Yes, he would try to schedule stops tomorrow to permit meals and allow for film deadlines.

Back at the Wayfarer, Trip walked with the President back to his suite.

"What do you think?" Rattigan said.

"They hate it," Trip said, meaning the reporters. "But I think it's good for you."

The President said nothing. He was holding his right hand slightly forward as he walked; Trip saw that it was rubbed red and raw by all the handshaking. Rattigan was breathing deeply, as if he were trying to throw off bodily the fatigue that weighed him down.

For a fleeting moment Triplitano remembered what Lisa Rattigan had said on the first night of this campaign: *Stop killing my husband.* He was glad Lisa had stayed in Washington.

They stopped outside the door of the President's suite.

"What time tomorrow, Trip?"

"We pull off at seven o'clock, Mr. President."

"Tell somebody to send Sorrel up. I want a rub."

Sorrel, the faithful medic. This was the part, Trip thought as he walked on to his own room, that they never knew about. And Triplitano pictured, as he lay in his own bed waiting for sleep, the last minutes of Rattigan's campaign day: Sorrel bathing and dressing with ointment the President's aching right hand; Sorrel pummeling the President's knotted, drawn-up muscles; Sorrel tapping out of a little amber vial a tiny yellow pill: something to help the President get to sleep.

Friday the Twenty-third

Late on Friday, Lisa Rattigan flew up from Washington to join the President for the weekend's campaigning. Triplitano had told her that the President would return from his afternoon of handshaking in time for a quiet dinner in their suite, but he was late.

Lisa ordered their dinner held. She changed from the black dress she had traveled in into a beige dressing gown, refreshed her makeup, then paced from room to room for the duration of three cork-tipped filter cigarettes.

At nine-thirty he came in, gray-faced and wet from the snow.

"Look at you," she said as she embraced him. "Just look at you."

She took his coat and tie, hung them on a gilt straight chair, and wordlessly went into the bathroom to draw a tubful of hot water.

While he soaked, Lisa ordered dinner sent in, and later they ate in silence—until Lisa could not keep from speaking her mind.

"I really wonder if it's worth all this."

"All what?"

"Your pushing yourself this way."

"I wonder too sometimes."

"Then stop it. Do it some other way."

He shook his head. "It's going better now, and we only have ten more days. I've got to use them. Ten days like the last two will put us over the top, I think."

Meanwhile, in one of the motel's small meeting rooms, the campaign's hired advertising men had set up a videotape machine for a final review of the campaign's new, hard-line television spots.

Triplitano and Cardwell arrived at ten-thirty, and Trip announced that the President would not attend. "He's just thoroughly bushed. He hopes you'll forgive him."

"Not coming? Not coming?" The agency president, a carefully barbered, too-nattily dressed man who had flown up from New York just for this moment, jumped to his feet. "Then we'll have to reschedule."

"No," Trip said. "We'll go ahead and he can see them later, tomorrow morning, maybe."

The agency man, crestfallen, sank back into his chair and waved to the projectionist. "Let's run 'em. All together, no pauses in between."

There were ten advertisements: six thirty-second and four ten-second spots. None of them mentioned the war in Bolivia or defended Carl Rattigan; every one was aimed precisely, savagely at Abner Hoffman. Half of them finished with a credit that read, "The Campaign for President Rattigan." The other half were attributed to "The Committee to Protect the Presidency."

Cardwell and Trip watched in the flickering darkness as the images danced, then died. Once or twice Triplitano whistled at the end of a spot—the low, wheezing sound of a man accepting a body blow.

When it was over and the lights went up, Trip whistled again.

"Jesus H. Christ," he said.

"We've got to wound Hoffman, Trip," Cardwell said. "We've got to destroy his credibility. Totally."

Trip whistled again. "This is pretty strong stuff."

The agency president leaped to his feet. "These are beautiful spots, beautiful spots! I'm very proud of them. If you don't like them, give them a chance to grow on you—to sink in. They have terrific impact, terrific impact. Stanley, let's run them again, so Mr. Triplitano can—"

"I didn't say I didn't like them," Trip said. "I just said they're pretty strong. Have you got the time bought? Can we go ahead and start airing them?"

"We have a terrific time buy, considering the short notice. Terrific. Do you think the President will have a chance to—"

"I think he'll like them," Triplitano said.

And the meeting was over.

"Jesus," Trip said as he and Cardwell walked back toward their rooms. "Old Abner's going to wet his pants!"

"My only worry is the press," said Cardwell. "We may get some flack from them. This is pretty hard stuff."

"Screw the press," Triplitano said. And with a wave to Cardwell, he walked into his room.

Saturday the Twenty-fourth

Carl Rattigan left his headquarters at ten on Saturday morning in a light snow, dragging his motorcade toward another long day of campaigning: nine days now until the vote.

Cardwell, his speeches written, his memos on the polls dispatched to Triplitano and the President, took off to ski.

He and Sarah, in a wine-red rented Ford, crunched through the light morning snow toward Franconia, snow chains chattering. Sarah was smoking, fiddling now and then with the radio dial, looking for music to match their holiday mood. And Cardwell, looking at her, suddenly found himself remembering his college days: weekends spent fleeing the campus, driving with the radio blaring and a girl beside him, her knees tucked up beneath her.

"I wonder if I'll score this weekend," he said slyly.

"No chance," Sarah said. "I'm saving myself for marriage."

She smiled and slid toward him, and Cardwell smiled back. But the word—marriage—had unsettled him, pricked a little blister of guilt in his mind.

By lunchtime they were at the fake-Alpine resort, sitting in the restaurant watching the skiers, a toiling insect colony on the mountain.

There was a television set in the bar; when Cardwell heard one of Rattigan's new thirty-second spots come on, he stopped Sarah in midsentence and moved closer to get a better view.

It was the one the ad men had nicknamed "the crumbling White

House spot." While the narrator assailed Ab Hoffman's campaign for the White House, an image of the White House began to crack, then crumble and collapse.

When it was over, Cardwell returned to his lunch without a word.

"Is that your handiwork?" Sarah asked.

"I'm the evil genius," Cardwell smiled. "Or one of them."

But Sarah did not smile. "I think it's dirty pool," she said.

"Then wait until you see the one that shows Abner making a speech, with scenes spliced in every second or two of demonstrators going wild. It's really evil, and it's thirty seconds long."

"So the issues in the campaign just get lost?" she said. "All the President's talk about taking his case to the people just goes out the window? The issue becomes Ab Hoffman and the demonstrators? You play tough, don't you?"

"It's a tough game, Sarah."

"So I see," she said coldly, and Cardwell realized how cynical his words had sounded.

"I don't worry about the big issues being forgotten, Sarah. The voters aren't idiots. They know what this campaign's about. Meanwhile, we use every device that will help. Every legitimate device. You can bet Hoffman will."

"I know. I know. I'm just disappointed."

"In me? In the President?"

She evaded his question. "In what a campaign like this forces you to do. I wonder what he's thinking. I wonder if he thinks it's worth all this."

"Rattigan? He'd probably tell you that if Churchill had been Prime Minister in the thirties, the Nazis would never have subjugated Poland."

"Oh, God! That's such utterly discredited claptrap! I'm surprised at you."

He laughed. "You asked me to tell you what Rattigan was thinking, not what I think."

"What do you think?"

"I'm not sure. I want him to win. I don't like what Abner's doing. I really believe the President did what he had to do."

"You think only he can save the country?"

"I don't know. But I know *he* feels that way. Every good national politician feels that way. Hoffman does: 'If I'm elected, we'll have peace.' Hell, Sarah, they all feel that way. And those kids in the street feel that way; they think they can save the world. Only you and I are wise enough to know the world is beyond saving."

Sarah said nothing. She was staring out toward the mountain, at the crowds of skiers crisscrossing the snow.

Cardwell felt almost as if he were talking to himself. "We do tend to get drawn away from the real issues. But don't be too critical of that TV commercial; it's not all crumbling plaster casts of the White House. One candidate runs his spots, the other runs his, and the voters somehow sense the real issues behind all the show biz. It's not such a bad system."

Unexpectedly, Sarah squeezed his hand and smiled. "Know what you are? You're a party hack!"

"I know," he smiled. "That's what bothers me. I thought I was cut out for something higher."

"Maybe you can be ambassador to Jamaica. Party hacks get jobs like that, don't they? And big contributors?"

"This," he said, "is the last political discussion we're going to have this weekend. Now get up and let's go skiing. I want to gag you with a fistful of snow."

"Why would you do such a thing?"

"Because you make my conscience bother me."

Cardwell forgot everything else and gave himself to the brief weekend with Sarah. He saw her warming, giving up her hesitation, and seeing that, he wooed her all the more intently.

She was not an expert skier, so he let her set the pace. Sarah wound uncertainly down the easier trails, working to stay away from the crowds. Behind her, Cardwell tried to let his muscles take over and remember; it had been years since he had skied. As he followed, he found himself staring hungrily at her hips, the fullness of them; silently he vowed to end the skiing early and take her to their room.

They were like children: When Sarah would wobble and fall, Cardwell would dive into the snow beside her, throwing his poles into the air, and they would roll together in a tangle of arms and legs and skis.

Once, lifting his face from hers, he saw that her lips were blue. He touched her cheek.

"You're freezing. Why do you punish yourself?"

"I'm pretty tough," she smiled.

"Well, let's go in."

So they headed, wet and cold and frosted with snow, for the lodge. Back in their room he piled logs on the fire and made a nest of pillows and blankets before the fireplace.

Sarah poured drinks, and soon they were lying together naked in the firelight.

They were too tired to make love. Instead they lay together feeling the warmth of the fire and each other, looking down at the patterns the fire threw onto their bodies.

"Let's play the word game," she whispered.

"Silence is better," he said.

"No, play. You say the word that's in your head."

"That's all? How do you win?"

"You don't win. It's just—revealing."

"Okay, I go first." He thought a moment. "Flesh." Gently he squeezed the ample bulge of her hips.

"Just the words," she said. "No acting out."

"You go."

"Illicit."

"Illicit? You feeling guilty?"

"No, I like it. It's a Victorian word: 'their illicit affair.' It's titillating. You never hear it anymore."

"Because nothing's illicit anymore."

A silence spread between them.

"You go now," she said.

"Sarah."

"That's not a word, it's a name."

"No, it's a word, like 'flesh.' All warm and ripe and full of sex. If you were named Emily, you'd have no sex, no fullness. Listen: 'Sarah.'" He spoke the name in exaggerated syllables.

"My turn now. 'Salacious.'"

"You trying to seduce me?"

"It's another Victorian word. Salacious. Disapproving and sensual at the same time, just like the Victorians."

"My turn." And he raised himself on one elbow to look down at her face. "I love you."

"That's a phrase."

"The game's over. Now, tell me what you're thinking. The truth."

"I love you. I really do," she murmured.

"No mental reservations or purpose of evasion?"

"I love you."

"You feel comfortable, loving me here amid the pillows in front of the fire, illicitly and salaciously?"

"Supremely comfortable."

He fell onto her, kissed her hair, and they clung together, listening to the fire.

In a little while he began to stroke her back, gently and tentatively, with his right hand.

She drew away and smiled at him. "Do you really want to, or do you just feel obligated?"

"Just feel obligated."

"You can relax, then. We have lots of time."

It was, he knew, a pledge: as much a pledge as she could give. Cardwell took his hand away, settled closer in beside her, and they fell asleep, without making love, to sleep until long past dinnertime.

Sunday the Twenty-fifth

The next morning, an hour before dawn, Sarah found herself awake. She fumbled on the nightstand for a cigarette, lighted it, and caught in the sudden glow made by her lighter a glimpse of Cardwell's sleeping face.

So like a child's face, she thought. He slept on his stomach, hugging a pillow, his hair hopelessly tousled. She stubbed out her cigarette, turned to watch him, and wondered if all women had the same feelings—part mother love, part desire—seeing their men asleep.

Then she let herself admit what she had been trying to deny: All right, I give up. I love you.

She loved him.

If wanting to touch was love. If wanting to talk, to tease, to argue with endless fascination was love. If feeling that her moments with Cardwell were somehow illuminated, like stop-frames from a film—if these were love, then, God knows, she loved him.

But something troubled Sarah. She could not imagine the future with Cardwell, and she could not tell him about her past.

Those two inhibitions were what had made her so hesitant, so guarded; what had brought her close to tears so often when she was with him.

Once she had said the word *ghosts,* and he had laughed at her.

But the ghosts were real.

And there in the half-dark winter dawn Sarah let the ghosts come back: probed her old pain the way a small boy gingerly presses a bruise, to feel the twinge.

It had happened a long, long time ago. Now, looking back upon herself as she had been then, Sarah saw not a woman but a girl wracked by the frustrations of loving a man she could not have: a man who was married to another woman—and to his ambition. It had been, for her, an affair of hurried meetings, abrupt good-byes, whispered telephone calls, unbearable intensity. They had never spent an entire night together.

The man's wife, finally, had ended it for them, in a way that Sarah could only admire: She had come to Sarah's apartment and reasoned with her, as an experienced woman reasons with a girl.

"I don't blame you for loving him," his wife had said. "He's an exciting man, and he thinks he loves you. But what he really loves is his ambition. I understand that; it's why we're perfect for each other."

"That," Sarah had answered, "is the most cynical thing I've ever heard." But the woman had been right.

"Suppose he left me and married you," the woman had said. "It might not ruin his career; we're not so old-fashioned now. But if something did go wrong, he'd start blaming you, you can see that. And an affair that started with such excitement would end in bitterness; he would hold you responsible for his failure, whether you were responsible or not."

And that is how it had ended—like an amputation. Sarah had known, the moment the woman left her apartment, that the affair was over. But even now the nerve ends still cried out occasionally.

Sarah marked the end of her life as a girl—the beginning of her life as a woman—from that strangely polite encounter with her lover's wife.

And why was all this untellable to Cardwell? Because Sarah knew with her unfailing intuition that he could never understand. For all his hardness about politics, for all his sophistication in the ways of campaigning, he was deeply innocent—as innocent as his sleeping face. He might try to understand, but it would be beyond him, try as he might.

Cardwell stirred in his sleep, breaking her reverie, and Sarah leaned on her elbow, studying his face.

"What are you doing?" he asked when he awakened.

"Watching you sleep."

"Sexy, isn't it?"

"Hold me. Please." She moved against him.

"Wanton woman. Won't even let a man sleep. Got to have it all the time."

"Please. Hold me."

He took her in his arms and Sarah burrowed in, trying to bury her age and her old memories in his innocence.

That night on the drive back to Manchester, Sarah sat close to Cardwell, lightly stroking the back of his neck. But neither of them spoke, as if to talk would somehow destroy the memory of their perfect weekend together.

For Cardwell, what had made the weekend perfect was something more than the snow, the skiing, the release from the tensions of the campaign: it was his sudden sense that Sarah had come through, had given up her resistance and was ready now to love him. That victory, along with the pleasant fatigue of the weekend, warmed his blood as he drove.

Sarah yawned; he pulled her head down into his lap, and soon she was asleep. The weight of her head made his leg ache, but Cardwell didn't mind. He drove with one hand, stroking her cheek with the other.

Much later, he pulled up in front of the Holiday Inn, and Sarah stirred.

"What's the matter?" she said, her voice thick with sleep.

"We're home, sweetheart. Back to reality."

"Oh, screw reality."

As he lifted her suitcase from the car trunk, she touched his hand. "Let's say good night here. Prying eyes in the lobby."

"Oh no," Cardwell said, "I'm not hiding a goddamn thing." And boldly he swept her inside.

The first person they saw was Gary Triplitano. He was standing by the bar, in conversation with Murphy Morrow.

Cardwell and Sarah passed to the elevator bank, too far from Trip to speak. But Trip had seen them, and they could feel on their backs his steady, comprehending gaze as they stood waiting to go upstairs.

"Screw it," Cardwell said in the elevator. "He's an adult. We're all adults. Why are you blushing?"

"It's all right," Sarah said. "I'm not blushing."

But as they parted with a long kiss at Sarah's door, Cardwell knew that everything was not all right.

He returned to his car to find Trip waiting, leaning against the fender in the cold.

"Can we talk, old man?" Trip said.

Cardwell motioned Trip into the car, switched on the engine, and the two of them sat for a moment, waiting for the heater to dispel the chill.

"How much has she told you?" Trip said.

"About what?"

"About herself"—Trip could see that Cardwell knew nothing —"and the President."

Cardwell stared at Triplitano for a moment, then closed his eyes.

"They met for the first time when he was in the Senate; he went to Vietnam on an inspection tour," Trip began. "Then she came back from Vietnam about a year before the war was over. He was starting his hearings on the war. She had her Pulitzer, she knew everything about Vietnam, knew everybody there. She started helping us—all very discreet, of course, since she was in the press. She gave us names, leads, questions to ask. She made him an expert—more of an expert than he already was. He admired her, she was beautiful, he came to depend on her—"

"And they had—" Cardwell couldn't finish the question.

"They had—a relationship," Trip said gently, and he reached out to lay a hand on Cardwell's shoulder. "It wasn't a sordid thing. He was devoted to her. He was devoted to her and devoted to his wife—and devoted to politics. It was a tough thing to watch."

"Who knew—about them?" Cardwell said hoarsely.

"Almost nobody. Me. Sheila, his secretary. There was never any scandal. It went on for a year, eighteen months. . . ."

"And then?"

"I don't know. All of a sudden—I don't know, she just broke it off. Realized there wasn't any future, I guess. He was like a zombie for about six months. The hearings were a big success, the presidential talk got started, and suddenly he was a national figure—but he was just a robot for a long time. Then he started running. He's been running ever since."

"Why are you telling me all this, Trip?"

"Because I think you should be careful. A man's wounds can stay open for a long time."

"I'm afraid that's too cryptic for me to understand, Trip."

"He sent her flowers. In December when she was at Walter Reed, he sent her flowers. He had me order them, and the card he sent said, 'The President'—not 'The President and Mrs. Rattigan.'"

"That doesn't mean a goddamn thing!"

"I'm not saying it does. I'm just telling you to be careful, in case it does mean something."

"All right, I'll be careful. Now, do you have any more juicy little tidbits, or can we end it?"

"Look, old man. I don't know what's happening between you two. I don't know whether it's serious or whether she's just using you to feel closer to him or whether you're just having a good time. I just think you should have your eyes open, okay?"

"Okay," Cardwell said tonelessly.

"You driving back to our place?"

"No, Trip. I think I'll stay here for a drink." He switched the engine off and they sat in the sudden silence for a moment. Then Trip opened his door.

"No hard feelings, Johnny?"

"No hard feelings."

And Trip was gone, crunching his way through the fresh snow in the parking lot.

Cardwell went straight to Sarah's room.

Sarah answered his knock with a look of surprise on her face, and he swept past her into the room. Sarah had not undressed; the Sunday New York *Times* lay scattered on her bed.

"You must take me for a colossal fool," he said.

"John, what's the matter?"

"I just talked to Trip."

She closed her eyes as if she were receiving a blow, and Cardwell read her expression as a confession of guilt.

"The sophisticated woman takes a lover," he said bitterly. "Oh, he's not what she wants, not a President or anything. He's a bit of a fool, but he's young and willing, and conveniently nearby."

"Please. Don't."

"It was all a lie, wasn't it, Sarah?"

"No, not at all. Not at all."

"Not to tell me was ten times worse than a lie."

"I was going to tell you. I kept looking for a way to tell you."

"Tell me what, for God's sake? 'Oh, by the way, I fucked the President for eighteen months, but it was just for fun'? I hope you won't let it come between you and your boss'?"

"Stop it!"

"How is it when you see him now, Sarah? Do you feel like you've been in bed with history? Had a tumble with the big one?"

Sarah brought her hands to her face, then suddenly took them away, straightened, and gazed at Cardwell.

"You are not going to speak to me this way," she said evenly.

Cardwell sank into the chair beside her bed.

"I was the one who resisted this," she said. "I was the one who saw the obstacles. I swore I'd never let myself be hurt again, and look at me now!"

"Sarah—"

"I've let myself fall hopelessly in love with you. And hopeless is the perfect word."

Cardwell's anger drained away; he knew she was telling the truth.

"Why didn't you tell me, Sarah?"

"When could I have told you in a way you'd understand?" She hesitated. Then: "All right, I'll tell you now."

He shook his head and raised his hand to stop her. But she would not be stopped.

"I never intended to fall in love with him. Who intends to fall in love? I'd had a great success in Vietnam; I was on fire against the war, and he was the leader of the opposition in the Senate. We just came together. He fell in love with me."

"And you?"

"I loved him. Of course I loved him. He was a decent, intelligent, very romantic man. I fell in love with him against my—"

"Against your better judgment."

"It's like a theme in my life, isn't it?" She seemed to be looking past him as she talked. "The first time we made love—"

"Sarah, please!"

"—was in his office, late one night. It was always in places like that. I brought a basket of food and some wine, to help him with a speech."

"Sarah."

"When it was over, I looked around his office and saw all the pictures: the Speaker of the House, all these politicians staring down. I felt as if we were in public. It was like an omen. I guess I knew then that it couldn't work, but I held on. Of course I loved him. I loved him very much."

"You don't have to tell me all this."

"Almost as much as I love you," she murmured. "I'm a very intelligent woman, but I'm a fool about some things."

"But you ended it."

"No, Lisa Rattigan ended it. She came to me and confronted me with—reality."

Cardwell stared at her, searching her face.

"Trip thinks Rattigan is still in love with you."

"No," she said.

"Or that he still feels something."

"I hope he does feel something still, because I do," she said. And seeing Cardwell's stricken face, she added, "But it's not love. It's pain. I'd like to think he feels some of that, because it would mean he puts some value on what we had."

"I understand," Cardwell said.

"I want you to understand," Sarah said. She sank onto the bed facing him and laid her hand on his. "I want you to realize that when I see him, I don't have the slightest feeling of having slept with history. I was a different person then, and he's a different person now. When I look at him I don't see the man I knew. I see this tortured political machine, just ticking away. Remember what somebody said about Lincoln? 'His ambition was a little engine that knew no rest.' "

"I don't want to talk about him," Cardwell said, and he stood up.

"Tell me what you're feeling," Sarah said.

"I don't know, Sarah. I thought I loved you. I was sure of it. I may still love you. But I can't see you until—"

"Until? Or anymore?"

"I don't know."

"I think I know the answer," Sarah said. She stood up, kissed him gravely on the lips, and pushed him toward the door. "Go and get some sleep," she said. And she held her tears until he was gone.

Monday the Twenty-sixth

What Cardwell felt first when he awakened seven hours later was the vast emptiness of his bed and heavy silence of his room. He had grown accustomed to having Sarah beside him, sensing even in his sleep the shape and weight of her presence, hearing her breathing. Now she has gone, and her absence weighed as heavily as her presence had.

Lying alone in the dead early morning of his room, Cardwell tried to decide whether what he remembered of last night—his encounter with Triplitano, his confrontation with Sarah—had been dreamed: flashed onto his mind's screen in a few tumbling seconds before he awakened. But the ache he felt told him otherwise; it had happened.

He propped himself against two pillows and sat for a long time staring across his disordered room.

Why not call Sarah? Cardwell had to force himself not to reach for the telephone beside his bed. What could he say? That what she had told him didn't matter after all? That would be a lie. What he had learned of Sarah's past life altered everything, changed the shape of everything. Sarah seemed a new person to him, a stranger who had admitted him into certain rooms of her house but had left other rooms locked. And he sensed now that he could never know Sarah fully: that behind those locked doors lay too many things he could never share with her.

Had Sarah deceived him? Cardwell shook his head. No, not really. She had not locked the doors—just kept them closed. She had never lied to him. She had simply understood that there was no way she could tell him, that the differences between them were too great for him to understand the hidden parts of her life. She had sensed that Cardwell could accept the delight of loving her, but not the pain.

Cardwell flung back the covers and swung himself to the edge of the bed, only to catch himself and sit motionless for a while, as if to stand up would require more strength than he could summon.

He felt guilty: Why had he been so small and unforgiving? Sarah had not lied. It had been a long time ago. It was over now, something to be forgotten. Why should it matter, after all?

He rose and padded to the bathroom.

It was fully ten minutes later, after Cardwell had emerged from a stinging shower and as he stood shaving, staring at his ravaged face in the mirror, that he suddenly understood: Why did it matter? Because he could not love Sarah and serve Carl Rattigan at the same time. Not because of Sarah—but because of Rattigan.

Not that the President still cared for Sarah or even wanted her—Cardwell doubted that. Their affair had been too long ago, and about one thing Sarah was right: Both she and the President were different people now.

But Carl Rattigan was accustomed to having what he wanted, and he would not easily tolerate seeing someone else—especially someone close to him—have what he had lost, even a long time ago.

That was what Trip had meant when he had said, "Be careful." Be careful. Be careful not to offend your powerful patron. Be careful not to claim what once was his—or almost his. Be careful not to forget—your place.

Suddenly his razor caught: A little thread of blood appeared on his chin, burning red. Cardwell cursed sharply—at the pain; at Rattigan.

He had wanted to become a part of the President's inner circle: a trusted aide and confidant. But he had never dreamed he might become enmeshed in Rattigan's private life. And now—Jesus!

He splashed cold water on his face, pressed a shred of tissue onto his bleeding chin, and stood for another moment staring at himself, finding his own face unfamiliar: older somehow.

All the warmth and richness of the past weekend had suddenly drained away. The grand sense of possibility that he had felt, knowing that Sarah had finally surrendered herself to him, now was gone, replaced by a burden of confusion and guilt.

Back in his room he dressed slowly, automatically.

How many days until the vote—seven? Eight. First things first. Work to be done. No need to decide anything yet—let matters run their course for a while. Back in Washington—well, who knows what can happen? Just keep going. Try not to think too much. Just keep busy, and—

He knotted his tie, found his slim briefcase and found the room key on its dull red tag, and headed for his door and the whirlwind of campaign headquarters.

Just keep busy.

As he waited for the elevator in the deserted motel corridor, he could hear Trip's words again. "He was like a zombie. . . . He was just a robot for a long time."

The elevator doors rolled open and Cardwell, robot-like, stepped on.

Tuesday the Twenty-seventh

On Cardwell's desk on Tuesday morning lay the results of yesterday's round of telephone polling: four hundred calls made by volunteers to homes across New Hampshire:

The President	53%
Hoffman	39%
Undecided	8%

He smiled a tight little grin: the smile of a man who feels himself vindicated. The numbers seemed to be proving him right: After only forty-eight hours, the saturation campaign on television was showing results. After two days of relentless attack upon Hoffman, the undecided were beginning to break toward Rattigan, and Hoffman's voters were looking a bit shaky.

It was still too early to make any hard conclusions, but Cardwell's instincts told him he was right. The spots were working, chipping away at Hoffman, casting doubt on his motives for opposing the President. And Rattigan was campaigning well: The new person-to-person campaign strategy had thrown the demonstrators off balance, taken them off the front pages.

Only eight days to go; eight days to keep the momentum going—to keep the pressure on.

Cardwell shouted from his cubicle to Dot Orme. "Can you come in here?"

"I want to call a meeting for twelve o'clock here," he told her. "Order soup and sandwiches to go around, and—"

"Today?"

"Today. I want Geiger, the pollster. Anders Martin. Stallings, the guy who's running the volunteers. Somebody from the ad agency. And—"

"Mr. Triplitano?"

Cardwell hesitated. Then: "All right, if he's not out campaigning."

"Shall I tell them what you're meeting about?"

"Tell them I'm giving them their marching orders for the final big push."

They met at noon: the handful of shirtsleeved men who were generals in Rattigan's New Hampshire army. Over tepid hamburgers and paper mugs of coffee, they studied copies of Cardwell's polls and congratulated one another.

Triplitano slipped in late, after Cardwell had started his monologue. Cardwell nodded toward an empty chair—grateful to Trip for coming late.

"How many extra volunteers can you raise?" Cardwell asked Stallings. "People to handle the phones, and some really presentable types to go door-to-door?"

"As many as you need. I've got senior citizens to do the phoning. We can set up another bank of twenty-five phones. Fifty, if you need them."

"I want at least fifty, twelve hours a day from now until the vote. What about foot soldiers?"

"We've got the unions in Manchester," Stallings said. "They can turn out an extra hundred volunteers a day."

"I don't want blue-collar types in white-collar neighborhoods, Cardwell said. "Get me some young lawyers and some women, for God's sake. You can fly them up from Washington if you have to."

For an hour Cardwell laid out his plans, stopping now and then to take a question, scarcely realizing that every one of the men he was directing now—Triplitano, Martin, each of the others—was older than he.

"Let's continue the sampling—four hundred calls every twenty-four hours. I'd like to find out which of these TV spots is having the biggest impact. Find out where Hoffman's weakest, which points he's most vulnerable on. Then we can pull off the weakest commercials and repeat the strongest. Hit him where it hurts."

He turned to Anders Martin. "I want to schedule a couple of big rallies. Balloons, bands, the whole works. Let's keep him out at the shopping centers for the most part. But I want to add just one or two extravaganzas—the last one on Sunday before the vote."

"What about demonstrators?" Martin asked.

"Let's not worry about them too much now. I think we're strong enough to handle them now, if he'll do it. And I'd like to see him face them down just once."

"The last time he faced them he told them to fuck themselves, and it almost got on nationwide TV."

"That's one reason I want him to face them again," Cardwell said. "I want to erase that impression if we can. Leave a picture of him facing them with dignity."

When the meeting was over, Triplitano waited until the others had left.

"Johnny, I'm sorry about last night. I didn't know what to do but to tell you."

"I know that."

"No hard feelings?"

"No hard feelings," Cardwell said, trying to sound convincing.

Triplitano laid a hand on Cardwell's shoulder and eyed him levelly. "Are you going to be all right?"

Cardwell sighed. "I'm trying to keep my balance, Trip. Maybe I can talk about it after some time passes."

Trip squeezed his shoulder and then was gone.

That night, moving casually through the Musket Room of the Holiday Inn in Manchester, Triplitano picked four of the nation's most influential reporters and quietly, carefully leaked the latest poll. Triplitano was an expert at his job. He knew the virtues of the soft sell; he made no claims for the accuracy of his figures. He simply passed the page of numbers to his chosen few reporters with a quiet admonition: "You can use this, attributed to 'high officials in the President's campaign.' It's the latest stuff we have."

And having performed his quiet little errand, Triplitano settled back to watch the unfolding of the story—and to wait for the Vice President's reaction.

Wednesday the Twenty-eighth

Abner Hoffman was handshaking his way through the streets of Concord, trailing his kite's-tail of reporters and Secret Service men, when a local reporter gave him the news.

"Mr. Vice President, a poll on the Associated Press wire this morning has the President leading you by 14 per cent in New Hampshire. Any comment on that?"

"I'd be interested in knowing the source of that poll," Hoffman said over his shoulder. He grabbed the hand of a gray-haired woman who had been waiting by her car for a chance to shake the candidate's hand.

"It appears to come from sources in the President's campaign," the reporter shouted, and Hoffman threw back his head to laugh.

"I thought so," he said, and chuckled. "I thought so."

"If the President beats you by a decisive margin, will you abandon your campaign?"

"Now, gentlemen, ladies! You know that I'm not going to comment on a hypothetical question based on a dubious poll that I haven't even read yet!" Hoffman's smile was less cheerful now—an expression accomplished with the mouth but not the eyes.

"What percentage of the vote in New Hampshire will it take to keep you in the race, Mr. Vice President?"

"I'm just not going to comment on that, Ray," Hoffman told his questioner. "I'm just not going to comment at all." His smile was gone now. So, seeing no more hands to shake and eager to avoid more questions, Hoffman pointed to the line of campaign cars waiting down the street and led his entourage on a slow sprint toward them. "We're running late!" he shouted to the puffing reporters.

Later, in the lead car, speeding westward toward New Hanover, Hoffman sat back panting for several seconds. Then he turned to Warren Jasper.

"Get me a copy of that poll," he said. "Try to get an afternoon paper at the next stop."

Jasper nodded, and they rode in silence for a time. Hoffman removed his brown leather gloves, rubbed his big hands warm, then pointed at Jasper beside him.

"I want to spike all these questions about losing. I want to give them something else to talk about. You have a suggestion?"

"Not yet," Jasper replied, "but I'm working on it."

That night, in a speech to a student group at Dartmouth, Hoffman departed from his text to add some words penned by Warren Jasper.

"More and more," the Vice President said, "the President's whole campaign begins to look like an exercise in political cowardice."

The reporters who had been listlessly following Hoffman's advance text suddenly darted glances at one another and began scribbling furiously.

"First we have his refusal even to campaign actively in this state until forced by events to do so."

A spatter of applause arose, then died in the audience as Hoffman rushed on.

"Then we have his resolute effort to discredit me and to impugn my motives."

Silence.

"And finally there is the President's equally resolute effort to avoid any discussion of the real issue in this campaign: the bloody war that we are involved in by his decision."

Hoffman paused now and let the cheers come. The students, eager for bold, fearless talk from their champion, stood and roared. And Hoffman's band of reporters looked on, shocked at the bluntness of Hoffman's attack.

When the noise subsided he went on.

"There's still an opportunity, before the vote on Tuesday, for the President to redeem himself and his campaign. I have authorized my aides to meet with the President's political managers to lay the ground rules and to make plans for a public debate between the President and myself. I am prepared, if the President accepts my invitation, to discuss the issues face to face, to bear all the costs of televising our discussion."

Back in Manchester, the President, bone-tired after a long day of campaigning, stayed up to watch the late news and hear Hoffman's challenge.

"The bastard," he said. "Political cowardice!"

Lisa, sitting beside him, raised a hand as if to warn him against getting angry, but Rattigan smiled.

"Don't worry," he said. "I'm not upset. We've got the bastard on the ropes. He's throwing wild punches. He's gotten the message about the polls and he's getting desperate, trying to breathe some fire into his campaign."

"What are you going to do?" Lisa said.

Rattigan laughed. "I'm not going to do a damned thing but let him squeal. I'm not about to debate with him. Not while I've got 53 per cent to his 39 per cent."

He stood up and snapped off the television set.

"And meanwhile, dear First Lady, I'm going to get a good night's sleep. I'm going to sleep, and I'm going to dream about the polls."

Thursday the Twenty-ninth

But the President's dreams were not to last the night.

An hour before dawn, the Signal Corps telephone beside his bed rang—two sharp rings—and Rattigan was instantly awake.

"Mr. President, this is Sheldon Karnow. I have something to report."

"What is it, Sheldon?"

"We have some serious fighting. I'm afraid a camp of ours down there has been hit pretty hard."

"Do you have any numbers on casualties?"

"We're still sorting it out, Mr. President. I'm afraid it won't be good news."

Karnow, with his coolly professional way of understating things: How merciful at five o'clock in the morning, Rattigan thought.

"Do you want me in Washington?"

"I think we may have to discuss a response, since this looks like direct action against a United States installation."

"Go ahead and call the National Security Council for this afternoon. I'll be there before lunch."

There was a long silence before Karnow spoke again.

"Mr. President, I'll do what you wish about including the Vice President."

Rattigan heaved a long sigh. "Of course we'll have him. If we don't, he'll make an issue of that." Rattigan was silent for a long moment. "Tell Abner he can fly down on the backup plane if he needs to."

Less than two hours later, Air Force One was roaring toward Washington.

When the big planes landed at Andrews, Triplitano found Hoffman and his aide Warren Jasper disembarking from the backup plane.

"We have a car for you, Mr. Vice President. The meeting's at one, in the Cabinet Room."

"Thank you, Trip."

There was a long black car at the head of the motorcade pulled up beside the plane: separate transportation for the Vice President. Hoffman and Rattigan never spoke to one another.

The tension was palpable in the Cabinet Room when Carl Rattigan strode in at ten minutes after one, followed by Brooks Healy.

The tension that they all could feel—all the members of the National Security Council—was not simply the blood-quickening tension caused by a crisis, but the wary unease caused by the presence of an enemy. And in this gathering, Abner Hoffman was the enemy.

Hoffman stood with the group when the President entered, but there was no trace of deference in his manner. He was half smiling, as if he knew how uncomfortable his presence made the others, and as if he did not care.

"Gentlemen." Rattigan signaled them to sit down, and they sank into their chairs. "Sheldon will give us a brief rundown on the situation, and then I'll have your comments."

Karnow, nodding, moved from his seat at the east end of the table to his easel. He took up his long pointer and aimed it at the pink heart of the map: Bolivia.

"Early this morning, Mr. President, at about four o'clock our time, there was a sudden fierce assault near this spot." Karnow jabbed his pointer, indicating the place near Cochabamba, and the President's men leaned forward, craning to see. "Eighty Americans are confirmed dead, forty wounded. Later, U.S. jets went after the attackers but hit a column of our own men, killing fifteen more and wounding twenty."

Now and then while Karnow spoke, reducing the bloody chaos in Bolivia into neat, summarizing phrases, the men around the table sneaked glances at Ab Hoffman, as if by studying his face they could read his private thoughts. But Hoffman gave them no clues: He, too, leaned forward, listening intently to Karnow's summary.

Karnow took only ten minutes. When he sat down, each of the others spoke, responding to Rattigan's nods of recognition; each one except Abner Hoffman, who sat directly across the table from the President. When his turn came, halfway through Rattigan's polling of the Council members, Hoffman simply nodded and said softly, "I'd prefer to save my comments until last."

Without exception, each of Rattigan's advisers agreed: The sudden killing of nearly a hundred American soldiers was a tragic happening; it demanded retaliation—a swift, precise demonstration of strength—but it justified neither massive retaliation against Chile nor a pullback of U.S. troops. Aside from this one tragedy, the war plan was going well. Indeed, as one general put it, the casualties until now—until now—had been "well within the manageable range."

The manageable range: Hearing the phrase fall so bloodlessly, so impersonally, from the general's lips, Brooks Healy stole a glance at Rattigan and saw the muscles in the President's cheeks go tense.

When it was over, the men around the big table were unanimous in their opinion: The United States must strike back, in a precisely limited but forceful way. Healy, Woodson, Karnow, the generals—they were unanimous, except for Abner Hoffman.

"Abner?" Rattigan acknowledged Hoffman with the barest inclination of his head.

"Thank you, Mr. President." Hoffman did not look up from the scratch pad in front of him. "There are several points I want to make. The first is this: It was bound to happen. If you put twenty thousand troops into a combat situation, there are going to be these kinds of tragedies. And there will be more. You know it and I know it. There's no way to avoid it. How many did we lose—ninety? A hundred? Next time it could be two hundred."

He paused, not looking up to see Rattigan's reaction. Then, speaking quietly, he went on. "I want the record of this meeting to reflect that I have opposed American military involvement in Bolivia from the beginning. I still do. And I differ from every man who has expressed an opinion here. I believe that in the light of these events we should withdraw our forces."

He paused again and a few impatient sighs were audible around the table. Old Abner, they seemed to say: He's making his campaign speech again.

"If that's not acceptable to you, Mr. President," Hoffman said, "then why not launch a major attack against Chile and end the war that way?"

He hesitated for a few seconds to let his words sink in.

"The only policy that's wholly unacceptable to me is the one you're following. Those boys are sitting ducks down there. They'll continue to be sitting ducks if you just string along the way you're going now."

"Abner," Rattigan said slowly, "are you willing to have tomorrow's papers quote you in this meeting as calling for a major attack on Chile?"

"Mr. President," Hoffman replied in a voice redolent with sarcasm, "knowing how deeply you value confidentiality of discussions among your closest advisers, I wouldn't expect to be quoted at all in tomorrow's papers."

Even Rattigan smiled, and a few of the men around the table, impressed by Hoffman's nerve, chuckled aloud.

"Well, then, Abner," said Rattigan, "suppose I decide to hit Chile hard. Would you want me to tell the American people I was doing it on your advice?"

"I think the American people know, Mr. President, that you're not in the habit of taking my advice."

"All right, Abner—" Rattigan tried to end the exchange, but Hoffman rushed on.

"My advice is that we get those boys the hell out of there. Now! Today! Yesterday! Anything else I say is in the nature of merely pointing out options, Carl." In his anger Hoffman dropped the formal, deferential, "Mr. President."

For a brief moment everyone in the room waited for Hoffman to correct himself, to apologize, to erase his error by saying the sacred title. But Hoffman, surprised by his own boldness and proud of it, said nothing.

"All right, let's end this," Rattigan said curtly. "I'm not going to make a decision now. If I did that, somebody—somebody just might tell a reporter and it would all be on the news before I walked back to the Mansion."

Every man in the room, including Abner Hoffman, knew whom the President meant when he said *somebody*.

"Thank you, gentlemen. I'll be in touch with you individually." Rattigan, beckoning to Brooks Healy to follow him, rose to leave, and once again the group stood.

When the President had left, none of the men lingered to talk, as they had done in times past. The Cabinet chiefs and generals fled to the West Basement entrance and their waiting limousines, and Abner Hoffman, shunned like a leper, walked with his bodyguards to his office a hundred yards away.

Back in the Mansion, a fire was burning in the Yellow Oval Room. Rattigan motioned Healy to a small sofa beside the fireplace, then stood for a moment warming his hands. Then, head bowed, he walked slowly to the tall french windows that looked down across the South Balcony toward the Ellipse and the Potomac. Rattigan stood for a moment gazing at the river in the distance, then abruptly turned to Healy.

"Can you imagine how he'll exploit this?" he said. "Every time a boy is killed down there, Abner sees a vote coming his way. Did you see him smiling in there, enjoying it so? I wish there'd been a television camera there, so people could have seen him smiling."

Healy nodded, saying nothing, choosing simply to let the President talk on.

Rattigan shook his head. "It's so easy for Abner," he said. "So goddamn easy. All he has to do is attack, attack, attack. If I hit back at Chile for these damn raids, he can attack. If I do nothing, he'll attack."

He clasped his hands and extended them before him. "Brooks, I feel as if my hands are tied as a candidate because I'm President—because I have to make decisions and answer for them. And Abner"—he unclasped his hands and swung them through the air—"Abner's as free as a bird."

"I know," Healy said softly. And seeing the President looking to him for comfort, for reassurance, Healy went on. "When I was a boy at school, Mr. President, I ran a little track. I started out in the sprints, and I ended up running cross-country: distance running. That turned out to be what I did best."

Now Rattigan was gazing quizzically at his old friend.

"I didn't understand until much later why I liked the distances so much better. And then I realized that I liked the freedom of it; liked the feeling of running by myself, against my own best record; liked not having the other runners so close to me. I did my best when I wasn't looking over my shoulder at the competition."

"I think I know what you're suggesting, Brooks," said Rattigan.

"I'm suggesting, Mr. President, that you forget about Ab Hoffman. Run the rest of this campaign like a long-distance race. Don't feel you have to answer Abner, respond to Abner, react to Abner. Just run your race. Do what you would do about this crisis if Ab Hoffman didn't exist—if there were no vote on Tuesday."

Rattigan smiled despite his gloom. "That's good advice, old friend," he said. "But it's hard, Brooks. So hard."

Healy eyed the President directly. "No one ever promised it would be easy, Mr. President."

But Rattigan had turned back to the window and was staring out again. In the distance the Tidal Basin and the Potomac glittered like dirty mirrors.

"You made me take him, didn't you, Brooks?" he said after a time. "Remember?"

"Sir?"

"Abner. You made me take him on the ticket. You told me that it was the only way to neutralize him. I was just standing here remembering that day back at the convention."

Now Healy stood up. "Well, Mr. President," he said, "if that piece of advice has to be on my head now, so be it. I'll take the blame."

Suddenly Rattigan turned, rushed over to Healy, and embraced him. "Brooks, I'm sorry," he said hoarsely. "You're the best man I know, and here I am giving you hell."

"It's all right, Mr. President," said Healy. "It's all right." And the two men stood together for a moment in an awkward embrace. Then Healy stepped back.

"I'd better go," he said, and he moved toward the door. "I'll be at my office if you—"

"No advice, Brooks?" Rattigan followed him.

"Only what I've given, Mr. President. Decide what you'd decide if there were no campaign, no primary in New Hampshire."

Rattigan's voice was weary: "Thanks, old man."

"Call me if you need me," Healy said, and he turned to leave. But then he paused in the doorway, turned, and looked at Rattigan: a long, appraising look.

"What is it, Brooks?"

"You have to do this, Mr. President. . . ."

"Do what?"

"You have to decide what you're going to do with the full knowledge that it may cause you to lose. That what you decide to do may give Abner the victory. And you have to go ahead and do what you must do, even so. You have to face the possibility of doing the right thing and losing because of it. Are you prepared to lose, Mr. President?" Healy's gaze was direct.

"I—I can't answer that, Brooks. Not right now," Rattigan said.

"I'll be at my office, Mr. President," Healy said. "Call me if you need me." And with a wave, the President's old friend was gone.

Late in the afternoon, just before the evening news broadcasts, Gary Triplitano called the White House reporters into the press room and read a tersely worded statement: The President had ordered a series of retaliatory air strikes against suspected concentrations of Chilean troops in Bolivia. The operations were already under way. Any further attacks by Chilean troops against United States personnel would meet with similar retaliation.

Triplitano, perspiring under hot floodlights, finished reading the statement. The reporters, shouting and jostling, hurled questions at him. Wasn't this a new departure? A change in policy? An escalation?

"I'm sorry," Trip said grimly. "I have nothing for you beyond this statement."

A few reporters, muttering curses, tried again. But their deadlines were near; the press corps shoved toward the doors and rushed to their typewriters and telephones.

The planes were in the air. Downstairs, in the warren of offices that surrounded the Situation Room, the lights burned late and teletype machines clattered incessantly.

Carl Rattigan, sequestered in the Mansion, limited himself to one drink this evening and prepared to wait: to spend a night of fitful, interrupted sleep—and to face, in the morning, the firestorm of outrage and vituperation.

MARCH

Against All Enemies

Friday the First

WAR ESCALATES, screamed the headline on the front page of the Friday *Post,* and the *Star* echoed: U.S. JETS ENTER WAR.

The Vice President called reporters to his Capitol office at noon to hear a statement.

"In a meeting of the National Security Council yesterday," he read, "I suggested to the President that he remove United States troops from combat in Bolivia as a step toward peace.

"The President rejected that course, as he has rejected taking military action against Chile sufficient to end the war decisively. Instead, he has chosen action that, in my judgment, can only prolong the war."

Hoffman cleared his throat and stared into the cameras, then went on.

"What is most disturbing to me, other than his unwillingness to end the war, is his unwillingness to face squarely those who disagree with him; his refusal to explain or defend his decisions in an open discussion.

"Instead, the President has chosen to vilify me and to impugn my motives in a primary campaign whose chief feature is not reasoned debate, but a series of inflammatory television commercials.

"I think the American people deserve better from their leaders. And so I am offering once again an opportunity for open discussion of the issues.

"The manager of my primary campaign in New Hampshire has scheduled television time on a network of New England television stations for my final campaign appeal on Sunday night. I am offering that time instead for a debate between the President and me, to be conducted under whatever ground rules his advisers and mine may devise. . . ."

At the White House, Gary Triplitano brought the wire service account of Hoffman's challenge into the Oval Office. Rattigan read it in silence, then tossed it without comment onto his desk.

"I talked to Cardwell in Manchester," Triplitano said. "He says you should avoid this like the plague; not let Abner lure you into this."

"And you agree?"

"I think so, yes," Trip said. The President, he thought, seemed curiously detached.

"Healy said the same thing yesterday," said Rattigan. "He told me I should run these last few days as if Abner isn't in the race. Do what I'd do if Abner didn't exist."

"That's good advice," said Trip. And after a long silence in which the President made no comment, Trip asked: "Are you going to take it?"

"No," Rattigan said.

Triplitano stared at him.

"I'm going up there," Rattigan said, "and I'm going to debate him."

"On his turf? His TV show?"

"There comes a time when you have to shove in your whole stack," Rattigan said. He was drumming silently on the arm of his big leather chair, but otherwise he seemed serene.

Triplitano expelled a long sigh. "Mr. President," he said, "I have to tell you I think you're making a mistake."

For a long time Rattigan only stared at Triplitano. Then he said softly, "That may be. It may be that I'm going to lose this thing, Trip, and it may be that I'll lose because I was foolish enough to let Abner put me on the defensive in a televised debate. But if I lose—" He sighed and spoke the words again. "—if I lose, it won't be because people thought I was too cowardly to face him."

Triplitano said nothing, and in a moment Rattigan waved his hand, dismissing him. "All right, go on. You've got a lot to do from now till Sunday night."

Sunday the Third

At seven forty-five on Sunday evening, when his motorcade was still a block away from the Memorial High School in Manchester, Carl Rattigan gazed ahead through the darkness, studying the scene. He saw the giant mobile television vans, then spotted the demonstrators: a forest of bobbing signs in the carnival glare of the television lights. Hoffman's kids.

"I thought the ground rules said no demonstrations," he said flatly to Cardwell.

"The ground rules apply to the debate inside," Cardwell said. "I'm afraid we didn't discuss—"

"Too late now," Rattigan said, and he peered at the throng in the distance. "Abner doesn't miss a trick, does he?"

Triplitano, hearing Rattigan's remark, stole a glance at Cardwell, but said nothing.

"Let's go in another way," Rattigan said. And a minute later, after a flurry of radioed exchanges between the motorcade and a Secret Service command post in the high school building, the President's car peeled off from the motorcade, swung around a corner, and headed for the rear of the building.

A crowd of agents hustled the President into the building, unseen by reporters or onlookers. But Cardwell, trotting after the group, could hear the crowd in the distance, chanting as they awaited their quarry: "Peace on Earth . . . Peace on Earth!" It had the steady, emphatic rhythm of a drumbeat.

The place they had chosen for the President to spend the last hour before his confrontation with Hoffman was a band room: a large room with green-painted walls adjoining the big auditorium. Two White House telephones had been installed, and Cardwell saw that someone had placed a mirror on a desk, leaning it against a wall and giving the place the air of a makeshift dressing room before the junior class play.

Rattigan ignored it. He sank into the swivel chair before the desk and fell immediately to studying his briefing book, a black-bound portfolio of facts and possible questions thrown together by his staff for the debate.

Neither Cardwell nor Triplitano spoke. Cardwell studied the room as if trying to memorize its every nondescript detail; Triplitano sat staring at the floor. Ten minutes passed, marked only by the occasional turning of a page in Rattigan's black book. Cardwell glanced at his watch. Eight o'clock: a half hour to go.

All three men jumped at the sudden noise: a sharp, insistent rapping at the door.

"Mr. President?" A young Secret Service agent stuck his head inside. "It's the Vice President, sir." And suddenly Abner Hoffman was in the room, beaming as if he were the host at a festive dinner.

"Hello, Abner," Rattigan said in surprise.

"Just a gentlemanly hello before we tangle," Hoffman said benignly, and he extended his hand. The President stood without extending his hand, but Hoffman ignored the snub.

"You saved my campaign a bundle by coming tonight," he said to Rattigan. "The networks are covering our meeting as a news event. Now I may come out in the black." He was still grinning.

"Thanks for coming, Abner," Rattigan said coldly. And he sat down, as if dismissing Hoffman.

"Actually, Mr. President, I have some business to discuss. Do you think these gentlemen could give us some time alone?"

Rattigan looked at his aides, then at Hoffman. "Anything you say to me, they can hear," he said. There was a long, uncomfortable silence; Hoffman studied the two of them.

"All right," he said finally. "I wanted to tell you, Carl, the way I see this thing tonight. The way I see it is, you're on the defensive. There's been a strong reaction to this latest flap down there, and the whole country's up in arms."

Hoffman was leaning against the door into the hall, his arms folded easily over his chest.

"So?" said Rattigan.

"So you're in trouble, Carl. And I have the initiative, don't I? I can hit you hard—really slam into you. Or I can ease off a little, make it easy on you; take a softer line."

"Tell me what you're getting at, Abner," Rattigan said, and Cardwell saw that his eyes were little points of hatred.

"I have two opening statements in my pocket," Hoffman said, patting his breast lightly with his right hand. "One calls you a decent man, a man of principle who's just misguided. Takes the high road. The other statement—well, the other is more direct."

Rattigan stared at Hoffman.

"You can decide which one I'll use, Mr. President."

"What do you want, Abner?"

"Just a little assurance from you, Mr. President. Your word that in the unlikely event that I should lose on Tuesday, you'll keep me on the ticket in November. In return for an assurance from me: my word that I won't enter any other primaries. That I'll call off my race."

Rattigan said nothing.

"It's in your interest, Carl," Hoffman said earnestly, bargaining hard now. "Without me, you go into a national election with the party split wide open. With me, there's a chance of—"

Suddenly Rattigan was grinning. "Old Abner." He shook his head, still smiling. "You want it both ways, don't you? If you win, you win. And if you lose, you still want to win."

But suddenly his smile went dead. "You bastard, you don't care about the principle of the thing. You just want to be President some day, isn't that it?"

"This does you good, too, Carl," Hoffman began. "You've got to consider that. . . ."

Rattigan leapt from his chair and lunged at Hoffman so fast that for a moment, Cardwell and Triplitano stood frozen as Rattigan seized Hoffman's lapels, then drew back a clenched fist.

"Stop it!" Triplitano shouted. He grabbed the President's wrist and Rattigan's blow fell with an empty thud on Hoffman's shoulder, and the two aides pushed him against the desk. Rattigan leaned there for a moment, glaring at Hoffman.

The Vice President, his breath coming in heavy, wheezing sighs, stood with his back pressed against the door, his eyes bright. His coat was still bunched up around his shoulder; after a moment he looked down and began patting his lapels.

"I can still beat you, Carl," he said, panting hard.

"Get out of here," Rattigan said dully. And then the Vice President was gone.

For a long time none of the three men spoke. Then Triplitano said softly, "We've got twenty minutes before air time, Mr. President. Do you want me to go down the hall and talk to him?"

"About what?" Rattigan said scornfully.

Trip hesitated. "I'd hate to have him leak it to the press that you —" Trip swung his right fist in a slow arc through the air.

"And have it get out in the bargain that he tried to make a sleazy deal with me? Forget it," Rattigan said. "He won't say a word."

They stood in silence for a minute, waiting for the tension in the air to dissipate. And then, with a last glance in the mirror to smooth his hair and straighten his tie, the President said, "Let's go."

Eight twenty-five.

A bright blue backdrop had been set up on the vast stage. Before it stood two identical lecterns, shaped like stubby cylinders and covered in dark blue burlap. Off to the side was a long desk: headquarters for the moderator and the four reporters who would question the candidates.

Cardwell could see from his place at the edge of the stage that the audience was already gathered. But this crowd had a strange scent: There was, in the air, none of the suppressed excitement that fills a theater before the curtain rises. This crowd was flat, silent: like a congregation gathered for a funeral. The orders given them were strict: no applause, no crowd reactions, no cheering.

Cardwell watched as the President was fitted for his microphone. A technician asked Rattigan to count aloud, while another adjusted a spotlight on the floor. Hoffman came onstage, took his place at his lectern, and Cardwell turned to Triplitano.

"I don't like this," he whispered. "Abner's rattled him. Look at his face." Rattigan's cheeks, caught in the hot white lights, were still red with anger.

"Forget it," Trip said.

"Forget it!"

"It's too late to worry. Whatever happens, he'll have the satisfaction of having taken a poke at Abner Hoffman. That should last him for a long time."

"Jesus, Trip. Sometimes I marvel at you—"

But Triplitano silenced him: It had begun.

"Tonight's debate," said Sam Niles, the moderator, "is unprecedented. Never before have a President and Vice President been pitted in a campaign against one another. And never before—"

Cardwell tuned out; he was watching Rattigan. The President, he saw, had assumed an expression of ease; he was following the moderator's words intently, a hint of a smile playing on his lips. He seemed utterly calm now. It was Cardwell who was nervous.

"A backstage flip of the coin," Mr. Niles said, "gives Vice President Abner Hoffman the first opening statement. Mr. Vice President."

Cardwell stared, riveted. *I have two opening statements in my pocket,* Hoffman had said. *You can decide which one I'll use.*

"The issue in this campaign," Hoffman was saying, "is simple enough. It is betrayal: the President's betrayal of his campaign promises. His betrayal of his oath to defend the Constitution, which reserves warmaking power to the Congress. And his betrayal, finally, of twenty thousand young Americans who are fighting and dying tonight in a country where they should not be."

Betrayal. Cardwell inhaled sharply, hearing the word repeated. *The other statement—well, the other is more direct.* Cardwell closed his eyes.

Strange. Hoffman was attacking viciously, using words that cut like switchblades. Yet his voice belied the content of his speech: He was speaking softly, casually, in a tone so gentle as to seem polite. "Old Abner," Rattigan had said more than once: "He doesn't miss a trick." And this, Cardwell realized, was a trick, a skillful performer's trick: Make the words hot, but keep the voice cool and temperate. Hoffman was a master.

"Many Americans believe," Hoffman was saying, "that the President, by taking matters into his own hands, forfeited his right to their support. They believe—" Another trick: Hoffman was subtly acting as spokesman, not just for himself, but for a vast, unseen body of opinion.

"I believe the choice on Tuesday is more than a choice between two men," Hoffman was saying. "It is a choice in which the people of New Hampshire speak for all America; a choice between a strategy that counsels peace—and one that plunges us ever deeper into more war, more killing, more dead men."

Jesus! Cardwell looked at Rattigan; the President's eyes were burning. Jesus Christ.

Then it was over, and Cardwell could feel, where he stood, the silent sigh of amazement and fascination from the audience. No one had expected Hoffman to cut so deeply.

"Mr. President?"

Rattigan would have two minutes to reply. Cardwell, who had written the statement, tensed—the old vicarious stage fright—waiting to hear his words.

"I have no opening statement," Rattigan said. This time, the sigh from the audience was an audible gasp.

No statement? Cardwell shot a glance at Triplitano, but Trip was transfixed. No statement? Was Rattigan too angry to speak? Or was he coolly, calculatedly allowing Hoffman more rope?

"Then we'll move to the questions," Niles said after a startled pause.

Andrea Warner of the *Wall Street Journal* had the first question. Cardwell sighed, relaxing. She was friendly. Good.

"Mr. Vice President, some of your more intense supporters, who have been highly visible as demonstrators in New Hampshire and elsewhere, have called your opponent, in effect, a murderer. Do you disavow such charges, sir, or do you endorse this as a characterization of the—"

Hoffman interrupted calmly, seizing the initiative. "No, Miss Warner, I don't accept that language. I think it's extreme. But I can sympathize with the emotions that lie behind it. Of course I don't think the President is a murderer. But I believe his policies are tantamount to murder. I believe a policy of—"

Tantamount to murder. Cardwell lost the words that followed; unconsciously he was holding his breath.

"Mr. President? You may reply."

Rattigan expelled a deep breath. "Until this moment," he said in a voice unnaturally calm, "until this moment I had hoped that we could discuss—calmly and civilly—the great questions on which this campaign turns." He was speaking to Hoffman, Cardwell saw, oblivious to the cameras and the crowd. "The question of when and how this nation's great power should be applied in the world. That's why I came here." He glared at Hoffman. "But I see we can't." He paused: a long, steady pause. Then he said, in a voice very deliberate and low: "You don't care, do you, Abner? You don't care what you do or say. You've turned the vice presidency of the United States into the kind of political weapon it was never meant to be—a weapon against the presidency. And you don't care about the danger that poses for the office, for the *country*—because you just want to win. You'll say anything, no matter how reckless, no matter how extreme. You'll call the President a murderer if you think that may stir up some emotion, sway a few votes, discredit the man who happens to hold in trust the office of the presidency. You just don't care." He took a deep breath. "Well, I *do* care. And I won't let you do it. I won't stand here another second while you do that. I won't take part in any discussion that demeans the office I hold. Not now, and not ever."

And Rattigan suddenly walked away from his lectern toward the wings, toward Trip and Cardwell, trailing his long microphone cord behind him. The cameras swung to follow him, and Cardwell heard the audience break its discipline—erupt into excited chatter.

"Mr. President!" Rattigan reached the spot where Cardwell stood. "Get back out there," Cardwell hissed. "You can't just walk out now! Get back out there and defend yourself!" Unaware, Cardwell was holding the President by his upper arms. "Jesus, you've got to—"

Calmly Rattigan broke free of Cardwell. "I don't have to do a goddamn thing," Rattigan said. He tugged off the little mike about his neck, and he was free. "Let's go."

Cardwell, his face burning, stood rooted to the spot. Rattigan, Triplitano, Anders Martin, and the President's gang of Secret Service agents disappeared through the door into the hall.

Back in the glare of the lights, all was confusion. "The scheduled debate between President Carl Rattigan and his challenger, Abner Hoffman, has ended in confusion," Niles was saying. Hoffman was staring at his lectern, a spectator now. Nearby a man in earphones waved his arms in confusion, then drew his finger across his throat in a slashing gesture. It was over—or almost over. Now the commentators would take over, trying to create some order from this sudden chaos.

Cardwell pushed through the door. The hall outside was empty except for two Secret Service agents who stood on guard. The President was gone. Cardwell could hear, from the distance outside the building, the muffled drumbeat of the demonstrators: "PEACE ON EARTH! PEACE ON EARTH!" There was no stopping them.

Outside in the churning crowd, Cardwell saw Sarah running with the press corps toward their bus.

"Sarah!" He waved wildly, and she stopped to wait for him.

"What do you think?" she said softly when he joined her.

"Jesus, he blew it. He blew it, blew it, blew it." Eyes closed, Cardwell shook his head from side to side.

Not knowing what to say, Sarah touched his hand. The crowd moved on. Sarah heard the press bus engine cough and roar. "I'll miss my bus," she said, pulling away.

"Forget the goddamn bus, Sarah. I've got to talk to you."

"About what?"

He gave her a look of surprise, then looked at the ground. "I don't know. About everything. About this incredible disaster. About my life. About us."

"No," she said softly, "You mustn't do this to me. You've spent the past week trying to forget me, trying to put me out of your mind, trying to write off everything we had as a bad investment, a mistake. And maybe you're right. Maybe I can accept that. But please don't play games with me now. Please don't reach out to me just because your world is caving in and you want someone for comfort." She was walking quickly toward the growling bus. Cardwell followed her and grabbed her arm.

"I have to file a story," she said defiantly.

"Sarah, for God's sake, I've got to talk to you! We can't just let it drop without saying another word."

She stopped. "All right," she said, "but not until all this is over. Not until . . ." Abruptly she turned her face away from him. "Call me," she said. "Call me then."

And suddenly she was gone, half running to the press bus, keeping her eyes averted so he could not see her tears.

Tuesday the Fifth

Election Day. Early on Tuesday morning, just as the rim of the sun surfaced over the horizon, an old farmer who lived near Pittsburg, New Hampshire, got into his pickup truck and headed for town, and for the voting booth. Driving along the hilly roads, he could look south into Canada: His neighborhood was one of the few spots in the United States with such a vantage point.

At lunch hour, at the Rumford Printing Company in Concord, the block-long Hoe rotary press came to a halt; a pressman removed his paper hat, gobbled a sandwich, and hurried down the street to his polling place downtown. In the breast pocket of his work shirt he carried a folded-up flyer; some student workers for Abner Hoffman had left it at his door the night before.

As dusk fell in Manchester, a French Canadian mill worker and his wife got out of their car and walked into the high arched hall of St. Cecilia's Church to receive their paper ballots. They went separately into two of the ten voting booths and quickly marked their ballots. Later, as they walked to the door, they were stopped by a handsome woman who identified herself as a reporter for the New York *Times.* She asked them if they had any difficulty making up their mind for whom to vote. "Nope," the man answered, "I can't recall that it's ever been so easy." But when Sarah Tolman asked them to reveal their choice, the couple shook their heads and walked away.

To the east, not far from Portsmouth, a fifty-year-old woman, the wife of a Boston insurance executive, parked her car and took a long walk on the sandy beach that fronted on the Atlantic. She thought of her only son—a college student, angrily opposed to Rattigan's war—and of her husband, just as angrily in favor of it. She looked out into the night, out beyond the waves, as if she were trying to find the line that separated the black Atlantic from the sky. After a few minutes she hurried back to her car and drove quickly to Portsmouth. She arrived at her polling place five minutes before the eight-o'clock closing time.

All day, all over the little state, similar scenes took place. Housewives, college students, blue-collar workers, old people—all made time in their day to record their preference between the two men who had turned their state into an angry political battlefield.

Then the polls closed, and it was over. There was nothing to do but wait.

John Cardwell chose to wait alone in his littered headquarters office, with two murmuring television sets for company. It would be late—ten o'clock or later, he suspected, before a trend began to show.

Meanwhile he made a series of telephone calls to campaign workers on his list of twelve bellwether precincts. He asked each of them for the count so far, totting up the numbers on a small yellow-and-black hand calculator.

On the fifth call he found himself talking to a sharp-voiced old woman.

"Well," she rasped in answer to his question, "it looks like your man has squeezed through at this box. Rattigan got 137 votes, and, let's see, Hoffman got 61. Rattigan squeezed through, y'see?"

Cardwell hung up, laid down his calculator, and laughed.

At nine-thirty Triplitano called, breezy as ever: "Does the oracle have a message for us mortals?"

"Are you with the President, Trip?"

"I am, and he's itching for news."

"Well, so far the news is good." He gave Triplitano the early, sketchy numbers, then warned him against excessive optimism. "It looks good, but it could still go either way."

"Old buddy," Trip said, "you're giving me figures from key precincts that show us winning by almost two to one, and you tell me it can go the other way?"

"Let's hang onto our caution, Trip," Cardwell said. "Call me in half an hour."

He settled back again, dialing the numbers on his list, jotting down the numbers and tapping out the totals: Rattigan 1,508, Hoffman 1,031, Rattigan 727, Hoffman 559.

Strange, he thought, that he should feel so little. This was the moment toward which he had been working for more than two months: two months of meetings, speech drafts, memos, pages of poll results; two months of coffee in cardboard cups, of silent agonies over Rattigan's misfortunes. Now Rattigan appeared to be winning: Yet Cardwell felt no excitement, no tension, no elation—only bone-weariness and a strange, detached, almost academic curiosity about the result. He wanted to know the final result—because he wanted it to be over, and knowing the result would mean that it was over.

By ten o'clock the numbers were pouring into the network computers: Rattigan was winning. Cardwell's telephone rang again.

"I say we've won it, baby," Triplitano said. "What's wrong with the networks?"

Before Cardwell could answer, Trip said, "Hey, wait, this is it!" Cardwell, still holding the receiver, stepped awkwardly around his desk to raise the volume on his television set. He heard the last part of the anchorman's pronouncement: "—by a much larger margin than anyone predicted. Our CBS election computer projects that Carlton Rattigan, embattled and perhaps embittered President, will be the winner in this New Hampshire primary vote. We go now to our correspondent in the President's election headquarters, Norman Townsend, for a report from—"

Cardwell spun the volume down.

"We won!" Trip shouted.

"In spite of everything," Cardwell said. Still he felt no elation.

"Do you think we should wait for Abner to concede?" Trip said.

"No, take advantage of prime time," Cardwell said. "Don't wait for Abner, he may not concede until tomorrow. Tell the President to come to campaign headquarters no later than ten-thirty."

"You're gonna join us, aren't you, buddy?" Triplitano said.

"I wouldn't miss it."

It didn't strike Cardwell until after he'd hung up that Triplitano, his mentor, had asked him for advice. And Cardwell, accustomed to running things, had told Trip what to do.

When Cardwell reached the teeming room downstairs the President was already speaking, his eyes glistening in the television lights.

Cardwell watched and listened, feeling like a visitor from a distant planet.

"—together now toward victory in November," Rattigan said, and the crowd erupted into whoops and cheers. The President's victory speech was over.

The same old words, Cardwell thought. A very unusual campaign, a very unusual victory—and yet the same old words. The situations change, but the words remain the same.

The still photographers moved in close to the stage. Rattigan, beaming, beckoned his campaign team up to join him, but Cardwell didn't move. He felt suddenly drained, and knew that to join the happy crowd around the President would make him feel like an impostor. So he stayed rooted to his spot on the rear fringe of the crowd.

Then he saw Sarah. And suddenly he pushed his way through the crowd to the place where she was standing, half leaning against the camera platform in the center of the room. She had no notebook; she was watching the scene like any other spectator.

He touched her shoulder. "You said we could talk when it was all over. Well, it's all over."

Sarah smiled. "Congratulations." Then, studying his face, she said, "Why aren't you cheering? You should be elated."

"I'm just very, very tired, Sarah."

"Do you want to stay here?" Sarah said.

"Don't you have a story to file?" he asked. Sarah laughed.

"I spent the day writing two stories," she said: "One reflecting on a Hoffman victory, and the other analyzing a triumph by the President. It's an old reporter's trick."

"Then let's go," he said, taking her elbow and steering her through the milling, joyous crowd.

The hotel bar, which had been filled all evening, was deserted now; its crowd had poured into the ballroom to see the President. They picked a table in the darkest corner, and Cardwell, without consulting Sarah, ordered champagne.

"Is this for celebration or for comfort?" she asked when the waiter left.

"Maybe we'd better answer that when we're finished," Cardwell said.

They were silent for a moment. Then Sarah touched his hand.

"I know you're tired," she said. "But this is your victory, isn't it? You whipped him into coming up here. You wrote the speeches, planned the strategy, masterminded those awful TV spots. You—"

"No, Sarah." He shook his head and drew his hand away. "In the end, it's his victory. He believed Abner was pulling a dangerous stunt; he won because he communicated that belief. He hoped that in a crisis people would still give a President the benefit of the doubt—and they did. He believes that this country still has a role to play in the world, and these people—a good majority of them, at least—agree. So it's his victory."

"And what about you? Why so pensive?"

Suddenly, with an intensity that startled Sarah, Cardwell leaned across the table and seized her hand. "Sarah," he said, "the other night—when you wouldn't talk to me, I wanted to say so much. I wanted to say I'm sorry—"

"Sorry for what?" she said softly.

"Sorry for treating you the way I did, when I found out about—"

She nodded, cutting him off; but he went on.

"I acted like a goddamn fool."

Sarah, her eyes downcast, said nothing.

"I was never really desperate for anything in my life," Cardwell went on. "Perhaps because I was so lucky. I had it all. I never had to grab or fight for anything. It was all just there, waiting for me like packages spread out on Christmas morning. I never thought about it until somebody"—he could not mention Nancy's name to Sarah

—"somebody told me I'd never had to *choose* anything. Everything was chosen for me. But I want you to know—"

He was interrupted by the waiter, who poured their champagne, then disappeared.

"I want you to know—" He stopped, groping for words. "Can you believe how much I wanted you?"

"Wanted—or loved?"

"Don't tease me, Sarah. I'm not as good with words as you are. Loved."

"You're using the past tense."

"Sarah, for God's sake! I'm not playing games with words. I'm asking you to marry me!"

She looked up, startled, and stared at him, her face grave.

"I had my little speech all worked out, and you got me all confused," he said.

"It's all right," she whispered.

"The script usually calls for an answer from the lady, Sarah."

"I know," she said almost inaudibly.

"Then say something."

She shook her head, tossing her dark hair, then took a long drink from her yet-untouched glass. And suddenly in a voice much firmer, she said, "I can't marry you, John."

He took her answer like a blow. "You don't have to decide now, Sarah. You can think about it. I've got a lot to do before I'm free."

She eyed him intently. "Just getting out of your marriage isn't going to make you free," she said.

He looked up sharply. "Sarah, I know I hurt you. I was hurt myself, and I kicked you hard. But that was only one hurt, wasn't it? Don't let being hurt one time keep you from—"

"It's not that," she said. "You hurt me. You hurt me very much. I humbled myself; told you the whole story about Carl and me, tried to make you understand that that was an old, gone part of my life. But you wouldn't understand."

"*Couldn't* understand, Sarah."

"And so you walked out. You were afraid that I would upset the applecart of your ambition. So you walked out."

"Sarah, I'm sorry. What can I—"

"That hurt, but it also set me thinking. And the sum total of all that I've been thinking for the past ten days is this: I don't want to live in this world any more."

"You what?"

"You know what I mean: your world; our world, this little world of politics and hustle and stop-at-nothing ambition. I once thought it was the most exciting thing in the world, and it may be. But I know now that it doesn't have the power to make me happy."

The tables around them were filling up with people once again: reporters, campaign workers, Rattigan supporters, all relaxed and talking loudly. Cardwell left a crumpled wad of bills on the table. "Get your coat," he said, and soon they were outside, walking down Elm Street on the way to her motel.

She walked with her hands jammed into the pockets of her warm fur coat, eyes cast down as she sought to explain herself.

"You know this little world, John. For the people in it, life isn't a matter of right or wrong, happiness or unhappiness. For them, it's only winning or losing. For Carl Rattigan, for Hoffman, for—"

"For me?" he said.

"All right, for you. You came into this world where ambition is *everything,* and it consumed you. You forgot that there are other things in life. It's an infection that's in the air, and you caught it."

"You're a harsh judge, aren't you, Sarah?" Cardwell said.

"I can say it because I caught the infection, too," she said. "I'm a fellow sufferer. I won the Pulitzer when I was still in my twenties. Do you have any idea how much cold, single-minded ambition went into that? I went to Vietnam and lived in fatigues for two years. Until I was thirty years old I didn't really have any possessions except my ambition and a portable typewriter. Nothing else mattered. I walk into Sans Souci and I'm not Sarah Tolman, *person*—I'm Sarah Tolman, prize-winning reporter. Sarah Tolman, well-known face. Sarah Tolman, *success.*" She shook her head fiercely. "Well, suddenly I realize that's not enough—or it's too much."

They were a block away now from her motel, crossing the dark river with its line of ancient factories. Cardwell, though he wore no coat, was oblivious to the chill.

"It's funny," Sarah said. "There was always a part of me that knew that. When I would write about politics or about the war, there was always this little voice that warned me to write about the *meaning* of an event and not just the end result, not just the externals. That's what made my writing good. It's what people wanted most to know. Yet in my life, I didn't really listen to that part of me. I let it control my writing, but not my life."

"So what are you going to do, Sarah? Chuck it all and join a convent?"

"I don't know. Maybe I can't change the external things about my life, but I am going to change my life. Maybe the *Times* will give me an assignment somewhere else: in Europe, Israel. I'm going to see if I can live a different way. See if I can find something more important than success. See if I can find someone who wants *me* most of all—more than winning an election or being President or—" Her voice trailed off.

"And the first step is to tell the poor fool who loves you that you don't love him," Cardwell said.

"No! The first step is to tell him that I can't marry him. I love him very much." She stopped, embraced him suddenly, and kissed his burning face.

"I'm telling you to go and look for the same things, John. Go and look for them before it's too late. Go home and join the human race again. Publish your father's newspaper if that's what you want to do. Try to remember why you once fell in love with your wife and do it all over again."

They reached the entrance to her motel and stood in the cold glare of its lights.

"And where does that leave us, Sarah? What if I come back? Do we ever see each other again?"

"Come back," she said slowly, "and we'll be old friends."

"Great," he said bitterly.

Her eyes were brimming. "Old friends," she said, "who once loved one another. And who learned a great deal together."

She embraced him impulsively, tightly, and pressed her head against his chest. Then she pushed him away, and Cardwell fled, never looking back.

Friday the Eighth

There was no time for rest or for celebrating: The President flew back to Washington early on Wednesday, leaving only Cardwell and a tiny staff to close down the campaign office. The press corps, after weeks of jouncing bus trips across New Hampshire, scattered and disappeared: The circus was over.

On Thursday, the White House announced that several member nations of the Organization of American States had agreed to increase their troop contingents in Bolivia. Accordingly, the statement said, phased withdrawals of certain American units from Bolivia would begin immediately.

Abner Hoffman, back home in Oklahoma to rest after his defeat, went before the cameras to boast that his campaign against the President had achieved its purpose, had forced Rattigan to call home the troops. He would challenge the President in no more primaries, he told the press.

Cardwell, watching the evening news in his hotel room in Manchester, studied Hoffman's face. Hoffman looked puffy-eyed and spent. There was a note of boredom in his voice, of going through the motions. He was not gallant in defeat, Cardwell thought, only forlorn: a sad figure after all.

Late on Friday Cardwell took a commercial flight to Washington. He closed his eyes when the plane took off, and he settled back in his seat, feeling the weight of the long campaign drop away as the airplane rose.

Back in Washington he went straight to the White House—as if to see for himself, after his long sojourn in New Hampshire, that it was still there. He didn't seek out anyone; he simply went to his deserted office in the West Basement and sat for a long time at his desk, thinking of nothing. It was over; there was nothing to do now. The long battle was over.

Then he turned his attention to the stack of letters on his desk. Among them he recognized Nancy's pale blue stationery; he picked her letter up, surprised by its weight and thickness.

"I've started several times," she wrote. "First, late last night after we watched the returns from New Hampshire. I kept thinking I might see you, standing by the President maybe, or in the crowd on television. I was disappointed. Anyway, I tried to write again today, and now it's 'late tonight' again.

"What's wrong? Things keep getting in the way—like 'congratulations,' or 'I've missed you.' Things that make it hard for me to go on to the main unhappy subject. So this time I'll just start right out.

"I had a long talk Friday with Hokey Norton." Norton was their lawyer: Cardwell's boyhood playmate. "We had a long, rambling, difficult discussion: How do you tell your lawyer you want to file for divorce, when actually that's the last thing on earth you want to do?

"Well, sweetheart, he was very understanding. He said our friends here had pretty well concluded that something unfortunate had happened in Washington; that we were separated: another 'perfect couple' has turned out not to be so perfect. Hokey said my instinct was a sound one: that sometimes, the actual filing is a sort of crisis that forces matters to a resolution when two people can't decide which way to jump.

"So that's why I'm writing, because the moment has come for us, hasn't it? Hokey is sending you the papers this week. Meanwhile, I am writing to say that nothing is final yet (his words), or for a long time. So if you think there is any chance for us, any hope, then all you have to do is—"

Here her letter broke off abruptly. And below, her neat script resumed in another ink.

"The problem is writing late at night, isn't it? That's when your emotions are closest to the surface. That's when the tiny little girl in me comes out, too ready to plead and cry. And I'm determined to be strong. Now I'm at school, sitting at my desk as the sunlight pours in through the classroom windows; stealing a few minutes while my little delinquents are out at play. Days are the best time for me; I am very good at this job—something I didn't have in Washington, to make me feel strong and competent. After half a day of playing the stern schoolmarm, I find I'm much more in control; I didn't even flinch this morning when a little black boy stood up and yelled, 'Hey, Miz Cardwell, where's your boyfriend?' And one of his sidekicks yelled, 'Shut up, she don't have no boyfriend.'

"No boyfriend? I think I can stand that. Sometimes I get shaky and upset, but please don't worry about me: Most of the time (like now) I'm pretty strong, can face squarely the possibility that you may choose—that WE may choose—not to be married anymore. I can face that because I know that when all is said and done, I tried. I tried to live in a world where you were somebody and I was not. I tried to get you to talk about it when I saw you slipping away from me into that other world. I tried to live alone and like it—when you were away, or worse, when you were at home but actually off somewhere in the distance; when you would wait for the phone to ring, or compose a speech in your head, or add up Gallup Poll numbers; when you did whatever it was that made it impossible for you to see me or listen to me or be with me.

"I tried through all that, and now I'm trying again. Because I love you, sweetheart. Still love you in spite of all the mistakes we made, all the silences we let grow up between us, all the hurts, all the pain of knowing that I may never be as accomplished or as witty or as interesting as I would like to be, or as you would like for me to be. But two people can love each other and inhabit slightly different worlds, can't they? If they word hard at it? I tell myself yes, of course.

"I've gone on too long, and it's your turn now. I'm willing to talk about it, *if you are*. Write me. Call me, or better still, come home for a while. I'll welcome you with half-open arms. And we could talk—about the good days. Or, if you're inclined to, about the future."

He folded her letter and laid it down. Then he saw the envelope from Norton's law firm: the neatly typed address, the firm's name engraved in black, icily precise letters. He reached for it, started to tear it open—then flung it unopened into the wastebasket by his desk. Not yet, he thought. Not without trying again.

I'd want you back, she had told him once—how long ago? *But only if you change.*

His telephone rang. The White House operator: "Mr. Triplitano for you, sir."

"Trip?"

"When did you get back, old buddy?"

"Just now. An hour ago."

"Well, you missed all the fun. Hoffman's back in town. He had a meeting with the boss."

"Off the record?"

"No, of course not. On the record. Healing the wounds and all that. The victor accepts tribute from the vanquished. Blah, blah, blah."

"How did it go?"

"Pretty stiff in private. The old man still hates Abner's guts, and Abner's pretty badly bruised, so it was hard for both of them. They smiled for the cameras, though."

"Poor Abner."

"Screw him."

"He's a strong man, Trip."

"You're right. I'll grant him that. The reporters tried to press him afterward. Asked him if he'll resign so the President can name a more compatible Vice President. Old Ab didn't bat an eye. He said he'd been elected by all the people and he'll fill out his term. Of course he knows he's finished. It's sort of sad."

"Who do you think the President will name at the convention?"

"I'd bet Brooks Healy."

Cardwell was silent for a moment. "He's never run for office, Trip."

"That's all right. The President trusts him. Hell, he loves him. Why not let him have the man he wants, for a change? He's an impressive guy. He knows how to make a speech. He's loyal. Hell, I'd—"

Triplitano wanted to talk. But Cardwell interrupted, made a polite excuse, and ended the conversation. Strange. He had no desire now to talk about politics, to compare political candidates. Even the news of the two bitter antagonists meeting upstairs like bruised, blood-flecked boxers touching gloves after a match, scarcely interested him. He felt as if he were watching it all from a great distance.

Triplitano called again.

"I forgot to tell you. You've been invited to the correspondents dinner tomorrow night."

"I'm going to beg off, Trip."

"No you're not. The old man is going. He wants you to send up some ideas for a speech. Nothing fancy, he's going to speak off the cuff. And get this: The rumor is that Abner's going to come."

His old curiosity stirred a little.

"Okay, Trip. I'll see you there."

Saturday the Ninth

The annual dinner of the White House Correspondents' Association was a tradition that reached back to 1914, when President Woodrow Wilson accepted an invitation to address the journalists and their guests—off the record. Since that time, the President had more often than not appeared at the festivities.

As Cardwell walked into the ballroom of the Sheraton-Park, Bill Tepper of the Los Angeles *Times* stopped him. "Did you write the speech?" Cardwell simply smiled and edged his way toward his table. In fact, he had done little but send up a short memo to the President labeled, "Possible Points to Make." Now he wondered himself what Rattigan might say, especially with Hoffman on the dais.

Cardwell found the round table near the front of the hall to which he had been assigned and joined the other guests: Senator Robert Fain of Missouri; a commissioner of the Federal Communications Commission; and four reporters from Long Island's *Newsday*. Their conversation swirled around Rattigan's landslide in New Hampshire —63 per cent to 37 per cent—and the tumble of the week's events.

Cardwell said little. He was studying the crowd in the ballroom—two thousand reporters and guests—and thinking of the treatment the press had given Rattigan's hard-won victory. Again and again in the past four days, Cardwell had read that the President's triumph reflected a deep, traditional impulse of the people to support their Presidents. It was, they seemed to be saying, part of a pattern. But then, he realized, the press was in the pattern-making business. For them it was not enough to report an *event;* they must always find a pattern, a *trend,* a *new direction.* The problem, of course, was that so very frequently events didn't fit into any noticeable sequence or trend. Rattigan's victory was a case in point. Did it really mean what they said it meant? Perhaps. But no one really knew—not yet. No matter: the patternmakers spun out their patterns; when the pundits were lucky and turned out to be correct, they reminded their readers of their remarkable prescience. When they were wrong, they said nothing about it; they fashioned a new pattern.

Toward dessert, Cardwell found himself looking often toward the far side of the great hall, to the side door through which Rattigan would pass on his way to the dais. Cardwell felt again the old familiar sensation, akin to stage fright, that always hit him before the President spoke.

The program began with the usual forced hilarity: The outgoing President of the Correspondents' Association made his farewell with a collection of jokes; his successor followed with more jokes. Cardwell half listened as the two newsmen recited their speeches; waiting for Rattigan's arrival, he studied the Vice President on the dais. Hoffman, sitting to the right of the podium, fidgeted with the little fork from his shrimp cocktail while he chatted, apparently affable and at ease, with the wife of the new club president.

Suddenly, a blare of trumpets: "Ruffles and Flourishes," followed by "Hail to the Chief." Rattigan entered the hall from the far side of the dais and strode briskly to the podium: Tall, ruddy, smiling, he paused only once and held his hands high above his head to acknowledge the sudden thunder of applause.

Cardwell rose to his feet along with the rest of the crowd, and clapped as Rattigan stood there in the spotlight. But his eyes were on Hoffman. The Vice President was clapping, too, and smiling, even if the smile was a bit wan. Good, Cardwell thought. The show must go on.

Rattigan held a hand up, bidding for silence, and the crowd obeyed.

"My friends," he said, "I hope you will forgive me tonight if I violate ancient tradition and begin on a serious rather than a light note."

Rattigan paused. "We are all professionals here: in politics or in the coverage of politics. We know, I think, just how difficult a profession it can be. Tonight I want to salute a man who is a serious, tough, and able practitioner of the political art: the Vice President of the United States."

Rattigan began the applause, and the crowd took it up.

Hoffman, surprised, stood; he smiled and waved at the crowd, and Rattigan walked from his place on the rostrum to Hoffman's, where the two men shook hands. The crowd roared at the display of unity.

Cardwell studied the faces around him: the smiles, the glistening eyes. How many of these people realized that this show of unity was, for the most part, a charade? Rattigan, to be sure, had not falsified himself: He had a large and deep respect for Hoffman's political skills, however grudging. And a scene like this one was necessary to restore civility after a bruising, angry political feud. But the two men, Cardwell knew, had never liked each other very much, and now they hated one another. No single moment of smiling for the cameras, of shaking hands and waving cheerfully, could change that fact. This was a papering over, not a healing.

The moment ended; the applause died, and Rattigan returned to the microphone: "My informants told me that Abner didn't accept your invitation to be here tonight until he had examined a copy of the bylaws of the White House Correspondents' Association. When he found the provision that your president could only serve one term, and that the president is *automatically* succeeded by your vice president—well, then, Abner decided to attend tonight and see what he could learn."

Hoffman erupted into laughter; the crowd roared too, and Rattigan continued: "I must also tell you that I too began to read those provisions. But my eyeglasses misted up, perspiration broke out on my forehead, and I just couldn't go on." Again they roared.

Beautiful, Cardwell thought. The lines weren't all that funny, but the tone was right. The crowds at such ritual gatherings in Washington are always generous with their laughter—and tonight they were as eager as Rattigan was to create good feeling.

Then abruptly, Rattigan changed the mood: As the laughter died, he held his right hand aloft, asking for quiet. Then he began to speak more slowly and emphatically.

"It is very good," he said, "that we can gather at a time like this and laugh. But I think we should remember that not many days ago, some of us were a long way from laughter: deeply embroiled in a serious, sometimes bitter, primary campaign that raised some critical questions for our country. I want to talk tonight about those questions, questions that I believe will affect our destiny in the months and years to come.

"The first issue concerns America's role in the world. Where in the world—and when—shall America use her great power to defend the values of personal freedom and national independence? As you know, men of good have sharply divergent views on this matter. In the campaign that is just over, a choice more clear-cut than usual was presented to the voters. And I believe they have tendered me a mandate to continue the policies that were in dispute. I would be less than honest were I to say I am not pleased to receive such a mandate."

Rattigan glanced at his notes and went on.

"The second issue that was resolved during the campaign was *not* resolved in the way that I had originally hoped for. When the Vice President announced that he would be running in the primaries, it was my judgment that he should resign from the vice presidency, allowing me to appoint a successor as the Constitution stipulates. I felt that it would be deeply harmful to the country to have a split Executive Branch, that it could set a catastrophic precedent. I can tell you now that I asked him to resign—and he refused."

There was a murmur in the hall; Rattigan continued: "As I look back now, and as I look out at this meeting tonight, where men of both parties, of all factions of both parties, are meeting in warm and friendly spirit, I think perhaps I was wrong. For neither the nation nor our political community have been torn apart. Why? Because this government and this nation, I have discovered, are knitted together with strong bonds of civility and honor, bonds that are stronger than the turmoils of the moment. It is a moving experience for me to see us all together now after a time of serious national strain.

"We have been through a great deal in the past few months. I think we have come out of it all right, perhaps even stronger: in the words of Ernest Hemingway, 'stronger in the broken places.' For that I thank you—and I thank God."

He paused, then indicated with a nod of his head that he had finished.

The applause burst forth; the crowd rose as one man, shouting;

Rattigan acknowledged their cheering with a wave. Then it was over: the Secret Service agents moved up and escorted the President off the platform amid the cheers.

When the house lights came on, the conversation at the tables was animated. They had been impressed, even moved, by Rattigan's words. And for the first time Cardwell relaxed, felt the satisfaction of the moment. In the hurried aftermath of the New Hampshire primary, there had been no time to savor the victory. Now there was time; this was the celebration.

Cardwell was shaking hands with the senator from Missouri when he felt a hard clap on his shoulder. It was Triplitano. "There's a man who wants to see you," Trip said. "At the White House."

Cardwell raised his eyebrows.

"He gave me a list of a few staff to round up. He wants us to join him for a few drinks and some talk. I think he just wants to say thank you. Can you come?"

"Of course," said Cardwell. "I'll see you there."

Twenty minutes later, Cardwell stepped off the little elevator into the broad second-floor hall of the Mansion where a little crowd was already gathering. Lisa Rattigan, who had not been at the Sheraton-Park, was elegant in a long black dress. Triplitano was in the West Hall, laughing with Brooks and Anna Healy, three of Rattigan's White House secretaries, and some old friends of the President. Two waiters served hors d'oeuvres; two more passed drinks on silver trays.

Cardwell smiled, but said little. He moved from group to group, listening to the conversation, enjoying their enjoyment.

After the party had drifted on for thirty minutes, Brooks Healy stepped to the center of the Yellow Oval Room, where the little crowd had gathered.

"I want to make a toast," he said. "All of us have felt the fatigue and elation of the past two months. But one of us has felt it more deeply than the rest. He has endured all the strains of holding on—and he has prevailed. The victory he won on Tuesday was an impressive personal victory. But it was also a victory for the high office he holds—and for the country. Ladies and gentlemen, a toast to a great victory—and to a great man."

There were applause and scattered shouts of "Hear, hear!" as the little band of loyalists raised their glasses. Lisa Rattigan, looking as if she might cry for joy or relief or pride, moved close to Brooks Healy and squeezed his elbow.

The President, who had been sitting through Healy's toast, stood now and raised his hand.

"Thank you, Brooks," Rattigan said, and Cardwell noticed that though everyone in the room was smiling, the President was not.

"Most of the people in this room I've known for a long time," Rattigan went on. "Especially you, Brooks. So I think you'll understand, and not accuse me of a lack of grace, if I don't make a pretty speech. I made a pretty speech earlier tonight. You all know me so well that you deserve to hear what I really think. So I'll respond to those generous words by telling you.

"The press, the country, and perhaps some of you here think we won a victory up there, that 63 per cent of the vote represents a vindication for me and a victory for the presidency. Well, that's wrong. Dead wrong."

Rattigan moved restlessly on his feet, ignoring the looks of puzzlement that spread over the faces of the group.

"Well, don't feel badly. Some very intelligent people missed what really happened, too. Maybe I'm the only one who really sees what happened. And the next person to realize it may be the poor bastard who takes this job after I leave.

"We didn't win a goddamn thing except votes, my friends. Votes, and some time: an option on this little piece of real estate for four more years."

There was total silence in the room.

"Think a minute about this wretched little war, this war that has torn us apart for all these months. Measured against every other war in our history, this one was tiny: little more than a show of force, really. Every promise I made when I sent those men, I've kept: I promised to limit our forces to twenty-five thousand, and I did. I promised to get other countries to send their troops, and I got them.

"So, measured by almost any yardstick, it's been a tiny, brief little war. And in spite of some terrible accidents, it's gone rather well for us. But what happened?"

Cardwell caught the sharp edge of bitterness in Rattigan's voice. He looked at Brooks Healy, who was staring at the floor, his brow furrowed.

"What happened?" Rattigan repeated. "The country was torn almost apart. We've had three months of protests and bitter politics. The Government of the United States has been divided at the top. The President was forced to spend eight weeks as a part-time President and a full-time candidate. And a dangerous precedent was set. Despite what I said earlier tonight, a precedent was set that will haunt every President who lives in this house after me."

Rattigan shook his head.

"Well, I won. I won in the sense that I got the most votes. So why am I complaining? Picture yourself as one of those leaders who doesn't wish good fortune to the United States. The lesson, if you're one of those people, is that the United States almost ousted a President over a very small war. A very small war indeed.

"The lesson is that from now on, this President may be a little more reluctant to risk making hard, unpopular decisions. And future Presidents may be even more reluctant.

"The lesson, my good friends, is that we're in deep trouble. The lesson is that Carl Rattigan won. But the country lost—lost badly. Because if the world's strongest nation isn't willing to defend its values—with steel, if necessary—you can kiss those values good-bye. You can kiss *freedom* good-bye."

Cardwell saw that Lisa Rattigan was frowning, her eyes narrowed. She was wishing the President were not saying what he was saying; wishing he would look at her so she could signal him: Go easy. Don't be bitter. And Cardwell found himself thinking, he shouldn't be saying all this, unburdening himself so carelessly before twenty people.

But Rattigan pressed on. "We're in trouble," he went on, "and it's going to be more apparent as time goes on. I'll work hard to keep a finger in the dike, to put some strength back in this battered office while I can. But the tide is running. And I'm not sure that I, or any other President, can hold it back."

He looked as if he had a great deal more to say, but suddenly he ended it—shook his head and walked back to his chair.

There was an awkward moment of silence; a pall had settled over the happy gathering. Soon the group began to talk again: a soft, aimless chatter. But Rattigan's words had chastened them, and the mood of happy celebration chilled abruptly.

In another half hour it was over. Couples began moving toward the elevator, murmuring good-byes to Lisa and the President. Cardwell, moving with the group, heard Brooks Healy saying to the President: "Remember one thing. Over the long pull, it's been the optimists who were right about this country."

Cardwell was eager to leave. But when he had said good-bye to Lisa Rattigan and was shaking hands with the President, Rattigan pulled him back.

"No, stay, I want to talk to you. Wait for me over there." He pointed to the West Hall, the family sitting room, to the same wing chair where Cardwell had sat one night four months before, during another midnight conversation with the President.

It was twelve-thirty when the party ended. Lisa Rattigan disappeared to her bedroom, leaving Cardwell and the President alone.

"I wanted to thank you," Rattigan said as he sank into his chair, "for making me do some things I didn't want to do."

"It's funny," Cardwell said. "I always had the feeling that you would have made the same decisions without me. You would have gone to New Hampshire when you saw that it was really necessary."

"I may have," said Rattigan, "but it was good to have you pushing. Are you going to take a vacation now?"

"I want to. I want to go home."

"Well," said Rattigan, "I want you to get plenty of rest. Because I want you to run the whole campaign. Nationally. You can take over when you get back."

Cardwell couldn't speak for a moment. Then he said, "I wish I could say yes, Mr. President, because that's a great honor. But I can't."

"Why not? You deserve it. You've proven yourself, God knows. You're a veteran now."

"What I'm saying, Mr. President, is that I'm leaving."

Now Rattigan didn't reply. There was no sound except the ticking of the big case clock in the hall, a sound Cardwell remembered from that night four months ago.

"Forgive me," Rattigan said finally, "but I don't understand. I don't understand at all."

"I've been away from my wife for two months. She's never liked Washington. I'm afraid we've grown apart." Cardwell could sense that Rattigan thought his answer strange, as if no personal reasons could suffice to explain. "My father is running a newspaper, and he's getting old. I—"

"I need your help."

"You'll always have my help, Mr. President. Any way I can give it. But I have to put my life together again."

"Why would you prefer to sit down there writing editorials when you could be running things here?"

"I don't prefer it," Cardwell said. "I'd stay here if I were doing what I wanted. I'm doing what I feel I have to do. And you're over the worst part. You'll win your second term. You don't really need me now."

For a long time Rattigan was silent. Then he stood up and stared down through the big fan-shaped window behind the sofa, down at the sleeping West Wing, bathed in the pearly light of streetlamps, deserted now except for guards and cleaning women.

"It's funny," he said finally. "When I finished Harvard Law and came to Washington, I clerked for a federal judge named Carrigan. I'd wanted to clerk for a Supreme Court justice, but it fell through. Carrigan had been in Congress. He was an old friend of Harry Truman's from a marginal district somewhere in Missouri. Every time he ran again, he came closer to losing; he was a good man but a poor politician, and Truman knew it. When Truman left office he appointed old Carrigan to the Court of Appeals."

Cardwell stared at Rattigan, wondering what the President was driving at.

"We used to sit in his chambers in the late afternoon, having a drink and watching the streetlights winking on, watching the people hurrying from their offices toward home. And one day, the old judge said to me, 'It's like a cruise ship, son. Washington is like a cruise ship. Some people on board are passengers who travel for a while, then disembark and go back home. But some of us are members of the crew. We stay and sail forever.'

"I was young then," Rattigan went on softly. "I didn't know what turns my life would take. I thought I was a passenger." He turned and looked at Cardwell. "It turns out I'm a member of the crew."

"You're the captain," Cardwell said.

Rattigan shook his head. "Sometimes I feel like the captain. And sometimes I feel like a prisoner tied to the mast."

For a long moment, both of them said nothing. Then Rattigan, still staring down through the window, began to speak again.

"There used to be some giants in this town. Men like Acheson and Marshall. Agree with them or disagree, any fair man would have to admit they were giants. They had a vision of what a great nation ought to be, of what a decent world should be—and they had brains and guts and muscle."

He shook his head. "And now they're gone. A few good men are left, like Healy. But the giants are gone, and most of the rest are small men—limited men: pygmies. A President—a country—needs giants to lean on, and life without them can be very lonely and very frightening."

Slowly, as if awakening, he turned to Cardwell.

"Would you find it hard to believe that I could envy you? Envy you your freedom to choose—to pick up and leave?"

"No, I understand perfectly, Mr. President."

Rattigan was staring past Cardwell, the expression on his face one of dreaming.

"There was a time when I loved this place," he said. "Loved everything about it. Hell, I even loved receiving the credentials of the ambassador of El Salvador. Now—" He sighed. "All during the campaign I kept having a fantasy—a fantasy of quitting and surprising Abner. Just giving the whole damn load to him. And you know what? Now that I've won, I have the same fantasy. I still want to give it to him. Quit and go home."

"I understand, sir."

"Do you? I wonder," he said, and looked sharply at Cardwell. "Carl Rattigan wants to quit. But the President has a job to do."

The big clock interrupted him and struck the hour: one o'clock.

"Have you thought of running for office?" Rattigan asked.

"I've thought about it, but that's not for now," Cardwell said. "But someday I may run. Come back here as my own man and try to be one of the giants."

"I'd come and campaign for you," Rattigan said. "I'd work almost as hard for you as you've worked for me."

"Thank you, Mr. President."

"Thank you. If you change your mind, I still want you to run the campaign."

"I won't change my mind."

Rattigan stood up, and Cardwell joined him.

"I'll call a car for you," the President said, and leaned toward the telephone beside his chair.

"No thanks, I want to walk," Cardwell replied, and they walked together to the elevator. Rattigan pressed the button, then turned to Cardwell. Wordlessly the two men shook hands.

The usher on duty in the great dim hall downstairs let him out. Cardwell stood for a moment beneath the chalk-white columns of the North Portico, then walked around the curving driveway to the Northwest Gate.

The guard who swung the gate open for him murmured, "Good night, sir." And Cardwell heard himself say in reply, not "Good night," but "Good-bye."

He was halfway across Lafayette Square before he noticed the snow: tiny, almost invisible flakes that disappeared when they touched the ground. It was winter's last, weak gasp. In three weeks' time, he knew, another of Washington's incomparable springs would be upon the city: first a pale spreading haze of green, followed by a burst of tulips and azaleas.

He walked a block on Sixteenth Street, heading north from the White House, his overcoat collar pulled up around his ears. Then, past the Capital Hilton, he cut over to Connecticut Avenue.

The city in this early hour of morning was almost desolate. Even the street in front of the Mayflower Hotel, usually crowded with taxis and conventioneers, was deserted and silent.

He walked north: up the hill between the sleeping canyons of apartment buildings, across the broad bridge that stretched over Rock Creek Park, past the steel gates of the zoo.

He thought about his long conversation with Rattigan, and suddenly he knew, as if he had second sight, that the President was not sleeping. Cardwell had a sharp, clear vision of the President as he must be now: sitting alone in the half darkness of the Yellow Oval Room, staring off toward the brooding Potomac.

A few cars plodded up the avenue. Cardwell stopped at the corner and then turned right: Macomb Street. Sarah's street.

He started toward her building, the low red-brick box less than a block away. It was late, but he had so much to tell her; so much was still unspoken between them.

But then he stopped and turned back toward the avenue, quickening his step as he walked. Sarah, he knew, had been right: Someday he would see her again. Someday he would reboard the cruise ship, come back to Washington, and they would have much to talk about —as old friends. Battle-scarred friends. But between now and then, he had a great deal to do.

The snow had given up now. He stepped out into Connecticut Avenue, hailed a cab, and gave the driver the address on Willow Lane, Bethesda.

The next day he flew home—to Louisville.